The Wrong Ocean

Also by Kathy Boyd Fellure

The Language of the Lake

Lake Cottage Book Haven

Upon These Azure Shores

Having first-hand experience with a loved one diagnosed with Alzheimer's, Fellure's book is right on point with the roller coaster emotions of watching your loved one lose themselves. An emotional journey of three generations navigating caregiving while dealing with life's many challenges. Her use of Cornish phrases and idioms is amusing and poignant. Each character is unique and someone with whom readers can personally identify. I highly recommend it.

JANE DALY, author of *The Caregiving Season, Finding Grace to Honor Your Aging Parent*; *The Girl in the Cardboard Box.*

Kathy Boyd Fellure, author of the lyrical *On the Water's Edge Tahoe Trilogy,* has done it again with her new *Across the Pond Series.* The first novel, *The Wrong Ocean* is a true page turner. The intimate tale of a family conflicted by financial ruin, cultural differences, and the dread of Alzheimer's. The captivating characters drew me into the story. I truly love this book.

ANTOINETTE MAY, author of *The Sacred Well, The Determined Heart, Witness to War,* and *the #1 New York Times Bestselling Pilot's Wife.*

Having experienced a family member with the downward spiral of Alzheimer's, I empathize with Ian's painful condition and the wrenching decisions his daughter Elisa and her family face in *The Wrong Ocean.* Add the strife of family disputes and the longing of a daughter who helplessly tries to restore her father's love and memories. Kathy Fellure has created a churning recipe for a poignant exploration of family dynamics in the throes of sorrow.

MONIKA ROSE, author of *River by the Glass ~ A Collection of Poetry,* and *Bed Bumps.* Editor at Manzanita Writers Press.

I've been anticipating this novel since I read the first chapter several years ago when the author first started developing the story. I knew then it was going to be wonderful because Kathy not only has an empathetic heart towards people, but she has a love for Britain and the British people that is warm and genuine. Reading the Wrong Ocean took me back to the many times in my life when I stood on the shores of the Cornish Coast, spent many happy times having tea with my family there, and enjoying their distinct accent, an accent that sounds like home to me. The novel isn't only an artfully woven story about the shores of Britain and America, it brings the reader into the challenges faced by family members who straddle two cultures and have to deal with the onslaught of aging and Alzheimer's, and the responsibilities and difficulty for all generations in navigating these life storms with grace. Good novels entertain us, great novels bring us into their worlds, force us to hold up a mirror to our own lives and teach us something about ourselves in the process. The Wrong Ocean is a great novel.

SARAH LUNSFORD, author of *Images of America ~ Wineries of the Gold Country,* and freelance journalist who has written for the *L.A. Times* and many other publications.

The Wrong Ocean

A Novel

Across the Pond Series

Kathy Boyd Fellure

The Wrong Ocean ~ Across the Pond Series

Copyright ©2022 Kathy Boyd Fellure

©Book Jacket Press – P.O. Box 1209, Ione, California 95640-9771
www.bookjacketpress.com   with KDP Amazon.

Scripture quotations marked KJV are taken from the Holy Bible, King James Version

Humpty Dumpty by William Carey Richards ©1843 public domain

Mother Goose Nursery Rhymes John Newbery's compilation 1760s public domain

The Jolly Tinners, Parish of St. Hilary Village Inn 1807 public domain

The Legend of King Arthur & His Knights by James T. Knowles ©1860 public domain

The Royal Ballet on Stage and Screen; The Book of the Royal Ballet Film by Maurice Moiseiwtsch public domain

Editor: Bonnie Miller
Cover design ©Kim Van Meter
Back cover editing ©Marcia Ehinger
Typographer ©Aaron Cameron
Cameroncreative.co
Author bio picture ©Farrell Photography
Interior sketch art ©Ann Balestreri Brune
Library of Congress Control Number 2022910833
ISBN 978-1-7347031-3-9 (ebook)
ISBN 978-1-7347031-2-2 (SC)

For my sister Shannon Boyd who became the mother,

when our mother became her child.

He maketh the storm calm,

so that the waves there of are still.

~ Psalm 107:29

Part One
Cornwall, England ~ 2017

Chapter One

The ocean knows the fishermen whose nets sweep her depths for the day's catch. The bottom of their boats leave fingerprints on the mighty waters. The hand from above intertwining with the fingers reaching up from down below where man neither sees nor hears the kept secrets of the abyss. ~ Village folklore from Cornwall, England.

Victoria Regina

Ian's yellow slicker weighed heavy, his boots sloshing in the rising level of salt water filling the keel. The roar and rush of frothy swells battered the trawler and the lone seafarer struggled against the continual onslaught of the increasing storm. Dark skies pelted unrelenting rain, stinging the fisherman's exposed cheeks and forehead. Whipping winds blew his hood back, drenching shoulder-length scraggly white hair that caught in his beard, blurring both vision and hope.

Reaching for the wheel he steered head-on, his hands slipping with each wash of waves. The old girl was not behaving. *Victoria Regina* balked at his commands and he grew more frustrated by the second.

"Will you not work with me here?" Hammered to his knees and bowed over, he bellowed, "We'll go down if you be keeping this up!" A sharp judder sent him sprawling on his back, his head slamming against the metal. Gasping, he gripped the rim of the boat,

1

drawing himself back on both feet, balancing against the sheer force and fierceness encompassing him.

His battered frame resignedly hung over the wheel. He prayed for a break, be it ahead or behind. "Save me!" The old Cornishman relinquished control of his vessel.

The shoreline bore the ravages of the squall across her sands. Seaweed strewn in clumps and long stringy strands stretched southward. Lobsters, crabs, and the stench of day old dead fish blasted the old man's nostrils where he lay amid the carnage. Sputtering and spewing from his lungs he crawled, digging his hands into the rock, sand and silt. Sunlight glared shards of light.

He knew she'd been swallowed whole, but first she'd thrown him out like a jilted lover despite his efforts, despite his pleas.

"Victoria." Weeping, he drew back to the earth. They were forever separated now, he on land and she claimed by the sea. She'd descended and left him behind. How cruel lovers can be when intimacy fades and time erodes the beauty one beheld for the other.

"Me meant to save us." He called out from the beach. "Me only meant to save us." He reached toward the calm waters, his fingers raking pebbles and grit.

Two old fishermen hovered over the still body.

"Hevva! He's here! Ian, can you hear me?"

"Where?" A voice bellowed from the craggy rocks above.

"Over here, Colin—Hurry!"

"Clear his mouth."

"He's chummed." Crouching close, the red-haired codger rolled Ian over, brushed bile away into the sandy beach, and leaned his ear to the man's chest. "He be breathing. He be alive."

"Barely, Mick."

"Blow the horn."

"No." Ian raised his head inches before sinking back to the unforgiving earth.

"Do it or we'll lose the bloody bugger!"

The village alarm sounded after the horn's bold call. Church bells echoed through the gray-stone and bright-colored stucco homes standing in tall curving rows leading to the shore.

"Ambulance be coming." The burly seaman on his knees whispered into his friend's ear, "Hang on, mate." His clammy calloused hand scooped sand and hair, angling the face upward.

The call of the ocean drowned the voices above him. Ian listened for one voice, but it did not respond. He tried to concentrate, remember her name. A siren rang in the distance, humming between his ears. Closing his eyes, he sought her image, the outline of her face, the softness of her skin. Conflicting and constricting spasms seized his heart. He stared into the bright ball of light in the sky and watched the boats in the bay sail by between blinking eyelids.

Chapter Two

The divide between ocean and land is but a mental state. Liquid and solid both support man. The bottom of the ocean is a hardened surface. When inland, the water is contained in large bodies and river runs bordered by the land mass. Feet touch both. Whether you float or sink, the mind decides. ~ Statement posted below an oil and canvas painting on exhibit at a seaside resort gallery in East Anglia, England.

Inland

"My dad is in hospital again." Elisa turned off her cell and turned to her husband. "They say I need to come fetch him before he kills himself."

"Who says?"

"His mates. They held an emergency meeting at the Maiden Voyage Pub." She tossed a fold of her silky ginger hair over a shoulder and stared deep into her husband's weary eyes. "They would never say to take him from the sea if there was any other solution." The drain in her voice was noticeable.

"We're already struggling with my mum here." Troy lowered his tone to a mere whisper glancing into the next room. "You know they loathe each other. It will be a nightmare to house them together under one roof." He twisted in his recliner and winced at the thought of such folly.

"You aren't telling me anything I don't already know." Elisa collapsed on the white sofa cushions beside his black leather chair and kicked at the raised foot rest. "It's not fair."

"How can we afford another cross-country flight, and jet across the pond to check up on him again?" Troy's mind spun forward to his current work problems.

"He needs to stay with us, Hon. He won't be returning to England." Elisa drew her knees to her chest and wrapped her slender arms tight around them. "Muriel took such good care of him after Mum passed. I never dreamed he'd outlive her too."

"That old goat." Troy chided. "He'll do in the next caregiver too."

"Be careful, Fiona has her own meddlesome ways." Elisa nodded toward her former office where the endless drone of her mum-in-law's long distance chat with her Londoner mates wagged on. The chirpy voice espousing expensive redecorating tips for their new Upper Belgrave Street flat was acutely unnerving. Elisa always thought of Fiona as 'Lady Kensington'. Rolling her eyes she drew all of herself into a tighter ball before bursting, spreading herself across the length of the sofa in an exasperated plunge.

"What's wrong with you?" Troy yanked the recliner lever and sat forward. "She'll hear you!"

"Good, let her."

"You're acting like a child." He fumed.

"My father can't live alone anymore. At least he didn't run out of money and show up on our doorstep like your mum. He still goes out fishing to earn his keep, and they have to haul him back in time after time."

"Yeah, he's become the catch of the day." Troy hurled the insult with intent to sting.

"He's an expert fisherman." Elisa rolled and bolted upright. "At least he has a trade other than shopping." Her delivery was cold enough to chill the stuffy, overheated air.

"What is becoming of us?" Troy closed his mouth, pursing his lips together. "This isn't who we are." Shoulders slumped, he wrung his hands in his lap, head hanging low.

Troy was right, she barely recognized either of them anymore. In the quiet of the moment Elisa realized the conversation in Fiona's bedroom had ceased. One look at the doorway sent icy shudders through every extremity of her body in slow ripples leaving a numbness she couldn't shake.

Fiona stood arms crossed over her chest, one hip pressed to the door molding, one foot with toes pointed in fifth position and the other flat on the floor. Her platinum-blonde hair lacquered in place without a strand daring to stray out of place. Her lithe frame looking younger than sixty-something was pinched in black spandex leggings. An old pink sweater from her days with the Royal Ballet hung loosely to her thighs. Fire blazed around the dark pupils of her slate-gray eyes, flames ready to ignite the room. "Going at another row?"

"This is private, Mum." Troy warned.

"This room needs color. I'm tired of this boring black and white theme." Fiona turned her back, released her waist-length hair from the bun piled on her head and sauntered down the hallway to her room. She glanced back and snapped the silk hair scrunchie around a wrist before her door slammed shut.

Elisa rose and curled up on Troy's lap waiting for his muscular arms to enfold her for the few moments before Fiona's re-entry and unrelenting lecture of how they should be living their lives, how they should be raising her granddaughter, and how Troy needed to demand a raise from his boss. The three-point barrage was within minutes of certain delivery with the usual follow-up offer to take Mia for a drive so they could discuss things.

"Good thing Mia's still at the slumber party. I'm sending Mum to a hotel for the night." Troy stated and stroked Elisa's cheek.

"She'll flip."

"We'll put it on a charge card. It will be worth the finance charge."

"I'll get a bottle of wine and a couple of glasses." Elisa coursed a fingertip around the curve of his ear to his lobe and cooed. "And wait for you upstairs."

"Better hurry, before round two." Troy smiled that coy, half-crooked, lips half-parted saucy grin that she'd noticed from across a room full of college students at the grad party in midtown Sacramento the night they'd met.

She was almost to the top step when the hinges of a door creaked open downstairs.

Fiona's voice rang shrilly through the walls and floor beneath Elisa's bare feet. Something about how she was not going to be sent off to some cheap hotel, and how dare her son trifle with her emotions. No one told her Mia was gone for the night! Maybe she should pack her bags and spend a fortnight with friends that missed her and wanted her.

Please, please—go back to London and stay! Elisa struck a match and lit candles.

Troy insisted, he argued, then he pleaded.

Elisa popped the cork and let the wine breathe. The voices downstairs continued without coming to an agreement. She lifted one glass and filled it half full, careful not to drip on the taupe duvet cover. She swirled the deep red merlot several times before inhaling the familiar scent from their favorite Napa Winery. Alas, tonight was not going to happen.

"Cheers." She raised her glass to the surrounding white walls and closed door before blowing out three tapered candles on her mahogany nightstand. Troy's empty glass almost disappeared from sight in the dark undertones of the early winter sky hovering through the bedroom window. Elisa took a slow sip, then another.

The garage door opener remained silent as did Fiona's 1962 Austin Healey Sprite.

Chapter Three

An anchor is more than a weight. It is also a lifesaver, a tool, a weapon and a friend. Ask any captain or crew. But make time to stay and listen to their stories and be prepared to learn more than you gave thought to. ~ Nautical Notations in a ships log book – 1995.

An Anchor

"You can't be serious." Fiona shot steely darts across the breakfast table with the poisoned tips centered at Elisa's unguarded heart. "That weathered old fool knows nothing about city life; he'll dodder about the house and never venture out." Lady Kensington bent her bow and sharpened the next arrow.

"It's settled." Troy brushed back the shock of thick sandy hair that always swept down his forehead and flopped over his right eyebrow. He knew it drove his mum to insanity. It fell when he shifted in the armchair and reached for his wife's hand which he clasped between his. "We made the call while you were sleeping."

Heat rose throughout Fiona's neck and flushed across her face, a good bloody red that a proper Englishwoman would never let show. *Control, control, control.* The only emotional outbursts she allowed were those aimed at her daughter-in-law, and other Brits that became Americans. Within seconds Fiona composed herself "When will he arrive?" She smoothed the already perfect pleats of her beige slacks and tugged the v-neckline of her cotton blouse.

"I'm flying over tomorrow to bring him home." Elisa answered, offering no other information.

"Are you flying into Heathrow?" Jealousy seethed under the cool temperament Fiona strained to maintain, her façade cracking under the scrutiny of the two pairs of eyes watching.

"Yes, I am." Elisa straightened her back and squared her jaw.

"You already purchased the ticket?"

"Troy did that too while you were still sleeping." The muscles in Elisa's neck pulled taut.

"I would have accompanied you, spent some time in London."

"This isn't a holiday, Mum. Ian has been in the hospital. His daughter is bringing him home since he's been discharged into Mick's care because the doctors will not release him to live alone."

"She may need help. Ian is a stubborn man."

"And how do you plan to help her if you are flat hopping in the boroughs of London?" Troy's irritation was growing. "You'll be helping me transform the guest room for Ian's permanent stay."

"You have time to book another seat."

"I got the last seat."

"Economy or first class?" Fiona pushed the limit, her tone softening.

"I'm flying economy. We're trying to save money, not spend it like we're rich."

"But Walter has a soiree at his Kensington Square pound house this weekend."

"Then buy a ticket and go." Troy threw his hands in the air.

"My charge cards are all maxed out." Fiona whined.

"Why don't you ask one of your gentlemen friends to buy you a first class ticket?" Elisa had no patience left for the spoiled socialite. *And don't come back.*

"They still think I'm rich." Fiona's left eyelid twitched until she ran a hand over it.

"What, or they won't be your friends anymore?" Elisa left the room not waiting for the answer. Money associates with money. There is no friendship outside of millions in pounds sterling, the trendy nightclubs, pubs, and fashionable boutiques to shop along Kings Road and the Thames River. That inner circle of the rich and famous knows who's in and who's out. Fiona was hiding on the California coast using their suburban Sacramento Land Park residence, and Lake Tahoe summer cabin addresses. The past two years she'd managed to pull it off. Twice when friends wanted to visit she begged off saying she was on holiday and had loaned out both places to other visiting friends. Oh, if they'd only told her in advance, she would have loved to accommodate them. Next time.

Trudging up the stairs, Elisa consoled herself with memories of last night when she and Troy checked into the Sheraton Grand Hotel. It was worth the splurge. He swooped her up and drove them in his mother's convertible, with the top down. Troy ordered room service, they sipped champagne in the spa tub and *slept* blissfully uninterrupted from nine p.m.to six a.m. Fiona was so preoccupied brooding with her telly volume tuned high, she'd never noticed them slip out or sneak back in.

Troy kept his promise to spend time alone with Elisa before she left for Cornwall. He'd even agreed that is was a good idea she let Sebastian take over her weekly column for the newspaper. Seb had been petitioning her to let him try out his new Sacramento Lifestyles idea. She would freelance again after they got her dad settled. Elisa hummed a favorite tune as she packed the luggage, drawing from two zippered storage bags of heavy winter clothing from the walk-in closet. Early January can nip to the bone on the Cornish Coast. Her California wardrobe would stay behind. She dug out boots for walking the shoreline and boating with her father. The boots were buried in the musty corner under a mountain of flip-flops and wedge sandals crammed under the sweater section and shoe shelves.

"Where is everyone?" Mia tossed her sleeping bag and back pack on the living room carpet, and waved good-bye to Mr. Reynolds. She stood tall for eight, but her Batman pajama bottoms dragged the floor though cuffed at the ankles. "Mom, Dad?"

"What about Grandmum?" Fiona rushed in from the kitchen for hugs.

Mia's nose scrunched against her grandmother's strong embrace. She squeezed her way under the lock of arms surrounding her and dashed to her father. "Daddy!"

"Welcome home." Troy waited, arms open wide. "Did you have fun?"

"We watched movies and made a giant tent city with blankets. Lily's dad hung Christmas lights across the ceiling to make a starry night. And a glowing ball for a moon. It was magical." She gasped, bent over with face tilted upward, fingers spanning the length and breadth of the room. "Can you do that here sometime? Pleaseeee!"

"I think maybe I can." Troy tossed Mia over his shoulder and walked to the base of the stairway. "Mom, your smidget has returned home to the Kensington Family Circus."

A wiggling, giggling Mia pretended to seek release and bounced upside-down, watching Elisa's feet descend the steps until her painted toes touched said smidget's bobbing head.

"And which performer are you, little one?"

"I'm the tiger that jumps through fiery hoops and lunges at the crowd! Grrrrrr..." Mia grabbed her mother's feet as Troy lowered her to the last step where she preceded to wrap herself around Elisa's legs before twisting to thump her imaginary tail and bare pointed teeth with a thunderous roar. "Roar!"

"Mia, your mom is going to England tomorrow to bring Gramps back to join the circus."

"The funny one with the Santa beard? Oh, I like him. He knows all about history and books, oceans and fish that swim in schools. 'They're educated'." She quoted him.

She dropped to the floor and ran to Fiona. "Grandmum, my other grandparent is coming to live under the Big Top." Dancing in circles like the ballerina that walks a trapeze, Mia pirouetted and ended with an arabesque, which usually pleased Fiona. Not today.

"Come, you can help me finish packing my make-up."

"Really?" Mia was seconds behind Elisa, then squirreled her way ahead.

Troy raised his palm and fanned it in front of Fiona's wide open mouth. "Don't start any trouble. This is happening whether you like it or not."

"But he reeks of fish, dead fish. All the time. We'll never get that stench out of the walls." She poised herself on the edge of her heels having forsaken her traditional ballet flats. "It lingers."

"Ian is joining the circus, Mum. Best buy your ticket at the booth for the next show and get a front row seat." Troy gave her a one-arm hug, then made himself comfortable in his recliner with the Sacramento Bee newspaper and his coffee cup.

"And who are you, the ringmaster?" She chided, bitterness salting her tongue. "That silly childhood dream of yours."

"That leaves you to hang with the other joeys in clown alley, in your spare time." Troy kidded. "Seriously, Mum. Give the old guy a chance. Let him land on friendly soil. It's been over for two hundred years, forgive the rebellion, the colonists won the revolution. So his daughter fell in love with and married your son. We're Americans now. Ian isn't a traitor." Troy toasted her with his paper cup and swallowed lukewarm brew.

A reluctant Fiona slouched on the white sofa she hated. "I'm buying turquoise and teal pillows while she's gone." She patted the empty space beside her.

"Good for you. Those shades of blue will remind him of Cornwall." Troy opened the newspaper to the center crease, covering his face from view. "Maybe your redecorating skills can be useful in the other downstairs room, across from your door."

"I'll never have any privacy."

Troy cleared his throat. "That ship sailed here a couple of years ago."

"But—"

"No buts. The tent is up and I'm still looking for a volunteer to shoot from the cannon."

Chapter Four

Slumbering boats bob on the restless waters under a full luminous moon at the midnight hour. Millions of stars pin the sky, dots of brilliant light punctuate the inky black of night. The village sleeps content after a successful day's catch; enough to feed the hungry mouths at home and plenty to sell and fetch a good price elsewhere. It looks to be a prosperous year for the Cornish Coast. And hope be what is needed after the past season of want. ~ A Cornish fisherman's log book.

Setting Sail Across the Sky

Elisa buckled up for the departure long before the lights flashed on and the flight attendant stood ready to run through her routine announcement. Glad the last available ticket was a window seat, she settled in for the first leg of her journey cross-country. After a smooth take-off, she watched the ascent through a cloudless, blue sky that spread out like an endless uncharted ocean.

Everything in her father's life related to water: either in the water, on the water, or the fish he sought under the water. Her life was grounded in a city she loved, a 1940s home of her dreams, and a growing family. Elisa reached to stop the uncontrollable twitch tweaking her eyelids the second Fiona entered her thoughts. Fiona the intruder, the uninvited busybody that landed on their doorstep with nothing more than her precious sport car and overflowing designer luggage.

"Blast her." Realizing she'd spoken out loud, Elisa strained to force all thought of Fiona back to Sacramento and leave her there. It was easy, she simply envisioned her loading dirty pots and pans in the dishwasher, then heading to the laundry room next with a jug of detergent. A slow smile inched across Elisa's face. Anticipating a restful Fiona-free slumber, her thoughts returned to her father.

The year she was ten, her father Ian Darrow was almost lost at sea. He'd taken on extra work to make ends meet in a lean year when the fish seemed to have disappeared to the ocean depths. He pursued them, farther and farther out.

"Thar not be where he casts his nets." Joan Darrow told old widow Farley when she wandered over from next door to help with Elisa while her dad sailed. "They've overfished the lot of them."

"You'd best hope that not be, or we'll all be looking for work at the tin mines." The local fishmonger stretched to straighten her hunched back, and leaned forward on her snarled willow cane. White wisps of hair dangled loose from her hair combs and rustled the mustache Elisa tried not to stare at, but centered in on. Fingers reached to touch it, pull it, and her mouth opened to ask why she had one like the old fishermen, but she knew better. Instead she tugged on her gray cloth skirt and nestled in for a hug, which was immediately given.

"Why do all the fathers either work the mines or sail the ocean?" Elisa twirled in and out of clothes billowing in the breeze on the clothesline where her mum had attached weathered clips that looked like long wooden fingers. The week's wash was out to dry. More chores awaited them.

"The men fish the open sea or dig in the dark earth underground. That is all there be, child."

Elisa frowned a deep crease in her pasty forehead. "There is nothing else? Anywhere?"

"Not here." Her mum sighed.

"Tell the girl cities have other work." Mrs. Farley nudged her friend.

"Is the city a curious place for you, Elisa?" Joanie gathered her willow basket and dropped a few unused pegs inside.

"I won't know until I see one of these cities." Elisa pondered the question for a brief moment, and squinted her eyes at the sunny sky. "Can we go on holiday?"

"If your father be bringing in a good catch."

"Everything is about those fishes." Elisa scrunched her face, disgruntled, and dug her heels in.

"Pilchard fill the nets, the boats, and bellies." Widow Farley turned from her cob cottage toward the Darrow's stone home, and took Elisa's hand. "Fishery be the Cornish life."

Elisa remained quiet long after the door closed behind them and the women began the work of cleaning, filleting and deboning the fish for the supper fry. The metal pail of guts, gills, fish heads and tails slopped next to the rough-hewn table and chairs. The odor permeating the kitchen and dining room made her stomach lurch and flip. If she pinched her nose, she couldn't breathe when she closed her mouth. Fish eyes looked up at her from the top of the mushy pile in the pail—blank, yellow, lifeless eyes.

Ian didn't return for days. His friends shipped out on a search and find mission swearing to her hysterical mother that they would not return without him. The neighboring Mousehole Harbour fishermen found him first and towed his impaired trawler in from where he'd sat dead in the water. He brought in a middling catch, but the cost to repair the storm damage was staggering. It was a full year before Elisa heard him admit to her Mum he'd almost capsized at the peak of the sudden squall. He was never to fish alone after that, yet he did anyway. Hard times required a switch to crustacean, lobster, and crab. But her dad always went back to the fish.

Elisa awakened from her sleep to memories of how she'd watched her father on her previous visit. When he used the tidal moorings of the harbour during that summer, they seemed one to her, the man, the boat, and the sea. She set sail with him a couple of times when he'd asked her. It was so easy to please him. He longed for her presence and conversation. Other times he seemed comforted knowing she'd be waiting when he docked after the tide rolled in. They shared long suppers with longer discussions that ended up with him trailing off or repeating the same thing he'd said ten minutes before. Flustered, Ian had tried to cover up his mistakes and he was good at catching himself mid-way and improvising to hide his struggles. Embarrassed, he'd simply walk away as if he meant to start a new project or go in a different direction. It didn't always work.

Once during her visit he came back hours late and empty-handed after offering to fetch the fish and chips. She'd assumed he'd boated to St. Ives, to his favorite pub where they add more beer to the batter and the cod are twice the size. She drove them there after he returned. Silent and sullen the entirety of the ride, Ian grumbled throughout the meal, ruining their last day together. He downed a couple of pints at the pub and drank more at home. Most unusual for him. She flew home confused and irritated after having to ring for a cab to get to Heathrow after her father refused to drive her there.

How could she have missed the memory problems? He seemed careful, taking time to draw thoughts forward, to relay information accurately and to retain what he'd accessed. She considered it an ordinary process of aging. Later she discovered he'd written notes, reminders, and stashed them throughout the home and his boat. Directions to places he'd frequented his entire life, walking, driving, boating, and riding the trains. She'd missed it all.

Chapter Five

Oceans are massive, but still bordered by the larger land masses, continents. Should the vastness and depth be so intimidating? Frequently traveled after being mapped as discovered, they become less and less a mystery, and more and more traceable as charted. Crossing over whether by air or sea, progress has improved the speed and mode of transportation from luxury cruises with swimming pools on board, to Lear jets that bridge the miles in record time. Technology has taken over. ~ Internet News Report

Across the Pond

After changing flights at Kennedy Airport in New York, Elisa buckled up to cross the Atlantic. What used to be her favorite ocean, was now second to the Pacific. This did not sit well with her father. His angry reaction to a casual conversation concerning the matter fueled an almost violent reaction that had frightened her. A calm man, it was out of character to the point she'd asked him to see his doctor at surgery. He declined, but seemed unsettled by the incident himself.

This flight Troy had booked an aisle seat and Elisa hoped to change with someone wanting more leg space. When a long-limbed basketball team boarded, she got her wish after a desperate six and a half foot player approached. Towering over her, his head scuffed the plane's ceiling as he slouched forward attempting to bypass her to the window seat.

After loading his travel-on bag in the overhead compartment, the young man said, "Excuse me, Miss."

Elisa looked ahead four packed rows, then answered him. "Your teammates all have seats together." She unbuckled and scooted over to the window past the irritated passenger seated in the middle. "You're welcome to take my place."

A toothy grin widened across his face. "We're not allowed to ask."

"You didn't." She clicked the buckle closed and tightened the belt. "I offered."

"Thank you." He sat and stretched his legs which accounted for most of his height, then stowed his gym bag under the seat after handing hers over.

The red-eye was on time and most passengers closed their window shades in preparation to sleep through the seven hour trans-Atlantic flight. Elisa left hers open. Lights remained on during the smooth ascent, until they leveled above the sparse clouds. Belts clacked open as soon as the attendant flashed the okay, and lights were dimmed or turned off except for where Elisa sat toward the rear of the plane. It was a crystal clear sky and she wanted to see all the twinkling stars and the brilliant full moon encircled by a hazy lunar ring.

Within minutes the snoring center passenger leaned his snowy head on Elisa's left shoulder. He somewhat resembled her father with a beard and mustache. A short man with stubby legs, his feet didn't quite touch the floor, but dangled an inch or so above. He was no fisherman. Dressed in Dockers and a loose sweater his clothing was neatly pressed and the shoes smelled of brand new leather. Ian always carried the scent of fish on his clothes, in his skin, under his fingernails, and in his hair. She breathed in a strong whiff of a heady musk cologne, then turned back to the gaze out the window.

A profusion of stars shone with miraculous intensity. One of the plane's wings was visible, gleaming silver under the heavenly light show. Elisa knew they'd be over the ocean for some time. When she was a young woman, that part of the flight used to frighten her, the possibility of crashing into the cavernous abyss below. The water looked as black as a starless midnight sky over Cornwall, no street lights illuminated the village cobblestone streets or seaside cliffs. Pitch black spread like an endless cover until morning light broke. She preferred the early dawn of day. Yet if she wanted to see her father, she had to rise when darkness still hovered.

The basketball player popped earplugs in and his music blared. Elisa expected rap, but heard classical instrumentals instead. Soothing and peaceful, the symphony lulled her to sleep.

"Be careful there little girl." Ian and Elisa walked side-by-side along the ragged-edged cliff above a roaring clash of rising cap swells during an unseasonable change of weather. On their way home from visiting the village next over, Ian got them moving early on. Fishermen read the sky, the air, and the ocean like librarians read books. Salt mingled on the tip of Elisa's tongue, a fine brine spray surrounded them. She trudged in her blue Wellies beside her father's larger yellow Wellingtons. She marched in the damp, tall grass trying to keep in step with him as his pace quickened and fell like lead on the earth.

"Daddy, slow down." She whined, her shiny boots light on the ground.

He swooped her up in his arms and started running. There on his shoulder she caught sight of the black beast in the clouds encroaching toward them. It belted out thunderous warnings and clamored heavy and burdensome. "Hold tight." Her father shouted.

A howling wind swept under his feet, knocking them off balance and tumbling into the whipping grasses which stung her cheeks. They rolled, matting down all foliage in their path. Ian steadied himself on his feet again and hauled Elisa up, pressing her close to his chest. Rain pelted in blinding sheets with such sheer force, the earth below transformed into a muddy bog that swallowed his big yellow boots by inches. Her father's arms crossed over Elisa's back braced tight and locked in place, the other hand covered her head.

"Home be over the hill." He bounced out the words between huffing breaths and tangles of strangling weeds seizing each step that he fought to securely land.

"Should we pray?" She whispered in his reddened, chilled ear.

"Yes." He muttered into the crying wind.

She prayed, eyes closed, heart pounding, clinging to Ian's slippery slicker. Thunder and lightning charged the murky skies darkening all around them and then a flash of jagged light blazed, yet she listened for an answer. Her heart stilled in the crescendo of the storm. Ian trenched forward, boots sinking under the weight of their bodies, muck seeping into the pours of their skin. A distant flickering light drew his attention just west of his present direction. He honed in and redirected his course. The light amplified brighter, a single beacon in the wild blindness thrashing upon them.

"Ready yerself." Ian tucked Elisa inward, bowed his head while cupping hers, and proceeded to backslide down a hill. Mud slopped and sloshed. The bumpy ride deposited them with a splash in a puddle near the cottage side door. They were home. And they were safe save half the countryside they snagged along the way.

A mixed euphoria overwhelmed Elisa. Though confident her father would protect her in the storm, she had succumbed to fear in the midst of the worst of it. A sense of shame pervaded. Did he know? A sudden pull into his arms answered her thoughts.

"You be me brave girl, Elisa Jean Darrow." He squeezed her snug against his thumping heart. "You be able to face anything in yer life now." Was it rain or tears streaming down his cheeks?

She remained in her father's hold, sitting in the muddy pond of water as the door to the cottage opened. They stood, removed their Wellington boots and dumped the liquid contents and assorted clods of dirt and grass before entering where the hearth blazed a warm welcome.

"Yer tarried too long yer daft bugger." One by one Joan cleaved both to her bosom.

And that was how it went between her Mum and Dad, never any complimentary or romantic banter. She knew they loved each other, but words were purposeful to accomplish chores, work, and church. Maybe on their weekly pub dates they chattered away. The local fishermen made plenty of noise when they gathered at The Maiden Voyage for pints of ale and the fortnight mates' meetings. Round after round of cheers rang out the propped open door throughout the center of the village. Dastardly rows over dart championships ushered fistfights to the cobblestone street, and back inside again.

Ian Clive Darrow, average in height, commanded great respect from his hard labor and resulting immense physical strength. Unless sodden, none challenged him lest the foolish blaggard suffer a momentary scuff or two.

"Yer father is a man of honour. His word be binding." Joan cheeks blushed a hint of red. "That be why me wed him." She kissed the fiery hair on the tip-top of Elisa's head. "One day yer be wed to a Cornishman too." Joan crinkled the corner of an eye and winked.

Well, that didn't happen. Troy's lineage hailed from London. Fiona traced it all the way back to the fourteenth century. There was a mite of the royal bloodline. Didn't matter. The Kensingtons' weren't Cornish. And many was the young man from the village that wooed Elisa right up until she moved away to board at college in America. Where of course she met, fell in love with, and committed the unforgiveable sin of later marrying, Troy. Not a fisherman, not a tin miner, or a shoppe keeper, but a bloody suit and tie businessman.

Falling from grace was swift, and it all but killed her Mum.

"A blimey Londoner—how could yer?" Joan spun on her heels. "This is that university nonsense. Next we know, yer be blooming staying across the pond!"

Chapter Six

Home is a place we try to return to after spending our youth longing to leave it behind. Though the dwelling may look the same, have the same furniture and décor, the person seeking the familiar, changes more and more between each subsequent visit. Now a visitor, and no longer a member of the residing family. Grown children come home seeking what they left behind, not realizing the person they took with them, long ago shed the skin that is now, uninhabitable. ~ Library book Ian checked out about empty nesters.

A Bit Dodgy

Her godfather Mick arranged in advance to pick Elisa up at Heathrow explaining the drive there would be unsettling for her father.

Ian now stayed within a certain radius of his cottage, and his radar spun off the charts if anyone forgot and exceeded his set perimeters. This rather odd behavior was new and far removed from his lifelong exploratory nature. That part of his personality, the spur of the moment adventurer, made them kindred spirits from her youth.

All spiffy in his Sunday duds, Elisa walked past Mick not once, but twice.

"Where in Land's End did you get that starched shirt and those pressed trousers?"

"Me be dating me bird now. Midge, she does the wash and ironing." He tugged with both hands on suspenders his tweed sport coat concealed. Brown suede elbow patches bended, stressing the hand-stitching until Mick lowered his arms to gather the luggage Elisa had already picked up from the turnstile. She'd slipped her shoes back on, and cleared all check points under the burdensome security measures.

"Don't care much for London." He gruffed, his voice drowned by the growing crowd.

"Yes, I know. I appreciate you picking me up, but I could have hailed a cab."

"No, Elisa. We be having a chat before you see your dad." Mick straightened after loading and strapping her bags on his pull-away cart. "You need be prepare yourself."

"Why?" She took in the halting expression etched in the weathered wrinkles on the fisherman's face. They called him 'Old Mick', but he was the youngest in her father's group by at least a full decade. Black thick wavy hair spackled with gray fell at shoulder-length, and framed worrisome sea foam green eyes. He was the lady's man, telling tall fish tales and dancing women across the pub floor until last call. Still he bore the crusted edges of the salt water and air.

"Let me check under the bonnet before we get on. Me heard some rattling on the way here" He towed her luggage, walking them past noisy, reveling travelers out to the parking lot, stopping in front of a royal blue Mini Cooper.

The slap of cold air after exiting the airport lobby proved an instant reminder California was half a world away. She clutched her sweater tight under her neck. "This is your car?"

"Midge loaned me her Mini so you wouldn't be riding in me 'fishmobil' as she calls it."

"I like her already." Elisa surrendered her purse and carry-on to be loaded with the rest of her bags. "Wait." She grabbed her cell phone with urgency. "I need to text home that I've arrived."

"Daft electronics rule the world now." Mick shuffled everything in the boot, then held the passenger door open as Elisa two-thumbed a quick, *Have arrived. All well*, before lowering herself in the two-door compact.

A symphony sonata began playing in short ring tones the minute Mick buckled up and turned on the ignition. Fumbling inside his jacket pocket, he retrieved and answered his mobile with a sheepish shrug of his broad shoulders. "Leaving London now, Luv." A deep blush seemed to warm his chilled round cheeks. "Bloody well." His tone softened. "Does Ian understand?" A scowl crossed and lined his brow. "Maybe when he sees her. Ta." He hesitated while backing out and said. "You be looking more and more like Joanie the older you be, girl."

"Thank you, Mick." Elisa knew how much they all missed her Mum. "Is my dad okay?" She studied the fisherman's face as he paused and leaned onto the steering wheel before turning.

"He still be Ian." His eyes pierced hers. "Somewhere in there."

Elisa tried not to panic as Mick drove the choked, unruly streets into the lamplight of the city before heading to the countryside. The first two hours of the drive thy both were quite subdued, not a lot of chatter. Returning home felt odd. She thought about how hard a life Fisherfolk live, they maneuver their boats navigating the raw power of the ocean, and the physical labor is intense before, during, and after their nets burst with the coveted catch they hunt. Danger is a constant and bravery almost a daily requirement though never mentioned until there is loss.

Elisa palmed her cell, both hands lay still in her lap. The quiet would end upon reaching their destination. Neither of them spoke but a few words to catch up early on in the journey. Mick knew what lay ahead of her. His silence was deafening.

She stared out the car window in deep thought. Much like on the plane, it held a clear visual. Mick drove past all her familiar landmarks. Traffic had slowed once they ventured out of the city limits. She loved the two-lane roads and hated the round-a-bouts with a passion. Lorries ploughed through recklessly causing accidents. It scared her. *At least they had jobs unlike Fiona who lived off everyone else's hard work and money*. The roadside trees took on shadowy forms, blending into a single elongated shape that appeared to be following them the deeper they drove into the woods. The faceless, mindless mass hovered, drawing closer.

"Ian, he be a mite confused." Mick's voice startled her. They were now but a short distance from Cornwall. The hours had blended and blurred.

"Will he know who I am?" She needed to know. She already knew. But maybe she could be wrong. Fathers know their daughters. They protect their little girls from harm. This she knew.

Mick's meaty hands gripped tight around the steering wheel, his back stiffened, and his head topped merely a scrape from touching the roof of the Mini. "No."

Elisa laced her fingers together over the cell phone. He'd told her as such long distance. Wasn't that why she'd come to take her father home? Well, to her home, in America. This would be the last visit to the house of her childhood, to put it on the market, to sell all he ever knew and go through his belongings and decide what to ship, to give away, sell, or toss in the rubbish bin. The scope of the task waiting was surreal at this point. As well as her responsibilities back home.

"Ian be having moments, spurts of recognition, when you'd swear he's all there. He can answer questions without hesitation. But," A wide crack broke the strength and reserve of Mick's words. "He drifts off without warning, like a lost ship at sea."

"I see." But she didn't. Last year her father could carry a conversation, answer her. Remember details with sharp accuracy. He shared stories she'd never heard before that delighted her—memories of her mum, when they'd courted, fallen in love. Humorous escapades from when he was a Cornish lad loose with his mates amuck in the various port villages, St Ives, Polperro, Padstow, Mevagissey, Looe. Nothing but trouble the lot of them. How she'd laughed and he'd laughed with her.

"He struggled for you last visit." Mick focused straight ahead. "Pretty much pulled it off." His tone lowered. "Right up to the end when his temper flared."

"Is that still a problem?" The road rumbled under the car, a steady bumpy grind since the round-a-bouts left them to the winding roads of Cornwall. Mick picked up the pace as they neared Cagwith. Elisa asked a second time. "Does he still have angry outbursts?"

"Yes." Mick conceded. "Doc says it be next stage. Intense for a year now."

"So, since I left?" She rolled her window down half-way, the moisture in the air flowing in cool against her skin, with the familiar scent of the ocean flooding the car.

"There be an incident a few months back." Mick hitched his neck sideways until a loud pop, pop, pop released pressure from his spine.

"An incident?"

"An arrest." He clenched his jaw and waited.

"Arrest?" Her entire body went rigid. She unbuckled her seatbelt and turned sideways, her cell dropped to the floor and she left it there.

"It be stricken from his record. All charges were eventually dropped." Mick bobbed his head and managed a weak smile while working out the creak in his neck.

"Record?" Her voice raised in pitch and tweaked. "My father has a police record?"

"Just a few offenses. The solicitor be working with us all to be clearing Ian's name." Mick looked to her for approval.

"Pull over, Mick." Her voice ordered wavered.

He kept to the road wide-eyed, and sped up.

"Pull over!"

The right indicator flashed on, the green arrow pointing in the same direction as Elisa's trembling finger. Mick slowed down as a couple of vehicles passed them on the narrow road. He parked on the widest stretch of dirt near a ditch next to the woods. He left the motor running.

"Turn it off." Elisa's tone was flat, her glare reflected in the rearview and side mirrors.

"It be like this," Mick preempted her and shut off the motor. "Ian be stealing boats. Nothing big and fancy, or costly, mind you. Mostly small trawlers docked, not exactly sea worthy either." He faced Elisa. "The first one looked to be like his trawler. It be an understandable mistake."

"There's a second one?" Her stomach acids flowed and a queasy, bile rose up her esophagus burning in her throat. Her shoe nicked the vibrating cell on the car floor matt.

"Three boats. But one be going to scrap so it don't really count." Mick's eyes brightened and he blinked while nodding, certain Elisa would consider the upside of this bit of information.

"Why didn't anyone tell me about this before? When it happened?" Heat flamed throughout her limbs. "You had three opportunities!" She yelled.

"We be taking care of our own here. Ian be as much our family as he be yours." Mick grew defensive and didn't attempt to stifle a bit of indignation in his next delivery. "You be an American now. We still be Cornish."

"Don't throw that in my face. There are legalities involved. Is there a possibility he can go to jail?" She sat back in her seat. The mere thought of it took her breath.

"He spent a night behind bars in Port Isaac. But that be a lack of communication." Mick continued. "All financial restitution has been made outside of the courts. Two charges were dropped after full payment. The last one is pending payment in full."

"How did he pay for all this?"

"Out of his ISA savings. Your dad had a good bit put away. Me said one boat was scrap, worthless. No one could figure out how he got her so far out to sea." Mick swiped sweat.

Stunned, Elisa sat mouth open, head spinning, stomach churning.

"Let it settle before you see him. He understands not what he have done. He would never steal another fisherman's boat."

"Wait a minute. Where is the *Victoria Regina*?"

Mick sighed a sorrowful lament. His head bowed forward and he shook his mop of hair. "She be the first to sink, a terrible loss that sent him to the depths of despair. He knows, but he remembers not. The confusion spiraled him out of control for next months." Mick looked up. "Me did call then, but that Fiona answered and yacked on trying to get me to give her the message. When you called not back, we dealt with everything here."

"When?" Elisa spoke in a whisper. "When did she sink?"

"Six months after you went back to the States. He almost went down with her. Me thinks part of him wanted to, but he swam to shore." Mick croaked out. "Ian's heart be broken since then."

A lorry sped by dangerously close. Gravel and dirt kicked up rattling the under carriage of the little car and a rock bounced off the windscreen as the car shook in the after draft. There were no words. Elisa grappled with the extent of the circumstances, rolling it out like an unraveling tapestry in her mind. Three boats stolen, one sunk. Two paid for. One full payment due. Criminal charges still pending. The *Victoria Regina,* gone forever.

"Where did he last sail the *Victoria?*"

"Off the Lizard."

"Out past the Devil's Frying Pan." Elisa gasped, her heart fluttered, and she grabbed Mick's arm. "He would never try to end his life," she squeezed and held on, "my father couldn't."

"Me thinks he meant to go down with her. We all do." Mick was careful with what he said next. "Ian be lost in and out of his mind. He would never knowingly be taking his own life, or another. Doc says dementia or Alzheimer's. Either way, he not be coming back to us."

Mick started up the car. "We need to go now. They be waiting."

"They?"

"Ian be with Midge at her flat." Mick pulled out on the dark empty road, no headlights either way, no streetlights. "We don't leave him alone anymore. He wanders at night and we have to lock him in with us. It be me fortnight with him. Everyone takes a turn. It be working out so far, except for the last escape."

"Escape?" Elisa bit her lower lip.

"He hailed a cab, slipped out, and went for quite the drive." Mick smiled. 'The cabbie realized something not be quite right and brought him back after an hour. Said your dad be, 'A bit dodgy.'"

They sat in silence while Elisa tried to absorb all she'd just learned. "We be almost there, another five minutes. You ready?" Mick urged.

Elisa said nothing. Who was this person she would be taking home? A stranger? How can someone disappear while standing before you? Mick thought he was helping, but she'd prepared herself for the father she last saw and sailed so expertly with. Just old age forgetfulness. Surely once in the States all would settle like before. The change will be good for him she decided. She hoped.

The car pulled in front of a small building of flats. All lights were on in a lower flat on the right side. A thin, clean shaven older man peered out the front sheers, one hand held the curtain back. After a prolong stare at the vehicle, he stepped away, sat in a wooden rocking chair looking straight ahead.

Chapter Seven

Somethings can be fixed, and some cannot. Broken objects need not necessarily be discarded. People are the same way. The world today holds a different viewpoint. One year warranties have replaced lifetime warranties. Your grandmother's fridge lasted fifty years, a brand new one, a single year, but you may purchase insurance as additional back-up. Everything has a chip now too. The trusty microchip. Next they'll decide people need to be chipped like our pets, debit cards, and vehicles. How long of a warranty will those chips have and who encodes them? What is the true value of the person with or without a chip? ~ Excerpt from an article in a *Seniors* magazine.

Coming Home

Elisa took slow measured steps walking the path banked by flourishing hydrangea bushes up to the bright red door. She instinctively knew it was the downstairs flat numbered two, with lights blazing into the darkening of the sky. Upstairs only the outside entry bulb illuminated a weak aura that ringed a halo of light above the door, then dissipated in the misty air.

"Does Midge have other company?" Elisa glanced at her wristwatch.

"No one but your father." Mick hoisted all the bags from the boot unto the pavement, caught up to and wrapped an arm around his reluctant passenger. "He be looking changed, but it be your Dad."

Stunned, Elisa didn't budge. The old man in the window bent forward and cocked his head sideway to get a better look at her. Squinting, he searched without any sign of recognition, any expression of surprise or delight she was home.

"He be up late nights, can't sleep, can't read his books anymore." Mick shook his head. "That be a great loss for Ian. He loved his stories." Mick rolled the luggage past her up two steps, and opened the door without knocking. "Me live here most times now." He answered her questioning gape.

Elisa wanted to run, no, fly across the Atlantic, the entire United States of America until she landed herself safely back in Sacramento where she belonged, home.

"There be no turning back." Mick urged again, almost reading her thoughts. "It be your dad, girl. Come in, say cheers."

Following the fisherman inside, the immediate absence of any fish odors struck her as odd. The strong familiar oily gills and scales ode de oceanic perfume that assaulted your nostrils and open mouth did not permeate the air. Midge emerged from the kitchen bleary-eyed but nice.

"Welcome, young Darrow." She took Elisa's limp hand and escorted her to the living room. "We have been waiting for you, haven't we, Ian."

"Yes." He stood to greet her rising from the overstuffed Chintz Queen Anne chair that dwarfed his slender body. His movements were stiff and deliberate, as though painful. "Cheers.

Happy to be meeting you." He stretched out a frail hand riddled with bulging blue veins and purplish blotchy spots.

Elisa took note of the disappointment on both Midge and Mick's faces. It appeared they too had been hoping for some form of acknowledgement, though they were quick to recover. She followed suit. "Nice to meet you too." She swallowed the lump stuck in her throat. "My name is Elisa Jean Darrow." Her eyes locked onto his.

"Ian. Me name be Ian." He gave her a firm shake and nod of the head seemingly not acknowledging their shared last name.

He seemed pleased but she couldn't tell if it was because he remembered his name or hearing her name sparked a flicker of memory. Her heart leapt. The firm shake and nod was his trademark gesture. And there was strength in his grip that belied the feeble frame standing before her. This man had no muscle, his trousers bagged, his neck sagged, and sunken eye sockets were overladen by flaps of loose skin and bushy eyebrows. Where the Land's End was her father?

"I'll put on a spot of tea." Midge offered. "I've fresh baked scones and made lemon curd."

"Some clotted cream too?" Ian perked up and released Elisa's hand with a pat.

Elisa gasped. That pat was their special parting since the day on the cliffs. It was followed with a peck on the cheek but right now half a recollection was better than none. She sat in the matching Queen Anne next to where Ian settled again. A polished cherry wood table and antique brass claw-footed lamp with a silk shade embellished by fringe and gimps separated father and daughter. "It's a lovely rose print." Elisa pointed to the lampshade. "Nice detail."

Ian, somewhat perplexed, said. "Midge be liking pretty things." He murmured. "No fish."

"Me be helping me bird while you two chat up." Mick left the room with a wink of those sea foam eyes.

The two fidgeted in awkward silence. Ian rummaged through his pockets and jingled change. Elisa smoothed out the wrinkles in her broadcloth travel skirt. Ian stole longer glances at the visitor but said nothing when their line of vision intersected. The mantle clock ticked each second of time. The burning fire emitted enough heat that the room was comfortable unlike most of the older, drafty Cornish homes. Elisa appreciated the cleanliness and décor and it was not what she'd expected. All the fishermen lived rather rustic lives. Most were widowers and their cottages suffered neglect.

"Me miss me pipe. Mick's bird don't allow smoking inside her flat." Ian struck up a conversation and pinched his nose up in the air.

"I thought you gave up smoking." It slipped out. She tried to regroup but he'd heard her plain and clear.

"Me did. Me miss me pipe. Still like to clench it between me teeth." He inclined toward her. "How you be knowing me used to smoke?"

"Mick must have mentioned it on the drive here." She hated lying to him. It felt wrong.

"Oh." He dropped the issue.

41

"Ready to take tea?" Midge carried a tray packed with fine china.

"Me thought me use only the pottery, in case me be breaking another fancy cup and saucer." A troubled frown clouded Ian's face that preceded nervous shakes.

"Tonight is special. In honour of our guest." Midge's voice hinged a bit on the edge of irritated frustration. She took a deep breath. "I made your favourite currant spice scones, Ian."

"Me like those?" His snowy white eyebrows arched.

"Yes you do, Mate." Mick served Elisa first and Ian second.

"Then let's get on and toast Queen Elizabeth." He raised his plate not waiting for a cuppa. "God save the Queen, and cheers to me daughter, Elisa Jean." He reached to clink plates. "Be a good girl now." He watched for her to reciprocate.

"Cheers." She was careful to tip her plate to his ever so lightly.

"When did you be coming home?" Ian asked. "Will you be staying a while this time?"

Pensive, Elisa gave a cautious reply, "I am home as long as you need me, Dad."

"That be making your Mum most happy." Ian took a lusty first bite.

Chapter Eight

Where do forgotten thoughts go? Are they stored somewhere in remote receptacles of the brain, floating about unheeded until one day they slip back to the frontal lobe? Do they disappear forever, evaporate, and dissipate as a vapor? Is there some secret retrieval system yet undiscovered that can restore the displaced, lost, and elusive memories? Why are there more questions than answers in a technological world advancing with break through medical studies earning accolades and awards, while minds continue to erode away into oblivion? ~ Memory Care Blog

Strange Surroundings

Elisa threw herself across the cabbage rose fluffy comforter and buried her face in the ruffle trimmed pillow shams. Her muffled cries soaked the cotton print fabric, absorbing her anguish amid great gulps of air and the drool and spit of harsh reality. The tiny guest room held her shock and grief within its plaster walls like a miniature shadow box housing keepsakes and mementos.

She rolled and turned on the twin mattress, hugging a pillow to her chest as a buffer warding off more pain, more revelations, more bewilderment. The white iron headboard pressed against wallpaper and she curled in a tight ball, her boot heels digging into the sagging mid-section of the bed.

"You alright in there?" Midge asked, tapping repeatedly on the door.

"Yes." Elisa strung the word out and caught her breath between sobs.

"Earl Gray at seven o'clock then, Luv." The tapping stopped. "'Nite now."

She didn't answer. Light footsteps padded away until she could hear nothing at all.

Here in this stranger's home, on a lumpy mattress she craved Troy and their massive king size memory foam bed and pillows. The lack of familiar was unsettling as was the man posing to be her father who resembled more of an escaped rest home resident. What could she say to him in the morning? What kind of polite conversation could possibly cover all the legal decisions they needed to address? What words would even matter if he couldn't remember she was his daughter from one minute to the next?

Elisa texted a quick message to Troy, "Help!" The feeling in her toes went numb when she hit send. A quick riffle through her carry-on luggage produced a hot water bottle wrapped in a woolen cable-knit covering. She quietly made her way down the hall to the loo and turned up the hot water until a steady stream of steam fogged up the oval wall mirror hanging above the pedestal sink. After filling and sealing the rubber companion, she tip-toed back to the bedroom.

Nestling under the covers barely warmed her extremities so she reached to slip the needed aid over her feet, then pulled every sheet and blanket up to her neck. Her teeth still chattered, enamel clicking on enamel at increasing speed. Childhood memories of freezing in bed at night because her parents refused to use more coal to heat the house flooded back. Hot water bottles are a Brit's best friend unless your parents are wealthy and shelled money out for expensive central heat. *Must pick up another warmer and red rubber bottle at market tomorrow.*

A sudden commotion down the hall awakened her just as she was drifting off to sleep. The scrape of furniture across the flooring and escalating argumentative voices rattled. She rose and strained to hear the words as she cracked open her door.

"You not be telling me not to be going!"

"Go back to bed, Ian."

"Me going to the pub so me can smoke me pipe."

"Maiden Voyage is closed until tomorrow, mate. We be going then and get you a fresh pouch of tobacco in the village. Back to bed now."

"Me have to go to the loo."

"It be across the hall."

What sounded like a push and shove interaction ensued, shoes or slippers scuffling on the tile, and a few expletives were exchanged.

"Me can manage myself."

"You were headed to the front door."

"Oh."

A door slammed, shaking the walls surrounding Elisa. She peered out the crevice of space before her and saw Mick leaning against the archway near the kitchen. He was bundled in flannel and thermals under a heavy robe. Wool slippers covered his big feet. Her father emerged, leaving the light on. Mick reached beyond Ian and flicked it off, but not before she noticed Ian was dressed in trousers and a shirt with the tail tucked half-in and half-out of his unbelted waistband. His heavy winter boots clomped over the tiles as he returned to his bedroom. A pipe remained clenched between his teeth the entire time.

"Bloody Bugger!" Ian yelled in passing before entering his room.

Mick sighed and quietly shut the door. He reached up and flipped a bronze lock at the upper right hand corner near the ceiling. He knocked his head in exasperation against the closed door three times before heading down the hallway and disappearing behind another door.

A cold shiver journeyed up Elisa's spine. She stood there staring at the empty room for a while before crawling back in the bed and repositioning the hot water bottle over her feet.

Chapter Nine

Words can hurt and sting long after the syllables have passed over the lips that uttered the sentences that cannot be erased. Memory is a strange friend. Most choose to remember the good and forget or temper the bad within tolerable boundaries. Others choose to dwell on the worst and replay the vocal delivery over and over again to the point of torment. When this strange friend decides to become a foe, all choices are snatched away without permission. Leaving an empty auditorium that echoes, distorting once familiar voices, and confusing the faces that spoke specific, sculpted sentences that either breathed life into the soul, or drained every essence out. ~ Poetic viewpoint in an article on Alzheimer's in a magazine left in a hospital waiting room.

Silent Sentences

Ian sat at the breakfast table smoothing out the rumpled clothing he was still wearing from the middle of the previous night. All that was missing was his pipe.

"Ta, Elisa Jean. Ready for a cuppa?" He stood and pulled out the chair next to him.

"You're quite chipper this morning." Mick mumbled, rubbing caked sleep out of the corners of his eyes. He tipped his mug under his chin missing his lips, before raising it again, and swallowing a long gulp.

Elisa pulled her sweater tight at the neck and sat beside her father. As he scooted her in, wooden legs etched grooves into the high-polished tiles, and she noticed his shoes were on the wrong feet. The laces, loosely tied, dragged across the flooring. She opened her mouth to tell him, but he tripped before she could form a single word. Ian smacked hard into the high-back of the empty chair by Mick. Gripping hard he held on and swayed sideways before steadying himself.

"Dad, you need to tie your shoelaces."

"Oh, look at that." He sat and bent down at the waist. Taking two laces between his fingers he looped over twice but couldn't tie a bow. Struggling repeatedly, his lean cheeks burned crimson. He released the laces and tried again. Huffing, he tugged the long strands of coiled nylon up high and let go with a disgruntled sigh.

Elisa resisted the urge to reach over and do it for him. She pressed her folded hands deep into the warmth of her flannel nightgown and clasped them together in her lap.

Mick shook his head, rose and left the room, sipping tea with each step away from the table to the hallway.

Ian's voice raised, and low guttural cursing flowed the more frustrated he grew.

Elisa scanned the house for Midge but she was nowhere to be seen. Brewed tea sat in the center of the table in a Brown Betty pot surrounded by a jar of orange marmalade, a slab of butter for the equivalent of American English muffins waiting untouched on a chipped platter of china. Running her finger tip over the nick on the plate and the roses blooming in a circular ring along the border, Elisa's ears perked up when Mick's heavy footsteps approached.

A pair of scuffed brown leather loafers fell directly beside Ian's feet.

Ian dropped the laces and glanced up the full length of his robed, to his be-speckled friend. With a quick shuffle of his slippers, Mick shoved the shoes closer, and adjusted his gold-rimmed eyeglasses back to the bridge of his nose. He chugged down the last of his tea, leaned over, and refilled his mug.

"Switch into the slip-ons, mate." He sat tightening his plaid belt until his mid-section bulged. "You be getting about easier at the pub later without shoestrings being a bother."

Ian stopped dead, his neck and face aflame. His jaw fell open and he appeared ready to hurl a disagreeing blast of objections at Mick when instead he closed his mouth. He looked at Elisa, then down at the two pairs of shoes, a perplexed expression lit his paling cheeks. Using the toe of one shoe, he pushed at the back heel until the shoe freely gave way, then liberated the other with his socked foot. For a moment he sat there without moving, staring at both pair of shoes. He mixed up the two pairs, then matched them together again.

Mick stood and scooped up the discarded shoes under one arm, nudging the loafers until they touched Ian's socks. Whistling, Mick made a slow-stride back down the hall.

Elisa watched to see which room he entered. "Dad that's your left foot." She motioned for him to slip the shoe on his other foot.

"Oh. Left foot, right foot." He matched the shoes in place with the correct feet, tapping his toes on the tile for a prolonged period of time.

As soon as he returned Mick dumped a stream of sugar from a restaurant-style container into Ian's mug. "If we be going for fish and chips at the pub, you need to wear shoes. No socked feet allowed. You know that." Mick had already poured the milk from a home-delivery dairy bottle when the mug was empty. He tapped his slipper next to the loafers. "Get to it, mate."

A puzzled look washed over Ian. He sat staring at his gray socks and brown loafers.

Elisa turned toward her father.

"No, let him. It just takes time." Mick encouraged.

After reversing the left and right placement, Ian slipped his feet in each shoe.

"Good job!" Mick interrupted.

"Never mind." Mick whispered in Elisa's ear. "I be switching them when he gets into his adult nappy before pub time."

"What?" Elisa's chest caved.

"We only use them when Ian be going out. Don't want him to be embarrassed again. It be too traumatic when he has an accident in public." Mick offered Ian a muffin that he split and slathered both sides with the orange marmalade.

Hand shaking, Ian poured tea in his mug. He winked with a self-satisfied grin at Elisa and offered to pour her a cup.

"Yes, please." A faint smile trembled on her lips.

Ian poured bracing one arm up with the other, then he replaced the pot on the warmer.

Midge emerged from her room, hair done, make-up applied, in a smart tweed pantsuit. The woven fabric and tailored-style enhanced her shape. She looked years younger than the night before and she knew it.

"What's the plan today?" She asked Mick.

"Fish and chips for lunch in St. Ives. And Ian has to be at surgery to see the Doc at three for his annual." Mick answered. "Any chance of bangers for breakfast?"

"I think I can manage that. Want to give me a hand, Luv?" She placed a hand on Elisa's shoulder.

"Who be yer guest?" Ian leaned over and asked Midge.

"Elisa Jean, from the States." Mick replied as Midge rolled her eyes and left the room.

Chapter Ten

There is much to be said for routine. Spontaneity calls for less discipline and offers no promises. It's a grab bag of sorts. ~ Memory Care blog entry Elisa brought up after morning tea.

The Pub

Ian poked at the Cornish cod on his plate. He'd doused it with malt vinegar, the chips too but spared the mushy peas. The pint of Tribute ale was empty. Ian flagged the waitress over for another with a double wink, waving the stack of pound notes he always carried.

"Slow down on the brew, Mate." Mick handed Ian his fork. "Get to work on the cod." He speared the crispy coated fish floating in the river of brown liquid. "Going to be too soggy to eat if you wait much longer."

"Did you know that the Sloop Inn here dates back to 1312?" Ian spoke directly to Elisa.

"No, I didn't."

"They've changed things a mite from the old days. Too modern in The Captain's Room for the likes of this fisherman. But the ale be good." He raised his second pint to her, "Cheers, young one."

Before he could put the glass to his lips Mick whisked it to the table with a stern, "Eat the fish."

"Me need to leave room for Willy Walley Ice Cream, for dessert."

"There be no dessert if you don't eat your lunch."

Midge glanced around as the two men's voices rose. None of the few other patrons were paying any attention. She tilted her pint ignoring the stink eye Mick shot her as he continued trying to get Ian to put his drink on the table. She downed a long swig of the draft.

"I like mine soaked in malt vinegar too." Elisa cut off a large piece cod. "And if you aren't hungry, I'll be stealing some off your plate."

Ian squinted at her, his forehead creased in three rows as he placed his ale down and picked up his fork. "Yer have to let it be sitting a mite before it be saturated to perfection."

Elisa engaged her father in polite conversation while they each consumed the entire contents in front of them until only puddles of malt vinegar stained the white pottery dishes. She knew she'd scored points. This was a constant battle at home with Mia, getting her to eat her meals, and one area Elisa excelled, good old reverse child phycology.

Midge's red lipstick smeared the rim of her half-empty glass of beer. She'd ordered the Sloop Smokies ~ Arbroath smoked haddock in a Mornay sauce topped with parmesan shavings and served with soldiers.

"Snob pub food." Ian pointed to Midge's plate, "Me know not how Mick here ended up with a Londoner." He snickered. "She be reminding me of Fiona."

Elisa choked on the ale sliding down her throat. "Fiona?"

"Yer Troy's Mum." Ian eyed Midge, casting a disparaging glance. "Me haven't forgotten everything yet." He shrugged. "She still be vegetarian? They cater to that here; she can be ordering a Mexican bean burger with lime yogurt, salsa and fries." The disgust on his face was duly noted by both Mick and Midge.

"I did notice chips are now referred to as fries on the menu, like in America." Elisa said.

"Me still order me chips."

"Me have to agree with you on that fact, mate. In Cornwall we eat chips, not french fries." Mick said.

"The world is changing, you might as well change with it." Midge interjected. "Chips, fries, who cares?" She fluffed the pile of hair on top of her head and sipped her beer.

"Yer better care if yer want not to be swallowed down the disposal of what no longer be considered of value!" Ian banged his fist on the table top, rattling the empty plates and glasses, a piece of flatware tumbled to the floor.

Mick snatched the knife up and placed it on the dish nearest him. "How about that dessert now?"

"Don't placate me old friend." Ian sneered past Mick to his bird.

"I'll have a bowl." Elisa called their waitress over from the bar. "One for you too, Dad?"

"If it be Cornish, me be joining you."

"Three Willy Wallers." Mick ordered.

"And you miss?"

"I'll have the Knickerbocker Glory parfait." Midge said, "With a glass of water, please."

"Of course yer be." Ian chuffed.

"Enough, mate." Mick warned.

Midge excused herself. "You want to go powder your nose with me?"

"No, me don't." Ian answered before Elisa could.

"Why don't we hit the loo." Mick patted something that crinkled and puffed out in his pocket. "Got Ellies with me."

"Ah, come on then." Ian conceded and took the lead, tromping off.

"Your Troy can help Ian out with these when you get back home." Mick flashed the white nappy at Elisa then discretely slipped it back under his shirt. "Now they sell more of the adult nappies in England than the nappies for babies." Mick spoke in a hushed tone. "Me Midge uses them too. She be chuffed to slay me for telling you." He hustled off to catch Ian.

Elisa sat alone trying to absorb the implications of the conversation. The pub was filling up with several young families, chattering voices talking about anything but the recent subject matter that seemed hardly appropriate for public mealtime discussion. This was not something she had considered, her father in diapers. How could she ever help with that? Troy would have to step up to the plate. Could he? She had no idea. This simply had not come up with Fiona. Would she be able to help her mum-in-law with this sensitive issue should the need arise?

Reaching for her cell, Elisa tried to get a quick text message off before anyone returned.

"Need to talk. Call me this evening. About six Cornwall time. Have appointments with a lawyer and real estate agent tomorrow."

"Running into problems?" Came a quick text reply.

"Heading to surgery soon for Dad's annual. Will know more after."

"Is this deeper than we realized?" Troy persisted.

Elisa hesitated before responding. The truth might put an end to it all. Would Troy ask her to leave her father behind if he knew the wide scope of things coming to light? "Just found out about Ellie. Trying to grasp it all. Love and miss you. Hugs."

"Ian has another girlfriend? He comes back without Ellie. No more room under the big top."

Chapter Eleven

Belongings often tie us down. There is freedom in downsizing possessions and property, people and pride. Easy to say if you are not the one weighing the balance while going through the process. Harder for the individual taking inventory of lifelong attachments. Holding onto things only secures the mathematics of the inevitable. Yet it is human nature to collect and add as if life itself depended on the accumulation of what the soul leaves behind. ~ How-to-book advice for the committed minimalist, adventuresome reduction novelist and all other haphazard seekers.

Stages

Elisa crawled into bed with sheer determination to shed the burden of the day's events and disclosures. The doctor at surgery made the facts clear: Stage two moderate Alzheimer's. Leaning toward stage three severe. Can no longer live alone. Round-the-clock caregiving is now essential. Can live with family, assisted living a present option, and skilled nursing not far down the road. Aphasia loss of language, could be on the horizon.

Troy's ringtone, the circus theme song, buzzed under Elisa's covers shattering the silent otherworld. She ran her finger over the touchscreen.

"Ringmaster checking in later than requested. Big top tent is under repairs."

"What?"

"The heater died. It's fifteen thousand for a new one. Being installed tomorrow. Have to knock out some drywall for a bigger unit. Savings now near depleted. How was your day?"

"About the same."

"Who is this new lady friend, Ellie?"

"Ellie is the brand name of adult nappies here." Elisa heaved a prolonged sigh.

A long silence followed. She let Troy absorb the full extent of her words before asking, "Can you help dad out with changes?"

"Is Ian incontinent?" The sarcastic tone in his initial greeting fell flat.

"No, he only uses nappies for outings, so far. But, that is coming."

"Anything else?"

"Stage two headed to stage three, Alzheimer's." Elisa raised her head above the blankets and shoved the hot water bottle off her feet. "My father remembers, then forgets me. He forgets himself. He can never live alone again."

"I see."

"Well you have more clarity than I do." The words choked out, broken and fearful. "And he doesn't sleep at night. Mick has a flip lock on the top of his door here."

"He's a wanderer? A sundowner?"

"Yes, how did you know?"

"I've been reading up, it is a total loss of self, not just memory." Troy tried to filter his sentence with caution and kindness. "I'm so sorry, Honey. This has to be breaking your heart."

"Nothing seems real, more like a bad dream and I can't make myself wake up." She rolled over to her back. "He doesn't look like my dad, talk like my dad, or smell like my dad." Elisa wanted to continue listing off all she'd learned in surgery, but thought it better to wait.

"I'll get a flip lock on his bedroom door tomorrow. And don't worry, I did okay with Mia's nappies. I can transition." Troy whispered, "Love you. Get some rest. Ta."

Before she could answer, their carrier dropped the call. Mouth open, she swallowed the words, "love you too."

The early morning appointment with Midge's real estate friend loomed overhead like a dark raincloud. The gentleman had prepared to list the home, already done his walk-through, and started Mick on minor repairs and boxing of clutter for Elisa to sift through. Dread swept over her the minute they walked into the messy ground floor office. Tidiness did not appear to be part of Mr. Breckenridge's forte. He rose to greet her and papers scattered on top his desk skittered to the floor. His limp handshake matched his nonchalant attitude.

"Mrs. Kensington, I've already discussed matters with Midge. And will list upon completion of the final details I recommended."

"I have legal power of attorney for my father, and my childhood home."

"Oh, I thought, well that makes a difference." He glanced at Mick and took note of the deepening scowl and raised eyebrows before clearing a corner of his desk and motioning Elisa to sit in the chair opposite him. Mick leaned against the doorframe.

"Come in and join us." Elisa asked him.

"Trying to be respectful."

"I know." She moved to the chair next to the wall and waited until Mick was beside her to precede. "Give me the basics first, please." Elisa addressed Breckenridge with formality. "We can hash over the negotiables next." She pulled her cell from my purse. "Do you mind if I record? It's easier than taking notes."

His demeanor transformed dramatically, his spine went rigid, his feet planted on the floor. "Recording is fine." He said succinctly, then opened a file with photographs. "The roof is good, the house is clean enough, just needs to be emptied as you aren't looking to rent it out, but to outright sell."

"Not necessarily. Storage is not feasible with me living in another country. I'd like to try to rent or sell the home fully furnished."

"But it's a fisherman's house." He argued. "The stench makes it harder to sell."

"Perhaps we should consider renting to another fisherman?" Elisa countered.

Mick turned his head away and a low snicker escaped his parted lips that he seemed unable to stifle until he covered his face with the entire palm of his hand.

"I understood this to be a sale." An edginess tweaked the realtor's comment. He did not appear to be amused.

"Mick, Dad's home is paid off isn't it?" Elisa faced her godfather.

He cleared his throat and stared directly into the agent's eyes. "Yes, Ian paid it off years ago, back when everyone else was remortgaging. He only pays taxes now. Bloody high taxes."

"We'll see what interest the house draws. Once word gets out among the fisher folk, we may be looking at a rental. A sale is fine too, but I want to keep my options open to do what is best for my Dad." Elisa lifted her spare keys out of her purse. "I'll just take a peek."

"You'll need this lockbox key to get in." Breckenridge's cheeks burned a fiery red. "Midge authorized the box." A single brass key dangled on a chain from his left thumb.

Elisa took the ring and stood to leave. "We'll sign papers after I get back from the barrister's office. I need to define details with her first. Thank you so much."

Once in the car, Mick piped up. "She meant to help, not meddle. Trying to save you time. He, on the other hand, seems to have a plan of his own for selling the property."

"I appreciate Midge's efforts. Not sure yet if I want to keep him on."

"Your decision. Are you ready to revisit your past?" Mick drove down familiar streets of cobblestone. Every bump in the road took Elisa's thoughts back to happier days when they were still a family of three. Life was less complicated. The safety net of their village, extended fisher family, and the love of her parents all contributed to the confidence and desire that led her to explore beyond the comfortable borders of home.

The road narrowed after the last bend before Mick turned onto Kings Station Road. Elisa stared ahead to the stark white cottage with the bright, red arched door. Matching shutters framed windows on both sides supported by the window boxes Ian made and painted upon Elisa's pleas for her potted geraniums to have a bigger home. Both boxes were now empty.

Mick parked by the front door. As if he could read her mind he said, "Too hard to tend to the flowers from all our different homes. Midge transplanted them into clay pots in the back patio where Ian can garden himself if he wishes. He be free to lug them about every two weeks."

"He still gardens?"

"So far that seems to be what gives him the most fulfillment and peace of mind."

"You want to go inside?" Mick stepped out and made a quick dash to open the passenger door.

"No, but it's not a choice is it?" Elisa answered. A biting wind lashed at her in the open air. Her long legs stretched out until her boots landed on the frosty walkway.

"No, Luv." Mick pulled her to his chest for big barrel hug. "As your Dad would say, 'you be the brave one.' He be proud of his girl." Mick gave her a long squeeze before letting go.

Hot tears streamed her frozen cheeks. "I'm not so brave, Mick."

He cupped her chin. "Bravery be a moment by moment dealing with your present circumstances."

"To be honest, if I could flee, I would."

"Naw, you be your Dad's girl. This be uncharted waters and a fearsome storm."

"Okay then." Elisa pulled the lockbox key from her coat pocket and opened the door.

The distinct absence of the smell of fish hit her first followed by a hint of lavender that floated like a spring breeze in the dead of winter. The house was spotless, not even a thin layer of dust settled on the polished wood furniture. All the old threadbare throw rugs had been replaced with colorful woven red, blue and yellow braided ovals of various sizes in the living room and kitchen. Elisa noticed a runner the full length of the small hallway.

Her father's floor-to-ceiling twin bookshelves were organized in neat rows according to size, hard or soft cover, and were alphabetized by author. Elisa ran her hand over a row of spines.

"I tried to tell Midge to leave the books be." Mick explained. "Ian's order was always in his head, the books a mess on the shelves, some open, some standing, and some lying flat."

"She did a good job. Made the place presentable."

"Saleable." Mick agreed. "Is that be what you want?"

Ian's maroon leather recliner sat in a far corner of the living room, one of his pipes and a hardback novel on the end table within reach from the chair. The closer Elisa drew, the stronger the scent of sweat, leather, and her father's special blend of tobacco permeated that sanctuary of the room. "Saleable is good."

"We bring him here in between the two week rotating visits with his mates." Mick said. "He used to go to his chair as soon as he entered the house. Not so much anymore."

"How did Midge get rid of the fish smell?"

"She aired out the house for weeks. Then cleaned with baking soda, vinegar and ammonia. Then she aired out again after tossing the old rugs."

"All hard work." Elisa walked from one room into the next scanning for anything to remind her of her mother. Other than framed black and white photographs on the wall, all that remained of Joan was her hope chest nestled at the foot of her parent's brass bed. The simple décor represented her parent's practical lifestyle which Ian continued after her mother died.

"Me bird scrubbed down the walls with that solution too."

"I expected a flood of emotions to overrun me." Elisa stuttered.

"I think that be coming. This is all familiar, except the rugs."

"The old ones needed tossing decades ago." She admitted.

"A lot of the fish stink went out with them rugs." Mick crunched up his nose and face.

Elisa giggled, and then she couldn't stop. She tumbled onto the couch and doubled over in hysterical bouts of ragged laughter that rolled out, hiccups intermingled until she realized she was crying. She groped for a pillow to muffle her increasing sobs.

"Here." Mick handed her a white pillow with tiny black anchors embroidered across it in neat little rows. "These be new too. Room accents I believe be what Midge called it."

"Oh," Elisa blubbered, "I need to let go, but what will happen if I do?"

"Your parents be just ordinary folks like the rest of us. Nothing fancy, no fuss. Except for you." He sat next to her and rested his elbows on his knees.

"They made every sacrifice for me, my whole life, especially college even though it meant taking me away from them." Elisa sniffled, straining to regain control.

"Ah, your Dad knew you have a fine mind, one to take you anywhere you were willing to work toward. And you did."

"I left them behind." She cried.

"Children are supposed to move on into their own lives. It be the natural order like the ocean waves rolling in and out." Mick took her hand, giving it a gentle press before releasing.

"Mum waited and waited for me to come home." Elisa stopped talking to blow her nose.

"Joanie would have rather you married Cornish, have four, maybe five children, and buy the cottage down at the end of the road. This be true." Mick agreed with a nod. "But she loved you enough to not stand in the way of your dreams."

"And Dad?" She stifled the rise of emotions overwhelming her. The pillow hit the floor.

"All Ian ever talked about was you changing the world for the better someday. He believed in you."

"That's past tense, Mick." Elisa whispered, head down.

"That it be, Luv. He lives mostly in his past now." A twinge of sadness played across the fisherman's face and clouded the twinkle of his seafaring eyes.

She cried until their eyes leveled. "Sometimes I feel you know him better than I do."

With a shake of his too thick hair, Mick replied. "Sailing the ocean bonds mates like brothers. Ian be my family too."

"I know." She tried to catch her breath between diminishing sobs.

"You and me be family too. We both want what is best for Ian, put him before ourselves." Mick handed her a box of tissues from the end table.

Elisa blew her runny nose and ploughed through several tissues before she leaned onto Mick and answered. "What do you think is best?"

He sat back. "Me thinks he should go with you to America to share the end of his life." He rubbed his palms together. "Then he has a good day, maybe two and I be certain he belongs here, with his blokes." Mick fought to keep calm and stopped before continuing. "This disease be a vicious beast. There be nothing good about it for anyone."

"It's so unfair. He's a good man." She dabbed her eyes with the used tissue wads.

"What I do know is Ian will keep drifting. I've seen ships at sea aimlessly adrift." Mick's voice trembled and tears pooled, then flowed. "He be lost in a way no one on earth can fix."

"Thank you for loving him, Mick." Elisa reclined until they sat shoulder to shoulder.

He wrapped his burly arm around her. "The magistrate may soon be making these decisions for us at his next court appearance. The fight be on."

Chapter Twelve

Fathers and daughters have a special bond. The tender heart of a man is forever changed the first time he sees his child. Little girls look up to their dads who are taller and seem larger than life from the moment their loving hands reach down to hold, protect, and guide. Whether from across a room or across miles, this relationship grows deeper and stronger as time passes. ~ Passage from a gift book Elisa gave to Ian on his birthday the year she moved to America with a handwritten inscription, "Nothing can ever separate us. We will only grow closer."

The Hero

A few days later Elisa flipped through the pages of the book she'd brought back to Midge's flat. Many pages were dog-eared, bulging with clippings and letters slipped in between. Ian must have saved every piece of mail she'd sent him. Teary-eyed she reread her letters reliving all the excitement of her early years in a new country. One envelope was stuffed with postcards starting from New York City, to Boston, Dover, New Orleans, Washington D.C., Austin, Denver, Los Angeles, and finally Sacramento. Each card depicted historical information she knew her father would love.

Photographs of her at every location filled another envelope. She stood before a famous monument or landmark dressed according to the seasons: Christmas in Colorado, Marti Gras time wearing a mask and beads, cherry blossoms in full bloom along the Potomac, waterskiing in Lake Tahoe.

"I was a pampered, spoiled girl." Elisa blurted out loud to no one in particular. Warm pools glistened and gathered in the corners of her eyes and held there fighting for release. "How could I have been so selfish?" The young woman staring at her didn't seem to care.

"Ah Luv, you lived the life your parents longed to give you." Mick spoke from behind her in the arched doorway between the parlor and living room. "Don't be haranguing yourself over your Dad's treasured memories. These all brought Ian joy."

"They never came over, not even once." The mist lifted from her glance toward him.

"Of course not. They wanted you to come home."

"I invited them over and over again." The pictures shook in her grasp.

"America wasn't for them. It be what you wanted." Mick reminded her of a simple truth. "After meeting Troy, America became the home of your heart."

"But I never stopped to think of what it must have done to them." She tucked the photographs back in the envelope and returned it between the same pages. "And how hard they saved to fly me to Cornwall any time I agreed to return a fortnight."

"No regrets now. Ian wanted the best for you, to be loved by the man you fell in love with. Like him and Joanie."

Elisa sat silent in thought. All her dreams came true when Troy entered her life. Mia completed the picture. She patted her mid-section.

Mick cast a mindful stare. "So it be true then. Midge says you be in a family way."

Heat rushed to Elisa's cheeks and generated out like a forest fire. "How did she know?"

"She used to midwife in her younger days. Been thinking about it again. Folks been asking her. Families today prefer midwives to hospital."

"Troy and Fiona don't know yet. I found out for sure the morning I left the States."

Mick sat across from her. "Ian will be gobsmacked. Always hoped for another grand."

"He's hoped for a grandson for a long time." Elisa swept her loose ginger hair behind an ear and pulled a barrette from her sweater pocket. Clipping the stray strands back, she sighed.

"Babies bring joy. We could use a bit of that these days." Mick grinned wide and long, in a shy kind of pleased way. "I wouldn't mind being godfather again."

"Oh Mick, how wonderful that would be."

"Why haven't you told your Troy?"

"He's experiencing conflicts at work—his boss's company is in financial trouble." She stood. "I wanted to be a hundred percent certain first, you know?"

"I see. Not a planned addition."

"No. After Fiona arrived so unexpected, we decided to wait until she left, if at all."

"I don't think she be planning on departing anytime soon. Has it nip and cozy there now."

"It's starting to take a toll. No privacy and we have to supplement her income as she has none and she won't work. What's a former almost prima ballerina to do?"

"Dance."

"We asked her to consider teaching dance lessons."

"There you go." Mick flung out his arms, and sported an exaggerated expression.

"She adamantly refused. As if it is beneath her."

"Rubbish! Londoners, they be a privileged lot the likes of them." Mick scowled and headed into the kitchen and called over his shoulder. "Can I fix you a sandwich? Ian be waking up anytime now from his kip and Midge will be back soon from market day."

"I'd like that." Elisa followed him. She filled the kettle with water and turned on the gas until flames licked around the copper pot, the orange and blue fire a mesmerizing glow.

"Why don't you check on your dad while I be frying these bangers? You want mash on top?"

"Sure, I'll give it a go." Elisa removed her shoes and padded down the hall in her stocking feet. She noticed Mick has already unlocked the brass flip so she opened the door and stepped in careful not to make any noise. Ian lie snuggled in his covers. She watched him sleep lost in a deep slumber. She'd heard him tossing about during the night, restless and grumbling loud enough for her to catch a few words through the thick old walls.

Right now he looked almost angelic. A sweet smile danced on his pale face as if a pleasant dream occupied his thoughts. Quilts tucked in close to his chin, his neck was fully covered, and his cheeks weren't the usual ruddy complexion from the cold. His trousers and shirt were neatly folded on a chair next to his bed. Loafers placed under the seat with woolen socks nestled in each shoe. He was a man of order. It made life less complicated he'd always told her. Nothing was uncomplicated now and if anyone did not deserve this tangled mess, he didn't.

Her father was her first hero. In America all the heroes don capes. They fly across the skies, use special powers to fight the bad guys, and set captives free. Ian didn't need a cape. He wore fisherman's gear and a commoner's clothes, sailed the ocean in a trawler, and mastered perilous waves on a daily basis. His word was all he needed, like gold on the streets, and of higher value than multiple zeros on a bank ledger.

Heroes put everyone before themselves. That commonality the caped fictional comic book characters-turned movie stars, shared with her father. As a child she thought he could save her from any harm, real or imagined. And he did. He still would, he would lay down his life for her. If he knew who she was.

Elisa sat on the foot of the bed waiting for the man to awaken who'd rescued her on the cliffs from falling into the ocean that frightening day in her youth. She scooted closer until she was but a breath away, leaned in and whispered in his ear. "Let's fly away Daddy. Come home to America with me. They need you there as much as I do."

Chapter Thirteen

I wanted a puppy when I was a little girl but Mum said no. Dad wanted one too but he was gone at sea so he wouldn't be home to help housebreak, feed, walk, or poop scoop. For five years I begged, manipulated, and employed my cute factor. This had no impact on Mum at all. On my tenth birthday Dad came home with a slobbering bulldog pup peeking out of his coat pocket. Oh the row that rumbled the walls of our home that night. They struck some kind of bargain by morning light because Chauncey remained with us until after I left for university. He soon became Mum's shadow and she was inconsolable when he passed at near fifteen. When Mum fell ill, Dad tucked a female Cocker Spaniel pup in the bedsheets next to her. Without looking, Mum placed her hand on the puppy's head and stroked. Queenie and Mum were inseparable in those cold, cancer-ridden winter months into remission the following summer. Dad housebroke, fed, walked, and poop scooped Queenie. Love allows space where before there wasn't any. ~ A page in one of her old diaries Elisa unlocked with a key found on her father's Welsh dresser.

Making Restitution

Midge blasted through the front door flustered. "The Magistrate's office rescheduled Ian's hearing without proper notice for two hours earlier than on the calendar. Daft buggers!" She threw her handbag across the settee and headed for the back of the flat. "At sixes and sevens I tell you! The bloody lot of them."

"At least it be over sooner now." Mick ushered Ian out the door and motioned for Elisa to join them in the car. "You stand firm, mate."

"Where are we going?" Ian shuffled along the cobblestone walkway, a brown leather valise pinched to his body under his right arm. Wind rustled thin wisps of gray-white hair across his forehead and forced the collar of his tweed jacket up against his neck. He hugged the valise closer and lowered his bony frame into the vinyl seat on the passenger side. Elisa sat behind him and closed her door before a powerful gust rocked the Mini.

Mick headed down the lane to the main road out of the village.

Great mahogany polished pillars lined the echoing hallways leading to the courtroom. Mick's boot heels clicked in a repetitive cadence against the black tile floors followed by the soft patter of Ian's loafers and the clack of Elisa's heels. Open double doors to the hearing room awaited when they rounded the corner and walked through the foyer for witnesses and interviews. A board listed the civil cases for the afternoon session. Lord Justice Albert Simpson presiding.

The trio filed in and sat on the wooden bench at the front of the public gallery. They all noted the resemblance to the pews from Saint Gundred Church back in the village.

Ian stared up at the arched ceiling panels above with a quizzical squint. He pondered whether he was in church or somewhere else. Then he settled into a more peaceful expression. "Be looking like the inverted bow of me ship." Ian grasped Elisa's hand in his and squeezed.

A hushed silence filled the previous mumbling in the room as the magistrate entered from the side door of his private chambers.

"This be it." Mick nodded to Elias.

"Where be his wig?' Ian blurted out. "Justices be wearing the white horse-hair wigs."

"Not in civil cases anymore. It be optional." Mick whispered and gave him a sharp jab.

"They bloody well be doing for the past five centuries!" Ian persisted.

"Dad, no more talking." Elisa spoke into her father's ear as the court declarations continued. They sat as directed when the first case was called, but Ian stepped forward.

"You're the next case." Mick lunged and called out.

"I have me papers." Ian clutched the valise and advanced to the testimony box.

"That's the old fool that stole my boat." Called a voice behind them.

Elisa turned to look at her father's accuser. The stodgy man who refused to negotiate out of court. The overweight bloated complainant sat four rows directly behind her. His steely deep-set gray eyes held her stare and glared back penetrating deeper than she'd intended to allow.

A hand pounded hard against the wooden justice's desk, resounding throughout the room. "Go back to your seat and wait for your case to be called."

"Your Honour, me be no thief!" Ian's voice thundered. He raised and shook the leather folder containing the evidence of his innocence. "It be all here you bloody blaggard!" He aimed the valise like a weapon at his accuser.

A loud voice called out again, but Ian paid no attention. He turned to face the Magistrate's desk with every intention of approaching. A burly probation officer rushed toward Ian as the Crown Prosecutor smirked, then shot a knowing glance at his client.

"Come and sit with me, mate." Mick stood, a look of desperation clouding his face, one arm reaching out, and his hand waving his friend over.

Ian briskly bypassed the Probation Officer and the local press box shuttered into action, snapping pictures of the disturbance, cameras zooming in on Ian.

"I told you the old coot is nutters." His accuser continued, also refusing to quiet down.

Elisa knew his name, Ronald Fawkner. She held her peace but only for her father's sake, to help calm him until he returned to the bench where he belonged. She rose and stepped aside so Ian could sit beside Mick. After he slumped in the seat, Elisa sat, sandwiching Ian between them, hoping they could control another outburst from disrupting the hearings any further as they blocked his physical departure. Elisa pursed her lips, turned and shot daggers at Fawkner.

The current case proceeded without incident. A local dispute between neighbours over the boundary between their homes and the storage of two unused vehicles on the wrong side of the property lines. After opposing arguments were presented, the judge found in favor of the complainant. After the judgment was read declaring the defendant was to remove his vehicles and adjust the fence line two feet back into his property, the disgruntled man left in a huff.

Ian's case was called next. Both Ian and Fawkner advanced with their lawyers who were waiting in the front of the room near the Magistrate's bench. Elisa remained in the public gallery with Mick and waited.

"Will the defendant Ian Darrow's solicitor, please approach the bench."

Ian was sworn in and asked to sit in the defendant's chair for questioning. He co-operated without incident and pulled the leather pouch on his lap, firmly clasping it in both hands.

"Ian, do you understand why you are in court today?" His counsel asked.

"Yes."

"You are charged with stealing Mr. Fawkner's trawler from where it was moored in Bucie Bay."

"Yes, me be so charged."

"Do you remember taking this boat out to sea?" The young solicitor's tone was gentle.

"Well, sort of." Ian fidgeted in his seat, and looked off to the side.

"Can you clarify, please?" The defense solicitor drew Ian's attention back to him.

"Me thought it be me boat. The *Victoria Regina.*"

"And why would you believe Mr. Fawkner's boat to be yours?"

Ian hung his head, the tip of his loafers scuffed against the wooden box enclosure where he sat. Hands ringing in his lap, he seemed to be struggling for words, but said nothing.

"Do you need me to repeat the question?" The solicitor lifted his glasses, held them in the air and waited for a response.

Ian hesitated then answered. "No, the answer be the same. I remember not. Me can only tell you what me have written down that me do remember, but…"

"Yes..," his solicitor prompted.

"Me don't remember why or when me wrote these sentences." A defeated expression clouded Ian's face. His head slumped lower, to his chest. Silence hung in the courtroom like a heavy fog rolling in off the coastal waters, relentlessly seeping inland. Then silence.

Hot, angry tears stung Elisa's cheeks. She longed to spare her father this unnecessary humiliation. The medical diagnosis had been properly submitted for review before the hearing. Why had the case advanced without dismissal?

Mick's grip tightened on Elisa's shoulder and he began to rise from the bench when Ian's counsel interrupted the questioning and requested permission to approach the Magistrate's desk with a thin yellow folder.

Irritated, the prosecutor objected only to be ordered to also approach.

"By order of a crown approved physician, I have Mr. Darrow's file denoting stage two advancing to three Alzheimer's. This explains my client's inability to remember the event, the timing and circumstances other than he thought it was his trawler. To be clear, Ian Darrow believed he was setting sail on his own property."

"Why was this transcript not submitted in advance?' The Justice's tone was reprimanding and terse.

"It was, but apparently it was somehow misplaced."

The Justice opened the new file and read through the first few pages. "This changes everything."

"My client seeks compensation for his sunken boat." Interjected the prosecutor.

"What I did read before this hearing was the report on the condition of your client's trawler." The Justice thundered. "It was not a sea-worthy vessel, it was scheduled to be scrapped, and it is something of a miracle that Mr. Darrow did not go down with it." Simpson shuffled the papers in front of him and declared. "Ian Darrow did offer financial compensation according to a scrap estimate based on the last time the *Titus* went in for repairs, but was declared scrap. I suggest Mr. Fawkner accept the out-of-court offer."

"Case dismissed." The Justice declared. "Next case."

Fawkner rose and shook a fist at Ian as he stepped away from the witness chair and walked toward the galley. "You bloody faker!"

Ian stumbled.

"Come on, mate." Mick stood. "Ignore him."

Elisa pulled her purse over her shoulder and stood beside Mick.

Ian passed them by and went straight toward his accuser. "You bloody hell liar!" With one swift movement he lunged, his hands extended for the man's throat. Face purple, he hurled an unintelligible barrage of curses. The valise flew in the air and struck the edge of the bench.

Mick grabbed Ian from the back by the scruff of his collar before he made contact. Fawkner threw the full weight of his body forward as Ian flung backward.

"You owe me for a sail-worthy boat!" Fawkner's fists grazed Elisa's face as she helped tug her father away from the wild punches.

"Bloody blaggard!" Ian shouted and tried to lurch into the attack.

"No, Dad!"

The probation officer inserted himself between the two parties and escorted Ian, Mick and Elisa out the court doors. The justice ordered Fawkner to be detained for physical violence as the doors slammed shut and echoed down the tile hallway.

"You best leave before he recalls you. Lord Justice Simpson doesn't tolerate outbursts in his courtroom." The officer's nametag fell and pinged on the floor.

"Thank you, mate." Mick picked the laminate badge up and glanced at the name—O'Keefe.

"Be on your way then." He urged them to the front exit of the building. "My wife has the same horrible disease, and the Justice—keep on, keep on." He stood in silence and watched the trio exit to the car park, then re-pinned his nameplate and disappeared from sight.

"Me be no thief!" Ian's roar succumbed to a faint whisper.

"We know, Dad." Elisa moved slowly and deliberately, placing her hand on his shoulder.

"Me remember not any of it. Nothing. And that be the truth. If you tell me I did this, then me will believe you." Ian trembled, from anger or fear, or both, neither Elisa nor Mick knew.

"You can pay the bugger off now and be done with him for good." Mick opened the passenger door for Ian and turned.

A balled fist undercut Mick's jaw, raw and jagged, followed by a second slug direct to the gut. Blood spattered a thin line across the glass windows as Mick fell back against the car and slid down to the pavement below in a heap.

"Dad!" Elisa stumbled backward from the blunt force of his attack.

"Me don't have any Alzheimer's!" Ian cheeks flamed a fierce red as he braced himself to take another swing. "Quit telling the village folk I be swallowed up by some memory disease."

Elisa caught Ian's arm in mid-air and held his elbow above hers. "Stop. How can you hit Mick after all he's done for you?"

"Still got a good right hook there, mate." Mick sat dazed and dabbed blood from the corner of his mouth with his jumper sleeve. His jaw cracked when he closed it, and popped as he opened it as wide as he could.

"Enough!" Elisa shouted. She let her arm fall down to her side and slid beside Mick on the ground. "Is your jaw broken?"

"Naw, he sucker-punched me good though."

"Has he done this before?" Stunned, Elisa gazed up at her father in disbelief.

"A couple of times when I let my guard down." Mick rolled his head to the side until it snapped, then he arched his back. "Back in alignment now. Let's head home."

Ian buckled up and remained silent most of the drive to Midge's flat.

"Dad," Elisa asked. "Are you upset with me?"

"He be asleep. The car usually lulls him to the Land of Nod." Mick's words were slurred and carefully delivered from one of side of his mouth. "Stings a mite."

"Do you need to go to the hospital?"

"No, need an ice pack. Should have applied one immediately. Keeps the swelling down." Mick drove down the cobblestone roads leading into the village. The car bounced on uneven stones and he winced with each bump.

"How often does Dad lose his temper?"

"Don't be troubled by what happened today."

"He can't explode like this in front of Mia." Elisa spoke with firm resolve. "It would terrify her. Change her opinion of him."

"Your Troy can handle it." Mick encouraged. "It be part of the disease. Some suffer worse than others. Ian has tapered down the more he forgets, the less frustrated he feels."

"I saw fear in his eyes, raging fear." Elisa pulled out her cell and scrolled through pictures of her daughter. She turned the cell off and slipped it in her purse.

"He does better when staying where his Reggie can sit at his feet. Midge won't allow a dog in her flat for any reason. Barry and William keep Reg for us. When it be their fortnight with Ian, he finds comfort petting old Reginald. They let him sleep with Ian, and he's allowed on the furniture. Things change up a bit when Ian comes to Midge's."

"I see." Elisa measured the pattern of her father's snoring. A gap lagged between every few breaths.

"She's not bad, just blasted picky." The car reeled around a bend in the road.

"I remember begging my mum for a dog. For years she said no, then Dad came home with a puppy in his pocket one day after he docked his boat. Mum was livid. Ranting about who was going to end up of taking care of the mutt." Elisa slung her hands in the air mimicking her mother's extreme discontent.

"The pair of them ended up dog folk," Mick laughed. "Ouch, that smarts."

"Midge isn't going to like this." Elisa recoiled back into the seat.

"She be of a mind to get over it." Mick parked the car then shut off the headlights. "Odds are Ian won't remember much of today by morning. And if he does, it be bits and pieces."

They sat in the dusk listening to Ian snore. His window fogged up, his face pressed on the glass. Steam rose and fell, then Ian snorkeled once or twice.

"Midge be trying to get me to the altar. She allows Ian to stay here to score points with me. She still has boundaries. So do I."

"You don't strike me as the marrying kind, Mick."

"It seems I be becoming more and more *trainable* in that direction." Mick winked.

"You mean like a dog?" Elisa quipped.

"Not funny." Mick groaned. "Her hints aren't subtle or lost on me. She leaves magazines with wedding pictures all around the flat. Drives us by stone or brick churches everywhere—city, county, seaside. She special ordered those M&M chocolates, for Mick & Midge, in her favorite colors, lavender and purple."

"But helping you with my Dad, that's the big one."

"Ian be her prize. But Luv, she wants us to be alone to get started."

"Oh. Is that why you called?"

"No, I thought he be better off to stay here, Cornwall."

"And now?"

"Soon he'll be forgetting where he is not just who he be."

"So now America rates?"

"Now I know either way—family, friend, home all be forgotten. Lost in his mind no matter how hard he be trying to retrieve any of us." Mick unlocked the car doors.

"We had a dog at home. Lulabelle, we just call her Lula." Elisa gathered her purse, Ian's valise, and the lunch hamper they'd taken on the road. "Dad would have liked her, she bore a striking resemblance to Chauncey, our first dog." Elisa sighed. "She passed last year."

"Oh, so sorry. He might not have remembered Chauncey anyway."

"Oh yeah." Elisa tried to appear unscathed by the reminder.

"He recalls farther back the best. Short term be toast."

"Silly of me. I thought the dog could have helped him with the adjustment from a move."

"We all have to adjust. No one escapes the clutches of this cruel thief." Mick called Midge's mobile. "All home and coming in." He nudged Ian awake and out under the lamppost.

"You get into a row at the pub, mate?" Ian eyeballed Mick's swollen jaw in the light.

"A bit of a scrap. Nothing broken."

Chapter Fourteen

Me mate once had photographic memory of Cornish history. He knew things I'd never heard of. Things like—an ancient cemetery once existed at Trevose where now new homes have sprouted. Bones are continually washed up by the sea as it encroaches. All church records of the burial site have been lost over time though the ruins of St. Cadoc's Chapel be a distant half mile away. Ian knew so many interesting bits of our past. All is now lost in a place where he cannot retrieve information nor see the snapshots once so vivid in his mind. In a sense, he is being buried alive, struggling to breathe, one trowel of earth at a time. I see him suffocating under the weight of an invisible heap of compost and mire. There be no rescuing him from this form of early death whilst living. ~ Mick's lament to mates at Maiden Voyage Pub over several rounds of pints.

Settling Accounts

"It be no shock that cowardly blaggard send his request for compensation by post!" Mick fumed, pacing the carpet, the crumpled papers balled up in his fist.

"At least it's the amount for scrap." Elisa countered. "That's one tenth the cost Fawkner wanted in court." Obvious relief overcame Elisa. They'd tucked her dad in for the night an hour before Midge popped in with the post. The two women sat on opposite sides of the settee.

"I can take Dad home with me now."

Mick sat across from them in silence. He opened his hand and smoothed out the paper work on his jeans. "Sorry to make a mess of it." He handed all over to Elisa.

"I'll call Troy to see when we can get a flight out. We have enough travel miles left to cover the trip, but then we'll be near zeroed out." Elisa folded the papers in half.

"So, you don't know when you'll be coming back to visit?" Midge asked, her eyes fixed on Mick. He remained stoic and she knew what that meant.

"We'll have to get Dad settled in and who knows how long that will take." Elisa hedged. "He might not return at all, you know that, Mick."

"I do."

"It will be quiet around here without him. No more late night escapades." Midge tried to lighten the mood. "Barry said he'll keep Reg. It's a six month quarantine for a dog to travel to the States." She rolled the fabric of her hemline up the side of her leg, then slowly let it fall.

"You have a pub in Sacramento to take him, so he doesn't get homesick for his ale."

"We do. 'The City of Westminster ~ The Streets of London Pub' on J street in downtown Sac. It was recently renamed ~ Streets. They fly the American and British flags."

"Good fish and chips for me mate there?" Mick's eyes met Elisa's. "And Cornish ale?"

"Oh he'll devour their fish 'n chips, but no Cornish beer." Elisa hesitated, then added, "Boddington's English Pale Ale, and well, Guinness."

"Ian won't be downing any Dry Irish Stout!"

"There are other foreign beers—from Germany, Belgium, the Netherlands, and American brews on their tap list." Elisa rattled off as if she'd memorized the listing. "France too."

"Ah—no bloody Cornishman will be drinking any of those pints."

"Maybe he won't notice the difference." Midge suggested.

"Don't even go there, Bird." Mick shook his head not so much in disgust, but in helplessness. "His mind isn't gone yet!" he snapped back. "They have any of his other favorites? Pasty and Bangers and Mash?" He turned to Elisa, his voice strained.

"Yes, and Cottage Pie with minced beef." Elisa replied.

"No Stargazy Pie?"

"No. I make it though, once a year. Troy likes it, Mia not so much."

"And Fiona?" Mick halted. "How will she treat me mate?"

"We'll keep her in check. She's going to be a good Mum or her son will shoot her from the cannon to another circus on the moon." Elisa promised. "Or Mars."

"So Troy still be the ringmaster." Mick laughed.

"Yes, and his troupe is growing. Dad should fit right in with the rest of us. We could use a new act, sell more tickets that way." Elisa stood and tussled the mop on Mick's head. "You're welcome to cross the pond for a fortnight and get front seats for the next show. It should be a doozy." She shoved her concerns about Troy's job to the back of her mind.

"Go to the States? Never thought I would, but you make it sound like entertainment."

"The Kensington Big Top always offers a show of some sort. Come over and see for yourself. Fish & Chips on me at Streets and all the pints you can drink." Elisa caught the glint in Mick's eye. He was intrigued. She knew she'd hooked him. He'd need to see Ian was okay. That he did indeed fit in.

"Troy got a ticket for flight out tomorrow night." Elisa announced somewhat stunned. "Is that too soon?" Her eyes flittered about the flat searching for her father. "Where's dad?"

"He was agitated so Midge took him for a drive early this morning."

"Is everything tied up enough for me to leave? I stayed with the solicitor Midge picked so we could rent rather than sell."

"Ian's signed the cheque for the trawler, the house be rented out to a Padstow Bay fisher family with me as their local legal contact as you designated, and you have your dad's medical files on disc. Midge and I will box Ian's personals." Mick stopped short. "I guess you be ready to go with this short notice."

A strange look of uncertainty crowded his features after the words left his mouth. Elisa realized it was the finality of his involvement in Ian's long journey. She wasn't sure how to handle the sudden change. Mick had been in charge here. She simply followed his lead, sought and trusted his guidance. Once in America, she'd be making all the decisions, right or wrong. Was she ready?

"Are you up for this, Luv?" Mick's eyes knowingly searched hers for any misgivings. "His passport and visa are ready to go."

"We basically have twenty-four hours to pack up all dad's belongings, sort through what personal things he may remember and want—until he forgets, and let everyone say good-bye."

"I can arrange a farewell at the pub tonight. His mates will be there. You pack for him and Midge can distract Ian as best she can. He doesn't like change so this could be a bugger." Mick headed for the kitchen to make his calls.

Elisa slumped in the overstuffed chair she'd avoided during her stay. It was too comfortable and she hadn't wanted to make herself at home. She was a visitor. Right now it was perfect though, she slipped her shoes off and stretched her feet up on the ottoman. Midge's cottage rose theme encompassed her like a royal garden in full bloom, an enticing fragrance floating, filling her head and influencing her thoughts. It was a girlie-girl room for the likes of Mick. He must truly love her to live amid all the pinks, mauves and dusty rose colors.

Mick's voice trailed out from the back of the flat. Elisa could hear enough to know one Cornishman was being asked to send the news down the pipeline that Ian's time with them will end tonight at the public house down the lane. Maiden Voyage Pub, her father's other home since she was a little girl, where all major decisions were discussed. More often than naught a row or two ensued before several pints were raised in agreement, then voted on most always in perfect accord. She knew this is where Mick had called from for her to come home. And not because she could hear the rabble rousing in the background. The villagers were a tight lot of crusty codgers and curmudgeons.

Smoothing a hand over the shiny chintz fabric belayed the cozy atmosphere of the room. It wasn't soft and had no give, but was taut and cold to the touch. The window before her framed the outside world, wooden molding and glass panes, in mini-pictures of a wider spectrum. Rain pelted a constant rhythm, blurring the images beyond into a watercolor painting. Blue hues blended and mixed into the greens, grays, browns and a hint of mustardy yellow. No clarity. She hadn't heard the rain before. Elisa rubbed her woolen socks together, arched her feet and pointed her toes.

"The pub be full tonight!" Mick emerged with a broad smile setting off his twinkling eyes and upbeat mood. "Ian be sleeping off a good one like a babe until morning."

She longed to share his enthusiasm and strained to feign some presentation of it to enhance Mick's spirit as an encouragement. But she came up empty, bankrupt to be exact. Devoid of any emotion except distinct underlying fear that heightened by the second. Bending forward Elisa wrapped her hands under her curled toes and held firm. She mumbled, not in disapproval, but in desperation. "That ought to make the cross-Atlantic flight interesting."

Chapter Fifteen

Ian spent the afternoon pottering about his garden in Midge's back yard after the rain stopped. He trifled away time as if he had an indeterminate amount to spend pinching back spent petunias heads and fertilizing the soil in every clay pot and pocket of earth that had been given him. He drew a sense of security and happiness bent over on his kneeler pad that he scooted about while dragging the heavy metal watering can, pot to pot. He nurtured each sprout and sprig as though he'd be there in the spring to see them grow into mature plants. Sunlight broke above, streaming through the straw hat covering his head. He removed one glove to be precise in pruning and plucking for the compost heap. He scouted for the usual lesser pests; ants, snails, and beetles under leaves and inching along struggling stems, and for slugs under the rocks. The activities of larger offenders, moles, rabbits, and squirrels were more noticeable along the borders of the flowering bed. There was a special allowance on his bank ledger to fund the expenses to properly tend his garden. To this, Mick purchased any supplies Ian loaded in the shopping cart. None went to waste and every plant bloomed as if a master gardener puttered over this patch of Cornish earth. No true gardener abandons their plot, they daily guard their sanctuary as they live and breathe. So it be and has been. ~ Elisa and Mick watching Ian muddy up his boots, trousers, and knees, at one with the dirt as he was with the sea. The day before leaving for America.

The Unknowing Wayfarer

"Don't work yourself into a tizzy." Mick admonished Midge. "Ian needs calm."

"The pub won't be a calming experience." She huffed and flounced herself on the settee.

"They need to say ta. We've had our time with him."

"Then you go." She sputtered out and waited. "I've had my time with Ian."

"Fine then." He slammed the flat door, lowered himself in the Mini, and sped off with Elisa and Ian who were already loaded up. "Me Bird be staying home."

"That be a mite prudish of her." Ian chided. "She don't approve of me. Me know." He clicked his pipe on the enamel of his front teeth before clenching it tight between molars in the corner of his mouth. "You brought me pouch of tobacco?" A worried expression straightened his crinkled brow and piqued his eyebrows.

"In me pocket." Mick exceeded the speed limit with a jolt.

The pub overflowed out the front door onto the cobblestone streets and smoke puffed a hazy welcome. The trio entered to excited applause. The room cloudy with cigarette, cigar and pipe fumes made it difficult to breathe. Mick motioned for a mate to prop the front door open. Darts speared across the room, piercing one of two round boards to the left on a wood paneled wall, hitting the center red bullseye. Cheers mingled with slurred greetings, most unintelligible, but the general mood was celebratory.

"I think they've been here drinking a while before we arrived." Elisa glanced around the crowd, pints were raised high and tables were full of empty mugs and glasses. The bar had a tray waiting for them with Ian's favorite Cornish ale and the only empty booth had a reserved for four sign in the middle of the table. They were seated under the Maiden Voyage massive figurehead of a mermaid carved in two-hundred year old wood. It was rescued from the foremost tip of the bow after a ship went down during a legendary storm. The superstitious crew claimed smugglers pirated and boarded, sinking her purposely after plundering her exotic wares from the east. Ian loved the tale though he discounted it as strictly legend and not historical fact.

It appeared the entire village inhabited the revered pub, except Midge. Her absence was notable and her empty seat filled within seconds.

"Came to say ta-ta, mate." Barry shoved his way next to Ian. "I be missing you."

"Why?" Ian asked perplexed. "Where you going? Off to a fortnight at St. Mawes? Calling on the grands?" He shrugged.

Mick shot Barry a warning glance and mouthed "No." with a shake of his head.

"You gadding about Mawes?" Ian asked again. He reached Barry's shoulder and gave it a powerful squeeze.

The scene repeated itself over the course of the next few hours. Voices called out across the room and the bloody lot of them offered condolences for having to ship off to America. The crowd thinned a little, but the pub still burst with drinking fishermen and their tales. Ian moved from table to table enjoying the attention and the free pints of ale. He ordered a Cottage Pie and scarfed it down in record time. Being out of Mick's extended control suited Ian.

"He needs to taper off the drinking or he'll float to California." Elisa yelled at Mick over the din. "He has to use that dinky airplane bathroom. Troy didn't buy first class tickets."

"I'll round him up for the night." Mick pulled the tobacco pouch from his shirt pocket. "Hate to when he's having such a good time. Too much alcohol might interfere with his meds."

"I know." She shouted. "They're singing the pub song already. Better hurry."

But it was too late.

♫*We sailed the seas fishing, for a mighty catch wishing. The ocean opened wide her mouth, schools come swimming from the south.*♫

Fishermen stood arms wrapped round each other, some holding pints of frothy ale spilling to the floor. Ruddy faces weathered by the salt air and water, aged beyond their years, queued-up swaying in the dead center of the pub.

The baritone, Bertie, sang the next stanza solo. ♪*Mend your nets and cast your cages. We Cornish be fishing pilchard for ages. Raise a pint when you get to shore, then we be going out for more.*♪ He tugged his tweed jacket, elbow patches butting up against mates on both sides.

A chorus rang out, ♫*Hevva! Hevva! The Huers call. From rocky cliff tops, the lookouts call!*♫ Ian stood in the center bolstered by his mates, singing along off-key. Red-haired Celts, grizzled and gray, retired blokes that still set sail when need arose in the village, chimed in.

The revelers belted out the chorus again, lines out of time, halting and screeching, without a care.

"They've downed enough ale the lot of them be thinking they sound like a church choir in perfect tune—after weeks of practice." Mick muttered in Elisa's ear as he pushed through the crowd to help her ease Ian out of the midst and whisk him away. "Come on now, mate."

Ian would have none of it. He planted his loafers, strengthened his double-looped arm hold, and winked from a safe distance like a naughty child taking advantage of a flustered parent.

"We have a parting gift for you here." Bertie broke free from the entanglement of Ian's lifelong mates and tripped his way to Mick. "This flask be your lifeline in America until you find a proper public house." He slipped a gleaming silver flash from his inside coat pocket and fell smack into Ian, tumbling the domino line of fishermen on their bums to the floor.

"America?" Ian laughed.

"Let's have a smoke on it." Mick waved the tobacco pouch and pulled out his own pipe.

"It be about bloody time." Ian propped himself up leaning on the nearest bench for support. It took some effort, but he rose on his own.

Ian startled awake in the dark of night, eyes open wide. His heart thumped against his ribcage, his head pounded. He listened for the ocean, strained to hear her call his name. Not a wave crashed, not a thunderous roar reprimanded, no wind howled. The room was hollow, empty and he shivered in the bleakness of a terrible chill that swept through flesh and bone to his very soul.

"Tell me again why I be flying to America." Ian questioned Mick with a distrustful scowl.

"To see if you like it at your daughter's home." A plane taxied away from the glass windows where they stood, and rolled down a flight lane toward the runway. The huge gray body lumbered in dissipating fog, a ghost with wings grounded until the boggy weather lifted.

"When did she go there?"

Tears blurred Mick's line of vision. "You remember our walk on the beach this morning?"

"Yes." Ian responded. "You took pictures, with that big camera."

"That's right."

"Mick, have you forgotten that me don't like the States?" Ian's shoes shuffled nervously on the slick high-gloss tile floor.

"No, mate. But you've never been before. Check it out and see what you think."

"All flights have been cleared for take-off. Check the boards for any departing gate number changes and have a safe journey." The bland electronic voice announced. Blinking lights lit up row after row on the suspended board beside them and eager passengers clamored over in a rush.

"Where be we Mick?" Ian's voice wavered. He walked away from the pressing crowd.

"At Heathrow International Airport. With your daughter Elisa." Mick moved in sync.

"Me want to stay with you." Ian pleaded over rising voices. "Me don't mind your bird."

"It be time to go be with your granddaughter Mia, and your daughter."

"Don't you want me anymore?"

"Of course I want you, but so do they."

Elisa ran up beside them, cheeks flushed and out of breath. "The flight is boarding and we can board first," she sucked in air, "have go through security now and take off your shoes."

"What do they want with me shoes?" Ian stared down at his feet and clicked his heels.

"You can put them right back on." Mick leaned in to Elisa's ear when Ian turned to look at the growing queue ahead. "I slipped him a mild sedative, Doc's order. Here's two more. He already took his memory meds."

"Thanks, Mick. How can I thank you for everything?" She lunged forward and wrapped her arms tight around him. He tucked the pills in her coat pocket when she let go.

Mick reached down and put Ian's hand in Elisa's. "You take care of each other. I be coming to America soon to check up on you, mate."

Ian burst forth and threw his arms around Mick's neck and clung close. "You be me best mate, Mick." He sobbed, resting his head on Mick's sturdy shoulder.

"Passengers for the trans-Atlantic flight 584 are boarding at gate 96. All class A passengers queue up, have your tickets ready. And thank you for your patience with the delays due to the heavy fog this morning."

"And you be mine." Mick choked out. Red and bleary-eyed he took Ian's hand and again placed it in Elisa's. "Go with your daughter." Tears trickled down his cheeks. He stepped back. "I can still ring you up from across the ocean." Mick's shoulders sagged, his hands trembled.

"Me be going to the other side, mate." Ian watched until Mick disappeared from sight.

Chapter Sixteen

"The Jolly Tinners" ~ *"Come all true Cornish boys, walk in. Here's Brandy, Beer, Rum, Shrub, and Gin. You cannot do less than drink success to copper, Fish, and Tin."* A local riddle asked: "As I went down by Hilary's steeple I met three people. They were not men, nor women, nor children. Who were they then?"~ One of Ian's favourite olde sing-songs and riddles.

By Air, Not by Sea

Once in their assigned seats, Ian fumbled with his safety belt to no avail. Frustration grew by the second. "Bloody well make me take off me shoes and take X-rays of old loafers, then me be cramped into these narrow chairs!" He repeatedly clacked metal against metal, missing the open slot, his face flaming beyond ruddy red to scarlet, sweat beaded at his brow.

"Is it okay if I help? I figured mine out a minute ago." Elisa waited for his answer.

"Oh, why not?" He quit wrestling and dropped the longer belt on his lap.

She was quick to pick it up and insert the flat metal base into the enclosure until a subtle click sounded. "You can pull here to tighten it so you're comfortable."

"You be a nice lady to help me out. Me usually steer me boat, and don't have these contraptions on board when sailing the sea." He yawned. "Excuse me. I had no intend to be rude, just tired."

"Oh, I understand. This is a long flight. I'll be taking a nap soon myself."

"Ian Darrow. What be your name?" He smiled and brushed strands of hair from his face.

"Elisa Kensington."

"That sounds a mite familiar"' He scratched the side of his head and squinted, then glanced at and studied her face. "Of course you be. Sorry, sometimes I forget things."

"I know." She clasped his weathered hand, the leathery skin rough and dry. "A fisher of the sea." She squeezed. Sorrow seized her heart but she dared not let it show.

Ian closed his eyes, his mind a jumble of people's faces, names, and bobbing boats moored in a bay. He searched for the *Victoria Regina*, unsure if she be docked at Port Issac, Padstow, or all the way around the tip to Mount's Bay. He needed to get his bearings. How else would he find her? Why be she docked so far away that they had to fly in the sky to look for her? The same fog creeping outside seeped inside his brain, clogging every thought. He tried to fight off an invading slumber but it was a powerful force to reckon with. Sleep soon became the victor. Wandering Cornwall to Land's End, the ship's captain shook the dirt off his boots and tread water along the shoreline. Calm seas called to him, her melodious voice entrancingly clear. Clearer than anything he be seeing or hearing for years. He followed the fading echo deep into still waters.

Not a wave rose to greet him. No frothy peaks, no foam. A pristine cerulean sea buoyed him, arms stretched out, feet dangling weightless. Once earthen land disappeared beyond the widening spread of the oceanic scape, he became aware he be sinking, slow but steady into the great abyss below.

He tried to swim but he couldn't remember how, what to do with his legs and arms? What motion would propel him to float on his back? He knew these actions. Water rose to his chin, lapping and tickling the edges of his ear lobes. She wanted him, was claiming him for herself. The word *stroke* flashed in his mind. *Stroke*. How?

Like glass, the sea stood under the sun reflecting rays of light, prisms glittering in exquisite, translucent beauty. A false sense of safety flooded through him as she kissed his lips, droplets moistening the tip of his tongue. The intensity of her embrace held him spellbound, breathless. He did not struggle when a gentle wave washed over him, covered his head, and the transparency of her being encompassed his body. The light near the surface of this liquid world was brilliant like a starry night, dimming the deeper he sank. His mind went blank.

Part Two

Sacramento, California

America

The Lone Cypress on the Pacific Coast

Chapter Seventeen

This continent of America is overrated. The Rebellionists of 1776 not be honourable men, but ungrateful rebels guilty of treason. Brave New World. Balderdash! The Land of Opportunity. Let them have their Wild West and Gold Rush. Countrymen foolish enough to hide behind Indian war paint and peacock feathers to dump tea in a harbour deserved separation from the United Kingdom. We Cornish know our roots. We stand firm on the soil 'neath our feet. And yet our youth be drawn to those traitorous shores, beguiled by inflated promises of financial freedom and entrepreneurial odyssey.

~ Joanie's lament to Ian and the villagers at Maiden Voyage Pub upon Elisa's announcement to venture to the United States.

Landing on Foreign Soil

JFK International Airport in New York was a frightening experience for Ian. He hung close to Elisa, shadowed her steps until they got to the bathroom.

"I'll be right out. Stand here and wait, okay, Dad?" Her eyes pleaded with his.

Ian answered, "yes," then nodded his head with a calm, full-lipped smile.

She hurried through the circular tiled entry pulling the handles of both their carry-on luggage with her, and disappeared down a long row of closed green stall doors.

Ian waited for her to reemerge at the open doorway until he grew impatient. He wandered a few feet forward to gaze in a shop window brandishing a wide array of men's hats, coats, and winter scarves draped over faceless mannequins sitting on shelves. When he turned around, an endless moving sea of people crushed forward enveloping him. He moved along with the quickened pace, constantly looking back for Elisa and the brightly lit up sign with the figure of a woman in a dress with the letters—WOMEN.

His heart thumped like the drum section in a symphony and sweat beads dampened the back of his flannel shirt collar, then trickled down his neck. Warmth flushed throughout his body. After passing several gates, he caught sight of a women's restroom sign on the opposite side of the walk. He dashed across, bounded in the same circular title entry and began pounding on one closed blue door after another. "Elisa!"

A young mother skillfully herding three little girls bundled in layers of woolen, hooded coats, and mittens, tapped him on the shoulder. "Sir, the men's room is just a few feet to the left. Do you need help to get there?"

Ian whirled around, a deranged look of exasperation plastered across his face, eyes wild with fear. "I lost me daughter."

"How old is she?"

"I, I don't remember." He sputtered out. "She looks like you."

The woman glanced at his wrist for an emergency medical band. By now several other women, both coming and going, were obviously displeased with his unwelcomed presence in their private sanctuary.

"I know someone who can find her for you." She reached out to him.

"Mommy, I have to go potty, *now*." The smallest child in their group tugged on her skirt.

"What's he doing in here? Someone call security!" A lady over six feet tall, dressed in a black business suit and Burlington raincoat, edged past him, her high heels clicked against the mosaic flooring. "Security!" She ordered as though accustomed to telling others what to do, and yanked out a cell phone from the outer side pouch of a shoulder purse, scrutinizing Ian while placing a call.

"Mommy!"

"I think he's lost." The young mother directed her girls toward a stall door that opened.

Ian fled. He stumbled into the end curve of tile, scanned the length of the restroom, the walls spun and slid sideways as he made a quick exit. Searching for anything familiar along the decorated shop windows and boarding lounges, he continued heading in the opposite direction. This was not Cornwall. This was not even England. It must be the gateway to hell.

"Dad, Dad!" Elisa cried out. She rushed through the crowd towing the bobbing luggage. "Ian Darrow!" Wheels bumped over the laminate floor panels and into other passengers. "I'm so sorry." She apologized while running forward. "Sorry." She knocked into one traveler after another and pressed on though she'd lost sight of her father.

"Oh God, where me be?" Ian backed up to a wooden column in front of a bookstore, swung around and placed his palms on the glass, then slumped to the ground in despair. He raised his hands and covered his face first, then moved them over his ears and head. Terrified sobs erupted, snot and tears staining his cheeks. The world hurried by him as if he wasn't there.

"Dad. Why didn't you wait for me?" Elisa knelt beside Ian and hovered protectively.

He turned and buried his head onto her shawl and coat, fingers gripped the fabric and clenched tight. His legs stretched forward, loafers sticking out in the path of the passersby.

"Are you his daughter?"

"What?" Elisa turned directly into a slender young stranger in black tights, ankle boots and a mid-calf corduroy skirt. Dark brown hair cascaded down her burgundy cable-knit sweater as she bent over. Three elementary school age girls huddled in a circle around her, the oldest one clutching an adult raincoat and an umbrella. The other two towed several carry-on pieces of wheeled luggage, their cherub ebony faces a welcome sight.

"He was looking for his daughter in a women's restroom. He seemed frightened by the crowd and surroundings. Is he okay now?" She tried to get a peek at Ian's face. "I recognize his shoes."

"I am so sorry." Elisa blurted out. "Did he scare your daughters?"

"Oh, no. My father lives with us. He has dementia and diabetes. Can get pretty moody, but he loves his grandgirls." She maneuvered closer. "I knew something was wrong."

"Thank you so much. He got a bit disoriented." Elisa moved her luggage aside.

Ian let go. He peered up at the little girls. A nervous smile accompanied his sniffles and he lifted an embroidered handkerchief from his tweed coat pocket, then promptly blew his nose.

"He sounds like Papa." The middle-size child with electric green eyes knelt beside Ian.

"This be Mia?" Ian asked, and rose to his feet taking her hand to hold him up.

"No, Dad. She's waiting for us in California."

"Are you on the Sacramento flight out?"

"Yes, I live there with my husband and daughter, and my mother-in-law."

"That's our flight home too. We live in the Land Park area near the zoo and Fairytale Town." She extended her hand. "I'm Madeline Tucker."

"And Funderland." The youngest added.

"Nice to meet you. I'm Elisa Kensington." She shook hands.

"And let me guess from your accents, you two hail from England."

"We be Cornish." Ian stated. "Me name be Ian Darrow. A pleasure to be meeting you and yer daughters. They be well-behaved like our Mia." He struggled to straighten his clothes and regain composure. "Apologies. Lost me bearings. Just be learning how to navigate on American soil."

110

"That's him!" The long tall woman in the black business suit pointed out Ian to an accompanying security officer. Her finger hung in mid-air like an enemy rocket ready to fire. Disdain tweaked her high-pitched voice and her ruby lipstick bled slightly over the defined lines of her lips. "He threatened all the women in the restroom."

"He most certainly did not!" Madeline retorted. "He was looking for his daughter and he has found her. All is settled."

"Sir, you need to come with me." The officer directed his comment to Ian.

"Why?" Elisa asked in shock. "We'll miss our connecting flight." She stood up.

"Ms. Foster is filing a formal complaint."

"Really, I'll match her formal complaint about him, with one about her." Madeline declared. "Threatening an elderly gentleman." She straightened to all of maybe five feet four inches in her heels, and planted herself in front of the trouble-maker.

"Well, I never." Foster gaped and took a step back. "Just forget it. I have a European jet to board." She shot Madeline a disapproving glance and huffed off.

"We okay here now?" The security officer asked. "No terrorist threats?"

"This man did not in any way threaten anyone." Madeline answered.

"He's a Papa." The oldest girl said.

"Your name Ma'am?" The officer drew out a pad and pen from his front shirt pocket.

"Mrs. Madeline Tucker, Sutterville Road, Sacramento, California. You have Ms. Foster's information too?" She offered him a business card. "Also has my phone number and email."

"And yours sir?" He turned to Ian.

"Ian Darrow, Parkridge Road, Sacramento, California." Elisa answered for her father and fished out one of her new freelance writer business cards. "I live at the same address ~ Mrs. Elisa Kensington. May we board our flight now?"

"There doesn't seem to be any real trouble here so go ahead." The officer tucked the cards in the notepad and put it back in his pocket before leaving.

Elisa heaved a sigh of relief. They still had time to make their plane. "Thank you again." She asked. "Do you want to walk to the gate with us?"

"Sure. Girls why don't you hold Mr. Darrow's hands. Is that okay?"

"Be good for me." Ian answered before Elisa could.

"Alzheimer's." Elisa whispered to Madeline as they kept pace behind a content Ian and his first friendly American acquaintances. "He's rather enjoying the rapt attention of your daughters."

"To them he's another Papa, and they have been missing my dad something awful."

"I hope my Mia and Dad hit it off as good as last time they saw each other."

"You only have one?"

"Yes, just Mia." Elisa kept her eyes trained on her father as she fought to keep her hand from straying to her belly. "He's forgetting all of us."

"I'm so sorry. It's a treacherous disease." Madeline spoke with what appeared to be a pained understanding. "My father is going through the angry stage. Struggling with all the new limitations."

"We'll just starting fresh. Spent some time at home in Cornwall with dad first." Elisa struggled with the suitcases and gave one a big tug. "The wheels stick."

Noise in the airport leveled off to an upbeat hum the closer they got to the boarding gate. Elisa couldn't help but notice all the children up way past their bedtime on red-eye cross-country flights. Jet lag was going to hang on for a couple of days.

"Do you use the adult daycare drop-ins?" Madeline asked. "Dad goes twice a week, four hours a day, and truly enjoys the companionship and activities."

"Never heard about it until now." Elisa thought it sounded odd.

"It's good stimulation for them, and it gives you a much needed break. I'll give you my card for 'Alternate Address' near Sac City College. You can look up their rating online and see what you think."

"Thank you." Elisa mumbled not sure she'd ever need or use such a place. But she wanted to be polite since Madeline had saved her father from being branded a terrorist first time he set foot on non-Cornish ground. Mick would have flipped had he witnessed the scene. Probably flown Ian back to Cagwith and sent Elisa packing for good.

"We have first class seating." Madeline mentioned when they reached the gate.

"Oh, we're traveling coach this time." Elisa and Ian got in queue behind Madeline and the girls for the 'A' seating which had started before their arrival. The line moved fast. She rubbed the two oblong sedatives between her finger tips in her coat pocket trying to decide whether to make sure her father used the bathroom to change before they buckled in and she gave him his meds. What would be worse? A drenched diaper or a drugged parent? She figured since they were seated at the very back of the plane, the tiny bathroom cubby won out of sheer convenience. Nausea gurgled in the back of her throat. So morning sickness was going to accompany this pregnancy too. It was time to tell Troy about the other family addition arriving seven months down the road. She'd be showing soon and all the world would know.

Chapter Eighteen

As a small child I prayed all the time while walking along the rolling hills behind our cottage. I talked out loud to God, and he listened because he never once interrupted like grown-ups did. I learned how to chat up God from Mum. She held long conversations with him especially when you were at sea. It didn't matter what she was doing or where she was—cooking, cleaning, gardening, shopping in another village on market day, or such. She knew him well, and shared her heart like she did with the widow Farley next door. Prayer is hardly a part of my life these days. There simply isn't any time in our busy schedules—Mia's school and ballet lessons, Troy's demanding job, and my former writing job. Except back in Cagwith I asked God to show you mercy in this terrible disease, this monster Alzheimer's that is devouring your mind and body. If God is real, maybe he can help you. ~ Elisa's conversation with Ian as he slept blissfully sedated beside her on the flight above the snowcapped Sierra Mountains over Nevada and into California.

California

Ian woke up quite refreshed from the cross-country flight. Once the landing and seatbelt sign lights went off, he excused himself to use the toilet cubby right away and put on a dry nappy. They had a long wait ahead of them to disembark so Elisa remained belted in until he returned about ten minutes later.

"Everything okay?" she asked, and released the buckle. "My turn." She hurried in and right back. She'd gone four times while he dozed. Good thing she got the aisle seat.

"Cramped quarters in there, much like the cabin on board me boat." Ian sat beside her after staring at the number of passengers still in their seats ahead of them. "I be used to taking care of business with next to no space." He gave her a cockeyed glance, then winked.

Overhead compartments snapped open and shut. The aisle filled with people grabbing their handled luggage on wheels and towing it behind them. Only half the plane had emptied out. Elisa looked but didn't see Madeline and her girls. They were long gone.

"Let me push me baggage." Ian more told Elisa than asked. "I should be a gentleman taking care of yours too." An embarrassed plead shadowed his lean, stubble-covered face.

"Thank you. I'd appreciate that." She relaxed and hoped this Ian would stick around for a while, at least until Mia got a chance to interact with him. Mia loved her Gramps, at least the one she used to know. Elisa had asked Troy to leave Fiona at the house. That encounter could be put off as long as possible. The airport greeting would be the four of them, a friendly welcoming committee. The initiation into the Kensington Family Circus would follow second, and the bearded lady was to be on her best behavior. No daggers, flame throwers, or stink bombs allowed. Period. Fiona argued this fact and that made Elisa uneasy to say the least.

"What be you thinking?" Ian asked.

"About home."

"Your home?"

"It will be your home now too."

"Cornwall always be me home." He sighed and stared out the portal window to the blacktop below. The skies outside were an overcast gray with billowing storm clouds racing in. No sea of blue above or beneath.

"I know this isn't England." Elisa held her breath a few seconds before exhaling. "Please give it a go here."

Ian noted her pale expression, the bloom of her youth disappeared a decade ago when she left. Now a Californian, she was bronze in the summer and autumn months, and colorless in the winter and spring. This he knew from the videos and photographs she faithfully posted. Though he'd encouraged her to explore, he missed her beyond what words were capable of expressing. "Aye, me daughter, for you me be willing to do this best way."

"I think this coast will grow on you, dad. Carmel and Monterey will remind you of the Cornish coast. And though it is a lake, Tahoe is enchanting." Elisa believed this to be true. She planned for them to set sail on every boat they could.

"The crowd be thinned out now. We can leave." A few stragglers remained when he stood and reached to unlatch the overhead. One by one he pulled down their carry-on and set them at his feet. He popped the handles up into place and pushed one ahead of him and towed one behind. Elisa followed down the now empty aisle to the crew's cabin doorway.

"Thank you for flying with us." A perky stewardess made eye contact with each of them as they passed. The captain stuck his head out to say thanks too, and stepped from the cockpit, offering to shake Ian's hand.

"Thank you, sir." Ian stopped and gave him a hearty shake before stepping over the threshold where a sliver of space peeked between the plane and the onramp connection. Once Elisa caught up with him in the exit walkway he turned and told her. "We captains be grateful when we bring our crew in safe to land again."

Elisa watched a proud grin break across his face and dock there. It was the first hint of real joy she'd seen him convey in America. A sense of comradery held her father's heart for this captain of the air and his ship with silver wings. He respected completion of responsibility with honor. A well-read bookish man, he read about travel all the time. He understood maps too, at least he used to. She believed he secretly desired to navigate the world in his youth. That the open sea invited him for adventures beyond his homeland shores, but he sacrificed those deep yearnings for the woman he loved and the daughter he cherished. It wasn't that he settled, but chose instead a different course. Yet she wondered did he ever regret the simpler life he led when he could have sailed across the pages of his own book into another story.

"Where we be going from here?" Ian turned to ask.

"Down the escalator to baggage pick-up. Troy and Mia are waiting there for us." Elisa paused, then looked directly in her father's eyes. "Are you ready?"

"As can be."

"Can you manage the escalator with both suitcases?"

"Maybe you should cart your own now." Ian passed the handle of the floral bag into his daughter's hand. "I be giving the heave ho this manly black piece ahead of you." He pushed the luggage onto the moving, metal stairs with care and stood behind it on a flat surface that boxed out into the next step. *Tricky,* thought Ian, *one wrong step on this shape-shifter and you be a goner.*

Elisa followed and as they descended she scanned the lower floor for any sign of her husband and daughter. She caught sight of their black and orange San Francisco Giants jackets and baseball caps over by the first turnstile. They were in their usual meeting spot next to the first of two floor-to-ceiling sandwich stacks of suitcases. An artful display of lost luggage that remained from the old Sac Metro days into the current Sac International ones. It made quite the overstatement and was a favorite sculpture for the locals.

"Mom!" Mia cried out and sprinted to her mother, chestnut ponytail bobbing out the back of the ball cap. "I missed you so much. Squeeze me so I know you're real!" She threw herself onto Elisa's coat and hugged with all her might, burying her face on the warm, soft fabric. "It smells like you." Mia gulped in a huge swig of air.

"I missed you too sweet daughter of mine." Elisa squeezed. "See, I'm real."

Troy encircled the two of them. He pulled a heavy raincoat from under his arm and fanned it out like a protective shield. "You do smell good." He planted a big kiss on Elisa's lips. And another. And another.

"Dad." Mia objected. You have to share Mom." She cozied up closer.

Ian observed the trio with delight. This be what he and Joanie wanted for Elisa. So what if America now be her home. She'd found happiness, or it found her. Without love you have nothing. He wanted to remember this moment, the reuniting of a family. He mentally focused on storing the image before him, the sound of their voices, the excitement, the reflection of Cornish life transplanted to root and grow. He snapped the photograph in vibrant colour and compartmentalized it in his brain, squinting to safeguard any chance of escape.

"Good to see you again, mate." Troy unfurled in a sudden hurry and drew Ian in a bear hug. "How was your first crossing of the pond?"

"Me took a kip though most of it." Ian stopped to think when his son-in-law released him. "Never felt any turbulence so guess it be smooth sailing." He angled toward Mia hoping she'd take note of his arms flung wide to embrace her.

"Gramps!" She rushed at him with increasing velocity. "I knew you'd come to the States like I asked you." Her thin arms wrapped around his back and shoulders until he was secured within her hold. "Stay and never go back. " She begged. "Promise."

"Oh, me thinks to be here into me old age." Ian swayed sideways within Mia's grasp. "You have room for me then, at the house?"

"Of course. Dad and Grandmum have been fixing up one of the downstairs bedrooms for you, and you get your own bathroom too." She wobbled until they steadied and she took his hand and pointed to the parking lot. "To the car, and then the big top."

"Let's wait for the luggage to spin around our way." Troy suggested when the flight number flashed on the overhead screen and bags began flopping out on the circular belt.

"I brought me entire life in two big suitcases. Your mom posted more to be delivered at your front door. Me brought you some books." Ian kept Mia near to him and marveled at how she mirrored Elisa at this same age. Tall and lanky yet she made it look fashionable if not intentional to be a good head above her peers. He hitched for a second—that would please Fiona. Mia loved ballet and moved with Fiona's grace and beauty. *Concentrate. You be here to be a part of this family. Fiona too.*

"Books! The ones from your shelves in Cornwall? I loved reading those stories." Mia gushed. "Oh Gramps, we'll have so much fun together." She nestled like a baby bird, then matched his gait, his loafers, her flats, step one and two, step three and four.

"Ian seems to be holding his own." Troy whispered in Elisa's ear.

"This is the best I've seen him do."

"What happened?"

"I don't know. He slept most the flight. Mick and I gave him the prescribed memory meds from the doctor, and sedatives for the flights. He's been taking his prescription for months now."

"It seems to be working."

"If only." Elisa experienced the first glimmer of hope, a surge of emotion flowed through her that fluttered like butterfly wings lifting light and airy. Or was it the baby, a flicker of movement, life growing inside her floating in amniotic fluid, weightless, protected?

"Mia is entranced with him." Troy commented, and listened to the ease of his daughter's laughter. She bonded with Ian as though they'd never been separated the past two years by becoming fast buddies. Troy was certain they were already conspiring, hatching exploratory plans far beyond Ian's new boundary lines that were soon to be imposed.

Chapter Nineteen

Seldom comes a season in one's life that brings unexpected joy. It arrives unceremoniously and at first glimpse there be an awareness of purity of purpose as there be no hidden schemes, no petitions, and no query of needed reciprocation. 'Tis a gift. Time unwraps the present, then advances into the future. Savour the hours and days, perhaps months and years. Take nothing for granted during the lingering interval. ~ 'Olde British adage.

Home

Ian marveled at the tall city buildings including a flat-top Egyptian pyramid. From the backseat of the SUV he observed a magnificent bridge all lit up in the night sky as if the Christmas holiday was still being celebrated. Pressed against the passenger window he watched rushing water near crest level roll with a life force of its own below the bridge out toward the city. He knew boats be nearby.

Elisa turned and said. "Quite the metropolis isn't it, Dad?" She relished the delight and wonder reflected in her father's sparkling eyes. "Sacramento is the capital city in California."

"How many stories high?"

"Thirty-one, then twenty-eight, twenty-six, twenty-five, then it drops about ten stories a building, so far. There are plans for a Capital Grand Tower from seventy-one to eighty-two stories."

"It be like stacking lighthouses one on top of 'nother." Ian stared turning from left to right as Troy took one of the freeways through town. "You not be living in one of these towers?"

"No, no." Troy answered.

"Bloody good news." Ian said with obvious relief. "Me heard of these skyscrapers." He stretched his neck to view all before they disappeared from sight when Troy took an exit off the freeway.

"We live off Sutterville Road, almost home, Gramps." Mia said. "We live near Fairytale Town, and a zoo." She scooted closer to Ian gazing up into his dancing eyes.

"Troy be having his circus then?" Ian asked.

"Oh, the big top is our personal residence." Troy mused. "You are most welcome to join."

"Me hope to fit in spot on. What job be available?" Ian quipped.

"Hmmm, the knife thrower is open, as is the lion tamer."

"Let Gramps get there and decide then, when he sees what he has to choose from." Mia suggested.

"Such wisdom from one so young." Elisa chimed in approving. "Let the child lead the old folks. That includes the two of us." She humored Troy.

"Speak for yourself, I am still early middle-aged. My mum has yet to claim her actual age. She has joined the ranks of those in their golden years though it remains unofficial and undeclared."

"Me be liking that, golden years." Ian echoed with thoughtful laughter. "Sounds a mite grand, more like a privilege than it be one's impending sentence of doom."

"No doom and gloom here in sunny California." Troy spoke and thunder clapped. "There you see, a little lightning and thunder show to reassure you that rain will fall on this recently drought-ridden state." He flipped on the blinker and made a sharp right into a neighborhood lined with full grown trees, flower trellises overladen with winter roses, and low front yard fences exposing bountiful gardens illuminated under interspersed street lamp posts.

Even under the night sky, Ian could see kindred gardeners made their homes here.

Troy rounded a slight curve in the road then slowed down to pull into a driveway. After he spoke to the dashboard and she answered, a garage door opened.

"Let's take Dad in the front door, so he can see the yard." Elisa motioned for Troy to wait before entering the garage.

"Good idea. Everyone you may now exit the vehicle. I'll bring in the luggage through the kitchen door after I park the car." Troy stopped and told the engine to shut off. He got out and was quick to open Ian's door. "Welcome to your new home in America."

Mia's seatbelt buckle clicked open and she hurried around without closing her door to the passenger side where her mother and Ian sat. "Yay! You are finally here!" She ran past her father to unfasten her grandfather's belt. "Come with me." She waited for him skipping in circles on the paver stone pathway leading to the entrance of the two story home.

Ian took a hold of Troy's extended hand and arm and gripped tight. "Me best not start this visit with a fall and risk me bones breaking. Am being stiff from the long flights and sitting in the car." He stepped down from the SUV and tried to use the platform intended for exiting the vehicle.

"Take your time. No one is in a hurry." Elisa encouraged her father from behind Troy.

"I am!" Mia announced with glee. "And Grandmum is inside waiting up for us."

"Fiona, oh goodie." Elisa muffled her disparaging tone with one hand over her mouth.

Ian struggled to angle his way off the runner with one hip leaning against the doorframe for extra support. He trusted Troy alright, but not his own creaky bones and weary joints. With a sudden thump both feet hit the ground and he straightened up with a sense of accomplishment. "It be a longer way down than it looks." He quipped and glanced about the garden before them.

"Gramps!" Mia leaped to his side and took his hand from her father. "Come inside with me. I'll show you all the flowers along the walkway." She led the way describing each winter bloom. "These are called perennials because they come back every year. And we have English daisies and primroses."

"We can all come out in the morning for a walk in the gardens." Elisa said.

Ian beamed. "You be the gardener?" He asked Elisa.

"Oh, no, Dad." She knew he would be disappointed, but better he hear it from her than blabber mouth Fiona or the gardener himself. From her youth Ian had taught her how to till the soil, plant the seeds, and tend the plants. To hire help was a disgrace.

The red front double doors flew open. Fiona was dressed all in black—leggings, turtleneck, ballet flats and if Elisa didn't know better, she could have sworn Fiona held in her hand a cone-shaped black hat pointed at the tip. She moved to the outer brick stairs and stood dead center on the top step. The porch light lit up Fiona's face like a full moon shining too close to the earth. She practically glowed with an eerie fluorescent aura.

"Cheers, Ian." Fiona shrieked. "Everyone come in. I have a surprise planned."

"Areah!" Ian exclaimed and faltered backward into Troy's quick grasp.

"What does that old Cornish gibberish mean?" Fiona snorted.

"It's an expression of surprise." Elisa retorted before ushering her father up the steps with Mia. "What's with the witch hat? Halloween was last October. I didn't think you'd been out flying since then." She grit her teeth. This was not the welcome over her threshold she wanted for her father.

Troy scowled as he passed his mum and snagged the hat with a swift swipe of her palm. Fiona reveled in their distress. She pranced about the entry and living room like a pampered actress on stage in front of worshipping fans.

"I ordered fish and chips from Streets. I wanted to make Ian's first meal here a memorable one." She sashayed into the kitchen keenly aware of the disturbance her melodrama produced.

"That was nice of you Grandmum." Mia yawned.

"Are you hungry, Dad?" Elisa asked.

"Tis a kind gesture." Ian answered. "But I be a mite knackered. Not so much hungry."

"That's called jet lag and it's totally understandable." Troy said. "I'll park the car in the garage and bring in the luggage so you two can freshen up for bed."

"Could manage a cuppa tea." Ian offered.

"I didn't think to brew a pot. And the food might need heated up." Fiona placed a tray full of soggy cod fillets and stone cold chips on the living room coffee table. "I can microwave the food."

"We'll reheat the chippies in the oven tomorrow." Elisa slipped into the kitchen and put a kettle of water on. "Tea in a few minutes, Dad."

"Much obliged." Ian's jaw opened and his head leaned back as he expelled a long, drawn out yawn followed by a deep sigh. He blinked when another yawn escaped before he sat on the sofa and held out open arms. "Join me, Beanie."

Mia snuggled close. "Sorry, Gramps. I started the yawns and I can't stop." She stretched her limbs straight out, kicked off her bright pink shoes with mini-tutus sewn on, then leaned in and asked in a timid voice. "Do you think I'm old enough now to be called, Bean?"

128

"Bean it tis from this day forth and forevermore." Ian hugged her.

"I love how your words always sound like part of a storybook."

Fiona moved to the doorway and glared. "He'll molly-coddle Mia." She muttered under her breath. "He'll ruin all the refining etiquette I've diligently worked to perfect in her speech and stance." Fiona's slender figure pressed against the archway molding like a black bishop chess piece ready to make the next move on a checkered board.

"Not to worry, Mum." Troy trotted up behind her hauling suitcases in and under his arms and hands. "Mia loves you both, you can share her affections." He pushed past her, dropped Elisa's luggage near the stairway, then deposited Ian's bags in his room.

Fiona remained rigid, her lips now stilled, yet her mind flashed at light-speed from one scenario to another where Mia choose Ian repeatedly over her. She envisioned them walking the Crooked Mile at Fairytale Town where he'd be fool enough to skitter down the winding slides and squirm through the holes in the big cheese. He'd win her heart by being an impish kid with her instead of applying appropriate pressure to mature her gracefully through dance class and symphony recitals. A droplet of blood trickled down her sharp chin before she realized she'd bitten a fissure in her lower lip. It soaked into the cotton of the turtleneck top.

"Dad," Elisa sat with him, "would you consider taking another of your meds before bed tonight? I think this medication is helping your memory." She held a square white prescription bottle in one hand.

"Me did better on the airplanes." He answered. "Don't think it can hurt."

Elisa popped the cap and rolled one small round white pill in her father's open hand. She gave him a mug. "Earl Gray, nothing added."

Ian studied the pill before swallowing it with a sip of the strong brew. The tea was comforting, strong enough to nip the tongue, but a soothing warmth going down the throat. He closed his eyes and remembered his cottage on Mumford Lane in the village of Cagwith with the cobblestone streets and flower pots he shuffled from one bloke's home to another. The garden out back at Midge's would need tending on the morrow. His heart grew heavy about leaving his patch of earth behind. Perhaps Elisa would let him tend a patch here, front or back garden he didn't mind. Just soil he can dig his fingers 'neath and nourish. It pleased him to consider this possibility as Mia fell asleep under the protection of his shoulder, tucked in like a pixie as when she was but a wee one, when he first nicknamed her Beanie. He drifted off curious about this real Town of Fairytales across the road, certain there be a grand garden of such glory tended by itsy-bitsy winged creatures of flight. If the Yanks had such a place, he might reconsider his former harsh assessment and give it a go here.

Chapter Twenty

Morning always brings another day to get things right, at least to ponder the past day's events. Where to go from there involves both choice and opportunity. The two don't necessarily share congenial agreement, but the option remains open. ~ Caption on the kitchen calendar with a photograph above of a great waterfall spilling over mighty granite stones under a brilliant setting sun. Eagle Falls, Lake Tahoe, California.

The Weekend

Ian woke up alone on the sofa, he figured Troy had carried Mia upstairs to her room. Two warm blankets covered him from head to toe. At some point in the night, he'd laid out across the sofa. It was more comfortable than any of the beds he'd slept on during his fortnight travels about one mate's home to another. Someone had slipped a feathery soft pillow under his head. He basked in the toasty warmth of the well-heated room and realized he'd slept through the night for the first time in ages, at least that he could remember.

A quiet commotion rumbled in the kitchen. Ian listened to the scuff of slippers cross the floor. Reluctant to emerge from his cozy cocoon he remained burrowed until he heard the humming of a familiar tune. He struggled to bring it to mind. *Greensleeves.* He thought it be his daughter so he rose to greet her and the new morn.

"Cheers, Dad." Elisa chirped. "I hope I didn't wake you." She placed a Brown Betty teapot on the table nook set for two with his favorite breakfast—bacon, runny eggs, sausages, beans, a fried mushroom and tomato slice, toast and marmalade. "Just the two of us this early. It's Saturday sleep-in."

"What time be it?" Ian glanced at his wrist.

"California time, it is 9 am. Cornwall time, 5 pm. You feeling it?"

"Me slept through." Ian noticed her slight pooch of a tummy in the clingy night frock, her robe loose.

Elisa tied the robe closed with a dangling sash. "Rested up enough then?"

"Have you told Troy yet that you be in a family way?" Ian raised the tea cup she'd filled to the brim and let the steam rise up his nostrils before taking several sips.

"I will today." She sat next to him, the plate in front of her bearing naught but a sparing portion of scrambled eggs and toast. "It will be a bit of a shock for him."

"Best he hear it from you and not his Mum. If Midge could tell, so can Fiona."

"Point well taken and advice soon to be heeded." Elisa promised. "I always keep my word." She forked the eggs from one side of her plate to the other, and drank her tea.

"Aye, you do." He said and relaxed in the chair and took a look about the kitchen. It was modern, not country at all. Stainless steel appliances and white walls with stark matching cabinets offered no creative bent, just clean cut edges. The dishes were white too. He started on his breakfast. "Good and hot." He dipped one soldier slice of toast into a yellow pool and sopped up the yolk.

"Dad, you almost seem to be your old self again." Elisa took a small bite of toast with marmalade.

"Me do?" He wolfed down the strips of bacon and speared a sausage link. "Hope it be lasting." Ian concentrated on the food before him. "Me be tired of Midge's porridge and stewed fruit every day. Blimey, change it up a mite!"

"Your appetite is back too." Elisa said, watching him devour every scrap of food while her stomach churned at the sight of it all. She struggled with the smells when cooking for him, but she wanted his first day to be special. He was a foodie and didn't know it, but her mum knew the way to Ian's heart and she indulged him. She was an excellent cook and baker and Ian loved her for it.

"Where did you find the marmalade?" He asked after polishing off the last smidge of crust."

"Touch of Britain in North Highlands. Chippy place, and food and sweets shop."

Ian stared straight ahead, "Me miss yer mum's homemade orange marmalade. Best it be in all of Cornwall." He smacked his lips as an endorsement.

"You won't find the likes of that here. I've searched for years." Elisa topped off their cups.

"Why be everything white?" Ian asked, glancing around the bright space.

"The home had been recently remodeled before we bought it. To be honest, I was disappointed with the kitchen, wanted more of a cozy décor."

"I see spurts of colour, red kettle, the wire basket of fruits, the sapphire glass canisters." Ian purposed to take in all he could whilst this period of clarity continued unfolding. Aware he was enjoying a phase of normalcy absent from his life for some time now, Ian wondered if he'd done anything different. He thought not, but other than traveling to a country he never desired to see, life be the same. He noticed his loafers were on the wrong feet, but that be an easy fix.

"Mia has big plans for you today, are you up for it?" Elisa stirred extra sugar in her tea.

"A bath be necessary first." Ian added. "And a kip."

"There's a dresser for your clothes if you want to go through your suitcases. I can press anything you need de-wrinkled." She took a slow sip from her cup, hoping for the right temp.

Ian rose and gave Elisa a kiss on the cheek and winked. "I hope to return clean-shaven, bathed, and the same bloke that walked in the front door. Now where be me room?"

Chapter Twenty-One

Change your life! Take charge and reclaim control of the things that have bogged you down in the past. The future is yours for the taking. Simply put one foot in front of the other and move forward. Take a risk and see where it leads you. ~ Motivational book on Troy's desk.

Things Are Not Always What They Seem

Ian rifled through his bags, pulled out clothing, and started to line the dresser drawers in neat, organized piles. Socks, boxers, and t-shirts—top drawer. Thermals and flannels—second drawer. Casual trousers and tops—third. Heavy jumpers—fourth, and a mish-mash of personal favourites he basically lived in on a daily basis—bottom drawer. Mission spot on.

After hanging his hooded anoraks and heavy coats in the empty closet, he dumped the remaining contents on the bed, and placed the luggage side-by-side on the closet floor. With great care, Ian arranged items on the dresser top—watch, wallet, glasses, British coins in a brass dish, pipes in a custom-made wooden six-hole shoe, tobacco pouch, pipe cleaners, and a portrait of Joanie the day he married her. He ran a hand over her face. The black and white picture depicted a striking young woman with a generous smile, soft curls that rested on her shoulders, and huge piercing eyes. Ian kissed his fingers, then tapped her lips.

The room around him floated with a nautical theme in shades of blue from deep navy to a pastel hue. Ian settled on the edge of the large bed to look out the window centered in the middle of the room over a small round table and an upholstered chair. The blinds were tied up exposing the back garden and patio surrounded by a dormant winter garden of flowerless stubs and stems.

"So this be Elisa's home in America." He sighed. "Not how me imagined." Nothing in the room was worn, but stiff and new, with more colour than be in the rest of the home.

An immediate shudder ran up Ian's spine shooting electric currents to his neck and across his shoulders blades. He gazed into the bright light of morning searching for a starry sky instead. A great awareness of his minute stature in the vast array of the universe held him spell bound. He thought how small his life be, even smaller due to his shrinking brain. Oh, he be listening to every word at surgery: diagnosis—Alzheimer's, diminishing comprehension capacity, invasive memory loss, communicative skills waning, and an eventual withdrawal to, what be it? Hard as he tried he could not remember that part. No matter. He heard the worst of it.

It was quite a while before he rose to venture into the connecting bathroom and deposit all his toiletries on the counter and in the cupboard above. A handy shaving kit carried all his needs. It was a thoughtful gift from his daughter. After laying out the last of his personal belongings on the marbled stone, he brushed his teeth. The aged reflection mirrored before him bore no resemblance to the man he knew. Some old codger with saggy, baggy pockets under bleary reddened eyes stared hard at him. "Who the bloody hell are you, you old goat?" He spit a bluish foam into the sink, ran the faucet to rinse it away, and slammed the cabinet door hard enough the glass rattled.

After selecting a pair of thermals and changing, he propped himself on top of the bedding and laid back against the rows of pillows. He'd never seen so many on one bed. Stretched headboard to the foot of the mattress, he wiggled his toes and his feet. With a shiver he rose to fetch his slippers from the closet, then returned to the bed. This be the jet lag they all spoke of? He looked about the room and got up again for his flannel robe. Glad for the red plaid amid all the blue, he tightened the belt snug and settled back again. A sudden thought brought a moment of panic—where be the hot water bottles he might need? He rose and stood, turned, waited, then walked over and took his favourite pipe from the shoe, clenched it between his back teeth, and relaxed deep into the pillows once more. The familiar aroma of his special blend filtered up his nostrils, and the taste bit strong on his tongue. Ian slipped his hands in his robe pockets and noticed the pale blue sky painted on the ceiling.

When Ian didn't answer her knock on the door, Elisa pushed it open to find her father in the middle of the bed sleeping in his robe and slippers, pipe dangling from the left corner of his mouth, head down on his chest. He didn't flinch when she removed the pipe and returned it to its proper place. She took a wool blanket from a quilt rack on the wall and tucked it about him, before slipping off his ratty old house shoes which she clutched against her heart.

He must be exhausted. Unable to take her eyes off him, she pondered what the day would bring when he awakened. How could he possibly have the energy for Mia's planned adventure at the park?

He laid on top of the comforter, he'd never crawled underneath. The pallor of his face was stark in contrast to the bright red flannel robe and dark gray woolen blanketing molded over his thin frame. His hands were both cold to her touch. A single tear trickled a slow journey down her cheek.

Elisa placed the slippers at the foot of the bed and pulled two hot water bottles from the bottom nightstand drawer. She knew he'd search for these faithful companions even though he wouldn't have a need to fill them because the central heater was set at sixty-five degrees. Old habits remain none the less. She left the winter warmers on the reading table along with the Daphne du Maurier paperback books from her pockets. She knew he couldn't read anymore, but it wasn't her father's room without books. Fiona had ignored her request to make sure books were waiting for him. Instead she purchased eight new pillows.

Chapter Twenty-Two

There are few places in the world like this magical corner of Sacramento's Land Park. For over a half-century, millions of children have streamed beneath Humpty Dumpty's stone archway and ventured into wondrous, undiscovered worlds – the worlds of their own imaginations. Favorite fairytales and nursery rhymes are the backdrop...all designed to inspire creativity and literacy in young children. ~ Excerpt from the Fairytale Town brochure and map, William Land Park.

"Play, Learn, and Grow With Us"

It was a sight to behold, the perfect bloke breakfast. No more lumpy, lukewarm porridge. "Be gone Midge and take your, 'Keep your mitts off the sugar bowl,' and 'No butter for you,' healthy ways with you!" Triumph at last.

"Be that me runny eggs, beans, and bacon?" Ian chirped.

"And sausage, tomato slice, mushroom, toast, and marmalade." Elisa patted the chair with a quite-satisfied smile. "Just like yesterday morning."

"Have me died and gone to Midge-free heaven?" Ian blinked twice.

"No, Dad. You're in America, land of the free."

"Me might be willing to give this America a go." Ian quipped and sat with a sudden hurry.

"Tea is brewed and ready." Elisa plopped the brown ceramic teapot in front of her eager new B&B resident. "You're looking chipper today all duded up to pop over to the park."

"Has everyone else eaten?" Ian asked. "Me fell back asleep yesterday. Though not be sure of that."

"Yes, you slept one day into another. I am pretty sure you are all caught up from jet lag now. It's just you and me, this morning. They ate hours ago." She poured them a cuppa.

Ian bowed his head and closed his eyes for a few seconds, then said, "No kip today. Me be ready to visit Bean's town of fairytales."

It was a short walk down the neighborhood street and across a two-lane road to this famed Fairytale Town in Sir William Land Park. Ian marveled at the cottages that dotted both sides of Parkridge Road. All the homes except one had front gardens and inviting porches. Trees formed a bridal path on the quaint and quiet street. Once they got to the Sutterville Road, it was busy with fast moving cars and lorries speeding by in both lanes. There the four of them crossed over to the park where endless green lawns and massive trees sprawled out like a forest sea. Ian was relieved that Fiona had buggered out. It would be more pleasant without her incessant corrections and unsolicited advice.

Mia sputtered forth with a string of questions from the moment they set foot out the front door. She seemed to be disappointed her Grandmum had chosen to stay behind, "to tidy up a bit." But she soldiered on with a cheery heart for her Gramps. Elisa and Troy did not hesitate when Fiona declined, nor did either of them plead for her to reconsider.

"Come on, Gramps. We're almost there!" Mia urged and tugged on the hand she'd been holding the entire walk. She twirled, her brunette hair flowing in ribbon curls, never letting go. "You just have to stoop under Humpty Dumpty."

"Me have to what?"

"You'll see when we turn around the bend." Troy said with a chuckle.

Sure enough there stood a stonewall archway with a huge Humpty Dumpty fellow leaning his egg-self side against one stone tower. The lad was painted with a bright wide-eyed face and spiffy blue duds, and a red bowtie. He greeted the little people with an open-mouth smile and a small straw hat on his egghead noggin. And only wee folk could fit through the open gates. This was not an adult-size paradise. "Ouch. Low Bridge" warning signs were posted on both sides of the archway entrance, with additional, "duck" signs on the two gates.

Ian removed his cap and bent down to follow Mia inside, his head scraping just below the arch. A gatekeeper sat in a stone booth and asked for the entrance fees posted. Children cost less than adults. Another sign stated that no adult could enter unless accompanied by a child. Mia danced as Troy paid up and they all advanced over a bridge with water flowing below. A young couple tried to gain admittance behind them, but were turned away for lack of a child. A twinge of compassion tweaked Ian's heart for the childless pair who left without insistence or complaint.

"The rule is for the children's protection." Elisa whispered.

"It be necessary?"

"It's a good precaution." Troy responded.

"Let's be pirates!" Mia pulled her grandfather toward a ship flying a black skull and cross bones flag docked permanently in the water to the left. Straight ahead a king's castle of stones rose from the ground with a lowered drawbridge and turret tower.

"Be yer not wanting to be a princess at the castle?" Ian asked.

"Pirates have more fun, matey." Mia altered her voice in a somewhat roguish manner.

"Off to pillage and plunder then." Ian followed pretending to raise a sword from a scabbard. "We be not Cornish pirates though, they brought harm to the people. We be American pirates instead."

Mia thought for a second then complied, "Okay." She plucked a dagger from its sheath. "Mom and Dad, I mean, you bushwhackers, be look-outs and don't let anyone lower the flag!"

"The girl be cheeky." Ian winked. *And she be Cornish, she be Cornish.*

"I think you mean, swashbucklers." Troy answered. "Not one bloody blaggard will board the ship!" He stood straddling in his Docker shoes, slacks, and polo shirt, hand held high.

Elisa tried to get in the mood, but she was stymied by her father's heightened ability to communicate. "Can dad's new meds work this good, this fast?" She asked Troy. "It's like he went to bed the stranger, and got up the father I know."

"At least for today, so let's go with it." Troy said. "Who knows what tomorrow has in store for us." He improvised his best Jack Sparrow imitation while Ian and Mia took the ship. Fortunately, no other people were headed their way so he did not have to sword fight nary a rival pirate nor an aristocrat. He kept watch for the Royal Navy's ships on the horizon lest they fire up their cannons.

And so the day went. Ian walked The Crooked Mile, with great care not to fall. There was one harrowing near slip on one of the winding curves but Troy caught his elbow just in time for him to steady himself. The lot of them sang-a-long with Mia's *Wizard of Oz* rendition of, "*Follow the Yellow Brick Road.*"

Ian found Fairytale Town lived up to all expectations for young and old alike. He preferred the farm animals at Farmer Brown's Barn—Daisy the cow and Eeyore the donkey, and yes, The Little Red Hen House. He never spied the Three Blind Mice, maybe they be blind to him as well. The barn smelled of the Cornish countryside—dank hay, upturned earth, and future fertilizer. He was comfortable there and the animals let him pet them. Mia was gentle with each creature, nurturing and sweet.

Mia's favourite was Sherwood Forest that soon filled with merry men and maidens romping though the trees and taking on a large climbing fort. She begged her mom for a party there on her next birthday. She'd already ruled as the queen of the castle for her fifth celebration with the entirety of her kindergarten class. And she was certain she'd found the secret magical stone in the castle.

There was a big top for Troy, but it was the Children's Theater, not a circus. He made the best of it and produced a one-act play with the available four actors and actresses. It was a new version of Peter Pan meets the Invisible Mermaids from Pirate's Cove. Mia made it up as they went along. Ian determined it to be a dramatic comedy of errors and fantastical fantasy—a strange mix of genres Ian was certain could be written into story, a novella at least. Perhaps Troy could sell it at the circus for peanuts.

The surprise of the day was Elisa and Cinderella's coach. Not that Ian saw her as the Old Woman in the Shoe, but she be more suited to the Mother Goose Stage in his way of thinking. She be the writer, the one he'd always thought to become an author. Mother Goose's stage be incased in storybooks stacked high. A grand place for a child or adult's imagination to grow. Yet Elisa sat in the orange pumpkin carriage and waited for a driver to lead the horses. By the time Troy finally obliged her, Mia moved everyone on over to Jack and the Beanstalk, next was the Cheese That Did Not Stand Alone because Mia asked her Gramps to wriggle though one of the holes next to her. It was a tight squeeze with the full breakfast in his belly.

Ian thought the interactive learning garden, or Mr. McGregor's Garden, to be the crowning success of Fairytale Town. It scored points with the old fisherman in other ways too. Beatrix Potter herself would give a stamp of approval for this teaching patch of earth where school children that might not have the opportunity at home, did have it here to till the soil and plant seeds to grow.

"I find this Town of Fairytales to be of British birth." Ian announced as the family came to Banbury Cross Station for a snack before heading home.

144

"What do you mean, Gramps?" Mia asked and ordered pink cotton candy for all, and bottled waters, "to wash it down."

"Your castle says it be of King Arthur's royal lineage, has a reproduction round table with surrounding murals of our Queen Guinevere, the King, his Guards, and Merlin the Magician." Ian stated and took an airy bite into the fluffy spun sugar.

"True enough." Troy agreed.

Ian continued between mouthfuls of the sweet. "Our Beatrix Potter's Peter Rabbit and His Sisters, Mr. McGregor's Garden, Sherwood Forest, and here we be at the Banbury Station."

"Dad has a point." Elisa conceded.

"Merlin's Cave be in Tintagel, Cornwall. There be magic all about Arthurian geography, near the rocks and cliffs where waves brought the infant to the shore. Many believe Arthur to be mere legend, but there is great validity to that fabled time of chivalry and right over might. A great honour it be to become a knight at the round table, to sit with the King at the famed citadel." Ian took a breath and sighed. He chugged his water in one successive gulp and tossed the empty bottle and white cone into a trash container. "Lancelot du Lac of France brought ruin to the good queen and Camelot. Love be Arthur's undoing, trusting those closest to him. Though it be said the king and his faithful knights disappeared inside a vast cavern at Alderley Edge, Cheshire, where they lie sleeping to this day with their mounts." Ian stopped and exhaled.

Mia sat at his feet, mouth gaping, eyes wide. "Is the legend true?"

"There be historical Arthur and Legendary Arthur. Each person must decide for themselves what be truth."

"What do you believe, Gramps?" Mia shifted and rested her head on one knee she bent, while sitting on the other leg.

"The land be an important part of the king's story. Cornwall be more than one layer of geography—what you see, the ocean, rivers, trees, valleys, hills, cliffs, forest. Then there be the hidden mysterious, mythical places. These be difficult to retrace over the ages as most names not be on any modern map."

Mia was captivated with her grandfather's love of Arthurian stories. To him they were never fairytales. "I wish I lived at Camelot and served the king as a knight at the round table." She stood and held Excalibur, her cotton candy paper cone, high, "Right before might!"

"Silly child, those old myths are nothing but the tattling of men foolish enough to believe in knights on white horses saving damsels in distress." Fiona stood hands on her hips, behind Mia. "It's sheer folly." The sun beat on her blonde ponytail and silver jogging suit.

"Good to see you popped over after all, Mum." Troy tossed the last remains of his sweet away and tilted his water bottle to down the final drops. "How did you get in?"

"We were about to walk home." Elisa said with a snarky edge.

"They know me by name here because I bring Mia all the time. The gatekeeper just charged me to join you. I didn't think you'd be gone this long." Fiona answered.

"Can we come back again soon?" Mia asked. "To Funderland? Please."

"There be another place like this?" Ian took a step back.

"Funderland is more of an amusement park, you know, roller coaster, choo choo train, merry-go-round." Elisa answered as they all headed for the front entrance.

"Like Brighton?"

"More like Brighton for little folk." Troy laughed.

"Must we duck under another wee fortress to enter?" Ian bent to exit Fairytale Land.

"Oh, no, you can stand straight up. The train tracks run by the front entrance so you have to wait if the red lights flash and the warning rail lowers until the train passes." Mia piped up. "That happens a lot. It's fun."

"There be a Ferris Wheel?"

"No, sorry Dad." Elisa answered. "Let's walk home."

"But there's an Octopus Oscar the Fisher ride with baby fishes, and a tea cup and saucer swirling in circles. One that you have to be careful what you eat first or,"

"That's enough, Mia." Fiona cut her off. "Your Gramps won't like the frilly tea cup ride." She took Mia's hand in hers and followed Elisa.

"Oh, yes me will," Ian interrupted. "So the Yanks learned how to celebrate tea time." He snickered. "It not be the coffee cup ride."

"Good point." Troy agreed. "Or we'd all be standing strapped in venti white paper cups bearing green mermaid emblems."

"Latte or mocha?" Elisa quipped.

"Who knows, that may be the next big attraction, at least in Seattle." Troy mused.

"It's called the Crazy Cup Ride." Fiona muttered. "Should be Ian's cup of tea."

"All I know is some giant Squirrel I've named Slappy is the big boss now." Mia giggled. "They call him Happy, but Slappy fits him better."

"Those rodents be darting up and down trees, and running amuck all over the park grounds." Ian scowled at Fiona. "Some walk upright on two legs, their pampered fluffy tails high in the air."

If Fiona heard the comment, she never let on. Her stride increased as did her chatter with Mia, head cocked sideways with a roving eye checking on Ian each chance she got.

Elisa fell back beside Troy and Ian, letting Mia and Fiona take the lead. "Dad, do you need another nap when we get home?"

"I still be working off me big breakfast." Ian shuffled along the sidewalk and onto the park greens. "Me slept a day and night already. No more kips for me this day."

The evening lulled on in low speed after a light supper salad, and rice and vegetable dish. Ian seemed antsy, almost anxious when they settled in the family room to watch the telly. A documentary filled the big screen and he relaxed able to follow some of the presentation on Baby Boomers and their Music. He listened as British and American bands played in succession, each one louder than the previous performers. If the night had ended there, all would be perfect. Fiona would have none of it. Nope, the quiet family night came to a screeching halt when she brought up that Elisa was in a family way and congratulated her son. Troy dropped his bucket of popcorn and it spilled in a heap on the carpet.

"Why didn't you tell me?" He turned to Elisa. "How did you find out?" He blasted Fiona.

"I was waiting for a romantic moment—alone." Elisa snapped at Fiona. "How could you stoop so low?"

Fiona maneuvered her way past Troy to the formal dining room arch opening, a coward's escape route after dropping the baby bomb. She glowered from a safe distance waiting for her prize. Troy sat dumbfounded. Elisa fell to her knees and began scooping up popcorn by the handfuls into the empty red and white striped tub.

A shrill squeal reverberated off the four white walls. It emanated from the smallest mouth and tiniest body. "A baby sister!" Mia chasséd, toes pointed, to her Gramps past Fiona, and rushed over to her parents. "I've been begging for two years, two long years." She helped Elisa shovel the last kernels into the bucket. "She can sleep with me. There's enough space for a crib too."

"Bloody good news!" Ian joined in, "Mick be sure to fly out for this miracle." He rose his bottled water in celebration. "Cheers!" He clinked the open air and swallowed a swig.

"Oh, Dad, Mom—thank you!" Mia leapt over and planted a big kiss on her father's forehead. "Cheeky, cheeky, cheeky!" She twirled.

Troy knelt beside Elisa. "Did you fly pregnant? At risk?"

"No risk. I found out for sure the morning I left. A repeated home pregnancy test."

Troy gathered her in his arms, drawing her close. "I know the timing seems crazy, but we can do this together. Girl or boy."

"Girl." Mia glided, dipped mid-demi-plié, and finished with a glissade.

Face blank, Fiona slumped against the plaster and squirmed in her flats. She dug the balls of her feet into the thick carpet. The merriment unnerved her. It was not supposed to play out this way. Troy should be angry, they can't afford a baby, and Elisa failed to trust him with the unexpected announcement. Mia should be jealous, displaced not joyful. And Ian, the old shipwrecked bag of ancient bones, he shouldn't even know what is going on. Who does he think he is toasting like it is a blessed event?

How had this upper hand been trumped? Finding the discarded pregnancy test in the outside rubbish bin had been the first victory. Realizing Elisa neglected to share the shocking news with her husband before leaving for an indeterminate amount of time was yet another. Not letting on she knew anything was her ace in the hole. Someone had stacked the deck.

"Not quite the soddened old fool you took me to be?" Ian sauntered by. "Hitting the loo before me next bottled water." A loud, vulgar belch burst forth tainting the air between the two.

150

"You odious, uncouth, vagrant." Fiona pinched her nose while turning her head away.

"What does odious mean?" Mia asked.

"Your Grandmum has opinions." Ian exited to his private bathroom humming a tune.

"Oh." Mia replied, forehead scrunched and eyes quizzical.

"Never mind, my little ballerina." Fiona assured her.

"I can look it up in the dictionary." Mia scurried off.

Fiona observed Troy and Elisa walk arm-in-arm into the kitchen with Mia tagging along. *I still have the ace of hearts up my sleeve. I won't play out my hand too soon next time.*

Chapter Twenty-Three

England is the mothership. America was born and flew off across an ocean. Even though spaceships weren't invented yet, that's how I see it, and it's easier to understand. Kind of like remakes of old movies, and covers of songs. I'm an American by birth, but Cornish by space travel, the captain of my own ship, The Intergalactic Cornwall Constellation ~ Mia's explanation of her U. S. citizenship to her Gramps.

Two Counties—One Allegiance

The few next weeks, Mia showed her Gramps around the 'hood': Funderland, The Sacramento Zoo, Sac City College, the William Land Park pond and amphitheater, and most important of all ~ Ford's Burgers down the street.

They took a walk everyday down Parkridge to Parkmead Road so Ian could check out all the neighborhood gardens.

"You're nibby. You touch all the plants and flowers and pinch snippets you put in your pockets." Mia shook her finger at her non-repentant grandparent.

"These cuttings will grow in me patch of earth in your mom's back garden she be lent to me."

"Why do kids have to ask permission and grown-ups don't?"

"Me have gotten the required approvals from each home. Whilst you be at school me pops about introducing Ian and chatting up. We be friends then." Ian snapped a tender stem off at a tri-leaf cluster and added that bud to his coat pocket.

"Gramps, you should ask each time you take a flower." Mia gazed over her shoulder to find Mrs. Peters at her front window with the drapes pulled back, watching them. "These are her prize camellias that she enters every year in the big deal of a flower show. She places and wins all the time." Mia waved and flashed an exaggerated smile, pointed to Ian, and shrugged. "You have to behave better or they won't let me lead you around for our alone time." Mia issued that statement with severe chastisement. Her sternest look of displeasure accompanied an abrupt tromping ahead without waiting.

"Bean, me be trying to fit in here." Ian followed Mia after giving Wendy Peters a friendly wave and raising his hand in toasting mode with a verbal, "Cheers."

"I looked up what Grandmum called you that day she blabbed about my sister." Mia turned, she stood hands on her hips, pink Wellies in a puddle of rain, a cross, but serious expression clouded her features. "It is not a compliment."

"Yes, well Fiona be tart-tongued and overtly meddlesome." Ian refuted.

"Why don't you two get along?"

"We have never, Bean."

"It will be nice for me if you try. And much more peaceful for Mom and Dad." She was unwavering in her stance, flecks of freckles burnt like tiny pit dots of fire on her fair-skin face.

"Of course me be willing to try, for you, but good luck with your granny." Ian snickered.

"She loses her temper when you call her that."

A glimmer of delight shone in Ian's eyes as he sighed. "No fun then today." He shuffled a couple of steps forward. "Me promise from this day forward to be tolerant, be nice to Fiona." He crossed his fingers behind his back and gave Mia a timid grin. "Whether or not she be agreeing, me be trying to do me best, dear Bean."

"Thank you, Gramps." She enfolded him in a California bear hug, the real deal. "I knew you'd listen." Her saucer blue eyes held him captive and she knew it.

"Me always be listening, Bean. But there come one day when, me won't remember everything quite right." Ian rested his hand on the top of her head. "Could even on the 'morrow."

"I've heard the talk. Something called Alheimer. It sounds like a person's name." She spoke in a soft tone, not so bossy anymore.

"Me be trying hard to remember things, people. It be easier since arriving in America." He brushed off his trousers and offered her a sweet from his shirt pocket. "Yes, yer Gramps went searching and found the sweets drawer in the kitchen."

"You won't forget me will you?" Mia strained to steady a quivering lower lip.

"Not be by the grace of God. And me be inquiring of Him concerning this subject." Ian struggled to remain calm, to reassure her so as not to be scaring her.

"We can pray about this together." Mia took his shaky hand in hers and started walking forward at a slower pace. "Gramps?"

"Yes, Bean." Ian's voice faltered. He be dreading this moment when she would understand.

"If the answer is no, I will remember for both of us. And I'll tell you all the stories about what we do together and where we've gone." She promised. "Like your first day at Fairytale Town."

"Ah, that be a good day. There be a bit of Cornwall in the Humpty Dumpty tower and good King Arthur's Castle." Ian held her small hand tight within his. He never wanted to let it go. He thought she be the stars and the moon, part of heaven here on earth. "Me be trusting you with that Bean. You be remembering the stories of us, then they not be forgotten."

Humpty Dumpty sat on a wall,

Humpty Dumpty had a great fall,

Four-score Men and Four-score more,

Could not make Humpty Dumpty

Where he was before.

William Carey Richards 1843

Chapter Twenty-Four

Books be holding the world in a hand. The reader be traveling to new places and meets people that sometimes be changing their lives. Whether fiction or non-fiction, the story be coming alive between the pages. There always be books. ~ Ian sharing his thoughts with Mia.

Novels, Memoirs, and Biographies

Ian pondered his and Mia's conversation later in the day. Her heart be pure, a rare and glorious wonder in the day and age her parents be raising her. It be an honour for Mia to find her Gramps interesting enough to be writing a book about him. He wondered what she might choose to record and what she might decide to leave out.

"What you thinking about, Dad?" Elisa wrapped her arms around Ian's neck and plucked a big kiss on his forehead.

"How blessed me be." He pat-patted the side of her cheek, then watched her open the fridge and gather food to prepare for the family lunch on this lazy Sunday.

"Why yer not be taking Mia to church?" He inquired.

Elisa froze. "What? Why do you ask?"

"Today she asked me if yer mum and me took you to church when you were a little girl."

"Oh."

"What be yer answer?" Ian shifted in the kitchen chair under the slice of sunlight streaming in from the curtain-less window with nary a smudge.

"We used to. Every Sunday. She was too young to remember." Elisa regrouped and spread out the lunch meats and cheeses for sandwiches across the marble slab of the island in the center of the room.

"Why do yer be going no longer?"

"Aren't you inquisitive?" Lining up an array of condiments and salad foods Ian detested but ate to appease his daughter's health concerns for his deep-fat fried diet, Elisa tried to redirect their discourse. "Would you like your ham and cheese heated, no rabbit food?"

"Yer mum and me quit going after your baby brother be born too early."

All movement ceased before him.

In but a mere whisper Elisa uttered. "My brother?"

"We never spoke of him. Too much heartache. Joanie asked we not make mention to yer, ever. Yer be not yet turned four when he came, and left our lives." Ian's hushed tone echoed a distant, unhealed sorrow.

"I don't understand, why never tell me?" Breathless, Elisa faltered and gripped the edge of the countertop until her knuckles whitened.

"Yer be too young, not able to understand the implications of a troubled pregnancy. We never made an official announcement

157

to anyone. He did not 'thrive' so the doc said. Joanie never showed to be in a family way at near six months." Tears pooled, then trickled. "Me delivered me son at home, in our bed. He came in the middle of a night. Me awakened to Joanie moaning in her sleep. Neither of us realized what be happening, until there he be with us."

Elisa walked to her father's side and knelt before him, clasping his hands in hers.

"For decades me pushed him to the back of me mind, a place only he lived." Slow sobs began to rock his body like the waves of the ocean rolling into shore.

"Did you name him?"

"Aye, we did. Michael, for the arch angel in heaven. The one who fights the battles here on earth when mankind be in need of a warrior. The Lord sends Michael." Bleary-eyed Ian cast his eyes upon Elisa. "Me thinks me forgot about me son. Then lost him again in the ravages of this dread disease. But he has come back to me memory." He kissed his daughter's teardrops and pulled her close to his heaving chest. "Be not turning away from God like me. We clung to yer after losing Michael, never wanted yer wandering too far away."

"And I left you, crossed the ocean." She rested her head on Ian's shoulder.

"As yer should 'of. Yer dreams be yer own." Ian stroked her hair, cupped her face in his weathered palms. "Children be meant to grow into their own lives. Michael would 'of one day too. He be formed perfect, me lad, but tiny."

"How did Mum deal with her grief?"

"In her silent prayers. She ached to understand. When the cancer came, she longed for her son again. Me used to carry her out to the garden. We buried him there near her roses." Ian let go a quiet sigh that weighed heavy in the air.

"The little statue of the sleeping angel? Mum used to sit there for hours when she gardened." Elisa gazed off to the side. "How could I not notice?"

"That be when yer mother no longer desired to go on Sundays. The church has some strange ways about her. Me agree with all the rituals and traditions. It be taking away from intimacy. 'Twas a long time before me came back to me faith."

"We have no such reason. Life got busy. We chose other things." Elisa stood and pulled a chair out to sit beside Ian. She smoothed out the creases in her slacks with long forward motions.

"Search yer heart, yer soul. Ask what be more important." Ian's voice deepened. "Pain lessens, but be never going away. That be the truth of it though many will speak otherwise." Ian sat straight in his chair. "Remembering helps and be hurting at the same time."

They sat next to each other, shoulder to shoulder in the quiet of the mid-day. The brightening sun filling the room with a wary winter warmth. The rest of the home did not stir. Troy was out working in the garage at his tool bench. Mia went next door offering weekend dog sitting services. Fiona was shut away in her room doing barre stretches. She'd join them for lunch but eat next to nothing—a couple leaves of lettuce and tomato slices. No meat, no cheese, no bread, maybe a small piece of fruit.

"Me can help prepare the meal." Ian realized he'd taken Elisa's hand in his. He gave her a gentle nudge. "Me can't burn down the house if it be cold meats."

"I'd like that." She stood with him. "Can we talk more about this later?"

"Yer be reminding me. If me forget." A sudden look of concern swept across Ian's face.

"Yes I will, Dad."

"We should 'of told you long ago, together. Before Joanie left this earth." Ian struggled for words. "She be close once, but not again. Yer forgive me, Elisa?"

"I forgive you dad." She answered. "I am not an only child."

Chapter Twenty-Five

Relish the present. Too many people be 'liven in the past. In their regrets, their mistakes. Today offers endless possibilities. The future be not promised, it be hoped for. ~ Ian's philosophy on a good day.

Friends

Troy answered the house vintage telephone and listened to an unfamiliar voice ramble on the other end. He waited politely until she finished talking and handed the phone to Elisa who was stretched out on the sofa reading a book.

"It's for you. Some woman named Madeline Tucker."

Elisa took the phone. "Hello, I was wondering when I'd hear from you."

"Meant to call sooner, but my dad took a tumble down the back patio steps a few days after the girls and I got home."

"Is he okay?" Elisa sat straight and lay the book splayed open on the coffee table.

"He is now. Spent some time at the hospital. He hit his head on the bricks and got a nasty bump with a double cerebral concussion. Not pretty I tell you. Projectile vomiting all the way to the emergency room by ambulance. He made no sense at all for a week."

"So sorry."

"Thanks, he's better now. Talking up a storm again and happy to be back home with us." Madeline paused. "How's your dad braving these Yankee shores?"

"He's actually doing better. The new drug is working, and he's more like his old self."

"It can be a wonder drug for some people in early onset, some even mid-stage." There was a brief silence. "Would you like to meet for a cup of coffee? There's a coffee shop at Land Park."

"Sure. When are you free?" Elisa surprised herself with the spontaneity of her reply.

"Tomorrow when the girls are at school. Is seven forty-five too early?"

"Not at all. Mia will be in school then too. By the way, what are your girl's names?"

"I'm sorry. I should have introduced them at the airport. My nine year old is Savannah, Shelby is seven, and Sybil is five."

"Your oldest is close to my Mia's age." Elisa added. "We get going here by six am."

"Oh good, fellow early risers. I have to run Dad to an appointment in a few minutes, but I'll see you in the morning." Madeline's voice faded under a booming, demanding man's words admonishing her to hurry or they'd be late for the movie.

"So, who is Madeline Tucker?" Troy asked before Elisa could return the handset to the vintage black Ma Bell rotary cradle.

The coil cord sprung and snapped when the phone clunked in place. "I don't understand why you love this old phone. It's so cumbersome."

"It still works which is more than I can say for all else that comes with a measly one year warranty." Elisa picked her book up and relaxed onto the sofa arm, her bare feet tucked against Troy's hips and legs. "She's the woman I met at the New York airport."

"She lives in Sac?" Troy picked up his novel and cozied in for a good read as well planting his socks on Elisa's legs, facing her from the opposite side. "That's coincidental."

"More providential. What are you reading?" She strained to get a look at his book cover.

"A new author. Good writing so far but I'm only a third of the way into the story. Historical. And you?" Troy grinned behind his paperback, his eyes focused in on his wife.

"The latest by that Australian author. Love her books." Elisa shifted her body weight. "I think meeting Madeline was meant to be."

"It's not like you to get chummy so fast."

"She's the one who stuck up for Dad. Remember, I told you."

"Her father has dementia too. What were the odds of you two connecting on the other side of the country?"

"I know. Her dad fell at their home. I hope Dad doesn't go through that too." Elisa expelled a breathy sigh and cast her stare to the ceiling.

"Ian's a pretty steady fellow. He even puts his shoes on the correct feet now." Troy prodded her with his toes.

"How's work going?"

Troy's legs stiffened. "Not good. Blair still won't take no for an answer."

"How can he expect you to do what he's asking? It's illegal to cook those books for him." Elisa drew in a sharp, short breath. "What can you do?"

"Stand by my word." Troy's chest tightened, his teeth clenched, and his relaxed mood evaporated. "He'll fire me. He's backed himself into a corner. He knows that I know too much."

"How did it come to this?" Elisa lowered her book. "He seemed so decent when he hired you. And you walked away from a better job offer to help him get his business going."

"I misjudged his character." Troy's shoulders slumped. "I saw what I wanted to see. All the signs were there from the beginning. Let me take care of this mess, okay."

"I want to support you." She persisted. "Is he going to go bankrupt?"

"He'll never do that." Troy deflected her concern. "You have your hands full with your dad. Have coffee with Madeline, enjoy your new friend. I'll deal with the facts and figures." He placed his book on the table and leaned toward her. "No way is my work going to ruin our morning alone. The merry trio will return soon."

Elisa glanced at her watch, almost eleven. She looked out at the winter sun struggling to peek through a cloudy sky. Splotches of blue hung in between the gray fluff crowding out hope for clear weather and an afternoon outing. The picture window across the room framed a moody day. It suited the present conversation.

"Let me be there for you." She offered. "That's my job."

"First you gave up your weekly newspaper column to fetch your dad, to freelance for a season after he settles in. And I know you miss your previous travel writing life." Troy drew her close.

She laid her head on his chest, his rapid heartbeat thumped against the ridge of her ear. Their legs tangled. The tension she'd sensed moments before disappeared as their bodies relaxed.

"This is what I need." Troy leaned back to make room. "I miss spooning with you any time I want. We're never alone anymore, never."

Elisa listened as the drum of his heartbeat slowed, like the end of a song toning down. He held her so close, arms enfolded like a second skin. She liked that, the hugging part. No man before him ever understood how important it was to her, or they didn't care. Troy knew. Raindrops danced across the window glass, a mesmerizing tango. Elisa closed her eyelids. A distant melody played in her head, guitar riffs strumming.

Long, luxurious kisses dulled her thinking. Troy's lips tasted sweet like honey. Time was theirs to share. She relished each second.

Thunder and lightning echoed throughout the smoldering skies. The world outside had darkened and no blue remained, only blackening shades of gray.

The front door flew open. Fiona stood arms bursting with recyclable grocery bags.

"I could use a hand or two." One bag hit the tile entryway.

Troy circled around to meet her and lifted the cloth bag off the floor. Ian and Mia hurried in dripping wet behind Fiona. They carried their bags into the kitchen.

"Welcome home." Elisa started unloading items into cupboards and the fridge. "Who did all the shopping?"

"We all did." Mia said. "Together. Gramps wants to make everyone dinner tonight, bangers and mash, but he promised, no mushy peas." She pointed her index finger directly at him. "We eat whole California garden grown peas here."

"I'm tossing a green salad." Fiona countered.

"Rubbish rabbit food." Ian huffed.

"What else did you do today?" Troy asked.

"We ventured to an indoor mall, a circus of sorts called the Arden Fair." Ian quipped. "Big junk food court filled with rude and impertinent folks who have forgotten manners their parents most assuredly taught them in their youth. Fiona shopped in nearly every store, on two levels."

"Really, Mum." Troy's words hinged with a distinct edge of disapproval.

"Ian led the way into every store, I just followed." Fiona shot the gloating fisherman daggers. "He knew what he was doing. It's blooming four in the afternoon."

"Thought you two needed time alone." Ian told Elisa. "Fiona didn't complain while she tried on clothes in those fancy shoppes."

Mia held up two colorful glossy handle bags bearing high-end store names.

"I needed new lingerie." Fiona grabbed her purchases and headed for the hall to her room.

Mia asked "Do you want me to bring in the rest from the car?"

"There's more?" Troy turned on his heels for the front door.

"Not to worry, I'll get that later." Fiona halted mid-step.

"Oh, let's fetch all your *needed* merchandise now, Mum."

"I picked up a few new outfits for my job interviews next week."

"Where?"

"The salesclerks told me they're hiring and I'd be perfect for one of the positions." Fiona twirled around with the bag handles dangling from her slender wrists like diamond jewelry. "Because I have flair and style. Plus, I get a discount on anything I buy."

"How did you pay for all this today?" Elisa asked suspiciously.

"Oh, they helped me open new charge accounts. Pitiful limits, but it will increase every six months, if I use my card." A sly smirk spread across Fiona's face.

"And pay your bill! Based on what income?" Troy fumed. "What were you thinking?"

"I was killing time. Ian road blocked every effort I made to come home earlier."

"You need therapy, Mum." Troy slammed the front door behind him.

Fiona trotted down the hall and closed her bedroom door.

Mia stood silent in the middle of the kitchen.

"Me only meant to give you husband and wife time." Ian leaned onto the granite island countertop in the kitchen and stopped gathering the items for his dinner menu.

"You did, Dad. And we both appreciate it. You aren't responsible for Fiona's shopping addiction. She is."

"I helped Grandmum pick out some of her new clothes." Mia hung her head, sensing she had contributed to the problem.

"You didn't do anything wrong, sweetie." Elisa rushed to her daughter's side and wrapped her arms around her in a tight squeeze. "Grandmum is a big girl. She can make her own decisions."

"Is she in trouble for buying new clothes?" Mia sniffled. "She bought me a new dress."

The front door opened and Troy appeared carrying about half a dozen bags. "She'll be at both of those interviews next week if I have to take her myself." His nostrils flared as he exhaled a disgusted grunt. "Mum's always looked down on shop girls, said they're mere servants to the upper class." Troy straightened, marched down the hall and deposited the bags in front of Fiona's door, hesitated, then grabbed it all up again and went back to his car.

"How about that dinner, Dad? Can you help your Gramps do the cooking, Mia?"

Ian pulled a skillet from the iron rack above the island. "Me could use a potato peeler, and masher while me fry up the bangers."

"Grandmum used your name on the applications." Mia wiped her eyes and looked up at Elisa.

"Go, you're a good helper. Remember to add milk and sea salt before you mash."

Mia scampered off after Elisa planted a kiss on the top of her head.

"I'll get the snap peas and show you how we steam them." Mia pulled a bag from the fridge. "But Gramps, if you want your mushy peas, that's okay too."

"Thanks, Bean. This old Cornishman needs me greens me way." He winked.

"Mom and I will set the dining room table." Troy rejoined them and motioned to Elisa. They stacked five of everything in piles, including placemats and matching cloth napkins.

The kitchen chatter volume increased to loud bouts of laughter and giggling as Ian told one joke after another. Sizzling bangers floated a savory aroma throughout the home.

Troy pulled a fist full of receipts from his shirt pocket. "Over two thousand dollars!" He muttered under his breath as Elisa placed the last fork on the table. "And that doesn't include the loot she took to her room." The last words sputtered out with fiery venom.

"Let it go for tonight." Elisa rubbed her palm over Troy's trembling hand. "She wants a battle, and she'll win." She kissed him hard on the lips. "Listen, Dad and Mia have made their peace and moved on. If we do too, we win." She kissed him softer and longer next, then stuffed the receipts in his back jeans pocket. "We win, this time."

Chapter Twenty-Six

Family be a mixture of birthright, marriage, divorce, and rebirth. Somewhere in that mix be a blend and border of bloodline and crossing the line. It be a balancing act of the utmost effort to find the measure of worth in each soul to live in peace together. A bloody brood to contend with. ~ Ian's comments after the Arden Fair Escapade.

Repercussions

Fiona grabbed her purse and stormed out the front door to sit and wait in the car for Troy. He took his time getting ready for work, gray suit, teal tie and a white starched shirt. The sedan was fully loaded with her purchases from the previous day. All tags attached, including the ones she intended to snip off when her son came to collect the bags she toted to her room.

Troy buckled up and voice commanded the engine to start. "You'll be returning everything and closing your accounts. Or should I say, Elisa's new accounts."

Seething in the passenger seat, Fiona bared her teeth, grinding the back molars with precision. "So what if I used her social security number and other information?"

"You forged her name. That's a criminal offence in this country. In any country."

"I need new accounts. Mine are maxed out." Her right eye twitched.

Troy glared in the rear view mirror after staring down his mum. Fiona was not her usual presentable self this morning. Stray blonde hairs stuck up and out the back of her loose bun. Mascara clumped and eye-liner ran wayward, like a make-up mask gone wild applied in reckless haste. It didn't matter. Troy was on a mission.

"You return all of it, or you check out of your current residence. It's that simple."

"She put you up to this." Fiona's lips flattened into a mere twist of a thin line.

"No Mum, you did this to yourself." Troy clicked the garage door open and slowly backed out into the street. He changed gears and headed toward the tail end of rush hour traffic to the mall. "I'll be late to work this morning because of this mess you've created."

"I said I would take care of it myself."

"You can't be trusted."

"There's no need to treat me like a child."

"Then act like a responsible adult."

"I need caffeine." Fiona ordered. "Go to the drive-thru window the on the way so I can buy my short soy latte." She checked her hair in the mirror and swept the stray wisps under the bun.

Troy heaved an exasperated sigh. "Are you even listening?"

"I have cash."

"That's not the point!"

Fiona watched his usual calm demeanor slip away as his shoulders tensed tight and he gripped the steering wheel firmly with both hands, fingers tapping. She opened her designer handbag and pulled the shimmering gold cosmetics pouch. With a quick flip of her travel magnifying mirror, she freshened her foundation and blush, then began to redefine her blotchy eye make-up.

"Don't miss the turn at Freeport Blvd or you'll have to go to the next location before the freeway exit. There isn't a drive-thru at that one."

Earlier that morning Elisa fled to drop off Mia at school and meet Madeline at the coffee house when Troy and Fiona hurled accusations back and forth. Her father headed out back to his garden, taking breakfast and a thermos of brewed tea with him. The row went on and on until Troy drew the line. Fiona had to leave that very evening if she did not comply. Period.

Madeline stood at her chair and waved.

"You made it ahead of me." Elisa gave her a quick hug.

"I took the liberty of ordering our coffees and a couple of pastries."

"Perfect. Let me get some sugar and cream." Elisa grabbed a cup and went to the coffee bar, returning in a flash. "Yum. I love their signature bread pudding." She helped herself to a thick gooey slice of wonderfulness on a white ceramic dish.

"We have similar taste." Madeline took the second plate of bread pudding and pushed the croissants aside. "I hoped you wouldn't have to cancel if it was a rough morning."

"Oh, it was one of those special beginnings of a day, but not why you would think. Not my dad anyway." Elisa stabbed her fork into a big chunk of cinnamon syrup coated breakfast.

"Yeah, some days you just need to go for a drive or slip away to pretty much anywhere."

"Is your dad getting worse?"

"This fall sent him into a tailspin. It's sad. The girls are struggling with the changes." Madeline took a long sip from her disposable cup leaving a red lipstick outline on the lid.

Elisa looked closer at the woman sitting across from her. Her long raven hair was gathered on one side with a clip. A dull sheen replaced the glossy highlights she'd noticed at the airport. Her eyelids sagged over pretty chocolate brown eyes, and darkened baggy puffs weighed below. Her stunning ebony skin tone seemed blotchy. The bright young woman she'd met two months ago didn't look aged, but wearied. "Are you getting enough sleep?" She asked.

"Ugh. No. Does it show?"

"I know I'm not getting as much sleep as I need."

"Don't worry. I look how I feel. Worn out." She slumped, elbows on the table in front of her cup and plate. "Exhaustion holds an entire new meaning in my life."

"This is from your dad, not your daughters?"

"Yep. Thank God I have the girls. They are a huge help. Can't take dad to the adult day-care again until he behaves better. No more picking fights, slapping the ladies on their bottoms, and heading out the door for home before I pick him up."

"Oh my." Elisa sat back in her chair and poked at her plate. The memory of her father's antics in Cornwall returned with vibrancy. "He'll come around though, won't he?"

"Maybe, maybe not."

"You weren't prepared for this were you?"

"I thought we had more time." Madeline's voice tweaked.

Elisa did not know what to say next so she said nothing, but she took Madeline's hand in hers and held it. The uncertainty of permanent memory loss terrified her. The coming and going of it all right now is bad enough. And she'd thought Madeline had it all figured out. How foolish to think such a thing.

"The irony is when we met, I thought I was supposed to be there to help you along, and here you are helping me." She squeezed Elisa's palm and pulled back with a gentle tug.

"We can help each other."

"I would like that. Your father is supposed to be there to take care of you, you know." Madeline wiped away a tear that straggled down her cheeks. "I was a Daddy's girl all my life."

"Yeah, I do know." Elisa ached inside. "Me too."

Picking up her fork, Madeline took a stab at the bread pudding. "I love this stuff. Tried to make it at home but it never comes out as good as here." She took a bite and swallowed.

"Sometimes it's just nice not to have to cook and bake for everyone."

"My hubs hired a maid to fill in for me at home, and offered to have someone help me with the meals for a while, until I get back on track." She choked back a threatening outburst. "Trouble is, I got derailed. No one expected it, least of all me."

"I was headed in the same direction. The new medication has temporarily changed that. Not sure for how long." Elisa drew in a deep breath and held it before exhaling.

"How strange and cruel this disease is. People forgetting themselves, their entire life history dissolving. As if they never existed." Madeline's voice fractured, her words halted.

"I wonder what the end will be like, for my father. And does he fear it?"

"I fear it." Madeline's face fell, her voice hushed.

"I do too."

Madeline admitted. "I think the cracks in my façade are showing. I can't fix this, or heal it, or even slow it down."

"Well, if we crumble, we'll go down together." Elisa added. "If my mother-in-law doesn't do us in first."

"Geeze, you have that too?" A long line knit across Madeline's brow.

"She may be out on her bum today if she doesn't." Elisa opened her mouth, then shut it. "Am I evil to want her gone? Hope she challenges Troy, because he will follow through."

"Not evil, honest."

"Yes, I sit here enjoying every bite of this delectable dessert for breakfast and leisurely sipping my coffee, knowing Troy is facing the dreaded Fiona dragon. And I really don't give a fig, except for Troy who has to endure her nonsense." Elisa consumed a couple more nibbles.

"Does she have somewhere else to go?"

"Back to London. One of her friends will take her in, for a while. Until they catch on that she's completely broke."

"Then what?"

"They'll pawn her off on another friend until the word gets around. Then no one will."

"How sad. What kind of friends dump one of their own?"

"Rich, selfish people just like her." Elisa shrugged. "Fiona told too many lies to back things up. Actually, I think they've figured it out already." With great relish she finished the last bites on her plate. "Thanks. Next time it's my turn to treat."

Troy stood at the mall entry and waited for the metal gates to be raised. He carried all the shopping bags in one hand. Fiona sat nearby at the little café with her soy latte.

"You could have stopped before we got here."

"Your coffee house was not our destination. Besides," he turned, "you have your cup of caffeine now, so fuel up, Mum."

The steely door retracted into the grate above and a man in a fashionably tailored suit and tie greeted them with a good morning wish and a flashy grin.

Fiona dumped her paper cup in the rubbish bin and followed her son up the escalator to the second floor, and directly in front of the ladies department. She flinched when the young woman addressed her personally.

"Elisa! So good to see you. Are you here to buy out the store again?" She gushed with a combination of enthusiasm and commission totals ringing.

"Actually, we're here to return everything and close the account." Troy answered.

Fiona huffed and turned away.

"Oh, I see." The petite brunette on spike heels moved back, and picked up a phone. She placed a call, then turned toward Troy and Fiona. "I can help you with your returns if all your tags are still attached and nothing has been worn." Her chirpy tone turned flat and sour. "You'll have to go to the business office on the third floor to close your newly opened account though."

Troy lifted the bags to register level and left them on the counter top. "All the receipts are inside, all tags are attached."

"And the reason for all these returns?" She asked curtly.

"Stephanie," Fiona read the sales girl's name tag. "I simply decided I don't need these for my wardrobe." She spoke with that air of superiority Troy remembered from his childhood. The one he detested, that made him feel, well snobbish. "The newer styles will be coming out, and I'd like to wait to see what is offered."

"Oh." The clerk perked up again. "Well I can help you with that too. Do you still have my card?"

"Why yes, I do." Fiona tilted her head off to the side and raised her chin just so. Her coquettish actions had the desired effect of endearing Stephanie to her once more.

"Why don't you have your husband head on up to the next floor to handle the charge account while we finish up here and chat a bit?"

"Actually, my mum will be going upstairs with me." Troy responded as each piece of clothing was credited to the new card. "Are we zeroed out now?"

"Almost, one more dress. And this looked simply stunning on you." Stephanie held up a green chiffon tea-length dress still on the hanger."

A slight gasp escaped Fiona's lips.

"Will you still be applying for a job?" The sales clerk asked.

"No, probably not at this time." Fiona dismissed the question with a wave of her hand.

"Well, let's still get together for that cup of tea."

"You didn't have to embarrass me like that in the store's business office!" Fiona mumbled more but Troy kept walking up the steps of the escalator to the third floor women's section. This time she toted the bags. "My financial status is my own personal business."

"Let's just get this done." He stated and landed at the final step onto the glossy polished tile floor. His heels clacked in unbroken cadence toward the register station. A glance over his shoulder set his jaw rigid. Fiona lagged farther and farther behind.

"We have some merchandise to return and an account to close." He addressed the sales associate before she could manage a cheery greeting.

"Do you have it with you?" She inquired with a curious look up and down.

"My mum does, she's almost here." Troy spun around and gestured for Fiona to join them at the counter.

Fiona took her time, then deposited the bags in front of the middle-aged woman strumming her French manicured nails impatiently on her side of the station's surface.

"And what have we here?"

"Oh, a few frivolous things I find no need to keep."

"All tags attached and receipts in the bags?"

Troy waited for his mum to respond before answering. "Yes."

"I can take care of your purchases, but you need to go to the business office to close your account, unless you wish to do that online."

"Online sounds fine." Fiona walked over to look at the closest rack of sweaters on the right. She lifted a hanger and held a rose colored one to her chest.

"Or you can exchange any merchandise you wish."

"No, we are returning everything." Troy replied.

The register hummed away and one by one each item was retrieved from multiple handle bags and scanned with a wand until a red light beeped. The procedure came to an abrupt end. The clerk closed and folded all but the last bag. She removed tissue paper, then flattened it out.

"Did you decide to keep the pantyhose?"

"What?" Troy lurched forward to examine the empty red bags. "I said everything."

"I have to have the merchandise to return it."

He stared at the name tag pinned and pressed to her bosom in a too tight blouse. "Angelica, did I pronounce your name correctly?"

She nodded in affirmation.

"Something is missing?" His jaw tightened but he spoke in a polite and calm voice.

"One package of forty dollar pantyhose, light beige, re-enforced heel and toe, size petite. To be precise." Her clipped tone edged icy with annoyance.

"Mum?"

"I forgot. I opened that package first thing yesterday to try the hosiery on."

Troy whipped out his wallet to pay for the nylons.

"You will have to take care of that in the business office by paying off the account in full. There is a remaining forty-three dollars and twenty cents on the charge." Angelica offered the return register receipt and credit card to Fiona, not Troy. "Thank you for shopping with us. We do hope you come back again soon. Our spring fashions are coming in daily now." With a coy snicker she left them and sauntered to the opposite side of the floor.

"Why didn't you tell me you opened a package?"

"Because you were talking abusively." She raised her voice to a high pitch. "I'm wearing the pantyhose. I needed new ones." She stared hard and long at him.

Troy leaned in. "Follow me upstairs and I'll pay off your account for you Mrs. Kensington."

He rushed by shelves and rounders of expensive winter and spring clothing, nearly bumping into a mannequin draped in bright bursts of color, and pointy toe, low heel shoes. Up the escalator he exited leaving Fiona trailing behind. By the time she arrived upstairs, he was seated with an elderly gentleman in a main office. She slid in the seat beside him.

"I understand we have a bit of a problem here." The white-haired man sat stoic, his face devoid of expression at the desk before them. "Let's see if I can take care of this without involving the authorities." He asked for the credit card and receipt from Fiona. From that point on, he only addressed Troy who paid off the bill in full by personal check. Fiona signed all the paperwork presented to her without reading a word.

"Is that all?" Fiona stood. A defiant smirk spread across her face and her body stiffened. She avoided direct eye contact with both men in the room.

"Wait a moment please." He rose and shredded the card in front of them. "The account has been paid in full and is now permanently closed."

"Thank you, William. I appreciate your help in this delicate matter." Troy stood and shook hands before passing his mum out the door.

"I do hope you will consider us for all your cash purposes in the future."

Fiona exited without any response and walked out the open door in a hurry to catch up to Troy.

"How could you?" Anger sharpened her tone. "I can never shop here again. This complete humiliation was unnecessary."

Troy's face reddened. "I used to have my slacks and shirts tailored here. You want to talk about humiliation. Thank God I knew William." He headed down the escalator. Fiona nipping at his heels. "I can't believe you aren't the least bit repentant!"

"I need some kind of freedom." She shouted.

"You want freedom, Mum? I'll set you free. You can pack your luggage and leave anytime. Go back to your friends in Belgrave Square or wherever they reside." Troy shouted. When they landed on the ground floor he realized people were pointing, stopping and staring at the public scene. Unwitting customers were subjected to endure their row, without any consent.

He pulled his wallet and thrust a twenty in Fiona's hand. "Call a cab. I have to get to work."

Chapter Twenty-Seven

Stories have a life of their own. You begin a journey at the turn of the first page and before you know it, you are no longer be the reader, but part of an adventure. Whether you travel to new worlds or visit someplace you have been before, you step into the pages and are transported elsewhere. Every reader sees and feels this differently. The author writes an invitation, and if it be a good book, the reader embarks on a sojourn through chapters that change their lives. ~ Ian's answers Mia's question about why he read so many books as they spend an afternoon browsing at a local bookshop.

Stranger than Fiction

Mia purchased a hardbound journal with blank lined pages. She wondered how long it would take her to write Gramp's story and fill in all those pages. The clerk rang up her small stack of books, all were from the discount bookshelves at the front of the store. Except for the one with the picture of pets with their humans. She paid full price for that paperback but it was only five dollars and ninety-nine cents, plus tax. She liked the illustration of the two people in a cozy bed reading an opened book with a cat on the front and back covers. They were reading to the six dogs.

Gramp's stack was twice as high as her four books. He'd found his from all over the store. The pretty, teenage salesclerk chatted away with him like they'd known each other for years. She batted long eyelashes and flicked her blonde hair back twice when she asked him where he was from in England. Silly girl. Mia interrupted and asked if they could have Mexican food for lunch.

"Gramps, are you done yet?"

Ian grabbed the burlap tote bag outlined with famous author faces in green ink. He turned to Mia. "Yes, all done." Then looked back. "And ta Miss for your interesting suggestions for me next visit." He shook the girls hand and she gushed after he let go.

"Hope you come chat Cornwall again soon, Mr. Darrow."

Mia wrapped her arm around his and led the way out of the store and across the floor to the Mexican restaurant. "I like their fish tacos. They have white sauce instead of a red one."

"Fish tacos sound good to me. Should you text your mom so she can join us if she's finished her business at the store?"

"Okay." Mia pulled her cell from her pink purse with the cat face. Her two thumbs moved with speed, then she slipped the phone back and zipped the vinyl closed. "Do you always chatter with the store clerks like that?"

"If they be interested enough." Ian opened one of the restaurant's double doors for Mia to enter. He scanned the surroundings and commented. "Colorful and quite southwestern. American."

"Yeah, I like that coyote the best." She pointed to a howling skinny purple and orange dog to the right. "The red kerchief around his neck makes a statement." She thrust her hip out and placed a hand on her waist. "I'm cool, I'm the main dog."

"Do yer mean, alpha dog?"

"Yeah, the alpha dog, coyote. Maybe I should ask Mom to dye my hair purple."

"Why not be streaking it orange too?"

Mia glanced at the wooden carving and paused in thought. "Naw. Too radical."

Ian cleared his throat and laughed. "Time we be ordering." They walked to the registers. "Three orders of fish tacos, please."

"Do you want the single taco or the three tacos?"

"Get the single, it comes with tortilla chips." Mia answered Ian's blank stare. "And we'll have a side of guacamole, rice, and three sodas."

"All be done then." Ian paid the total and they scouted for a table after filling their glasses at a massive soda machine. Mia gathered forks and napkins at the end of a salsa bar.

"It's loud in here when it fills up." Mia warned. "I'd like to start interviewing you." She sipped root beer from her straw before Ian pulled a chair out for her.

"What be you thinking of asking me?" He sat beside her and hung his bag of books on the back post of his chair. She did the same with her plastic bag, but first she grabbed the journal.

"Well, I already know you read lots of books. Why?" She quickly reached into her shoulder strap purse and clicked a pen that she placed behind one ear.

"Me love to read. Read me first book when I be a young lad."

"How old?"

Ian squinted at the high ceiling and stretched in his seat. "About six. Words be easy for me. Me first books had big pictures with one sentence on the page." A happy grin spread slowly across his wrinkled face.

"When did you start reading chapter books, about third grade?" Mia ran a finger around the rim of her glass.

"Me never nicked any though me family be poor. Me head master lent me some of his books." Ian sipped his soda without a straw. "We learnt the alphabet at four, me be reading at six, be hooked on books at eight."

"Like Mom." Mia noted.

"She be a reader like me."

"And me."

"Me thinks either you be a reader, or you not be. Not much betwixt."

Mia pondered the statement. "True, not many in the bookstore who don't like books. And in the classroom."

A waitress appeared and scooped up the metal stand on their table with the number twenty-two, and placed three red baskets and the side dishes in front of them. Elisa followed behind her. Ian stood to pull out her chair.

"Thanks, Dad."

"All taken care of now."

"Yes, finished at the giant discount warehouse store." She blew a wisp of hair from her eyes and relaxed.

"Now we relax and savor our meal." He let go a sigh. "Me bought you a novel. Historical."

"I should have time to read it now."

"Why doesn't Grandmum care much to read books?"

"Me know not the answer to that question. Do you?" Ian asked Elisa.

"Too busy with dance practice, rehearsals, and performances. Ballet was her entire life. Still is, really." She lifted a taco and took a bite.

"She has all kinds of big books about ballet, mostly with pictures, but she doesn't read them." Mia nibbled on some chips. "She flips through and looks at the photographs for a long time." She stood and waited. "I'm going to get some salsa, spicy or mild?"

"Spicy."

"Dad," Elisa whispered, "This is more complicated than we thought. Fiona could have been prosecuted. Troy texted me after he got to work." She watched Mia fill little clear plastic cups with assorted salsas. "He gave Fiona an ultimatum, or she has to leave."

"Me thought yer said it be done."

"We're done. Troy won't help her this time. She's on her own from now on."

"Me see."

"Please understand, this has been going on for two solid years. From the moment she arrived, she's plummeted us into debt, and we simply can't afford it anymore."

Mia returned balancing containers with red and green salsa on her forearms.

"Yer could be in a circus act." Ian took several of the cups.

"I am." She grinned. "I'm trying out for a new act though."

"Me be guessing the tightrope?" Ian lay the array of homemade special selections out in a straight line across the middle of the table. "All spicy?"

"A couple of medium, just for variety." She winked. "And, yes, the tightrope."

"That be a dangerous new endeavor, Bean." Concern filled his words.

"It's the next step up. There has to be a bit of danger. Isn't that why you love to read mystery? For the thrill." Mia settled back in her chair and dumped the corn and black bean salsa on rice she spooned into her wax-paper lined basket. "That's the fun of it all."

"There be a twinkle in your eyes me Bean."

Elisa remained silent and ate her taco. Ian looked to her for some sort of backup.

"The Kensington Big Top needs a show stopper. So we can sell more tickets." Mia chowed down and spoke between bites. "You know, like when the lion closes his mouth on the tamer's head and the crowd gasps until he slowly opens it, his teeth never touching the skin. It just looks like it."

Ian cast his glance sideways, away from his daughter. *Bean be too aware of the unspoken, the stress in the house that be far more visible than the adults be able to disguise. She be a smart one, Bean. No fooling her.*

"What is the novel about that you bought me?" Elisa asked.

"It be a civil war era mystery travels from Virginia to the west, be here in California. A debut author me think you might enjoy reading. A woman about your age." Ian answered.

"Sounds interesting."

"Maybe we can start a family reading night." Mia quickly suggested. "Dad has his westerns, though I've never understood his fascination with the old west." She hedged for a moment. "Grandmum has her Royal Ballet books, and I can start my journal."

Ian thought, *Oh the wisdom of the very young. She be calling us to task this miniature psychologist.* We all to be family. Fiona be in, not out. She be a part, however flawed, of we fledgling band of circus performers. One clown with a disappearing memory, one lion tamer in the family way, one ringmaster be trying to keep the tent from collapsing, one young tiger be jumping through fiery hoops and over hurdles, and one wayward, prima ballerina tightrope walker be in danger of falling into the unsuspecting crowd below.

Chapter Twenty-Eight

I miss home. London. Big Ben. Parliament. Trafalgar Square, the River Thames, the National, Tate Modern, and Natural History Museums. Oh to stroll through The Victoria and Albert, to revisit the Old Masters and Impressionists at Somerset House, the Embankment Galleries. These heathen Americans know nothing about centuries old architecture, art, or sculpture. They boast in false pride knowing little of their former Queen, royalty, and privilege by birth. Two hundred years ~ poppy cock! Mere tourists in their homeland booking river cruises and taking double-decker bus tours. Even if the lot of them knelt in repentance at Saint Paul's Cathedral there'd be no redemption. All these years later and they still don't realize the depth, and width, and length of what they rebelled against and forfeited. I do. I know what I left behind. And I will return. ~ Fiona's rant to the Earl of Herefordshire upon his offer of a flat to sublet.

Birthright Has its Privileges

Fiona adored the sapphire satin and velour dress that she'd charged for Mia. It was the final straw when Troy made her return it with everything else. She'd begged Troy to let Mia keep the frock. Literally begged. But to no avail. Worse yet, he was adamant that she would have to tell Mia after they got back home.

The garage door slammed downstairs.

Fiona brushed droplets aside, straightened her back, and squared her shoulders where she sat waiting on Mia's canopy, poster bed. The pastel pink comforter and fluffy pillow shams supported her aching back. She leaned into them and elevated her tired feet. The black of her ballet slip-ons highlighted exposed pale skin rippled with blue veins from her toes to her mid-shin capri-leggings. Long white tresses cascaded loose framing the sharp features on her thin face, and she snapped a suede hair scrunchie that encircled her slender wrist.

Mia's footsteps bounded up the carpeted stairway. Fiona's heart raced like a wild bird about to take flight the closer to the second floor landing the sound traveled.

"Hello, Grandmumsie!" Mia walked through the open door and threw herself on the foot of the bed, dropping her backpack on the floor. "How was your day?" She rolled to one side.

"It could have been better." Fiona forced a faint smile. "Come here close to me." She scooted over to make room next to her. "Remember the dress I bought for the symphony?"

Mia's enthusiasm faded. "Oh." She kicked off her yellow shoes.

"Those are pretty purple hippo socks."

"Thank you." Mia worked her way up the bed until they lay shoulder-to-shoulder.

Fiona discarded her flats off the side of the mattress and moved her bare feet next to Mia's socks. "I need to talk with you about the dress I bought for you to wear next week." She'd been playing over in her head what to say, to make it as easy as she could, but there really was nothing to do but come out with it. "I had to return it."

"I know." Mia fidgeted with the crocheted trim on the pillow sham, and avoided looking in Fiona's searching eyes.

"You didn't do anything wrong." She caught her breath and stalled. "I wanted you to have that dress and wear it to many concerts and recitals."

"My dad wanted you to return everything from the shopping that day at the mall."

"Yes. Your dad and your mom."

Mia poked at Fiona's cold feet with her warm socks. "Why do you have those bumps on the sides of your big toes?" She'd seen them before but had never asked.

"Those unsightly growths are called bunions. These are what remains from my dancing career. Ugly, lumpy, need-to-be surgically removed *Hallux Valgus*. Sounds as hideous as it looks."

"Are they painful?" Mia touched one with the tip of her little toe.

"Yes, inflamed and painful. I've tried many home remedies over the years. We ballerinas try to go natural while still dancing, but after they retire you, surgery is always inevitable."

"I'm sorry the bumps hurt."

"Part of the job, mostly from my pointe shoes. I used to get blisters all the time."

"Ouch." Mia crinkled her nose and pulled her foot away.

"The dancing was worth all of it." Fiona set her gaze in direct alignment with Mia's evasive eyes. "I would do it all over again if I could. Even with the deformity."

"I took the dress out of the bag from your room and tried it on and danced around my room. I didn't take off the tags off though." Mia confessed.

"You looked lovely when you tried it on at the mall. That's why I wanted to buy it for you."

"But it was wrong, what you did. Wasn't it?" Mia asked.

Fiona sat forward. "Yes, it was wrong of me to purchase it the way I did. But," she choked up, "Grandmums are allowed to do nice things for their granddaughters."

"It's okay. I understand." Mia dug her heels into the full thickness of the bedding.

"I have tickets for the concert. Will you still go with me?" Fiona rose and gathered her ballet flats.

"Of course I will."

"Thank you my dear Mia. And,"

"Yes?" She answered.

"I am so sorry."

"It's okay. You just wanted to buy me a dress." Mia sat up and wrapped her arms around her legs, her purple toes wiggling in the air. "I appreciate that." Her soulful, saucer eyes penetrated across the room from where she rested her chin on her knees.

"I'll see you at supper." Fiona padded out of the room and down the steps. Tears trickled on her cheeks in an unbroken flow that she couldn't stop. She made quick haste in the hallway to her bedroom and closed the door. The lock clicked. All blurred around her as she grabbed the empty velvet hanger on her oval mirror.

Exiting out the front door she averted any contact with Elisa who was working in the kitchen, and hurried to her car in the driveway. With a quick toss her purse landed on the passenger seat. Fiona grabbed tissues from the center console and blew her nose while backing out onto the street. She turned the radio on full blast to a local 80s station. Her favourite British band, belted out a song from the early nineteen sixties as she headed out of the neighborhood for the freeway. Struggling to regain composure, Fiona shut off the radio, and made her decision.

"I'm going to miss you, Mia."

Chapter Twenty-Nine

Going on holiday is something we Kensingtons look forward to during the summer and winter months. It is a get-away of sorts that offers both respite and adventure. Troy charts the location and makes all the reservations way in advance. The upcoming trip to Lake Tahoe, an annual combination of skiing at Mt. Rose and hibernating at our north shore Tahoe cabin, is what I think Dad will most enjoy. Minus the skiing. Minus the snowshoeing. Minus the ice skating. But boating and snow fishing, that will appeal to him. ~ Elisa's hopes for the end of winter holiday.

Tahoe, Cornwall, Hevva, Hevva!

Ian packed his small suitcase for the four-day weekend holiday. Now his thermal under ware and layers of flannel would be put to good use. This lake Elisa goes on non-stop about where the waters remind her of home, he had to see this for himself. Snow boots were not necessary in the valley of Sacramento. Not even close. He tied his untwined snow boot laces around the luggage handle.

"Will you be ready by seven in the morning, Dad?" Elisa poked her head in the open doorway. "I'm going up to bed. Do you need anything?"

"By hook or by crook me be ready." Ian rolled his baggage to the hallway wall. "Where be your luggage?"

"Already loaded in the trunk of the car."

"You mean boot?"

"Yes, the boot." Elisa kissed the top of his head. "Nite-nite."

"Me be looking forward to meeting this lake you speak of so fondly. The one as blue as the Cornish coasts along the Atlantic Ocean and English Channel."

"Ah, you still be doubting your daughter, Mr. Darrow?"

"Tomorrow be telling." Ian winked at Elisa, then climbed into his comfy bed.

A grumpy lot of souls loaded up in the SUV the next morn. Coffee mugs in hand, baggage crammed in the boot, and a hamper packed with snacks under the glove box of the cramped vehicle. Fiona claimed her seat first, behind the driver. Mia sandwiched in between her grandparents. Troy sat in the driver's seat, Giants baseball cap on backwards, GPS on, and ready for departure. Elisa squished in last riding shotgun after locking up the house.

"Ian, you smacked me with your arm. Ouch—that hurt!" Fiona whined.

"Come on folks. We have a couple hours on the road ahead of us. Let's get along." Troy called out and turned around to his mum. "You can manage this."

"I need my coffee house." Fiona placed her travel thermos in the holder on her door panel."

"Elisa brewed your favorite blend. It's in your mug. We're not stopping to buy coffee."

"Posh." A good-sized pout blew out both sides of Fiona's mouth.

"You don't hear your daughter-in-law complaining and she has the wicker hamper stashed under her feet." Troy tooted the horn for silence before the weighted down rear end of the SUV sagged, hit, and scraped the curb when he pulled out. "Tally Ho!" And off he drove leaving suburbia behind, heading for an altitude at about six thousand feet above sea level.

"Destination—Sierra Nevada Mountains, Dad." Elisa said over her shoulder.

"How then can it be like me ocean?" Ian sipped his hot java blend carefully in case the car hit a bump.

"That will burn if it spills." Mia cautioned when Troy swerved to miss a squirrel.

"Too close for comfort." Elisa said. "I'll start Slappy squirrel watch now. *Bambi* watch the closer we get to the mountains.*"

"Look at it race up that tree." Mia strained to see past her grandmum to follow the fluffy-tailed rodent's escape route back into the Land Park forest. "They never make up their little minds quite fast enough." She shrugged when another darted in front of them, and froze. This time her father kept driving.

Fiona blurted out, "Just hit the bloody blaggard and get on with it."

"That be the spirit of adventure." Ian quipped. "Righto. You used to fox hunt on the Queen's grounds at Sandringham in Norfolk."

"No fighting, for the next four days. No quibbling, quarreling, no rows." Mia crossed her arms over her chest and jutted her elbows to the right and to the left. Her cheeky attitude duly noted. "This is a vacation. That implies people having fun together, with their granddaughter."

Up front Troy and Elisa shared a wide-eyed look of approval.

"Listen to the child." Elisa heard her own mum's voice respond from her mouth. She leaned against the leather neck rest and burrowed deep into the heated seat.

Ian startled. "Where we be? This bloke knackered off."

"Auburn. Still have a ways to go." Troy answered looking into the rearview mirror.

"You were snoring, loud." Fiona interjected.

"I didn't hear a thing." Ian rubbed his eyes and squinted out the window.

"You wouldn't you old coot." Fiona yanked bright orange plugs from her purse. The soft sponge disappeared into the cavities of her outer ears. An uneven smirk swept the length of her pursed lips.

"Can you stay awake with me, Gramps?" Mia hooked her arm in his. "I want to show you all our favorite spots."

"Lots of historical landmarks too, Dad." Elisa piped up.

"California Gold Rush period." Troy pointed ahead to the right where a five foot tall bronze monument stood encased in polished river stones. He passed a turn-out, then slowed down and pulled into the rest area so Ian could see while he drove by. "I can stop if you want to get out and read it."

Fiona sighed with indignant displeasure, and rolled her eyes. "Can we keep on?"

"It not be needed to stop." Ian answered as he pressed against the window. "Me still be a bit drowsy."

"Next big monument is where the Donner party ate each other." Mia shuddered.

"Cannibalism be in the rustic old west?" Ian arched a brow. "That be disturbing."

"Yes." Troy answered. The wagon train hit a blizzard they weren't prepared for. It got brutal when the food source depleted, and the search party waited too long to rescue survivors.

"There's a museum and movie to watch before we get to Tahoe. Donner Lake is smaller." Mia stated. "I've been there before." She hesitated. "Children traveled with the Donner Party."

Fiona's eyelids remained closed throughout the ensuing conversation. The local history bored her. She tweaked the earplugs until all the surrounding voices muffled into one.

Ian took advantage of his adversary's silence. The landscape changed before his eyes as they climbed higher in altitude to Colfax. He read all the green signage posting what towns came next—Gold Run, Dutch Flat, Alta, Crystal Springs. Valley vegetation changed from low brush bushes and scraggly oak trees to magnificent pines with lofty evergreen-needled arms that branched upward toward the slate blue sky. Some bore clusters of prickly pines cones. He cracked his window to inhale the earthy scent that a recent rain intensified.

"Baxter, Blue Canyon. These be sounding like western towns. Awfully American. John Wayne lived here?"

"No, Dad."

Ian stared out his window. "Kind of spotty on the snow."

"That's what several years of drought does. Last year we had almost no snow at all."

Packed embankments of dirty snow stood all of four feet high along both sides of the highway. The road had been recently salted and a slushy mix still potholed in the uneven blacktop. Troy had snow tires on the SUV, but the ride was bumpy and the Interstate was jammed bumper to bumper with weekend travelers.

"The forest be deep, mysterious. Like there be a story to tell that be not yet written."

"Those are profound words, Dad." Elisa elbowed Troy, her eyes widening and brows raised. "Most people just see trees and the white stuff."

"Gramps, what do you think needs to be written about this forest?"

"Not sure yet. Have to see the rest of it. But me be knowing before we leave." Ian gave Mia a thoughtful glance, then gazed back through the window as the miles passed endlessly by.

Fiona tugged at her purse, retrieved a black velvet eye mask that she pulled over her head and snapped the elastic band in place behind her ears. She yawned and adjusted the smooth fabric over her eyes, blocking out all light and movement.

Mia cradled a journal in her lap. She tapped a pen on the outer cover before opening it when the four adults in the car were otherwise preoccupied. Head down, her chestnut hair draped like a curtain over a stage as she wrote in careful print on one line after another. The traffic moved at twenty-five miles an hour for about half an hour, a slow snail's pace otherwise known as the weekend tourist bumper to bumper grind.

"That's Donner up ahead!" Mia sprung forward in her seat belt. She tucked the pen on the upper curve of her ear and closed the book. "Can we stop?"

"We'll stop on the way home this time. I want to get to the cabin by 10 o'clock." Troy moved from the right lane and sped up."

"We turn after Boreal Ridge, Gramps. Some of the ski resorts make their own snow when they need more." Mia pointed to strange looking machines along the side of the road.

"Fake snow?" Ian blinked.

"Well, not really fake. It is frozen water. It just didn't fall from the sky."

"Think of it as California-style, got-to-make-a-living, machines assisting the natural environment, kind of snow." Troy quipped with a nip of sarcasm.

"We ski in that manufactured soft powder. And you have the Eden Project in Cornwall." Elisa reminded Ian. "Not everyone in Britain is keen on the biomes experiment. 'A stimulated rainforest or Mediterranean climate' under plastic and steel in Cornwall isn't exactly natural."

"That be true." Ian conceded. "Eden be considered a tourist attraction. All those different plants, some indigenous, most not. Offering a backstory, some with supposed pre-historic heritage to draw in the masses."

"Yes, well those plastic domes don't fit the Cornwall image that I grew up in." Elisa huffed. "I don't care if they call them glorified greenhouses."

"Sounds like a science fiction experiment for the future." Mia's interest piqued.

"It's dangerous to play with the natural order of things." Fiona removed her mask and earplugs. "Something is bound to go wrong."

"What?" Troy zoomed in on her in his rear view mirror.

"Greed will be the end of this planet." She deposited her travel aids in her purse and zipped it shut, the metal teeth grinding closed.

Ian gaped at her. His jaw open and locked. No words formed in alignment with his collective thoughts. She caught him quite off guard. This he would have to think about.

"Careful old man. Drool is not an attractive feature."

"Perhaps the mystery be within as much as it be tarrying in the woods." Ian stated.

"I am entitled to my own opinions." Fiona fluffed her hair through her fingers to one side, her hand waving as if bidding farewell to someone passing by.

Mia grabbed her pen and jotted down something in the journal. She was quick to close it, and slip pen and book into her tote bag on the floor under her feet. "We're almost where the winter Olympics were held long before I was born, then we follow the Truckee River into Tahoe City. Our cabin is not far after the Y."

"It's on the lake, Dad." Elisa reached over her seat back to tap Ian on the knee.

"Yer be introducing me upon our arrival."

"You two talk as if the lake is an actual person." Fiona edged forward as far as the seatbelt allowed. "It's a lake, a body of water, not a living breathing being."

"How be yer certain?" Ian challenged.

"Don't be daft. I've been swimming in it, and boating on it. It does not speak and cannot hear." Fiona was more than annoyed. "Rubbish."

"Why not? The ocean speaks to sailors." Ian answered. "A listening heart and mind be all required. Fishermen know the language." He turned to Fiona. "It be not too late to learn."

She withdrew from the conversation and did not respond. Her tone of disgust lingered. Ian and Elisa carried on in their conversation until Troy pulled up in the recently snowplowed driveway. He circled around and parked. Ian stepped out and walked over to the wide view of the lake.

"She be beautiful."

Elisa came up beside him. "I knew you would have eyes to see her beauty."

"And not frozen over."

"Too deep, Dad. That has never happened, so far."

"From here she seems be as wide as the sea. We will get along, Tahoe and me. Me thinks there not be a language barrier between us." His boots crunched on a mash of pine twigs and clumps of packed snow. He took Elisa's arm in his and led her closer to the water's edge.

"This is my father. I have yearned to introduce you two for a long time."

They stood silent. The air about was chilled and the wind nipped. Neither father nor daughter seemed bothered. Rather, the cold bore a familiarity they embraced like an old friend.

"Me be thinking about me Mick."

"You miss him, don't you?"

"Aye." Ian scanned the lake from the east to the west shore. "He be a true mate."

"I've asked him to come. To America. Though I fear the two of you in cahoots here might do the Yanks in for good." Elisa laughed and shook her head.

"He be coming soon then?" Ian's hopeful countenance gave way to a sudden frown. "Alone?"

"Oh, you mean without Midge?" Elisa toyed a bit. "She has a Royal tea to attend at Buckingham Palace, by official invitation. She has waited her entire life for this. So—"

"When?"

"Day after tomorrow. He'll fly into Reno, less than an hour away."

Ian drew Elisa close. "Bless you, me girl." Ian led her toward the cabin, his boots slushing fresh tracks in the snow. "How we be taking him to Sacramento with us?"

"Tie him to the roof." She threw her arms high in the air.

"Me Mick might be liking that."

Elisa giggled. "He just might, but—Troy rented a car for the men. He'll pick it up at the airport. She tugged on his arm. "We three ladies shall venture home in the SUV."

"Best that way." Ian guffawed. "Mick and Fiona might spar if be left to each other."

"That is a crystal clear visual." Elisa turned a thoughtful glance. "One I'd unashamedly might somewhat enjoy. Seeing Fiona receive her comeuppance." She dipped forward, her face alight with a mischievous glow when she straightened.

"It be a bloody battle with neither be willing to give in." He winked.

"Gramps!" Mia bounded up. "Hurry, I want to show you all the rooms. Yours is next to mine." She whisked him away and trudged up the slope to the stairway. "Careful not to trip. It gets tricksy here."

"What sort of word be that? Tricksy?" Ian asked as he side-stepped the wooden planks.

"From J.R.R. Tolkien"

"The books or the movies?"

"Come on!" Mia stomped ahead, and waited on the porch. Her diminutive figure was quite imposing from six steps higher. Clad in powder blue ski boots trimmed in fur, jet black leggings, and a matching blue jacket with fur ringing the hood and cuffs, she stood poised against the railing post.

"You be looking like a page from a fashion magazine, Bean." Ian huffed, catching his breath as he ascended the last step, and stomped snow off the waffled soles of his boots.

"Grandmum got this for me last winter."

"Fiona has an identical outfit." Elisa commented and joined them. "Take him inside then." She followed through the open door and shouted. "All boots in the mud room to thaw after you change." Fiona was nowhere to be found. "Probably won't be helping me unpack this time either." Elisa mumbled.

A fire was already started in the hearth and Troy was hauling in luggage and supplies. Bulging grocery bags and a large crockpot lined the kitchen countertop. A few suitcases stood at the foot of the pine stairway for the second floor bedrooms.

"You know the routine. I haul everything in. You put it all away." Troy headed back to the car.

"I'd like to help." Fiona emerged from the living room. "I started a fire and brought in these groceries." She brushed her hands on her ski slacks, smearing soot in long streaks. "Let me wash first." She disappeared down the hall to the bathroom.

Let me help? I started the fire. Soot on her slacks? Elisa leaned back and watched the empty hallway not certain what was going to happen next.

Elisa placed her hand over her belly when the baby fluttered. It was definitely a good, strong flutter, maybe even a somersault. It was quiet in the cabin, the clock ticked, almost midnight. She stretched out in bed with Troy longing to awaken him to share the moment. But she lay still breathing in low whispers. He was sprawled out on his back snoring in exhaustion from the day's road trip and all the packing up and unpacking. Movement continued in her womb. *This little one's playtime is always at the midnight hour.* Reaching over, she took Troy's hand and placed it with hers on the epicenter of activity. Warmth flooded throughout her body, a flush of joy and wonder. Soft moon light glowed through the window beside them illuminating the bed. *Thrive and grow baby Kensington, take your time before entering this family circus troupe of performers.* A twinge tightened, then relaxed in her chest. The same sensation squeezed a second time. Elisa instinctively clasped her other hand over her tummy until the episode subsided.

"Wake up, wake up!" Mia bounded on the bed. "Gramps is already out at the lake."

Troy stirred and checked the clock. Eight. Late for all of them, except his mum.

"Grandmum made the coffee and put cinnamon rolls in the oven." She inhaled deeply before scurrying down the stairs. "Hurry!" A flash of her braided hair and bright red sweater disappeared.

"Fiona made coffee and pastry?" Elisa sat, glancing sideways at her disheveled image in the mirror, and combed her fingers through her tangled strands of hair.

"Not sure the munchkin has that right." Troy rose in the jeans from yesterday he was still wearing when he'd collapsed onto the bed.

"Yummy, I do smell coffee brewing and yeast." Elisa's nose tweaked in the air. "Dad is excited to pick up Mick tomorrow." Elisa slipped into leggings and a sweater.

"You already said something? I thought we were surprising him today?" Troy headed to the bathroom. "I'm taking a quick shower. Meet you downstairs."

"I did yesterday. Couldn't wait to surprise him." Elisa called out more excited than she realized. "See you downstairs."

A heady aroma of cinnamon and Elisa's favorite Columbian dark roast floated up to greet her and guide her steps to the first floor. Someone had ground beans and brewed strong coffee to fill the cabin with the doubly intoxicating scent that brought joy to her mornings. But Fiona? Why would she start being nice out of nowhere? At the moment Elisa didn't care. Breakfast waited, someone else had thoughtfully prepared it and she would just as thoughtfully accommodate them by savoring several cups of coffee with cream and sugar, and devouring a couple of those gooey rolls.

"Good morning." Fiona chirped.

Elisa sat at the already set table. A large platter spilled over with several dozen warm doughy spirals of frosting drizzled pastries. Five mugs encircled a carafe of hot coffee, and a large pitcher of orange juice sat next to it with five glasses. All encompassed a huge bowl of fresh fruits in the center. Wild Oats Wedgewood stoneware graced pinecone placemats with matching napkins. A tall glass held stainless forks and spoons for each person. A butter dish and knife backed up to the platter. Fiona had thought of everything.

"Good morning." Elisa responded trying not to let her complete shock show through.

Placing the sugar and creamer in front of her plate, Fiona pulled the chair out next to Elisa. She never sat that close to her. Ever. Then, she sat waiting for Elisa to eat.

"Oh, let me pour you a cuppa." Fiona reached for the carafe and filled Elisa's cup to the three-fourths mark, leaving room for cream. "That's how you like it, right?"

"Exactly right."

"Good. Where's Troy?"

"In the shower."

"Should we wait for everyone else or get started while the rolls are still oven hot?"

"Not sure when Dad and Mia are coming back. So let's eat." Elisa sat stunned as her, I-never-eat-carbs, underweight mother-in-law put two cinnamon rolls on each of their dishes, poured herself a full cup of coffee, and engaged her in light-hearted conversation.

"These aren't homemade, but this gourmet brand is quite tasty." Fiona polished off her first one and started on the second. "Goes good with black coffee."

"Uh-huh." Elisa nodded, then added. "Not bad with frou-frou coffee either."

Troy stood in the doorway, one hand on his hip, one arm raised as he leaned against the molding, watching the two women converse. "Well ladies, what have we here?"

"Breakfast." Elisa looked over with a sheepish expression.

"I see your favorite dessert roll and smell your favorite caffeinated beverage." He sat on the other side of his wife. "What's the occasion?"

"Just wanted to make the first day here special." Fiona answered matter-of-factly as she finished off her roll with a swallow from her mug.

"Breads don't usually pass over your lips, Mum." Troy stated with conviction.

Fiona passed the platter to her son. Troy took three rolls and handed it back. "You know I like spices with yeast breads. For so long I dare not touch them when dancing. Why not now?" She rose. "I'm going to call Ian and Mia for breakfast."

"What's going on?" Troy asked closely eyeing the pastry in his hand before taking a bite.

"I have no idea, but this was nice of her."

"Mum doesn't do nice."

"Well, she did this morning."

"She has to have some ulterior motive."

"Time will tell." Elisa sipped her dark roast and kissed Troy smack on the lips.

Chapter Thirty

Friendship endures the best and worst of times. A person be getting through life with just one true mate beside them. A gaggle of fair-weather friends brings heartache. A mate that has your back be the only bloke you need. ~ Ian's lifelong philosophy as shared with Mia for their book.

Soulmates

Ian chatted up Troy's ear the entire drive to the airport. He sat in the front passenger seat because Elisa wanted him to see the forest as they drove over Mount Rose. It was such a beautiful route in comparison to the Highway 80, though that was quicker.

"More snow here." Ian turned to Mia in the backseat.

"You're happy to see your friend, Gramps." She leaned forward. "I can't wait to meet him. I bet he's just like you."

"You know, Dad, Mick is a lot like you when you think about it."

"Except for Midge." He answered.

"True."

"Look at the planes coming in for a landing!" Mia squealed with delight.

Troy pulled into the airport and parked the SUV. "I'll go pick up the paperwork for the rental while you three walk over to the luggage area. I'll join you there."

"Me mate be here soon?" Ian stepped out into a near sprint for the main building.

"Slow down, Dad." Elisa caught up to him with Mia and Fiona close behind.

The overhead boards showed all the incoming and outgoing flights as soon as they entered the building. Departure and arrival times lit up in red and green.

"Looks like Mick's flight is twenty minutes early." Elisa stood reading while Ian jetted toward the first turn-style. "Not sure which one is for flight 546 from New York, but it will tell us soon. Dad!"

"Hurry, Mick be looking for us if we not be there waiting."

"They've landed so he'll be coming our way."

The crowd crushed back and forth around them, two flights had arrived and were waiting for their luggage. Ian pushed past a tall burly fellow in a knee-length raincoat and bumped into another man in khaki shorts, a Hawaiian hula girl shirt, and sandals.

Flight New York 546 flashed on turn-style number three. Elisa pointed up, Ian read it and rushed over past turn-styles one and two into a moving body of people. No luggage dumped onto the belt after it turned on. It circled around several times before a backpack toppled on followed by black soft baggage, then three hard-sided pieces smacked onto each other and rolled out next.

"Mick!" Ian called out over the blare of flight announcements. "Mick!"

"Do you see him?" Elisa shouted over the increasing volume of voices surrounding them. She held Mia's hand tight in hers and looked for Fiona who was nowhere to be seen.

"Can't find him."

"Me see you, mate." Mick's voice boomed over the din. His hand waved high in the air, like a distress beacon in the open sea. "Hevva!"

"Hevva!"

Mick rushed to Ian through the disinterested throng. His arms wrapped around him in a huge hug and he held strong. The two men rocked back and forth forming a formidable blockade for those trying to bypass them.

Ian looked up to familiar ruddy cheeks and a head full of the early Beatles style mop of black hair, and took a step back. "You be real me mate. You be real." He hugged him again.

"We be two blokes on Yankee soil now." Mick said. "You got me across the pond."

Troy stepped in. "Welcome to America." Then ushered Mia and Elisa forward.

"This be your Bean you be writing about." Mick reached out to a suddenly shy Mia.

"Gramps talks about you all the time." Mia offered her hand.

Mick lifted her high off the floor as he pulled Elisa close. "We be a family again."

The five of them huddled together waiting for luggage and catching up. Mia descended to touch the ground only to get propelled up again.

Fiona observed from a distance. Tears threatened to trickle down her cheeks and she strived to hold them at bay. Hidden by a pillar, she could hear Mick's resounding voice rise above all else. It was safe where she stood, away from the outpouring of excitement. Ian had something she didn't, a true friend. One who crossed an ocean, left home, fiancée, all he knew, to be here for his mate. He knew Ian's state of mind was failing. He'd get nothing in return for this act of faithfulness. He came to give. Simply to be available for a man that could awaken tomorrow and not even know who he was. This friendship, this sacrificial love, she knew nothing about. She had to perform, to have money, lots of money, to hold social status, to keep her friends.

The group trouped off without looking for her after collecting all Mick's luggage.

Mia spun on her heels and called out, "Grandmum, where are you hiding?"

Fiona stepped into the crushing swarm of holiday travelers and blended in. "Over here." She waved to Mia as she advanced inch by inch to where they'd come to a halt waiting for her. "Water closet necessities." She brushed a wisp of hair behind the small curl of an ear and plastered a semi-smile on her face.

"I was worried about you." Mia ran and hugged her. "You have to keep up." She took Fiona's hand and led to the front of the troupe. "Uncle Mick, this is my Grandmum."

"So this be the infamous Fiona!" Mick took the other hand and shook vigorously, almost lifting her right out of her ballet flats.

"I've heard much about you too." She landed back on solid ground.

"Don't believe a word they told you. Give it a go, then make up your mind." Mick flashed his best flirtatious school boy grin, winked, then turned back to Ian.

Fiona thought. *Same here. Don't listen to anything you've heard about this beastly Londoner.*

Ian rambled on, adhered to Mick's side as they made their way out to the car park.

"Blokes in the rental car with me. Ladies back to the SUV. Elisa's driving. We'll meet at Rosie's in Tahoe City for brunch." Troy herded the senior chaps and suitcases straight ahead.

Elisa led Fiona and Mia in the opposite direction, they lagged behind, still holding hands. She double-clicked the doors open, and her two passengers got in the back seat. "No one's riding up front with me?" She cast a surprised expression at Mia while opening her door.

"I'm sitting with Grandmum to chat. You have to keep your eyes on the road."

"True."

Fiona scooted to the middle seat so she and Mia were next to each other. She buckled both their seatbelts, then leaned her head against the leather seat.

"Do you need me to turn the heater on and warm you up?" Elisa asked.

"That will be nice." Fiona replied without looking at her.

"Alright then, back to Tahoe City." Elisa pulled out and followed a long line of cars out of the parking lot and back to the highway. She cracked her window to let crisp air stimulate her senses after adjusting the heater to the back seat only. Inhaling a long, deep breath, she savored the cold snap before exhaling. Fiona preferred heat, probably because she had no insulation, no body fat whatsoever. They dueled over the thermostat at home, Fiona turned it up, and Elisa zapped it down. Most of the heat rose upstairs, so Fiona's room held a steady chill. Elisa cooked on the top floor.

Constant chatter filtered through the vehicle. Elisa only picked up bits and pieces of the conversation, but enough to figure out they were making plans for an outing. Something fairly soon. Fiona had tickets. Mia appeared to be delighted about the event. Neither of them included Elisa so she assumed it was a grands only excursion. Anything for peace on the home front, especially during Mick's visit. He'd be observing the circus performer's interaction. Rightly so, he wanted to be certain Ian was in a safe and loving environment. Good thing Midge did not accompany him. Fiona and Midge—Elisa shuddered out loud at the thought of that encounter.

Chapter Thirty-One

Majestic Lake Tahoe captivates hearts at first sight. Her blue shores seem as endless as the mighty oceans of the world. Fishermen appreciate the depth and clarity of her waters. They also are wise to the dangers that accompany such depth. The cold will take you under in minutes. Though her beauty far surpasses possible perils, it is best to use wisdom when boating across the miles of sapphire, teal, and azure. Only fools would not heed the uncertainty of her nature. ~ Ian's and Mick's shared thoughts on the ocean in a lake they admired.

Bodies of Water, Lands of Light

Mick and Ian sat up late that night in the living room, logs in the fireplace crackling and popping, the cured oak burned down to ash with the passing hours. The two friends hadn't stopped talking from the airport, to the car, to the restaurant, and back to the cabin. They were polite to all around them, but they had much to catch up on, and even more to share.

"Dad, we're going up to bed." Elisa fought off a long yawn, but it had its way with her as she stretched an arm forward and her neck back.

"'Nite." Ian answered.

Troy carried a sleeping Mia in his arms while climbing the stairway. "'Nite."

Mick stood to offer assistance. "Need a hand, mate?"

Troy whispered. "No, but thanks. I'm used to this sack of potatoes."

"Righto."

"Where did this Fiona go?" Mick asked.

"She slipped off to her room hours ago." Ian answered.

"What's her story?"

"Here by default. Money's spent. Arrived with her Austin Healey, and baggage."

Mick's anxious eyes asked the question, searched for answers that remained untold. An awkward silence settled between them. He shook his head, ran fingers through his wild tussle of hair, and struggled to get words out. "Me hear yer voice and the old Ian speaks, as if we never lost him before."

"The drug be working for now."

"How long?"

Ian contemplated the question and stared toward the window where the dark night filled the large glass with curtains still pulled back. "It be different with every patient." A mist glazed his eyes. "Some longer than others."

"We be taking what we get, and be thankful."

"Each morning me wake up never knowing what sort of bloke me be that day." Ian shuffled his feet in plain view, brown leathers with soft soles. "If me put my shoes on the correct feet and can tie me laces, Me be cheeky." Thinning white hair on the crown of his head fell aside, exposing a sprinkling of brown age spots on his scalp when he bowed down to look at his shoes.

"No more loafers." Mick noted.

"Not if me be having a say."

"About Fiona."

"She be toff, a bit of a quandary she be. Me see more buried deep than the others do, except for Bean." Ian sat forward, an elbow braced on the sofa arm, hand cupping his chin. "Fiona be sarcastic, bossy, and missing her old life, but me think the reality of the shallowness hasn't swallowed her whole, not yet." Arms raised behind his head, he leaned onto the comfy sofa.

"She going back to London?"

"Absobloodylootely!"

"That a good thing?"

"We row. She be at war with her Troy and with Elisa time being. But she loves our Bean, and Bean loves her." Ian laughed. "Though quarrelsome, it be a loss to all of us if Fiona absconds, especially with the wee one on the way."

"You be my concern."

"Mick, the Yanks here not be so bad after all. Sacramento be too warm for the likes of this fisherman, but Tahoe be all Elisa promised."

"Have you been out on a boat yet?"

"Tomorrow, weather be permitting. Troy's boat be moored down the road at a marina."

Mick placed his boots on the coffee table and stretched. "Me bird won't have this at her flat. Her fancy furniture is constructed for dainty teas, and ladies' gossip."

"Aye, but yer love her, mate."

"I do."

Ian roared. "Midge been trying to pry those words from your mouth for years!"

"True enough." Mick looked over his shoulder. "She be a Thornton soon."

"You two be making a good, long life together." Ian positioned his shoes alongside Mick's. He pulled a pipe from his shirt pocket, a pouch of tobacco, then searched for matches.

"I brought some from Maiden Voyage." Mick drew a book from his jeans pocket. "Yer okay to light up in here?" He glanced around. "No ashtrays about."

"No lighting up allowed outside, ever. Summer or winter. Fire danger." Ian dug the bowl through the pouch and pushed his thumb down to tamp the tobacco, then dropped the pouch in his pocket. He struck a match until a blue-orange flame ignited. Clenching the stem in his mouth, he drew in and puffed until amber bits of his special shredded blend filled the room with a licorice, cherry smoke. "Come on, mate."

Mick pulled his pipe and pouch from his red flannel shirt pocket and lit up. "It be your blend. I braved customs for you." Little puff clouds rose to the ceiling.

Ian got up and flipped the fan switch. It began to whirl, catching the smoke and slicing through the air, dispersing it downstairs. "They have a smoke alarm here. It be the law. We not be wanting to be setting that noisy bugger off."

"Well, look at you two school boys." Fiona's voice admonished from the hallway.

Mick jumped to his feet.

Ian coughed. "Elisa knows me smoke me pipe."

"You promised Mia that you would quit." She tightened the belt of her worn cashmere robe around her tiny waist, walked past them into the kitchen, and knelt below the counter.

"You be looking for yer midnight snack?" Ian didn't mince words as he puffed. "The Cadbury sweets be moved." The slightest nick of a smirk toyed upon his lips when he stood to face her.

Her hand froze on the bottom cabinet handle. Steely eyes met his as she rose and stood, palms of her hands gripping the granite edge. "Where's my Fruit and Nut bar, old man?"

"When me missing pouches of tobacco reappear, the sweets be returned."

"Who do you think you are?" Fiona whipped around the barstools and headed straight for the firmly planted Cornishman.

Mick stepped between the two. His broad shoulders blocked both their paths as he stretched his arms out both ways. "We need bobbies to mediate? It be chocolate and tobacco."

"You have a stash in your room." Ian offered.

"How dare you enter my room without permission!" Fiona edged to the right and left to get past Mick who remained anchored like a battleship.

"I saw you unload a bag of sweeties after last market day at the British shoppe. Your door be open." Ian shot her a knowing look. "So be mine across the hall."

In one swift graceful movement Fiona dipped under and spun by Mick. She flew past Ian without so much as a sideways glance, and kept going until the echo of a door slam resounded in her absence.

"A might bit of anger for one so petite." Mick lowered his arms and sat back down shaking his head.

"She be the queen of mood swings with her steady diet of coffee and chocolates." Ian reclined on the sofa. "We each be having our habits." He puffed away on his pipe.

"Did yer promise Mia yer be quitting?"

"That me did." Ian huffed a long sigh.

"So Fiona be hiding your tobacco, to help you?"

"Perhaps she sees it so." Ian snuffed out his bowl and dumped the remaining ash in the residual cold tea of a nearby mug. "It be harder than me thought to outright quit as Bean asked."

"You did it once before, for Joanie. Remember?"

"Bygone memories still come to me." Ian hoisted himself up and went into the kitchen to wash out the cup. He squirt plenty of liquid dish soap after dumping the contents down the disposal. "Recent, be harder to recall." Streams of hot water poured out of the faucet as steam rose fogging up the window above the sink. Ian cleaned the few stray dishes on the counter too.

Mick grabbed the cotton towel hanging on the oven door handle, and dried dishes as Ian washed. A state of the art electric dishwasher nestled under the counter where the two men stood.

"Like back home."

"Me never be operating the modern machine at the house in Sacramento either."

"Not all new ways be better. Sometimes backalong be simpler and richer. "

"Yer ever feel—outdated?" Ian paused to look at Mick.

Robust laughter tumbled as Mick answered. "I be a decade younger, but yes. When the young lads come 'round playing those games on their mobiles. Their thumbs be flying faster than I can think." He flipped the towel out in the air and gestured with his hands at a wild speed.

"Me hopes me Bean stays good-natured in this progressive world."

"She be a delight, that one." Mick opened a cupboard to put away the glasses and plates.

"Maybe she be writing you into me story."

"She be writing about you?" Mick chuckled. "Then you be on your best behaviour."

"It be a true tale. The best and the worst of her Gramps." Ian wiped the granite clean with the special spray bottle cleaner left next to the sponge and scrubber.

"Yer mates at the pub be happy to assist her in this literary endeavour."

"That lot of sodden blokes be full of rumors and prattle her innocent ears need be protecting from." Ian rolled his eyes.

"They knew yer when but a lad full of mischievous pranks. That be fodder for any chapter book like you bury your face in reading all the time." Mick yawned, stretching until he touched the ceiling. "Time I head on up to the loft bed, mate."

"It be tomorrow already," Ian glanced at his wrist watch. "Sleep be calling us both."

"Looking forward to going out sailing on the boat. What kind of boat does Troy have?"

Ian shrugged and raised an eyebrow. "Find out when we board."

"Elisa said the waters be calm on the morrow." Mick pulled Ian into a big hug. The bulk of his muscle engulfed Ian's frail frame like a jolly giant would a village waif. "Yer need anything before I nod off?"

"All be well."

Mick was slow going up the stairs. He kept watch on Ian while he shut all the lights off and made his way down the hall. As he approached Fiona's door, Ian slipped a shiny purple foil wrapped rectangular chocolate bar from his pocket and slid it under her door. He padded across to his room after noticing a thin line of light flash on, then off under the doorway.

He inserted his pipe in its proper place on the rack, sat on his bed, kicked off his shoes, and neatly lined them up as usual. Fighting off sleep Ian strived to stay awake and read a chapter in a novel Elisa had given him when they arrived at the cabin. Leaning deep into the stack of pillows to buffer his boney back, he nudged reading glasses that had slid down the slope of his nose.

He paused holding the book and realized there was much his Bean would never know about him. Parts he wished she would, when he and Joanie tended young Elisa. She so reminded him of her at eight—all spunk and curiosity. Smart and cheeky. Savvy and silly. *Me must remember to tell Bean about the great tin mine exploration. Not a miner among we fisher folk.*

Book spine open on his chest, glasses crimping the tip of his nose, Ian dozed off half-way through the second chapter. The door creaked open and two pouches of tobacco were deposited on the dresser top. One slipper foot stepped inside, and a slender hand shut off the light switch. *She's worth giving it up for. I know you can do it.*

Chapter Thirty-Two

Change be rarely invited and usually arrives an uninvited guest. Plans can be mapped out over a period of time, but reality be altered in an instant. Weather, logistics, luck, divine intervention, call it what you choose, it plays a role in the ordinary becoming the extraordinary, a defined moment birthing history. ~ Excerpt from Ian's new book, The History of Lake Tahoe.

Snowfall

The first snowflakes fluttered in silent dance across a pitch black sky like the Royal Ballet's Swan Lake. The sleeping world knew not of the unannounced performance pirouetting in graceful, gentle gusts blowing in with the northern wind. White flecks dusted extended pine tree limbs blanketing the forest and sandy shoreline of the lake. Cabin rooftops settled under layers of snow like crisp linen sheets, light as air. The dark of night disappeared, hushed by frozen jetés and grand-pliés. Like miniature stars from the heavens, flurries created light and wonder.

"Wake up, wake up it snowed!" Mia rushed room to room, opening doors and jumping on beds. "It's magical!"

"Thought it was just a possibility of snow." Elisa mumbled and strained to see through blurry vision.

Troy buried his head under down pillows. A lone feather fluffed outward, freefalling back down to the mattress. "One more hour. Sleep."

"Get dressed, Dad. Hurry before it melts." Mia pounced between her immobile parents.

"Coffee." Elisa patted her rumbling tummy. "Did someone turn on the coffee maker last night?" She rolled over to Troy's side of the bed after Mia stepped over and bounced off to the floor. Her thunderous footsteps pounded down the stairs at record speed and ended with a jump.

"Uncle Mick!" Mia called up to the loft from the landing. "It's your first California snow!" She scurried toward Fiona's room, slowing her pace and entering with caution. "Grandmum, the symphony played last night." She whispered. "It's a premiere, a new ballet."

"I'll get my ski slacks and jacket." Fiona peeked from under her eye mask.

"The one with the furry hood." Mia responded.

"Yes."

"I'll get mine too." She squeezed a chilly hand that popped out from the quilts.

"Is it a Royal Ballet?" Fiona sat up, exposing her plaid flannel jimjams and bedhead.

"I do believe it is." Mia caught a glimpse, an unguarded moment of excitement so unlike her grandmother as she scampered to her closet and pulled out snow boots. She didn't seem to care her wild hair flared in lacquered wings, flying in all directions.

"I'll be ready in a jiffy."

Ian did not stir when Mia sat on the bed beside him. She stared at his wrinkled face, sagging white eyebrows, and budding mustache. He looked to be a Cornish version of Father Christmas. One eye opened, then the other as his labored breathing steadied.

"Morning, Bean. What be the story today?"

"It snowed last night." She beamed.

"Then we best dress extra warm. I be leaving one set of thermals on for the day."

Mia leaned in and kissed his forehead before running back upstairs.

Ian realized this meant there be no boats out on the water today. It be a huge disappointment.

About eight inches had fallen. Enough to stick. Plenty for play. Fiona was the first out with Mia, no coffee, no breakfast. In matching fur-trimmed jackets and boots, and sky blue ski pants, they rolled snowballs on the side slope of the property below the deck and sliding glass door. Elisa filled Thermoses full of hot caffeinated coffee and packed Fiona's leftover rewarmed cinnamon rolls in foil to take outside. She poured hot cocoa topped with whipped cream into the last Thermos, a hot pink and orange paisley print, for Mia.

"Sorry, Dad. No boat today." Elisa handed Ian his Thermos.

"The snow makes me Bean happy. That be enough for me." He winked.

"I know you were looking forward to going out with Mick and Troy." She hugged the rest of the containers to her chest and pulled the slider open. "Let's join the snow bunnies."

Troy grabbed the foil package and followed Mick and Ian out. A brisk stream of icy cold greeted them.

"Feels like me home." Mick cupped his gloved hands to his mouth and blew warm breath into the pocket of captured air. "The sky be clear and the sun be shining like on a good Cornish day."

The men hung back, but Elisa lined the coffees on the railing and trudged down to help build a snowman. He was a stout fella, short of stature yet rotund in girth. Mia supervised the construction until Mr. Snowman soon bore a resemblance to his Cornish brethren donned in a fisherman's smock, boots, and knit wool beanie. Fiona pulled one of Ian's pirated pipes from her jacket side pocket.

Mia reached for it and etched an upturned smile for lips with the stem before dangling it from a missing mouth. She pressed two small flat rocks for eyes and mushed one small pinecone for a nose.

"Something is missing." She stood back surveying the burly bloke. "He needs sticks. The smock arms are hanging lifelessly."

Fiona gathered boughs from the far end of the yard, shaking off snow and ice. "These look like hands with fingers and thumbs at the end of the limbs." She presented her finds for scrutiny.

"Perfect, Grandmum!" Mia went to work to fit the prosthetic limbs into the packed snow-body, measuring for level accuracy with her mittens.

Mick called out. "Where be his fishing pole or net?"

"Troy, go get one from the downstairs closet." Elisa yelled and waved.

With a forlorn sigh, Troy retraced his steps to the glass door, and shook his boots before entering. In his absence Fiona filched a lipstick from a zipper breast pocket. She scrolled the red tube up, then rubbed it in a circular motion creating ruddy cheeks on the snowman. Pleased, she smeared it across her lips next, capped the tube, and returned the shiny silver casing from sight.

With a worn net strung on an aluminum pole and a rod and reel, Troy emerged from the heated cabin and crunched his way to the top of the slope where the Cagwith Codger faced the freezing water.

"You ladies built a true fisherman." Troy angled the pole and rod between twigs and dug the ends deep into caked snow and hardened earth. "He's ready to board and set sail."

"Gramps wanted to take the boat out today." Mia commented.

"Not a safe navigation day, choppy waters, and an increasing wind." Troy pointed to the lake. Not a boat was in sight. Not even the Coast Guard.

"We go home tomorrow night." She protested.

"Your gramps is a seasoned fisherman. He knows when to go out and when to stay on land." Fiona urged. "Why don't you go drink your hot cocoa with him?"

"Okay." Mia bounded up the hill.

"What?" Fiona shrugged in answer to Troy and Elisa's blank stares.

The shadowy cover of night moved in from the Nevada shore bearing a strong northeastern wind dropping the temperature to twenty-four degrees. A warm glow filtered throughout the cabin, a combination of the new electric heater and a blazing fire on the hearth. A quiet day at home had not been the original plan, nor was a homemade family meal shared with extra chairs around the dining room table instead of boating to a local restaurant for a lakeside supper. The evening conversation bridged three generations, though opinions differed. Mia made notations in her journal, asked for quotes, and made careful entries based on the answers. She asked each adult to write a few words of wisdom, advice for those yet to be born. She designated five separate pages for this, each titled with the person's proper full name, beginning with her Gramps ~ Ian Clive Darrow of Cagwith, Cornwall, England. Born early morn, September 16 of 1941.

Chapter Thirty-Three

What does it mean to be old? To be aged in years beyond what the corporate and industrial work force considers of value before being labeled, obsolete? Retirement is more than oft a forced requirement than a personal decision. Physical labor whether artistic or in the elements takes a toll making the bones brittle, and the flesh weak, after decades of strength and vigor. The mind once sharp, the voice once articulate, loses focus. This is aging, maturing, becoming a senior. Once respected in society, now expendable, disposable, unessential. ~ Fiona's discussion with Mick and Ian the last evening on Tahoe's shores.

Decisions Made in Haste

The return to Sacramento arrived too soon. The lake beckoned Ian's name, called to him in the midst of his dreams every nightfall of their stay. Yet he remained on land, his boots laced and tied, his heart yearning, his dreams fading in clarity.

Mia went back to school over a week later full of contentment, eager to share all aspects of her wonderful vacation and Mick's visit with any peer that would listen. Elisa dropped her off and met Madeline for coffee at their hangout. She offered her the keys to the cabin for the following weekend, a get-away for her and her husband Ben, with or without their daughters.

"Just go." She encouraged. "I brought the key on purpose. You need the break as much, or more than I did." She sipped an extra hot latte.

"Are you sure? You trust us with your Tahoe cabin?"

Elisa placed the keychain in Maddie's palm and closed it, noticing her manicured fingernails chipped and breaking on most of the tips. "There's a key for the private pier too, if it warms up pack a picnic lunch." She urged. "Just go, hire a senior sitter."

Maddie didn't struggle for long. "Thank you." She choked back emotion, striving to keep her composure under control. "I never thought I'd need a break from my father. You know?"

"No guilt. A respite will revive you." Elisa stated.

"Dad is so angry these days. I miss the man I used to know, that I loved."

Maddie grasped the keys tight in her slender hand.

"Easy directions, I 8o to 89, to 28 into Tahoe City, go straight at the 'Y'. Non-smoking, all linens and towels are provided. We even have maid service. Just lock up when you leave."

"The Senior agency found a woman who can handle my father. She's firm, but gentle. He likes her, submits rather than fights her. Beatrice. She's half his age, yet wise beyond her years." Maddie teared-up. "Her mother fought this vicious disease for eleven years."

"Where and when does it end?" Elisa asked.

"I guess when they leave us."

"I can't imagine my life without my dad. We've had this conversation before haven't we?" Elisa sighed. "There isn't any escaping the inevitable."

"Yes we have because it is never not in our thoughts. The fear of the end is always there." Maddie's deep-set eyes drifted off.

Elisa observed the tilt of her friend's head, her long neck and dark ebony skin, both striking. The sorrow clouding her eyes did not detract from her outward beauty, smooth skin and sharp features accentuated an elegant figure with graceful movements. Though she no longer possessed the carefree manner like when they first met. Maddie wore the burden of responsibility that waged war both within and without for all those who love a family member suffering the relentless, progressive effects of dementia. Fine, thin lines already creased her brow and etched at the corners of each eye. Early aging. Stress. Part of the consequences caregivers experience for their lack of sleep, and morning, noon and night commitment.

"What are you thinking?" Maddie asked.

"How changed our lives and our families have become." Elisa apologized. "I didn't mean to stare."

"I know."

"I'm grateful for the opportunity to escape with my husband. I think we'll go alone, get reacquainted. It's too easy to lose yourself." Her heavy eyelids fell upon her friend. "To lose your marriage."

"Troy is under tremendous pressure at his job." Elisa hedged with nervous contemplation, sharing more than she intended to. "He may lose his job."

"Oh I hope not. My hubby is weary from all of it. Especially my lack of attention."

With deepened concern Elisa ignored the booming voices in the packed restaurant, and the rowdy table spilling over with teens beside them. "Go, send your girls to friend's homes for the weekend. I'll take your oldest, she's close to Mia's age. Get working on the other two. Make this happen."

"They should meet first."

"How about tomorrow, after school. Bring Savannah to the house."

"Okay, are you sure?"

"I've never been surer of anything. They'll get along."

"I still have your address."

"See you about four." Elisa stood and grabbed her cold cup of coffee.

"You should have checked with me first." Troy argued. "Why did you wait until today to mention we have company this weekend?" His irritation grew by the second.

"I didn't think you'd mind. She and Mia connected immediately."

"There's so much else going on. Mick flies back to Cornwall Monday morning. It's been nearly a fortnight now. It's been a great visit, but we need to get back to normal whatever that is these days." Troy hurried out the kitchen door to the garage to get in his car with

Elisa following close behind. "Is my mum up early for something today?"

"Not that I know about. Why?"

"Look around, her Sprite isn't parked here in the garage."

"Maybe she had a date last night."

"Don't think so, she's been sticking close to home, and Mia. Even chatting away with Mick and Ian. Who knew she could be social and nice?"

"I'll check after I fix breakfast for bloke one and bloke two, as Fiona refers to them."

"Text me and let me know what's going on." Troy planted a kiss on Elisa's cheek and patted her tummy. "Love you." He climbed into his car and clicked the garage door opener, voice commanded the engine on, then backed out.

The door lowered after she lingered watching him drive off for the day. She had an obstetrician appointment after dropping Mia off at school. Mick and Ian had big plans to spend the day at the Sacramento marina. They were still going on about the day boating trips to the Carmel and Monterey coasts. The ocean had breathed new life back into her father. Mick shot pictures everywhere they went for all the village to see when he went back home.

The blokes wanted to hail a taxi and venture out on their own today, and hit Streets for fish and chips. Who knew what Fiona had going? Elisa went back into the kitchen, grabbed her list of questions for her doctor and tossed it in her purse. "Mia, you ready for school?" She packed the sandwich she'd made before Troy's objection to the weekend overnight visitor. She should have said something during the course of the week, but it slipped away day by day. Still, he was right. She threw an apple and pack of cashews into the insulated bag Mia toted back and forth.

"Ready." Mia appeared in the kitchen doorway.

"I'm picking up Savannah this afternoon after I pick you up. She goes to the private school. You know that brick building we pass every day."

"Yeah, she told me. She likes it there."

"Your room tidy for the weekend?"

"All cleaned." Mia scooped up her lunch sack. "What do you think of the shirt?"

Elisa stopped to take a good look at the hot pink, short sleeve, top. She read the imprint—"*I Dance with Ballerinas in Pointe Shoes*.' Catchy and cute. New?"

"Grandmum gave it to me last night."

"Looks good with your black leggings. Do you have a sweater?"

"In my backpack. In case it gets cold."

"Let's go." Elisa called out, "Dad, Mick, we're off."

Ian and Mick popped in the kitchen. "Have a bloody good day, Bean." They said in unison.

"I'm going to Gramps. Ta, Uncle Mick." Mia followed Elisa to the SUV Troy had left parked in the front circular driveway for them.

"Have you seen your Grandmum this morning?" Elisa asked as she pulled onto the street.

"Not since last night. She came up to my room with some shirts and her compact mirror."

Elisa slowed down at the corner stoplight, braked, then looked at Mia. "The sterling silver one from your Grandfather George?"

"Yeah, the one I've always admired that she lets me use when we do make-up together."

A horn blared three loud times behind them. Elisa checked her rearview mirror, and oncoming traffic before pulling into the left turn lane. The horn blasted again for several seconds before the driver laid off. "Okay, okay. I'm moving." She mouthed.

"Kind of funny with Grandmum, huh." Mia fidgeted with her hair scrunchie.

"Yes. Apparently, she left quite early this morning before your dad went to work."

"Where?"

"Don't know. I'll catch up with her later this afternoon."

"You seeing the baby doctor today?" Excitement flooded Mia's voice. "Can you ask if it's a boy or a girl yet?"

"Not today. Next time I have an ultrasound. Dad is going with me."

"I can't wait!"

All lanes of traffic came to a standstill on both sides of the road. Elisa sighed and checked her watch. She was barely going to make it across town for her appointment. This was an important one with lab results and discussion about the delivery options. She couldn't miss it.

"Can I tell you something?" Mia asked tentatively.

"Sure."

"I know all the men want a boy, but I really want a girl." Mia stated each word with clarity. "I haven't said anything when the men start talking. Especially about a boy playing ball with them and stuff like that."

"I'm hoping for a healthy baby, boy or girl." Elisa agreed. "Actually, I'm praying."

"I'll pray with you." Mia's voice softened.

"A prayer partner will be a big help." The car inched forward. When the light turned green, Elisa pulled to the left and passed the car holding the morning commuter traffic in slow mo. "Almost there. I'll be in the parking lot on time so we can swing by for Savannah at the parish school."

"Righto." Mia unbuckled her seatbelt when the car stopped. "What's for supper tonight?"

"Salmon, spinach, and potatoes for the fellas."

"Love you." Mia called out as she exited.

Elisa tried to get an, "I love you too," in response, but the door slammed and Mia was swallowed by a carpool of kids piling out of a big SUV. Instant regret surged through her. She wanted her daughter to know she still had time for her amid the chaos of their increasingly changing lives. Quick maneuvering got her out of the busy school parking lot and headed toward the freeway. Doctor Allegra's office was doable if she stayed the course. Then grocery shopping to buy the salmon for supper was just the beginning of a busy day. Her list was long, the bank, the post office, her mommy exercise group back in Land Park, the pharmacy to pick up her dad's meds, Fiona's blood pressure pills, and more of those giant stones they call pre-natal vitamins, and nasty iron supplements. Ugh, she'd sworn she'd never take either of those hard to swallow prescriptions again because of the major side-effect—constipation, double ugh.

Women in varying stages of pregnancy packed the small doctor's office lobby. Elisa scanned the room to no avail for a vacant seat. She sidled near the doorway to the examining room exit and stood waiting. When the next name was called she hustled to the empty chair. Once seated, she couldn't help but notice the bulging waistlines and swollen cankles most of the obvious third trimester women were dealing with.

A peculiar smell permeated her corner of the room. A sickening sweet rush of honeysuckle, like a Georgia southern garden in full bloom saturated the air to the point she had to cover her mouth and nose. No one else appeared to be bothered by the strong perfume odor.

A second glance took her by surprise. The average age of each patient was barely mid-twenties. She had to be the oldest mother-to-be present. Maybe the woman with green-tinged, spiked hair sitting next to her was closer to her age, then maybe not. She struck up a conversation with the sole intent of finding out.

"Is this your first baby?" Elisa asked.

"No, my second."

"Mine too. I have a daughter." She paused and waited for a courteous response.

"Uh huh."

Elisa squirmed to the left side of her mauve vinyl arm chair. She debated pursuing any deeper level of banter as she crossed her legs and kicked her foot back and forth.

"You'll get varicose veins if you do that."

"Oh, thanks." She lowered her legs, turning her toes inward.

"The stretch marks are bad enough." The woman flipped her lime green hair out of her eyes. "I have a three year old son that basically wrecked my body. This is another boy."

"My daughter is eight." Elisa listened to rustling pages of magazines turning at rapid speed across the all too quiet room.

"You're a lucky dog. This is it for me. Not risking another boy."

"We weren't expecting our little surprise. I'm thirty-five."

"Wow, that's really old." She blinked and turned full face toward Elisa. "I had Trevor at nineteen. We got married the year after he was born." She twisted a swirl of hair around her finger and held it taut. "Are you married?" She squinted.

"Yes."

"That's good."

A young man in burgundy smock and pants emerged from behind the door. He stepped forward in squeak-less orange athletic shoes and called the name, "Eleonore Watkins."

"Here."

Green hair rose and waved her hand high. She gathered a huge black purse with disposable diapers poking out of an open zipper. A couple of beat-up paperbacks fell out which she scooped up and tossed back in what looked to be a bottomless abyss.

"You should read this hysterical book I just finished by an author learning how to take care of her son by herself."

The overpowering scent of honeysuckle followed her past the door and down the hall to an unsuspecting obstetrician. Elisa was grateful for the hollow wood now separating them. *Did she just tell me that I'm old?* No one batted an eye in disbelief or even paid attention. The women not flipping through magazines were head down, thumbs flying on their cell phones despite the sign posted requesting all phones be turned off. Not another conversation was to be heard the rest of her visit.

The young doctor also commented on her age once she was placed in room number four. After her exam and question and answer period, she was herded out so the next expectant mother would have her pre-designated twenty minutes. Leaving the serene watercolor paintings of relaxing ocean scenes behind, Elisa had to find the restroom, fast. She paid her insurance co-payment by credit card at the open window in the waiting room and scheduled her next appointment for the following month, with an ultrasound at the hospital in two weeks. Her list of semi-answered questions still in hand, Elisa exited and took the elevator down the three floors instead of the stairs like she did when she first arrived. *Old women take the elevator. Young women race up and down the stairwell.*

The rest of the day's chores tediously wore on like a large wool overcoat on a too warm day. None of the wild sockeye salmon looked the right shade of pink, and the lines at the bank were long and slow. She hit the pharmacy only to face more horrendous lines of rude, impatient people, so she skipped the exercise group, and drove through for a fast food burger. She ate in her car. Her diet coke was flat, the fries were cold as was the cheeseburger. She forgot to ask for the onions to be grilled and tossed half her meal in the garbage. Nothing seemed to taste right anymore. The scent of old french fries lingered in the car as she left to pick up the girls.

Fiona's Austin Healy was still not in the garage when she brought the girls home and parked in her space. Elisa unlocked the door to the kitchen and noticed a note she'd missed earlier pinned under two Sacramento Zoo magnets on the fridge door. The girls dumped their backpacks on the floor and foraged for a snack in the pantry.

"I sold the Sprite on Craig's list and bought a first class one-way ticket to London. Left by cab early this morning. There is a letter for Mia in my room. Please wait to give it to her until her friend goes back home. I'll call her from my new flat in Chelsea about seven your time Sunday night."

Elisa watched the girls rush up the stairs two at a time, laughing. Mia's door closed with a bang.

Chapter Thirty-Four

Medical technology has changed since our daughter's birth. You don't just get a hazy instamatic black and white photograph of your unborn offspring. You get a video, a magical movie that can determine sex, length, the circumference of the skull, show the pulsating umbilical cord, and the heartbeat. The star of the movie is a content tiny person sucking their thumb while doing somersaults that feel like mere digestive flutters. ~ Elisa's take on new OB technology.

Siblings

Mick longed to stay for the baby's ultrasound, but he returned home to an anxious Midge and an ultimatum—marry her or fetch himself a new bird. The wedding invitation arrived by post the day of the big hospital test.

Ian accompanied the parents, but waited in the family lounge area. It had been an emotional farewell when his mate flew home. They all were still somewhat bowled over by Fiona's sudden and silent departure. Mia though, was devastated. She'd become sullen and withdrawn to the point of concern. Today's revelation held the promise of new hope and a possible road to at least partial recovery for all.

Elisa used her cell phone to call her dad to ask one more time. "Do you want to come in?"

"No, this be for be for you and Troy. I be watching the movie with Bean at home tonight." Ian tried to hit the red disconnect on his mobile but clicked the speaker on by accident instead. He pressed different buttons on the keypad until it finally clicked off.

Ian rifled through the various magazines scattered throughout the waiting room. He patted his pipe and tobacco pouch in his shirt pocket but resisted the temptation to head outside for a smoke. He'd cut way down, lighting up every other day now. His plan to smoke once a week, like a celebration, then once a month, turned out to be much more difficult than simply leaving his pipes on the rack and walking past them to start his day. *Might have to pack it all away.*

The tick tock of the huge wall clock above him accentuated time crawling by. He glanced at his watch, an hour had passed and it was a twenty minute procedure. He determined to keep his mind from dwelling on any possibility of complications. Instead he focused on Elisa's joyful birth. Nothing went as planned then either. Her conception surprised and delighted him and Joanie. They'd resigned themselves to a childless marriage due to a decade of trying to be in a family way with one disappointment after another. Her full-term gestation was interrupted by a slightly early arrival. She was but a wee one, smaller than most, but healthy. Oh, could she wail.

Ian pulled a paperback from his coat pocket. He was enjoying a new author even if she did choose to reside in Brisbane, Australia rather than Great Britain. She wrote lyrical words and crafted stories he savored that left him waiting with anticipation for the next book. Always the sign of a good author. Though his favourite authors be British.

When Troy did not appear at the stroke of the second hour, Ian put the book down and tilted his spectacles higher on his nose, then he lowered them. He repeated this several times whilst watching for the door to radiology to open. Ten minutes later Troy emerged.

"Elisa and the baby be well?"

"Yes—sorry about the delay. There was a bit of excitement for a while."

"Can yer share?" Ian's nose twitched under his heavy glass frames.

Troy wiped his brow with a paper towel from the treatment room. "They thought there might be twins, an echo sounded like two heartbeats."

Ian shot up and looked Troy directly in the eyes. "But there be only one baby. One healthy baby." Knees shaking and hands sweating Ian asked again. "One healthy baby?"

"Definitely, one healthy baby." A wash of shock cast a pallor from the top of Troy's head to an exposed V-neck and chest where'd he'd unbuttoned his shirt under a green tie-in-the-back gown he was in the process of shedding.

"Congratulations, Gramps, it's another beanie girl. If I didn't know better, I'd say she was occupied reading a book during the entire exam."

"Elisa always longed for a sister. I think me Bean does too."

"We gents are now officially outnumbered." Troy added. "They've bumped up her due date between three and four weeks, as of this ultrasound."

"Will they do another?"

"They want to do at least one more." Troy held the hospital gown in his hand and collapsed in one of the lounge chairs. "We'll see."

Ian sat beside him and asked. "It be not a good thing?"

"Elisa did some research on the correlation between childhood ear infections and multiple ultrasounds during pregnancy."

Ian observed Troy's color begin filling in, a faint pinkish twinge to his cheeks and forehead. He appeared to be just a lad himself at the moment, more likely to skip off to the school play yard than to become a father again.

"The heart be working right?" Ian had to ask.

"A perfect, single heartbeat."

"Why then did they think there be two?" Ian was quite perplexed and persistent.

"There was an echo, and not a clear image at first, like a blurry second outline shadowing the visible baby."

"That all be on the movie?"

"Yes." Troy stood. "I'm going back to get Elisa. She'll have the video with her."

"Righto." Ian reached out for Troy's hand and shook it vigorously. "Cheers!" He watched until Troy disappeared behind the same door, his squeaky shoes sticking to the tacky polished tile floor. The irritating sound offered a welcome distraction, a sort of focal point moving in the opposite direction. Away. Not closer, but distant.

Ian sat and folded his hands on his lap. *No grandson, no lad to carry on into the next generation the coat of arms and legacy of Troy's surname.* What be it mattering? His daughter be well, his granddaughter be well. Better this than to lose another babe and endure the sorrow that brings, that sorrow never truly goes away.

Chapter Thirty-Five

Integrity is everything in a job. You interview trying to put forth your absolute best, an honest presentation of your value to the company courting you. Convince them you are an asset and the game is on. It may be a stretch, a giant leap from your comfort zone, but in the long run it will be worth all the effort. Then when you beat the best of your competition to land the job, you keep pushing forward learning new procedures and protocol. Your confidence builds as you tackle challenges and hurdles, until at last you know the job. You own it. You can do it blindfolded and walking backwards. Then you can relax a little. Just a smidge. At least, that's how it's supposed to go. You work towards retirement, medical care, and accumulated vacation time. ~ Troy.

The Fall-Out

Troy went over the numbers again and again. His figures were correct, his math added up, but not to the sums his boss reported on the past four quarter statements. A cold sweat broke across the palms of his hands and chilled him to the bone. The deficit was undeniable. Now it looked as though Troy had cooked the books. Blair had lied. He had cheated and embezzled two and a half million from his own company over the past year.

It appeared to be a perfect frame, plotted to the finest detail. Troy glanced at his office door to make sure it was locked. He scanned the room for possible planted cameras, and lifted the landline receiver to check for bugs. He didn't even know what he was looking for but it seemed the thing to do. Icy rivulets rolled down his back under his starched white shirt and gathered at his belt. He sat frozen at his desk realizing his fingerprints were now all over the ledger, the one he'd taken from his boss's office after he left for lunch. Why hadn't he used gloves? *Because I do not have a criminal mind.* So this is why Blair required he keep both a computer spread sheet, and a hand written ledger. Troy now knew he had to prepare his defense at home on his personal computer. He had already printed out copies of the spread sheets and taken them home.

Heart pounding, Troy rose and carried the book with him, unlocked his door and returned the ledger to his boss's office. He lingered, pouring himself a cup of gourmet coffee from the copper urn where he and Blair usually shared their morning caffeine fix. He took a sheet of paper from his pocket and left it on the desk before heading back to his own office.

Had his boss left the building empty so Troy could check the safe for the books? Troy's eyes shot across the room to the plate glass window where he thought he caught a glint of light in the right corner under the blinds. *Could it be a camera?* He walked over and shoved the aluminum levers until the entire shade bent to his touch. No camera, just a tiny crack in the glass reflecting the afternoon sunlight. Troy released the blinds, then exhaled a deep sigh.

This was insane. Blair Goodwin was a personal friend, not just the boss who paid him six figures to do his job. They golfed at the same country club, bought each other lunches at Esquire Grill, and ordered shaken but not stirred martinis at Lucca's on J Street.

Both of their families shared barbeque meals together on warm weekends and Blair's sons played croquet with Mia. Elisa and Marilyn weren't the best of friends, but they got along fine.

Someone deserved to go to jail for this, and he knew it would never be Blair. That left only one person. *Good thing I have a lawyer already going over everything I've handed over. He'll need these new figures too.*

"Hey, did you ever grab a bite?" Blair knocked on the door as he entered. He stood almost regal in his charcoal Armani suit and gray paisley tie.

"Not yet. Going home for lunch today. Elisa has some big surprise planned to celebrate the new baby. Mia has a half-day for parent-teacher conferences tonight." Troy forced a practiced smile and tried to make contact with Blair's shifting cobalt eyes.

"You finally getting a male child? Good work for an English bloke like you." Blair turned away toward the extended hall. "Real men make sons, not daughters."

Troy passed Blair on his way out. "I may not make it back in today. But we can go over those figures next week for sure." He stopped by the secretary's desk in the front lobby and left another paper he'd been holding while he gulped down the last of his coffee.

"Why wait until next week?" Blair shouted.

"I'll work on the figures at home over the weekend, put in some overtime on my laptop." Troy turned and stopped, then added. "Family weekend, you know, with the ultrasound."

Blair zoomed in his gaze on Troy's facial features as if searching for something.

"You are pretty caught up with this new baby."

"Yeah, I am. It was a bit of a surprise at first, but now Mia will have a sibling, and she has wanted that for a long time." Troy laughed. "I'll be handing out cigars soon enough."

"What's the due date?"

"The docs bumped it up to early August after the test."

Blair hesitated before speaking. "Will Elisa have help? Your mom?"

"She'll have me. My mum moved back to London. Elisa's still her dad's caregiver, and we have no idea how long his improvement will last."

Blair stretched out both hands and scrutinized his pristine manicured nails. "Well, your wife is a capable woman. She'll do fine." He buffed his nails on his suit lapel, then flicked them against his thumbs, as if expelling some invisible dust or grit. An odd repetitive, daily habit.

Troy grinded his teeth, and took in a deep breath before swinging around to walk back and engage his boss. The two men stood head-to-head at Troy's office doorway, Troy a couple of inches taller, leaner, and more muscular.

"By the way, we found out early—it's a girl."

Part Three

London and the Cotswolds

Chapter Thirty-Six

London is a world unto itself. Royalty and refinement contrast the touristy invasion needed to build the economy. Modern new architecture stands side-by-side with century old construction and offers the best of both realms. The wealthy hobnob amongst themselves at gala affairs and political soirees. Fiona was back in her element. She chose to ignore the commoners and riffraff that perhaps walked the same streets and boulevards, but did not dine in ritzy restaurants and order five hundred pound sterling bottles of vintage wine and champagne. The fully furnished flat in Chelsea suited her exquisite taste. Leasing it from her friend and former lover the Earl made living bearable again. The past fortnight of parties, spa resorts, and leisurely shopping made home, home again. ~ Fiona's London.

Once a Londoner—Always a Londoner

Fiona slept in late, past noon. Her swollen feet ached from the high heels she hadn't worn for a couple of years. Not quite the ballet flats that were her signature statement in the States. It almost seemed as though she'd never left. She'd slipped back into her old lifestyle like a ballerina into her favourite pointe shoes.

Her friends hadn't let her pay for drinks and dinner since her return. Last night at the after show party one of the younger women announced it was Fiona's turn to throw the next soiree at her place.

A barely-twenty year old socialite named Elizabeth had all the gents wrapped around her anorexic finger. She never paid for anything, ever. Soon Fiona would be expected to throw around money like the rest of them. She glanced at the cheque book ledger laying at the foot of her bed. Her account had dwindled down by a third of her original deposit. And she was being frugal.

Troy, you would be proud of your mum. I've learned how to balance and not overdraft.

The room was silent save the low hum of classical music on her iPod. She played it all night long to soothe her to sleep and battle the insomnia that had set in soon after her arrival. A job was necessary to remain in London. None of her class worked except politicians, and those famous in the arts and film. She needed a believable excuse for employment.

Her mobile rang out Beethoven's Fifth. She lifted it off the Baroque nightstand to see if she recognized the number flashing across the screen without her reading glasses. The number looked close enough to be the Earl's cell.

"Cheers!"

"Oh, did I wake you? It's past noon."

"Elizabeth?" Fiona so hoped she was wrong.

"Yes. I'm over at Edward's and asked him why don't we ring you up and ask about your party."

"Oh, I'm on my way out for a lunch date and some shopping. We can chat up later. Ta, Elizabeth. Do remember me to dear Edward."

"Happy to."

Fiona smacked the mobile down, chipping the vintage paint on the edge of the stand. She licked her fingertip and dipped it on the flake where it had fallen to the hardwood floor. With great care she dropped it into an antique Limoges dish until she could glue the chip back in place.

She knows I'm broke, the impertinent twerp.

"You young strumpet! I'm certain you entertained the Earl last night, and this morning." Fiona shouted out loud, jumped off the bed and stomped her swollen bare feet on the floor. "I can't afford to host a party, pay for caterers, and offer a full bar." She limped into the bathroom, turned on the faucet in the claw-foot tub, and poured in a generous amount of Epsom salts. The room steamed up. After lowering herself in for a good, long soak her tensions began to fade.

At Barrafinas for dinner that night, Fiona dined alone by choice. She ordered the Carabineros and devoured the gigantic bright red prawns, enjoying her solitude. Mia had been on her mind throughout the day as she avoided her usual crowd everywhere she ventured. That had been easier than it should have been. No one had rung her up to join them. Elizabeth probably played a hand in this new development, but for today it worked.

Fiona appreciated the Barcelona-style tapas restaurant and its amazing atmosphere. It reminded her of the years she and George spent in Spain. Those early, happy years when Troy was a young boy and the three of them traveled on holiday just to spend time alone as a family. If only their lives hadn't drifted apart as Troy grew older and George's attention wandered toward any younger woman who made time for him while Fiona danced away from her family. Every plié and jeté she perfected as she strived to advance to the prized prima ballerina assoluta position absorbed her completely, until the knee injury. She slowly fell back down in the ranks.

"Waiter!" She snapped her fingers then immediately regretted the impatience of her action.

"How may I serve you?" The handsome man responded.

"May I have the cheque, please?" Fiona lowered her tone to a pleasant, grateful even keel as a peace offering. "You have been most gracious." She struggled to remember his name from the night they'd come as a group the week before.

"That's my job, Fiona." He bowed.

"You know my name?"

"Yes, I used to go with my grandmother to watch you dance with the Royal Ballet."

She blushed with embarrassment, realizing he was aware of her age, and by the unexpected joy that rushed through her for his acknowledgement of her once important status.

"Many years ago now." She answered with a demure glance.

"We followed your career until you left the ballet." He lingered. "My mother was a ballerina too, in Poland."

"Thank you, young man." Fiona patted his arm.

"You are one of the most graceful dancers I have ever seen. And my name is Frederick Townsend." He paused before leaving to get her cheque.

A deep stirring within caught her off guard. It had not all been a mistake, all those sacrifices were not for nothing. Losing her husband had been devastating. Losing her son's respect, now that was still something from which she had not recovered.

A single red rose descended to the table to rest in front of her. She'd noticed vases full of them throughout the restaurant.

"A gift from one of your faithful admirers, though not the splendid bouquets you were used to receiving at the close of your performances. Your meal and drinks have been paid. It is my way to show gratitude for all those years my mother and grandmother treasured your dancing. Swan Lake was their favourite." Frederick took her hand and brushed a gentle kiss on her thinning skin. "I must get back to work." He bowed once more and left.

Crystal clear droplets fell upon the rose she held to her heart.

"Mia?"

"Grandmum? Is that you? I miss you so much."

"I miss you too."

Static crackled across the phone line. Fiona was certain that Mia said something she didn't hear. "Mia, can you hear me?"

"Yes, it's a bad connection like last time, but please don't go."

"I called to tell you I love you and I miss our ballets and symphonies."

"Are you coming to visit soon? Please, please say yes."

"Not for a while. I have a new job and I start work next week."

"Oh, that sounds like you are going to stay permanently." Mia sighed.

"I'll try to come when the baby is born in September. I promise."

"August, the baby is coming early in August. Did you know it's a girl?"

"No. I am so happy for you to have a sister." Fiona waited a few seconds. "Mia, why is the baby coming early?"

"The dates were wrong whatever that means."

"Your mom is okay, everything is okay, right?" Fiona was careful not to alarm Mia.

"Oh yeah, it's the usual circus here, but we could use one more clown." she paraphrased her father.

"I am staying in London for now."

"Are you okay there, you usually call on Sunday afternoons and it's the middle of the week."

Tell her the truth. She loves you, she'll understand.

"I just missed you before the weekend." Fiona told a half-truth.

"Every day I wish you were here with us. Your room is waiting when you're ready."

"I'll come when your sister is born. Is your mom being scheduled for surgery?"

"I don't think so, at least nobody has told me that yet." Mia waited for a reply.

"That's good. Have you decided on a name?" Fiona sniffled.

"They're all talking about names, you know, ridiculous names like Bertha and Henrietta so the guys can call her Henry." Mia laughed.

"You can do better than that."

"There's a name pool. Why don't you put in your dollars and pick a name? First and middle."

"I'll have to look up what a couple of names mean. Have you entered one?"

"Yep, I like Annalisa. When I earn more money, I'll come up with another." Mia hushed before speaking. "Please come home. We all miss you."

I highly doubt that.

"Maybe you can come visit me during your summer break?" Fiona suggested.

"I would like that. Then you can come back with me!" Fiona could hear the excitement in her granddaughter's voice. "That would be perfect."

"I'll call your parents this weekend and discuss the details. Where are your parents?"

"At some meeting downtown where Dad works. Something about his job."

Fiona wanted to keep talking, but the doorbell rang at her flat. She raked her fingers through her newly shorn short hair and imagined the length was still there. "I have to go now, Mia. I love you my precious girl."

"I love you too. Buh-bye. I mean, ta!"

Fiona clicked the red phone emblem until the mobile cycled off. Who could it be? She wasn't expecting anyone. One peek through the peephole made her cringe. She opened the door reluctantly and droned. "Hello, Elizabeth."

"That wasn't a very friendly greeting." Elizabeth sauntered in without an invitation. "You ready for your soiree on Saturday?" After glancing around the flat she asked. "How are we ever going to dance in such a small place?"

"We've danced in smaller spaces both at friend's homes and out on the town."

"But this is tiny. I heard you used to have a palace."

"I had a large home before. Now it's just me. I don't need or want all that space. I hear your flat isn't much bigger than mine."

"I don't plan on staying there for long."

"You moving to a bigger flat?"

"I certainly hope so. And sooner than later. So who is your caterer?"

"I'm hiring a young man from Barrafina, if you must know."

"That's pricey, and one of the number one restaurants in London." Elizabeth headed straight into the kitchen to scope it out. "Adequate, but elegant."

"The Earl knows I appreciate antiques."

"I hear you two were once an item."

"We were once close friends." Fiona tapped her ballet slipper on the wood floor in rhythm to the song blasting in her head.

"And more." Elizabeth sneered. Her blonde hair cascaded down her skinny back and swayed when she moved. She flashed her green eyes like missiles honing in on their target.

"Edward tells me you spend most of your time at his place now. Day and night." Fiona sneered right back.

"I do. I find him fascinating. He's led an exciting life both here and abroad."

"There is a slight age difference between the two of you, forty, almost fifty years."

"Age means nothing when two people love each other. He does still speak of you quite fondly though." The superior smile faded from her lips and washed away the color in her face.

"We remain friends. He came to my rescue when George passed away quite suddenly. It was a shock for both Troy and me. He is fond of my son also, like a father figure."

"Well, I've told him it bothers me him subletting to a past girlfriend, so he'll be asking you to vacate after the soiree. ASAP."

Fiona lost her balance and tilted to the left, into the arched doorway where the two women stood opposite each other.

"What?"

"You heard me. It was decided last evening."

"I've spent all this money for a party you insisted I hostess."

Elizabeth closed the gap separating them until her warm breath fell upon Fiona's face. Her stiletto heels clicked against the wood grain of the floor, just missing crunching Fiona's toes. "Things changed while you were in the States. Love trumps friendship." Her short black dress inched up her backside when she turned to leave. "It is nice of you to spend your precious pounds sterling for the rest of us to enjoy as much as you have enjoyed all our money."

"You never spend a pence." Fiona sputtered.

"No, I don't, do I? And you are basically bankrupt. We've all figured it out. I've never seen anyone so tight with pound notes."

Fiona opened the door. "You may leave now."

Elizabeth spit out venomous words at Fiona. "Did you think a washed up, old former ballerina like you could steal Edward back?"

"Oh foolish child, that is the last of my desires. I'm going to be a Grandmum again." Fiona started to shut the door before the young woman cleared the threshold, to help her along her way.

Chapter Thirty-Seven

Betrayal hits hard whether you know it is coming or it blindsides you. Denial can't linger around for long. If you don't face the attack head-on, you will lose. You win when you face the onslaught even if the enemy is way ahead of you. Not fighting at all is the worst choice possible. Sounds easy, but truth be told, it's grueling. It may be the hardest thing you may ever deal with in your lifetime, but so worth the effort, energy, and humiliation. ~ Newspaper advice column.

Accused

Troy entered the room with his lawyer. Blair appeared shocked and disheveled. The papers Troy left on both his boss and the secretary's desks, had also been faxed to the lawyer Troy retained, the State of California Department of Consumer Affairs, and to the District Attorney.

Elisa sat with Ian in the lounge area by the secretary's desk. They came as support, no matter what happened, they would stand by Troy.

"I'm Robert Stanton, Attorney at Law, and I'm here to represent your former employee, Troy Kensington. I believe you received his letter of resignation last week."

"I received no such letter." Blair leered at Troy.

"Copies were sent to the agencies and departments listed on the forms I sent you by registered mail. Did you receive that mail?" The lawyer repeated.

"Yes, I did."

"And you still chose to not have your lawyer represent with you at this time as suggested in said mail?" Robert remained standing.

"Cut the nonsense, Troy. We don't need lawyers between friends." Blair ignored Stanton, but he couldn't look Troy in the eye either.

Robert motioned for Troy to sit across the conference table where his former boss sat. He then seated himself beside his client and opened a brown leather briefcase with a brass keyboard.

"All comments and or questions will be solely directed to me, not my client, Troy Kensington. Is that clear?" Stanton asked but Blair ignored him. Stanton continued. Troy made photo copies of the accounting ledgers you asked him to alter to reflect incorrect numbers and sums of money you reported making over the course of a four-quarter year. He also copied the annual reports. He printed out the computer spread sheets from this same period of time. These figures mirrored the falsified documents for the previous income tax year and the opening books for the present year." Robert took a long breath and waited, when he received no response from Blair he picked up where he'd left off.

"I am willing to fax all copies of this paperwork to any lawyer you retain. If you are willing to settle out of court with your former employee to clear his name of any wrong doing. He is prepared to do so. Otherwise we will prosecute to the full extent of the law. Do you understand these terms?" Robert's Italian shoes shuffled on the looped carpet.

Blair sat speechless. His baggy eye sockets and wrinkled suit looked like he'd slept in the office the night before and hadn't showered and shaved. Had he gone home? Troy wondered if Marilyn had figured out Blair's affair with his secretary Beverly. Bev would lie for Blair. She was barely twenty and not smart enough to realize the consequences for being an accomplice to Blair's deceptions. Marilyn on the other hand was a Rhodes Scholar. She was not just a stay-at-home mom as Blair referred to his wife. She probably figured the embezzlement out about the same time Troy became suspicious.

"Why did you do this to me, man? I gave you a great job with fringe benefits and travel miles." Blair stared steely-eyed into Robert's expressionless face. "My employee cooked the books and stole over two million dollars from me and my family."

Robert snapped the briefcase shut. "Then we are done here for today."

"Wait!' Blair cried out.

"Me be remembering a day like this back in Cornwall." Ian patted Elisa's back. "Me be accused of stealing boats and sinking them, so Mick told me."

"Yes, we did sit together in British court." Elisa dried the inside corners of her eyes with the tissue from her sweater pocket. "It was pretty scary."

"As it be good then, so it be sure to go here." Ian tried to encourage her. "Troy be innocent, me be praying for him."

"I am too, Dad. I am too." Elisa wanted to ease the concern etched deep in her father's raspy voice. This was one time she wished he wasn't aware of the circumstances and the meaning of their surroundings. Troy was presently unemployed and their savings was extensively exhausted between supplementing Fiona and all the flights to Cornwall to check on her father. All they had left were their investments to cash in. They would probably have to sell the Tahoe cabin and maybe even move into a smaller, less expensive home. Just where did Blair intend to accuse Troy of stashing two million dollars?

The conference room door flew open and Troy and his lawyer stepped out. An angry Blair followed close behind. "This isn't how this was supposed to go down!"

"I am certain this is not what you had carefully plotted and planned for my client, Mr. Goodwin. The District Attorney will be contacting you next. I suggest you retain a lawyer."

Blair blasted past Elisa and Ian without a word and stormed into his office. They heard the door slam causing the glass window beside it to rattle and ripple as if it was going to shatter. They exited the building, never to return. Stanton had sent a younger associate to clear out all Troy's belongings and box them for the police to eventually go through. Troy never touched a thing, not even the family photographs.

The ride down the elevator was quiet at first, then Ian piped up. "Well it could be worse, you not be accused of trying to sink the building too."

A resistant grin broke across Elisa face, and a low laugh escaped.

Troy responded. "Yeah, we are on dry land and that could be an advantage."

Robert exhibited a lack of understanding and opened his mouth to ask.

"Inside joke." Elisa muttered under her breath.

"I see."

Ian hung back with Elisa while the two men strode ahead talking over details of the strategy to take on Blair full force.

"It be a good thing Troy moved first, turned his boss in for fraud." Ian said.

"Yes, a very good thing, and it will help in his defense."

"This be too much for you today?"

"I'm glad it is behind us now. We can move forward to clear Troy." Elisa offered something positive.

"He be interviewing for new jobs now."

"It will be a difficult process. He certainly will not have a reference from his last job." An encompassing nausea rumbled through Elisa in the elevator and got stronger in the parking lot. "I think I need to munch on a snack, some protein." She riffled through her purse and pulled a baggie with nuts, raisins, and cubes of cheddar cheese. Her shaky hands made opening the airtight bag challenging, but she managed to control the tremors and rip it open.

Troy parted ways with his lawyer and rushed over to help Elisa and Ian board the SUV. "He thinks we can win this case. Blair made some giant blunders in his own math, in his handwriting. No matter how hard he tried to make it look like mine." He assisted Elisa into the front passenger seat and gently belted her in before hurrying over to the driver's side after Ian got in the seat behind him. "They have handwriting experts that can differentiate between the two of us. He also kept a little black book for himself with figures he didn't want to forget. None of it adds up to the real numbers. It is full of the cooked figures, all in his pen."

"He's going to lie, isn't he?" Elisa pressed.

"He'll lie, that's why he asked me to change the figures for him."

"And the rest of the office?" She pursued the point.

"Only Bev had any involvement. She'll cover for him. She thinks he's going to divorce Marilyn for her." Troy started the vehicle and headed for home. "Mia is waiting for us with Madeline and Savannah. Let's pick up some sushi on 16th Street, go home, and just be a family."

Elisa texted Mia. "She'd like some California rolls."

"I can do that."

"I be taking me cod and chips." Ian put in his request.

"Tempura." Troy and Elisa said at the same time.

"The baby is going to come right in the middle of this mess and it could heat up fast." Troy glanced sideways at Elisa, then back to the road ahead.

"We'll make our way as Dad likes to say."

"I could go to jail, if we lose."

"I know." She rolled down her window and let the chilly air blow against her face. She'd over-bundled, misjudged the temperature, again. Spring was coming. New life and rebirth. Hope.

Chapter Thirty-Eight

Londontown. London's night life is legend. Clubs offer cavernous dancefloors for dusk to dawn dancing. Gastropubs like the Old Crown on Oxford Street in Covent Garden are low-lit, with art-festooned rooms boasting high-end beer and gourmet foods. Entertainment ranges from comedy and jazz clubs, to classical music, musicals, and art centres. Tonight all will be incorporated and squeezed into my Chelsea flat. Lavish and indulgent. By invitation only. Frenemies rampant. ~ Fiona's Soiree.

Soiree

The *répondez s'il vous plaît* cards flooded in a rush at first, had trickled down to a complete stop by the evening before the party. Many never responded at all. Fiona expected as much after Elizabeth's unveiled visit. The question was would Edward make an appearance out of friendship? Or had lifelong intimacies fallen by the wayside too?

The older women assured Fiona they would rally about her, whether or not their wandering-eyed male peers accompanied them. It might end up being a "Birds Night Only," but that suited all of them to a tea.

Frederick headed the Barrafina catering staff. A crystal vase overflowing with three dozen long stem roses had been delivered by Hayford and Rhodes, one of the finest florists in London, an hour

275

before the party. It was the sole arrangement in the foyer where Fiona would greet her guests. Normally the hostess received multiple such deliveries. The exquisite vase with blue forget-me-nots artfully woven among the velvet red opening buds caused her heart to soar. The card enclosed simply read ~ Fiona, the Royal's most elegant ballerina. Fondly, Frederick.

"Your kindness means much to me." Fiona whispered in Frederick's ear. "Ta."

"My pleasure." He answered, and asked a woman standing nearby to join them.

"Will you introduce me to your beautiful wife?"

"Tessa, I am honoured for you to meet the ballerina you have heard so much about all these years, Fiona Rose Kensington." He beamed.

"I am most grateful for your invitation and hospitality this evening." Tessa offered her hand and dipped ever so slightly in a polite curtsey. The kindness of the gesture made Fiona's heart soar even higher.

"It is I who am grateful." Fiona reciprocated. "How lovely you are." She marveled at the petite creature before her in an elegant gown of spun blue starlight that draped down her back in an open V, and clung like silk on her slender figure. Waves of soft hazel curls fell regally on her bare shoulders and highlighted her azure almond eyes.

"Frederick said we might be waltzing till dawn." Tessa sounded hopeful.

"The musicians know all my favourites. This shall be the evening of waltzes." Fiona assured her.

The kitchen buzzed with last minute activity, preparing tiered-silver trays for the formal dining room. An Irish lace tablecloth graced the polished mahogany wood, and all of the ornate sideboard shelves bore Waterford crystal dishes of curry, shrimp, and caviar. Fiona nodded to Frederick to light each candle in the vintage candelabrum under the glittering, tinkling chandelier.

Fiona sauntered to the foyer when the grandfather clock struck the eight o'clock hour. Alone, she awaited whatever may transpire. She stood in tasteful black low heels, and a sapphire satin gown with a layered sash wrapped around her tiny waist. Her bodice of delicate black handmade lace formed a scoop neckline, and extended to snug three-quarter length sleeves with a scalloped trim. Her mother's sapphire necklace and dangling earrings shimmered gracefully under the dazzling low-light of a smaller chandelier hanging from the frescoed ceiling.

The minute hand denoted a quarter past the hour. No one arrived. Tessa brought Fiona a glass of champagne.

"A toast. To our lovely hostess. "She raised and clinked her crystal when Fiona raised hers.

"I fear I am being boycotted." She tilted and sipped the chilled French sparkling wine.

The musicians began playing classical instrumentals. A fire blazed in the granite hearth in the formal living room where all furniture had been moved along side of the walls to create a temporary ballroom.

"I hope you don't mind that Frederick and I acted upon your permission to invite some of our friends. We told them to arrive at half past the hour."

"I will be pleased to meet them."

A three bell chime rang in the hallway. Fiona left her glass to go open the door.

"Apologies for being tardy. We haven't missed a waltz yet have we?" Six elderly women stood in the outer hall. Their coats and stoles covered full-length flowing gowns of silk and organza. Snow-white and gray hair was pinned in salon coifed buns and curls.

"Do come in." Fiona kissed each one on the cheek. She had the gentleman who came to assist her callers take their coats to a designated guest bedroom. No one carried a purse, but there was a silver tray waiting for the lipsticks and compacts tucked in their coat pockets.

"My dearie." Her friend Louise held back as the others moved to the ballroom. "Elizabeth has invited all to do Londontown for an evening of gastropubs and clubbing. A few more may break away, but her intent is to shun this party she insisted you host." She kissed her forehead.

"The insolent tart."

"I am so sorry." Louise hugged her close, and Fiona let her.

Tessa had politely excused herself and joined the women in the other room. Melodious strains from the small orchestra filled the house with glorious classical notes; violins, cello, double bass, and viola. Fiona's friends found rest on the settees while the music played. The flat echoed each chord from the stringed-instruments across the empty dance floor.

Frederick appeared and ushered his four tuxedo-clad servers to where the women sat chatting. He and Tessa started to dance first. The ladies gladly accepted each request from the young men that requested to waltz. The two remaining guests rose and danced with each other. First Chopin, Brahms, and Tchaikovsky. Mesmerizing music for both concert and dancing.

Fiona watched from the foyer. *At least the evening is not a total disaster. There are fifty of us, fifty in our group of friends. Now we are but seven.*

Near the nine o'clock hour she rose from her chair by the door when the chime rang out again. Once ajar, she gazed down the long hallway gaping at the line of people.

"Much appreciate opening your home to us. We are Tessa and Frederick's friends from the Royal Opera House. It is such an honour to meet you in person. An honour." The young man who looked to be in his early thirties embraced her warmly.

"Ta." She gazed over his shoulder. "Are all of you from the opera house?"

"Some are also from the Royal Ballet. Many used to dance with you as I understand."

"Welcome, please do come in." She stepped aside as people poured in, taking her hand, kissing her, hugging her; young teens, middle-age couples, elderly gentlemen and women.

"I'm Veronica. We studied for years as soloists." A dimpled-cheeked matron hugged her.

"I remember you." Fiona hugged her back, quite surprised. "We studied to reach Principle Character Artist rank, and danced in many performances together."

As the room filled, Frederick called his servers back to the kitchen and make-shift bar.

"I learned how to glissade gracefully watching you. Leonard Farnsworth." He kissed her cheek, a long lingering brush of his lips, before following direction to the coat room.

"Come, come and dance tonight, Leonard." Fiona blushed.

One by one Fiona welcomed people she hadn't seen for decades, and met many faithful supporters of the ballet. Each greeting brought to memory laborious practices, private sessions to help each other past failed auditions, shining performances, old injuries that halted careers like hers, and endless wrapping of painful, bleeding, and broken feet to dance another day.

"Dame Edith, is that you?" Fiona escorted her hunched-over former teacher who could barely walk, to her bedroom where they sat on her chaise lounge. "It is quiet to talk here."

"My favourite student. My protégée." The elderly woman basked in their private moment. "How often I've wondered how you were. I've not heard back from you since you moved to the States. Not even the annual Christmas card. Did you consider my suggestion to teach dance across the pond?" Her gnarled palm sought Fiona's and grasped it tight. "Never for pounds sterling." She placed their interlocked fingers on her heart. "For the passion."

"Oh." Fiona struggled to hold back suddenly surfacing emotions. "I do not come close to you in talent."

"You are the dame now." Edith leaned her snowy head on Fiona's neck and shoulder. "You must believe in yourself as I have believed in you since you were young. How I've missed our visits. Come, take tea with me tomorrow. I have retired to a cottage in the Cotswolds."

Fiona drew the cherished mentor to her chest, and heaved a deep sigh. She ached with a profound intensity that startled her. "There is still much I need to learn from you. I will come."

Edith stroked Fiona's face. "The lessons in life are a bit dear, but worth the price." The wise woman said.

Fiona's home teemed with contagious laughter, and a crowded ballroom floor. All the food she feared she'd have to toss out now filled stacks of white china tea plates in her guests' hands.

At midnight the clock chimed in a new day. That is when she caught a glimpse of the Earl. He was moving about the room and chatting up a young ballerina named Lydia she'd just met who seemed quite taken with him. *They always are his first choice as I was so many years ago.* "Edward, when did you appear?" Fiona guided him over to herself.

"About an hour ago. You seemed occupied. I did not want to disturb you."

"Where is your Elizabeth?"

"I left her on Oxford Street when I was told what she had done to you. I had no part in this." He spoke with contrived sincerity.

"She wants to move in with me. Sell her place. Permanent. If I didn't know better, I'd think she has marriage in mind." Sweat beaded at his temples where black hair dye had missed covering numerous wild strands of gray.

Fiona had fallen prey to his philandering ways for years. Too many years she realized, and too easily, as she observed his slick demeanor and practiced speech.

"Why did you wait so late to join us?"

"It was harder than I thought to break away." His eyes followed the young ballerina across the room as they spoke. He winked at her in that charming way Fiona used to find irresistible.

"Lydia is quite graceful." Fiona half-turned.

"Like you once were. Almost the Prima ballerina assoluta. If only you hadn't fallen."

"I was dropped." Fiona corrected him.

Lydia walked up and interrupted to say her good-bye to Fiona whilst slipping a paper in Edward's coat pocket and bidding him an affectionate farewell. "Wicked bash." She called out before exiting the front door.

"If you hurry, you may catch up to her."

His eyes scanned the room before he led Fiona to the door. "You do not have to vacate after this soiree. You stay as long as you wish."

"I will stay a while longer. Ta for popping by."

"I wasn't sure how long I could visit. Ta, my Fiona." He rushed out and left the door open. His pace quickened to a hurried jog, then he ran like a marathon runner nearing the finish line in a race.

"You never took off your coat." She uttered to the growing space between them.

"Fiona."

"Yes, Frederick?" She closed the door, and locked it for the first time during the soiree.

"I have danced the Blue Danube with Tessa. May I take a break and ask you for the Second Waltz?" He reached an arm out to her.

"Dmitri Shostakovich?" Fiona looped her arm in his and walked onto the crowded ballroom floor as the orchestra began to tune up. She followed Frederick's lead in fluid, effortless movement, step by step, glad she'd slipped into her ballet flats hours ago.

The morning sun rose casting a soft red-orange glow through the open arched window. Fiona padded from her bed to the bench seat to watch the sunrise. Gathering her robe close, she sat, leaning her back against the wall, her legs stretched across the cushions. The play of light on the waxed wood floor and white plaster gave the room a restful, comfortable ambiance.

So this is contentment.

She pressed forward to absorb the rays of light warming her face, and pulled her knees to her chest. She longed to share this with Mia. Yet Troy and Elisa would never trust her to do so. Place their precious daughter on a cross-country flight followed by an overseas jaunt? To spend time alone with horrible, wretched Fiona in Londontown? Never.

I missed too many sunrises. I never cared to notice.

The alarm sounded, breaking her concentration. She let the musical refrain play out before shutting it down. No time for a leisurely bath soak if she was to join Edith at her cottage for tea. Fiona took a quick shower, applied minimal make-up and dressed in casual black leggings and an oversized cashmere pastel pink sweater. She glanced at her jewelry stand, but left without opening the box.

The drive in the countryside was breathtaking. She spent more time glancing out the rented Mini's windows than training her eyes on the road ahead of her. It was her first venture outside London since her arrival. Lush rolling hillsides with lavender patches swaying in the breeze reminded her of the paintings in the National Gallery. Thatched cottages with window boxes bursting with delicate blue, and vibrant yellow and purple blooms, flowers for which she did not know the proper names, beckoned her. It was an exhilarating solicitation that she accepted.

Her roadmap indicated Edith's retirement abode was mere kilometers in distance. She pulled off the roadside to double check the route she'd penciled in.

"I should have penned it with ink." Fiona spoke out loud and raised the spectacles dangling on a silver chain about her neck. "Oakshire Lane. That's better." She let her glasses fall. "It was a left turn, yes, this road, then I take the first right onto—" she scooped her frames up leaving a thumbprint smack in the center of the lens. "Posh." She let go of the wheel to swipe the glass lens between the folds of her sweater. "Manchester Road. That's it."

The day's journey to the Cotswolds' charted to be one hour and fifty-nine minutes from her London flat. She'd forgotten how picturesque the landscape was from back when her family went on holiday during her childhood. Quaint cottages quintessentially represented sixteenth century England. A far cry from the city roots she'd planted in her teens and grew her into adulthood.

Two quick turns and she arrived.

Edith greeted her at the door. "You found me."

Fiona gave her a potted geranium that rode in the passenger seat for the journey. She'd purchased the gift at the neighborhood flower shoppe on a whim before leaving the city behind.

"How lovely. Welcome to my cottage." Edith held the bright red heavy door open.

Fiona hugged the dear lady and deposited the large plant on the doorstep, then entered with a mix of anticipation and curiosity.

"Not what you envisioned for one so entrenched in the Royal Ballet and Opera House?"

"It's completely charming in every way." Fiona glanced about.

"A cozy fit for this old dancer." Edith guided her to the snug living room where a tea for two tray dressed with fine bone china, scones, clotted cream and jam sat waiting. "How was your adventure down our one car dusty lanes?"

"Peaceful, relaxing. I could have kept driving for hours." Fiona settled on the sofa across from where Edith positioned herself in an overstuffed worn arm chair. It cradled her like a child in a mother's loving arms. The soles of her clunky shoes grazed the throw rug.

"Twas delightful to be included in your celebration last evening."

"You made it special."

"I rarely travel to the city for performances these past years. Once in a great while, I'll board the train at Morton-in-Marsh Railway Station. Just to ride through the Cotswolds."

"You prefer it here now?" Fiona poured their tea and placed a cup within Edith's reach.

"There is a season for everything. I could not return to my former life if I wished to, which I no longer do." Shaking hands lifted, then balanced the cup and saucer on her knee.

"It no longer holds enchantment for me either, as I thought it would."

"We were blessed to be a part of something unique." Edith's eyes twinkled.

"Years and years of hard work and short, glorious performances." Fiona reminisced as she sipped her tea.

"And yet, we'd both do it all over again in our youth."

"True."

"Tell me about your granddaughter. You hold her dear to your heart?"

"I miss her terribly. More than I knew I could."

"Bring her for holiday." Edith picked up a brochure from her coffee table, and read. "Show her the 'hidden villages here where all is unspoilt. The Secret Cotswold Cottages. They are inaccessible to public transport. Take the train at Morton Station'."

"You know, I've never done that in my own lifetime."

"We aren't getting younger my dear Fiona." Edith spooned cream and jam on their scones, and handed one plate across the table. "Take her to the ballet and museums in London too. Walk along the Thames. Make memories."

"Her grandfather moved in from Cornwall with us. He has Alzheimer's and will soon lose all he once knew." A lump caught in Fiona's throat and lodged. Her eyes welled up and spilled over. She tried to continue the conversation, but found herself unable to speak.

"It is a tragic loss to lose one's self, and all those you love." Edith paused. "Do you care for him, her grandfather?"

A silence fell before she answered. "I disdained Ian, passionately. I worked hard at it. Now I find I miss him too." Her voice softened. "He is a man of integrity. A rare gem in this vain and shallow world. I did not know," she faltered, "that I had any love in my heart for him, until I left him behind."

Chapter Thirty-Nine

Mia writes in her journal after every family meal and discussion. Mick told her some pretty tall fish tales while he was here and Dad didn't deny a single one. She interviews her Gramps any chance she gets. He's sharing stories with her I've never heard before. It's almost like I'm learning my family history for the first time. And Fiona, she was the biggest surprise of all. She opened up to Mia before she abandoned our circus act. Mia couldn't put pen to paper fast enough when she got the three seniors together at the same time. They seemed to connect on another level, a generational plane exempt from what even Troy and I can relate to. Mia got Fiona to reveal her true age, and in front of two men she casually disclosed her most closely guarded and fibbed about birthdate. And all Mia did was ask. ~ Elisa's lunch topic confided to Maddie

Confidences

Maddie returned the cabin key with gifts including a case of Napa wine, a dinner certificate for two at Troy's favorite steakhouse restaurant at the Pavilions, and four Music Circus tickets for a couple of the season's musicals. There was also a small wrapped present for Mia for sharing her room with Savannah.

"You didn't have to do all this."

"But we want to." She pressed an envelope in Elisa's hand. "Read it later tonight."

"Okay." Elisa slipped the stationary in her open purse. "You look beyond refreshed. Sort of glowing."

"And that is exactly how I feel." Maddie cooed. "To say it was romantic, isn't descriptive enough. Fires in the morning, and fires at night. No schedules to follow, no responsibilities, just the two of us curled up on the sofa in each other's arms."

Elisa observed a contented sigh passed over her friend's ruby lips, and her exotic sable eyes shone like polished precious gemstones. "It is so easy to forget how important it is to be husband and wife."

"We needed to remember." Maddie returned to planet earth. "Thank you."

"Make it last. Spring is here and summer soon follows."

"Our kiddos will be out of school in May, not even June these days."

Elisa looked out the picture window where her father was busy scooting about on his kneeler pad from plant to plant, and pot to pot, fertilizing and clipping dead leaves so new ones can grow. "Dad says gardening is therapeutic. We should all take turns planting and tilling the dirt in a garden." He toiled in worn out, holey jeans, muckers, and an old shirt with the tail hanging lose, dragging in the mud. She knew he couldn't be happier.

"I imagine it is a sort of therapy." Maddie paused. "We were talking divorce before Tahoe. We got that distant."

"I am so sorry." Elisa tried to not show her complete shock.

"Don't be. We have a fighting chance now. We talked about making changes." She sniffled. "It was so subtle, so insidiously slow-motion, you know?"

"We're struggling too, with the embezzlement charges, Mick's visit, Fiona leaving, and the baby on the way." Elisa cut herself off at that point.

"Gets to be too much."

"Before Dad started responding to his current medication, when he was lost, nothing in my life seemed real anymore. He'd become a shell of the person he used to be."

"My father is there now, since the fall. It's an accelerated downhill slide to—the end."

A hush canopied over the two women. A quiet agreement that neither wanted, sought, nor could ignore. It was unavoidable in every aspect. The booming voice whether spoken or not. Alzheimer's rules, it controls, it destroys. It is a ticking bomb that will implode, explode.

Maddie spoke first. "Until I met you, not one of my friends really understood how crazy my life had become." She half-laughed, half-cried. "At one girlfriend's birthday lunch, my circle of friends decided I'm not fun anymore. And it's true. I have to cancel on them all the time, and I try to reschedule, but that falls through too."

"I don't have friends. Some work acquaintances, and literary colleagues I seldom see because now I freelance from home, on my laptop, in a corner of our bedroom." Elisa's composure wavered. "Don't even have an office anymore. My mother-in-law moved in it, and I moved out."

"What is it about this disease that people don't understand? If my dad had cancer, it would be different. People support families dealing with cancer."

"Maybe there is a lack of knowledge?"

"I am so tired of hearing, 'Why don't you just put him in a home?' How compassionate is that?" Maddie threw her hands in the air. "It's like he's *something* to be discarded."

"Like the person becomes invisible to society, loses their value as a human being." Elisa's voice cracked. "That part I do understand. I see it in faces when we're in public."

"My dad fought in World War II, served his country. He worked hard all his life, the same boring job for 45 years, for me and my mom. He doesn't deserve this." Maddie gulped and held her breath.

Elisa nodded. "What can I do to help?"

"Someone listening helps. The Tahoe cabin was a huge help. And perfect timing. Ben and I hadn't laughed together in way too long. I'd forgotten how funny he can be. It was fun to be silly together and not have to be so serious all the time. All Ben ever saw anymore was a messy puddle of emotions instead of the wife he missed.

"I so get that." Elisa assured her. "Sometimes I start to laugh when life gets insane, you know? Being pregnant my hormones are already all over the place. Then I cry for no reason."

"It is too easy to forget who you are as a person. Caregivers can lose the whole of themselves. Married couples kind of shift into survival mode, but not necessarily together. And the children, how can their minds wrap around the enormity of it all?" Maddie rose, her eyes reddened and nose runny. "Do you have a box of tissues?"

"Yes." Elisa stretched to reach a box on the end table.

"Thank you." Maddie grabbed a handful, and blew her nose several times. "May I wash up in the bathroom?"

"Sure, first door to the right. Next to my old office." Elisa laughed. "Let's make a pact to remember to laugh when we get together too. I know some pretty bad jokes that only I get."

"That is a great idea." Maddie agreed. "I'm not much of a jokester but I really do believe that laughter is the best medicine. I think we both need an overdose." She disappeared behind the beige paneled door she didn't close all the way.

A rush of water from the sink faucet gushed. Elisa knew it took a while to warm up. She rose and poured them the cups of coffee they hadn't gotten to yet. Ian waved to her from where he gardened near the kitchen window. He'd made considerable headway prodding along. He looked quite the character towing his mini weeding wheelbarrow and wearing a makeshift master gardener belt he had strapped about his midsection. It held a trowel, cultivator, and transplanter ready to draw like a gun from a holster. Most of all he looked relaxed, knee pads digging into the gentle give of the earth, gloves coated in layers of fertilizer and top soil. A satisfied expression from a place deep within carried his bowed and bent frame scooting along, humming or whistling one of his favourite tunes. *I need to remember this.* Elisa told herself.

Elisa became aware of Maddie standing beside her when she picked up one of the mugs, and offered her the other. She tore her sugar packets to dump in, and added cream.

"Thanks. How I wish your dad could hold onto that part of himself that brings this kind of joy."

"I'm hoping it lasts until the baby is born." Elisa sipped a couple of swallows. "I want longer, but I at least want him to meet her and know who she is, if only a short time."

"Does his doctor say how long he thinks Ian's meds will work?"

"There's no definite timeline. I notice every once in a while he slips, says something a little off in a conversation, skips a beat, and can't pick it up right away." Elisa walked back to the living room and Maddie followed. "Or I notice him staring off with a blank glaze in his eyes, and he doesn't come back for seconds or even a minute or two." Elisa rubbed back and forth on her tummy.

"And you try not to let panic seize your own mind and heart."

"Yes."

Maddie shifted on the sofa cushion. "But it does."

"When I was a little girl. My father was invincible. I looked at him the way Mia looks to Troy." Elisa stumbled on her words. "Back in Cornwall this past visit, my dad was a stranger to me, and I was lost without him, drifting aimlessly." She hesitated. "Does that make sense?"

"Perfect sense. I see it in my daughters' faces, the disappointment that when their Papa fell, he never really got up again. Not the Papa they knew and loved." Maddie ran her fingertip over the rim of her cup. "It's hardest for Savannah, she had him the longest."

"Do you think our girls talked about it, with each other?"

"I hope so. They need someone who understands too."

"Mia is writing a book about Dad, parts about all of us too. That's how she's chosen to deal with it."

"My younger two have started to pull away from their Papa. They don't have Savannah's level of comprehension." Maddie put the mug to her lips. "Sophia asked me if Papa keeps wetting the bed, am I going to made him go to the rehab house again."

"She sees it as a punishment?"

"Pretty much. His Depends leak a lot. So I wash sheets several times a week."

"The things you don't realize go through their child minds." Elisa shook her head.

"I know. On a lighter note, he'll sit and listen to her read for hours, the same thing over and over. It helps her with her homework." Laughter rolled out and Maddie sighed. "Dad has no sense of time, so it's all new to him minute by minute. Soph is a slow reader, so it works."

"There are blessings in the middle of the heartache." Elisa acknowledged.

"And we need those marvelous moments." Maddie agreed.

"Elisa." Ian popped his head in the French slider door, his dirty gloves smudging the glass and handle. "Me planted a flat of the yellow and purple pansies, and a flat of the melon ones. But me think what you be making for lunch be next on my list today."

"Okay, Dad. Come on in and you can change your clothes."

"I don't want to muck up the carpet so I be leaving me boots outside, and step in with me socks. Do you want me to leave the rest out on the porch?"

Elisa looked at the caked-on mud covering his kneelers, his shirt cuffs, and under his fingernails. "You have time for a quick shower before I make the grilled cheese sandwiches and soup."

Ian rolled the screen door open and shoved the heavy glass panel until it swooshed with a big heave-ho. "Wait, me should come in through the garage. Less traffic that way." He closed both doors and walked away.

"He'll remember to shower, but will most likely forget that he was coming in to eat lunch." Elisa told Maddie. "He forgets to eat meals unless one of us reminds him and he can't afford to lose any more weight. Some days he only shaves half his face."

"He speaks so clearly."

"I am enjoying this phase."

"I can help you prepare lunch. I make a mean grilled three-cheese."

"And I heat up a delicious deli tomato basil soup." Elisa rose.

"Sounds good to me. What kind of bread do you have?" She shadowed her into the kitchen, and went to the sink to wash up after chugging down the last of her coffee.

"Potato or sourdough."

"Good choices."

"Troy is on a no preservatives kick. Makes it difficult for a die-hard bread connoisseur." Elisa pointed to the fridge. "Just poke around in there until you find what you need. Here's a fry pan for the sandwiches. I am headed to the pantry."

Maddie took it and stacked ingredients in both arms, cheeses, butter, mayonnaise, and turned to find Ian directly behind her. She let the fridge door automatically close. He stood in smudged gray gardening socks that slouched under his hairy, knobby knees. A tightly-belted red flannel robe hung just above those unsightly knees. His trusty straw hat perched on top of wild patches of snowy hair tilted down on the crest of his bushy gray and white eyebrows. Pinched between a dirt-stained finger and thumb he held six delicate pansy faces on broken stems.

"Three for you, and three for Elisa. They be living in water for about a week. Me be not able to bear throwing them away." Ian reached out to her, and held his hand toward hers.

Maddie set all the food in her arms down on the granite countertop without breaking visual contact with him. "Thank you, Mr. Darrow." Her eyes misted. She took the clippings.

"Sometime fathers want to give daughters flowers." Ian disappeared down the hall.   Maddie held the petals like a beautiful bouquet. "How I have missed this, the flowers my father brought me from his garden." She pressed the blooms to her lips and asked. "How did he know?"

Chapter Forty

Gramps is different than I remember him. He forgets things, times, people, sometimes, even me. But there is much he still knows—his books, his garden, and his funny bone. Right now he's taking a drug that helps his memory. I want it to last forever, but I know it won't. I can tell from the way all the adults are around him. Kind of like he is a little kid, not like them anymore. What I do know is that he misses Cornwall and all his mates. Mom is right that Uncle Mick's visit was good medicine for Gramps. But it also made him sad. "I be Cornish." is his favorite thing to say. He's a good teacher and I've learned a lot from him since he came to America for the first time in his life. I wish he'd come sooner, but I know he's staying until—right now I'm not going to write that part. It can wait. Whenever it does come, it will be too soon for all of us. ~ Mia's journal entry when Savannah went home after her weekend visit

Children of the Cornish

"Bean, why be we doing this? Your mobile takes pictures, and it be a telephone? And people think me be the one nutters." Ian held the mini machine out at full arm's length, and tried to push the button she'd shown him while aiming the little box above the two of them.

"Just smile like we're having fun."

"Well, me not be having fun. This be work."

"Push the button, Gramps." Mia spoke through gritted teeth frozen in a fixed smile.

A brilliant flash coincided with a mechanical click.

"Good, take another one."

"Me be blinded!" Ian started to pull his arm in.

"Take a few more. It's best to be able to choose from a couple of shots." Mia adjusted her burgundy tutu by snapping the elastic waist band. Her multi-colored striped leg warmers had fallen to her shins, so she yanked them up over her knees and smoothed her black tights and leotard until all wrinkles vanished. "Take a few more." Her smile returned.

"Why yer be dressing up and me be wearing these duddy clothes?" Ian stepped back to give her a full view of his drab brown rumpled old trousers and the pastel hand-knitted jumper Midge gave him last Christmas. He'd dug it out during Mick's visit, a show of appreciation more than a desire to be photographed sporting it for all posterity.

He clicked before their heads touched and accidentally held the button down too long. The camera went in to repeat mode and kept shooting. Ian brought the mobile closer and aimed at Mia, then him, then at them together, then at them apart.

"Wait! You've probably shot a hundred pics." Mia stood on her tip-toes and stretched her fingers out. "Turn it off." It kept clicking away.

"How?" Ian looked directly into the screen.

"I can help you."

"Okay, Bean." He handed it over as it continued to fire away.

Click. Mia shut it down. "Well that should be an interesting photo shoot."

"So me did a good job?" Ian looked pleased, but waited for her reply.

"Yes, you did."

"Ta, Bean. Me be glad to be of assistance. No charge for me expertise."

"I don't think I could afford you, Gramps."

"Can we be having a look then?" He rested on the wrought iron garden bench.

"Well, I may have to photo shop first." Mia glanced at her photo gallery, then plunked beside him. She flashed one picture on the scene faster than he could see, before the next one popped up, and another, and another. "Hey, these are actually pretty awesome."

"They be awesome? Awesome be a good thing?"

"You've definitely have your own style." She showed him a close-up of his right eyeball.

Ian leaned back onto the iron lattice behind him. "Me don't think that be the angle me was going for."

"It's a great shot." She cozied up, and gave him a private screening, one hundred and twenty-four shots in all. "Ears, nose with numerous hairs, their heads wedged to one side, and then to the other. Her ballet flats, a forty-five degree angle shot of Mia from head to toe, arms stretching to reach her phone with a gasp of exasperation on her face.

"I really like this one of the two of us." Mia hit a box of tools and selected chrome, and the color flashed five times more vibrant on the original frame.

"How did yer do that?" Ian asked. "It be most impressive."

"Ta Gramps, but the credit goes to the photo shop fix option. I can make some of these black and whites if you want."

"Show me."

"Here, you do this one." She selected a picture very similar to the one before it, and placed the phone in his hand. "So, I press this edit symbol, then hit the color box, then pick one of the options in this line. Yep," she added with confidence, "that's all there is to it. Unless you crop, or zoom in."

Sunlight settled on the two of them when a cloud moved away from overhead.

"Okay, Bean." Ian skipped past the first two words, mono and tonal. He saw preview images of what the pictures would look like altered by that choice. He tapped on the word noir, and almost instantly they appeared in shadowy tones of black, gray, and whites. "Oh, me like this."

"And you can hit revert, if you change your mind to go back to the original picture."

"Bean, this be near magical. In the olden days in Cornwall, this be considered witchcraft."

Mia giggled. "It's just modern technology."

"And the blooming trees be in some of the pictures. Me not be trying to do that, so I can't be taking credit. But, me be liking the effect of colour though only half our faces appear on the outer edges." Ian grinned quite near ear to ear with satisfaction.

"I'd say your photos look like a professional took them. I do hope you will give me a fair deal that includes your permission to use all of these at my discretion." Mia tried her best to sound like a professional herself.

"Of course." Ian beamed.

"May I get that in writing? Your signature, please." She drew a thin line across her journal page with a huge X at the beginning. "Sign here and add today's date, kind sir."

Ian took her pen in hand and signed his name in clear cursive, careful to include all the information she'd requested. His hand was a bit shaky, and it took longer than he wanted, but it was important to him to be doing a good job of it. To be spot on.

"You have pretty handwriting, Gramps."

"That be important in me school days. The teacher had to be able to read it or you be starting all over again until it be legible. Not one of us in the class be having handwriting same as another. Like fingerprints." He hugged Mia close and wrote. "I love you, Bean."

Chapter Forty-One

Truth is a vanishing virtue. There are no little untruths. It is either true, or it is not true. Black and white. Yet most of the world lives in the gray matter. Sifting through that, is near impossible. ~ Troy's attorney, Robert Stanton—a statement concerning the lies Blair Goodwin has, and continues spreading.

On the TV News

Elisa picked up the landline after the fourth ring. "Hello?"

"It's Maddie, turn on the Channel 2 evening news, quick."

"Why? We're on our way out the door to the school for Mia's play."

"Troy's boss Blair is giving an exclusive interview, about Troy. Hurry. I recorded what you've already missed." Maddie hung up.

Elisa stood stunned holding the receiver, her mouth hanging open. "Troy, wait." She stuttered. "Turn on Channel 2."

"We'll be late."

"Maddie says your boss is on the news talking about you."

Troy closed the front door. He and Ian rushed into the family room and he flipped on the TV with the remote control he grabbed off the coffee table. The 54" flat screen flashed an instant image of

Blair Goodwin being interviewed by one of the top reporters. Blair looked like father-of-the-year with his two sons clinging to him. One on the right and the other on his left. The boys would draw sympathy from anyone watching. Their questioning, innocent faces looking up to their dad as they each hung on a pant leg of one of Blair's expensive suits. His hands rested on the top of their recently barber-clipped haircuts. His wife Marilyn was nowhere in sight.

"You are having Mr. Kensington served for embezzling from Goodwin Solar. This was once a trusted friend and employee?"

"Yes, yes." Blair hung his head and shook it. "The betrayal is beyond description."

"He was the company accountant?"

"He was more than that. Our families did everything together; our wives, our children." Blair raised his head with a hurt look of shock, and stared straight into the young female reporter's face. "I had to ask him to leave."

"So you initiated the proceedings." prompted the journalist.

"Someone had to once the money drain was discovered by my secretary Beverly."

"Thank you for your time, Mr. Goodwin." The woman turned toward the cameras. "Sad to bring you the story of one local entrepreneur's heartbreak. The bankruptcy of his lifelong dream, owning and running his business." She tossed her long blonde hair off to the side as the camera zoomed in for a close-up, to capture her downcast baby blue eyes. "This just goes to show that you have to be careful in choosing who handles the money in a private business." Kaycee Bridges for Channel 2 TV. Back to you, Ken and Jackie.

The TV station news desk appeared on the screen with two evening anchors seated, shaking their heads. Troy repeatedly pressed the remote's power button until all went blank.

"What the bloody hell be happening?" Ian collapsed on the couch.

"How could he lie like that?" Elisa fumed. "You started everything, you turned him in."

"My lawyer warned me Blair would counter-attack." Troy held the remote, still pointing it at the big screen. "But, I didn't see this coming."

"What can we do?" Elisa threw her hands up in the air.

"I should probably call Robert before I do, or say anything." Troy pocketed the remote and exchanged it for his vibrating cell. He glanced at the name and answered, then hit speaker.

"It's Stanton. Hello? Troy, are you there?"

Elisa sat with Ian. "Dad."

"Let Troy be talking with his solicitor. He knows what to be doing. Yer and the baby be not needing any extra stress." Ian tucked her under his arm and held tight while Troy paced the hallway, mostly listening on the phone.

"Yes, I understand. I do. Thanks." Troy clicked off his cell. "He says I talk with no one, none of us do. Not even to say 'no comment'. He'll prepare a statement for the morning news report."

"We say nothing? No counter with the truth?" Elisa sat forward.

"No. I give Blair nothing to twist and make me sound like a guilty person trying to defend myself."

"That be making sense." Ian agreed. "Liars keep lying."

"But, honey." Elisa started.

"Please, trust me on this. I want to do exactly as my counsel is advising me." Troy sat on the arm of the couch. "He knows how to handle situations like this. I don't. I agree. My first inclination is to defend myself."

"You are telling the truth." Elisa argued.

"He went public with lies. This may actually come back on him, his own words, not my accusations. Please, Elisa. Let's go with what my lawyer is telling me to do."

"So if we're asked, we just zip it?"

"For now, pretty much. The statement will be released in the morning. Let's go to Mia's play, sit and watch it, come home and go to bed. When we wake up, it will be a new day." He snagged her sweater from an entryway hook, and draped it over her shoulders.

Ian headed to the door and waited. "Mia be watching for us."

Troy and Elisa joined him. "My purse."

"It's on your shoulder, honey." Troy kissed her. "Take a deep breath."

The three of them stepped out the front door.

A cameraman stood on their front porch with the Channel 2 reporter Ralph Moore. "Troy Kensington, Blair Goodwin has gone public with your alleged embezzlement from his solar company. Do you have a comment at this time?" He shoved a mic in front of Troy's mouth, and stood waiting.

Troy motioned Ian and Elisa to the parked SUV just feet away, escorting them past both men. He opened the passenger door, and Elisa buckled up. Ian sat in the middle of the back seat. Troy made his way to the driver's seat where the cameraman and reporter situated themselves in front of his door.

"Any comment for our viewers. Mr. Kensington?" The mic thrust in his face a second time. "What did you do with all the money?"

Troy wedged his way under the arm holding the mic and strained to open the door as the reporter's body weight pressed against it. He turned sideways and got an arm and a leg in, then pushed out to get his other half inside the vehicle. The engine started on his voice command and he hit the hazard lights.

Elisa teared up. "This is inexcusable. A complete invasion of our privacy." She sniffled and looked out the window down the street, trying not to let either of the news crew see her crying. "What if Mia had been with us?"

Troy honked before backing out. Only then did the news team back off.

"Roll right over their bloody shoes." Ian huffed.

"Don't let them see an emotional outburst. They're still filming. Zooming in." Troy followed all traffic laws as he drove off at the residential twenty-five miles an hour speed limit.

"You don't think they know about the school play? Will they try to follow us there?" Elisa's distress showed. She checked the side mirror in time to observe the two men jump in a clearly marked station van with a satellite dish spinning. "They're going to follow us!" She shrieked.

"Stay calm, Honey." Troy tried to comfort her. "I'll take an alternate route, just in case. I can give them the slip."

"Listen to you. We sound like criminals on the run."

Ian got his mobile. "Me be texting Mia so she knows we be running late."

Troy weaved in and out of the neighborhood streets. If Channel 2 could tail him through this maze, he figured he'd head home and use the electric garage door opener. He'd seen reports on the six o'clock news where they stood on doorsteps of people's homes, ringing the door bell, announcing, so-and-so won't answer to talk with us. He was concerned Elisa might crack.

"I'm going the back way and I'll drop you two off at the side auditorium doors. No one has been behind us for the last five streets."

"Are you sure it's safe to go to Mia's school? I don't want her exposed to any of this."

"I don't either." Troy gripped the steering wheel and clenched tight. "Ian, can you help Elisa to go in so she doesn't miss Mia's play. I'm sure your Bean has been trying to find us."

"Aye, mate." He hopped out when Troy stopped and opened the door for a frazzled and teary Elisa. "Come with me, we be off to go find our seats." He glanced at his watch. "We be but fifteen minutes into the show."

"Troy."

"Go with your dad, I'll be in shortly. I'm phoning this into my attorney when I park."

She hesitated, and scanned the school lot. "My heart is thundering."

"Get your seats and calm down. It will be okay."

Ian urged her out of the car and into his arms as he closed the door. They proceeded a few feet away so Troy could head down the packed rows of parked cars.

Troy kept them in his sight until they entered the school building. Then he squeezed into a small space in the last row. After he told the engine to shut down, he pounded his forehead on the steering wheel twice. "Why does my family have to suffer because of me?" He yelled out loud.

It took several minutes before he could make the call. "Robert, there was a news team waiting for us on my front doorsteps! My daughter could have been with us. What? No, none of us said a word. I'm at the school for Mia's play. Yes, I'm sure they didn't follow me, but it certainly wasn't for lack of trying. I'm listening."

Troy let the cool evening air slap his face as he walked into the front of the auditorium. He has his prepaid ticket and the number of his seat which was in the mid-section. He made polite excuses as he pressed past people seated in the outer chairs of his row.

Mia came on the stage as he sat next to Elisa. She clasped tissues in her lap, and he could tell, even in the darkened room, she'd been crying. He took her hand and slid his other hand in his pocket and fidgeted, then pulled out the TV remote. With a double take and a shake of his head, he immediately slipped it back in the pocket. He looked around, no one had noticed.

"You made it just in time." Elisa whispered and ran her fingers through Troy's. Mia only had a minor role in the play her class had written themselves. The important thing was that they hadn't missed her part. She said her lines perfectly, with voice inflections in all the right places, and clarity that made Elisa proud of her daughter.

She was glad Mia had been spared the ordeal at the house. But would she be the next time? As of tonight Troy was already on trial in the public eye. Blair had seen to that with his calculated manipulation of the local news media. He was back in control.

Sitting in the room full of parents excited to see their child in a performance made transitioning back to their true life easier. Here they were simply another family enjoying the school production, a drop of water in a large pool. Expectant parents, a proud Gramps, and a child who knew nothing about embezzlement. Soon they would have to sit Mia down and tell her enough to protect her from the gossip that would descend upon her too.

Chapter Forty-Two

Fiona's phone call caught both Troy and me by surprise. She'd moved from London to a cottage in the Cotswolds with her former mentor Dame Edith. She has a small room there and is helping the elderly woman by cooking and cleaning. She sounded different, her voice was soft and well, kind. Neither of us had ever heard that peacefulness in any form of communication with her. She had a king size request—Mia to come for a fortnight holiday in late June to early July, for Fiona's seventieth birthday. She'd send the airfare, and pay for everything. She asked for permission to take her on a train trip through the Cotswolds, to East Anglia for tea at the Queen's summer home, and a brief trip into London for a day and night to go to a Royal Ballet performance. She was specific and responsible in giving us an itinerary for approval, subject to any changes we ask for. After deliberation, we agreed. That would take Mia out of the country during the first court hearings. She would miss all newscasts and media coverage. Fiona immediately purchased the ticket when I gave my consent. ~ Elisa's response to Troy and Ian's pleas on Fiona's behalf.

On Summer Holiday

Sending their daughter off alone for the first time in her life proved to be more of an emotional upheaval than anticipated. The good-bye at the airport was even harder on Dad. His Bean was going back to England without him. He moped about the house all day without her to cheer him up. Finally he rang up a cab to take him to Streets Pub for fish and chips. Once there he rounded up the other local Brit transplants for a game of darts which he later shared in detail.

Elisa's concern had been changing planes in New York, where she'd had so much trouble returning to the States with Ian. She wouldn't be there if Mia needed her. The airline was excellent, offering a special program for children traveling alone. So Elisa remained behind, pregnant and showing her baby bump. Her secret plan to fly with Mia to New York and see her off from there got the kibosh from Troy at first mention. Righto. The pregnancy progressively held her back from more and more. She was considered high risk since the ultrasound, though only Troy and she know that at this point.

"Mum Skyped while you were at your OB appointment. Mia arrived safely at Heathrow." said Troy.

"You got to see her?" Elisa groaned. "How does she look?" She joined him on the sofa.

"Like we are a distant memory. She is elated to be with her Grandmum again. Loved traveling on her own. God help us. She bought a travel journal in New York, just for this trip. She's planning others." Troy laughed. "Reminds me of another travel writer I know."

"She should remember more of England this time." Elisa sighed, remembering an earlier together trip when Mia was at a younger age. "I feel left out."

"Oh, that independent spirit. I have to wonder who she inherited that attitude from." Troy teased.

"She took the Nikon with her too, but said she'll use the cell for pics to send right away."

"Turn on your phone. She sent a group text to you, me, and Ian with a few pictures from the airport of her and Mum."

Elisa grabbed her cell from her purse and checked. "Oh, my, word—she doesn't look like an eight year old, she looks like a teenager. Is that your mum? With short hair?"

"Yes. Hard to believe." Troy brought up the same text. "She's showing her age too. That is huge for her." Troy added. "I'm certain we've made the right choice to let Mia spend this time alone there with her wayward grandmum."

"That must be Dame Edith in the wheelchair. What a kind soul she appears to be."

"My guess is she's a good influence on Mum. I remember her always encouraging her to dance, but also to make time for family."

"Wise woman. Too bad Fiona only listened to half of the advice." Elisa kept bringing up the pictures one after the other. "When did our little girl grow up?"

"I don't know, but she sure has. No denying that." Troy peeked over Elisa's shoulder. "Your dad's napping so he hasn't opened these yet. Do you think he'll be okay seeing her across the pond without him, with her other grandparent?"

"I don't think it will bother him. He just misses his Bean."

"They've each built very different relationships with Mia."

"She loves them both. He'll be happy for her."

"That's more than I would have said for my mother before. She seemed quite jealous of Ian at times." Troy cozied up close to Elisa on the sofa.

"Maybe she's gotten over that now." Elisa burrowed into his embrace.

"The fact she's left London behind is a good thing for her personally." Troy nuzzled and gave Elisa's lips a quick peck. "I never thought I'd live to see her break away."

"Maybe she's finding herself, apart from all her monied, so-called friends."

"To pay for all this she has to be on a budget, or she'd already be broke. Life in the country is simpler, quieter, not Mum's usual speed."

"I hope she has peace, Troy. How can she not in a quaint cottage in the Cotswolds?"

"Edith was a real friend in the past. She sent Christmas cards every year even when my mum walked away from the intimacy of their friendship. I would like to have a better relationship with my mum one day." Troy lamented. "Sooner than later."

"You will." Elisa kissed him. "Keep loving her."

"It's hard for me to believe in anything during this sham of false accusations." He sat forward and wrung his hands together. "My reputation is ruined even if Blair doesn't get away with this. I've already been publically slandered. That sticks with people, you know. They remember the worst." Troy got up and walked to the front window. "None of it is fair."

Elisa struggled to get off the sofa. "Whoa, seven months and I'm a cow."

"Sorry, Hon." Troy went over to help her up, but she pulled him down beside her. "You are beautiful." He cupped her face and kissed her, a sweet lingering kiss. "I don't mean to be negative. You are the only one I can share with, and not be judged." He stretched out.

"You're right, everything about this is unfair. Some days I think we'll get through, and other days I think we're done for." She moved with great effort before laying her head on his chest. "What I do know for sure is that we are in it together, not alone."

"I'll go with that." Troy held her as close as he could with an extended belly in-between. "I thought of a name for our daughter." He patted the baby bump. "Not one of the fun names in the pool, but one I like."

"What?"

"Hope—Hope Elizabeth."

"I like that name." Elisa pulled Troy into a hug.

"No matter what happens," he said, "she is our gift of hope."

Chapter Forty-Three

Journals can later become books. Travel journals open the world for adventure. I know this because my mom was a travel news journalist before taking the job as a columnist for a local newspaper. She used to go everywhere, and later write about it. I could hardly sleep on the airplane because I wanted to see everything. The Cotswolds are different than Cornwall. One is ocean and fishing, and the other is inland and countryside. I like both, and I want to see more. ~ Mia's entry on the first page of her 'Map of the World' journal.

England

Mia was entranced. The quaint little cottage where she stayed was like a page out of a storybook or a fairytale. Cotswolds roads are lined with numerous unique cottages capped under straw-thatched roofs. Window-boxes burst with flowers of every color, and picket fence gates open up to flourishing gardens that greet you before entering brightly-painted wooden doors.

Dame Edith and Grandmum fixed up a guest room for Mia. It was tiny, had a twin bed, dresser drawers with an old mirror hanging above, and not much else. Rosebud wallpaper covered all the walls but not the ceiling. Decorative plates with English flowers and countryside scenes hung in rows. The room smelled heavenly with drying bunches of lavender.

Mia unpacked her luggage and crammed full all but one drawer. Edith suggested she leave one empty to fill with what keepsakes she might purchase to take home. For now she placed her two journals in there.

At four o'clock, tea awaited her in the living room.

"Are you sure you don't need a kip? The jet lag will catch up with you." Fiona poured the strong brew into teacups.

"It will probably hit me soon, but right now I'm wide awake." Mia took the saucer blooming with pink English roses presented to her.

"Earl Gray for today. We can try different loose leaf blends daily, or teabags if you prefer." Dame Edith uncovered the sugar bowl and showed Mia how to pinch a sprinkle instead of spooning a bigger serving. "Milk is poured in the cup before the tea. Fiona said you like it the English way."

"I do. Thank you so much." Mia was on her best behavior. She perched herself on the outer edge of the settee cushion. She gazed about the room, not to be nibby, but because every nook and cranny held photographs from ballet performances that seemed to span decades.

"Ta, petite ballerina."

"Am I properly dressed?" Mia tugged at the baggy smock overlaying her green leggings.

"You are lovely."

"Are you in any of these pictures, Grandmum?"

"Yes, many of them. Have a look about, and see if you recognize her." Edith suggested.

Mia set her cup and saucer on the end table with great care, and gave herself a private tour. "Oh, there you are, and here too." She ran her fingertips over the glass. "How beautiful you are." Pictures of the royal family intermingled on all four walls. "Is this both of you with the Queen Mother?" Mia stood awestruck.

"That was at the height of my career. Before..." Fiona stopped herself.

"Before the sky fell." Edith finished.

"Your china pieces are lovely." Mia admired the unique collection.

"All gifts while I was with the Royal Ballet and the Opera House in London."

"Are we going there while I am here?"

"Why yes we are, for a special performance and reception." Edith promised. "Now come dear, take tea with us and tell all about your journey, every detail like the good writer your grandmum boasts you to be."

Dame Edith claimed the walking tours would be too much for her, even in the wheelchair so she sent Fiona and Mia off on their own to board the train at Moreton-in-Marsh Railway Station. Besides, she said she'd traveled this adventure many a time before.

It was a six hour excursion of hidden villages called, The Secret Cottage Tour. After disembarking the train, guests board a Mercedes minibus. Fiona booked it for the two of them, alone. They were invited on a personal sightsee in a real thatched home owned by woman named Karen. It was called the Secret Cottage. Mia fell in love with the inglenook fireplaces where open log fires were blazing in June, unheard of in Sacramento where it was most likely already one hundred plus degrees. A buffet lunch and a traditional cream tea were included.

Described as a remarkable experience, both Fiona and Mia had to agree it was enchanting. The driver stopped every place Mia requested to take pictures of the mostly honey coloured limestone houses, and an array of other magnificent sights—historic manor houses, ancient churches, fords, all the wildlife roaming near brooks and streams, and amazing National Trust homes. There was so much more, almost like going back in time to the sixteenth century. Mia scratched away in her travel journal making notes and asking the names of what she didn't understand, like 'chocolate box' cottages.

"Gramps would love all these gardens."

"Yes, Ian appreciates such beauty and knows what is involved to grow and maintain the grounds." Fiona agreed.

"Are you still angry with him?" Mia turned to ask after clicking away with the Nikon.

"No, no. That has long since subsided." Fiona assured her with a turn of a hand in mid-air. "I've come to appreciate Ian more since I've returned.

"That makes me happy." Mia leaned into her Grandmum's side. "I knew you could be friends."

"How is he doing?" Fiona politely inquired.

"Better. I hope it lasts a long time. It will be hard to lose him."

"I am coming on holiday when your sister is born. Maybe Ian and I can catch up then, mend our differences." Fiona hesitated with a shyness unfamiliar. "Become friends."

"That will be wonderful!" Mia stated it with certainty. "And you know I've prayed for it a long time."

"Yes, warring grandparents are not what grandchildren dream about."

"Not this one."

"May I have a picture with you on the mobile so we can Instagram it to your parents? Let's stand over here by this grouping of trees." Fiona coaxed Mia over. "This landscaped parkland is breathtaking. Let's get the country house in the background."

Mia unstrapped her Nikon and left it on the ground. She leaned under her Grandmum's arm, held her cell phone high in the air, and angled it down. "Say cheese." She clicked three times.

"We can change it up and trade places." Mia ran around Fiona and posed from a profile stance instead of their previous up front and personal pic directly facing the camera. "Turn this way so we have a different background with the trees and the old car parked in the driveway."

Fiona copied Mia's positioning and spaced herself so the car was visible. "That's a vintage 1939 Vauxhall DX14 coupe, a rare one of six."

Mia spun around. "What?"

"I love vintage cars, especially pre-World War II." Fiona shrugged, then flashed a big smile showing her bleached white teeth.

"I didn't know that." Mia shot a repeated string of pictures. "Finished."

"I am sad to admit in the old days, I only dated men who owned these expensive vehicles and could take me for long rides in London." With a heavy sigh Fiona added. "I hope you won't judge too harshly for such vanity."

"What do I know about dating?" Mia checked the frames and deleted two.

"How did we turn out?"

"Looking spiffy."

"Is that a new word or is it slang?"

"Depends on your definition of slang." Mia winked.

"You sound like your Gramps. And you wink like him too."

"Thank you. I'll take that as a compliment." Mia snagged her digital Nikon.

The driver motioned them back to the minibus.

Walking across the manicured grassy lawn, Fiona continued their conversation. "You are gifted with words. That is a connection with Ian. Writing and reading."

"Like ballet and symphonies are with you." Mia pointed out.

"I used to consider Ian—unrefined."

"And now?"

"He has more class than most of the people I know in London and Sacramento."

"Have you ever told him that?" Mia arched an eyebrow.

"Oh, no." Fiona shook her head and fanned out her hands.

"Why not?"

"I wouldn't want to give him any ideas."

"Like?"

"Well, you know."

"Maybe that he has class?" Mia got to the car first and stared up into Fiona's eyes. "That he isn't just a smelly old, undereducated fisherman?"

"Oh dear. You knew that was my opinion?"

"Everyone around knew, Grandmum. It showed."

"I am so sorry." Fiona opened the door for Mia. "I am truly sorry."

"You can tell him when you come home."

"You make it sound simple."

"Because it is." Mia belted herself in. "You tell the truth."

Fiona stood still holding onto the door handle. She opened her mouth to speak, then closed it and shut the door. She walked around to the other side and got in. While belting in she said. "Was I as terrible as I am beginning to realize?"

"We love you. Nobody is perfect."

"For one so short and young, you make a lot more sense than the crowd I've been hanging around for far too long." The Mercedes rolled back onto the dusty one-lane road hitting a couple of bumps before getting on the way. The driver apologized from the front seat.

"It's quite okay." Fiona waved off his concern. "Where to next?"

"We're leaving Oxfordshire and heading to Gloucestesrshire."

"This adult is learning from this youngster." Fiona tapped Mia on the top of her head.

"And I learn a lot from you."

"Such as?"

"You have to make sacrifices to pursue your dreams. To work hard and practice to achieve your goals." Mia took Fiona's hand in hers.

The driver smiled in the rear view mirror and drove past a well, and a barn. "This is what we call a dovecote." He told Mia. "It's a small building for birds."

Fiona picked up the travel journal and handed it over with a pen. "New word."

A field of lavender wafted by. Mia blurted out. "There aren't any traffic lights, anywhere." She recorded her observation with an illustration of roadside signage.

"Round-a-bouts and roads barely wide enough for a lorry. No electric lights." The chauffeur noted. "The cities have the traffic, and stop and go lights."

"America must have been like this a while ago. And full of the old cars you like, Grandmum." Mia watched out the window. "It's quiet here too. Cows moo. I've heard ducks quack, and birds chirping in the trees on the parklands."

"Nobody rushes about in the Cotswolds. You've probably noticed villagers riding their bicycles, and strolling roadside paths." The driver pointed to a young couple walking together.

"What are those brown baskets strapped on the front or back of the bicycles?" Mia asked. "And all the bikes are no-speeders. No wires and brake grips on the handlebars."

"Most are hand-woven wicker or cane." The driver answered. "Basket weavers were once quite popular in each village. The back basket is usually a hamper for tea time. What you Americans call a picnic."

"Thank you, sir." Mia wrote furiously as he spoke.

"Call me Roger. A pleasure to be of assistance with any other inquiries."

"Ta." Fiona answered.

"I'm happy to be with you again." Mia held her breath for a few seconds. "It hurt my feelings when you left and didn't say good-bye." Tiny crystal clear pearls clustered in the corners of her eyes. "Mom gave me your letter, but I didn't understand why you left."

"Please forgive me for my foolishness." Fiona cast her glance down. "It was a selfish thing to do. I hope our time together here can mend any breaches I caused."

"I forgive you." Mia answered. "I don't know what 'breaches' means, but I can look it up in the dictionary." She propped herself against Fiona and nested like a baby bird. "You are my dovecote, Grandmum."

Chapter Forty-Four

Carrying another human life within you changes choices you make about what you do, and don't do. It's that simple. I haven't had an alcoholic drink since my test was positive. I don't even take a baby aspirin, just vitamins and iron horse pills. Naps are one of my daily activities. Six mini-meals are spaced apart instead of the traditional three big ones. Weather permitting, I walk in our neighborhood, usually with my dad, so we aren't power walking, more of a senior and prego pace with sudden bursts of speed that peter out when either of us needs to recharge. We cover a couple of miles and chat the entire time. I've gleaned much from my dad during these treks, and I treasure getting to know him more intimately. The baby hears these conversations. It comforts me to know she will recognize the sound of Dad's voice by the time she's born. ~ Elisa's heart.

Family Matters

Elisa stroked the tiny pink dress and pressed it to her heart. Mia had worn it home from the hospital, a gift from her then editor and boss who had since passed away from cancer. She and Troy had given away most of Mia's baby clothes and furniture, not expecting to have another child. The plan had been to wait two or three years and try again. Then it became four to five years. This box held what she'd saved as mementos to give Mia one day when she had her first baby.

"I'd forgotten how little the wee ones arrive." She told her father.

"Aye, yer be that small one time too, but you wailed loud enough to bring the cottage tumbling down." Ian laughed at the memory.

"Life passes so fast, like a whirlwind circling, almost like a tease, then whoosh, it leaves without asking." She folded the dress and laid it on the yellowed tissue paper at the top of the stack of clothing.

"That be a prolific statement." Ian adjusted his glasses on the middle of his nose, and looked up from the novel he'd gone back to reading. "You be a woman of wisdom."

"Oh, Dad. I am a woman lacking wisdom." Elisa sighed and closed the lid on the box.

"How can you say that?"

"Because it's true. I've made some major blunders, especially lately."

"Tell me." Ian pulled the recliner lever which lowered the raised footrest with a cranking thud. He sat upright in the chair. "What unwise things be you thinking yer be doing?"

"I talked Troy into waiting to turn Blair in, hoping his boss would admit to his indiscretions and fix it so the company wouldn't go under." Elisa admitted. "I was more concerned about Troy's job and our loss of such a lucrative income." She shifted on the loveseat and pushed the box aside.

"That be human nature."

327

"Well, it's costing us more than I ever imagined."

"Blair be bringing this on all involved. How sad for his wife and sons. You and Troy did nothing wrong." Ian held her gaze.

"But I did, Dad. I focused on the money. We live quite comfortably, we always have. I don't know what it means to struggle." She winced and placed a fist behind her at the small of her back. "It was a self-motivated demand. I didn't listen to my husband's wisdom."

"There yer be rocking a marital topic of the ages. Spouses heeding one another's advice." Ian's brow creased in layers of consideration.

"In this case, I was wrong. And you and Troy convinced me to let Mia go on holiday with Fiona. I was a firm no. Yet, every text, every picture tells me it was the best thing that could happen for the two of them." She held out her cell and showed him the last pictures that had come in an hour ago—happy faces, a jimjam pillow fight, tea with Edith, some kind of a reception.

Ian took the phone and swished his finger to the side on the screen to view each photograph. "These be smashing pictures. What a time they be having! Mia be not wanting to be coming home." He grinned, toothy and wide.

"She flies in the day after tomorrow." Elisa let her excitement show.

"Me have missed me Bean too." He returned her mobile.

"I guess we should get ready for our doctor appointments."

Ian took a long look at his watch. "We be having a couple of hours yet."

"Actually we need to leave in about thirty minutes in case of traffic." She rose and took the multi-colored, lettered, *It's a girl,* wrapped box with her. "Do you need to shower?"

"Did me getting ready last night to save time." Ian looked to his watch again, and scowled.

"Okay then, your doc first and mine next." Elisa called out from the stairs.

Ian shook his wrist several times and put the ticking face to his ear. "Perfect rhythm." He stood and looked down the hallway to his room, and scrunched his face in quizzical contemplation before sitting back down and reading his book.

Ian's appointment only lasted fifteen minutes. The doctor asked questions, he answered while Elisa sat and listened. Just a quick check of his heart rate, blood pressure, vision, and hearing, then blood and urine labs they did next door. They scheduled his next appointment and left.

"That was, quick. Did she weigh you in?" Elisa started the SUV.

"Not this time." Ian responded.

"So they usually do weigh you in." She persisted.

"Yes. Last time they told me be losing too much weight in a month."

"All the more reason to weigh you in today. Being pregnant I can say that it's not my favorite part of my visit, but necessary."

"Maybe they can be putting me on the scales at your doctor's office? Still, they measure by pounds, not stones." Ian countered.

"I can convert it for you."

"We be almost there?" Ian rolled down his window and poked his head out.

"Just around the block. I guess we could have walked for exercise." Elisa's stomach growled. "Maybe grab lunch after we leave? I schedule these that way, I eat after, not before."

"Because you be weighing more?" He popped his head back inside the car and the electric window went up.

"Pretty much." She laughed. "I guess you're onto me."

They parked right in front of the entrance and hurried inside.

"Ten minutes early. Not bad." Elisa checked in at the window, grabbed a magazine and placed it in the chair next to her until Ian got there after a pit stop to the bathroom. "You have to be quick here or you stand."

He viewed the room and commented. "This be cheerier than me doc's. Nice surgery. Nice paintings and comfortable chairs." He ran his palms over the thick padding of the high back chair and scooted in the seat until positioned in the center. "Made for short legs."

"Get comfy, they run behind an hour or so here."

"Brought me book." He reached to take it from one of his cargo pant pockets. "Be liking these trousers Troy got me more and more. Lots of compartments for storage."

Elisa raised her hand to cover a laugh. "You can never have too many pockets."

"How long you be in the family way?" Ian struck up a conversation with the young woman the other side of him.

The pudgy blonde responded. "If that means pregnant, I'm eight months, due in twenty-nine more days." She reached out to shake. "I'm Delia. And who might you be, and from where?"

"Ian Darrow, and me be Cornish. Cagwith, Cornwall, England." He answered. "Here with me daughter Elisa, she be seven months."

"Hello, Ian's daughter." Delia leaned forward and waved.

"Elisa Kensington, nice to meet you."

Ian continued conversing, asking questions and answering just as many. Within minutes he had a following of expectant mothers encircling him, chairs pulled from across the room to face him. The office transitioned from quiet to a bit rowdy, laughter prevalent, when the nurse came to announce the next patient's turn—no one got up.

"Delia Hamilton?" A young man in green scrubs called out a third time.

"Oh no, over here." She stood and bear hugged Ian on her way by. "Bring your dad to all your future visits." She made Elisa promise before departing to the weigh station on the other side of the oak door. "Wonderful to meet you Ian from Cornwall!" Delia shouted. "Thank you for sharing about your fishing days."

Elisa rolled her eyes, huffed, and raised the magazine she was reading to eyebrow height. Her eyes darted from one inquisitive woman to another, and their focus. One of the women standing grabbed Delia's chair and scooted deeper into the inner circle. Ian was demonstrating by hand gestures how to steer in the open sea, and reciting poetry by ancient mariners.

"Your father is fascinating." A woman loomed closer to Elisa. "I'd keep one like him all to myself. I'm Virginia."

"I'm the fascinating fisherman's daughter." She answered but no one was paying attention to her. "Elisa, my name is Elisa." She babbled on.

Basking in the moment, Ian halted when Elisa's name was called.

"Come now. It be your turn in the queue." He bid farewell to the room full of hormonal soon-to-be-mommies and ushered a reluctant Elisa past the door to the awaiting scales. "Cheers ladies, and to your wee ones too." Ian waved to a gush of sighs, and well wishes asking him to return.

"Ugh. Up four pounds." Elisa groaned stepping down.

"It be less in stones." Ian encouraged her.

Once settled in the fourth exam room, the two sat beside each other along a side wall.

"The doctor will be in with you soon." The nurse took vitals, then left.

"Dad, what were you doing out there?"

"Socializing. What else be there for a man my age to do in a surgery waiting room?"

She mulled over the response. "Spend time with your daughter."

"Me be right next to you." He pointed out.

"You had a room full of third trimester groupies hanging on your every word."

"It be the accent. Yank women love the accent." He shrugged. "What be a bloke to do?"

The doctor interrupted their discussion. "Hello, Mrs. Kensington. And who háve we here? Could this possibly be the gentleman entertaining a packed waiting room of late term pregnant women? Well, if you didn't make my usually aggravating behind schedule lull more interesting today, Mr.—?"

"My father, Ian."

"Sir, I should pay you to come and sit here on a weekly basis." She introduced herself, "Dr. Winona Farrell. I am Dr. Allegra's partner and filling in while she's on vacation. Now Elisa, Let's go over your last lab results. Your blood sugar is elevated high enough it was flagged. Since it's the only time this pregnancy, I'll check weekly from now on. Your blood pressure is up too. Under any stress lately?"

"Yes, definitely more stress than usual."

"Can you manage that stress level to get it down?"

"I can try."

"Best for the baby to be as calm as possible until delivery. And are we still considering a Caesarean-Section?"

"Troy and I are still discussing that possibility."

"Okay." She cocked her head and reread the computer screen. "Troy Kensington is your husband? I see."

Elisa paused, then asked, "Did you watch the news broadcast?"

"Yes I did. I can see why you are under stress at this time. You need to find a way to not let it interfere with your pregnancy. Do you practice any form of meditation?"

"I pray."

"That works too. My job is to help you bring your baby to full-term, and experience a safe delivery." She checked her screen again. "It says you go to a mommy exercise class?"

"Yes, two to three times a week." Elisa took a list out of her purse.

"Good. You have some questions for me?"

"A few." She handed over the list.

Dr. Farrell scanned the list and said. "Excellent questions. You are pro-active in self-care. I'll email you these answers this evening after I do some research. You have the same email?"

"Everything is the same."

"Well then, Ian, may I ask you to step in the hall while I examine your daughter?"

"Everything be okay?" Ian stood to leave.

"Yes. It's a routine exam." Dr. Farrell stood and opened the door.

Elisa was quiet on the drive home. After lunch they'd picked up a roasted chicken at the market for dinner. Ian threw salad mixings in the shopping cart with some broccoli.

"You be telling me if something be wrong with the baby." Ian said, more of a statement than a question.

"I would, Dad. They're being cautious with me. I'm thirty-five. It's a magic number for pregnancy. Puts me in a higher risk bracket."

"What be the meaning of that? All be okay, or not okay?"

"It means that they will be diligently keeping tabs. I go in every week from now on, have labs done. Things like that." A long yawn overtook her and she gave into the stretch of it.

"How will you be destressing during this legal battle?" He persisted.

"Prayer, meditation, walking with you, Mommy exercise, letting you men do all the cooking." She watched for his reaction. "Just seeing if you were listening."

"Troy knows?"

"Yes. He would have come with me today, but the lawyer called him in for a briefing. They're getting to serious business. Found holes in Blair's statements and figures that have nothing to do with Troy." She added. "This could be our saving grace."

"I be hoping so for both your sakes." Ian watched the lawns of Sir William Land Park flow by. He grew to love this patch of green across from the city university. He frequently visited the zoo nearby the Town of Fairytales from the King Arthurian Courts. Even the Fun Land where children were the kings and queens that ruled within the railway borders of that adventure kingdom now be feeling like home.

He went on walks along the pond where the swans and ducks raised their cygnets and ducklings peacefully together in protected beauty. He dearly admired the commitment the surrounding neighbourhoods shared to preserve these landmark treasures for their children.

"Dad." Elisa repeated. "Dad."

"You be needing something, Bean?"

"No, Dad it's me, Elisa."

"So it be." Ian answered.

"I thought we could go for a walk while we wait for Troy."

"Let me put the food away inside the fridge, then me be meeting you on the porch."

"Leave the chicken on the stovetop. It's just for fifteen minutes. I don't want to have to reheat it. Troy is coming home for an early dinner."

"Righto." Ian shuffled along with the grocery bags.

Elisa waddled to the red wicker chair on the sprawling brick porch, and plunked herself down with an exasperated heave-ho. "I'm the Fat Cow Lady of Land Park. My besmirched royal title. Even my obstetrician saw the slanderous news report. Who else saw it? And there's more to come. But I have to destress. That's easy enough, just check out of the reality I'm living. Don't you dare cry, that won't solve anything. And here you are talking out loud to yourself like a lunatic." She flipped a potted plant with her foot and watched it roll to the steps but stop short of traveling the distance below.

She massaged her belly in long circular stokes and felt the baby kick against the motion. "Even you have something to say. Not a lot of room left in that sack." Elisa traced each kick and fist jab. Then came the summersault, a complete flip that extended her skin's stretch ability to a new limit. She watched knees, and a big head tuck and roll. Then nothing. Quiet. Stillness.

Chapter Forty-Five

Ballet is pure grace in movement. The dancer makes the most strenuous physical action appear to be effortless, fluid balance in unbroken rhythm. Performers are storytellers. They speak with each step and leap. A lifetime of practice absorbs all of the person committed to this talent, perfected with their troupe family. There is precious little left outside of the inner circle. It is a high price to pay for physical pain and the isolation from relationships that may have existed before. That loss is most times, irreparable. ~ Dame Edith's warning to young Fiona at the beginning of her career.

London ~ The Company

The reception had been a complete surprise as Dame Edith had intended. Fiona stepped into the banquet room holding Mia's hand while they pushed Edith's wheelchair with the sole purpose to honour her former mentor for years of faithful instruction and guidance. As the crowd rose clapping, she assumed it was for all for The Royal's beloved sentinel. Not until she reached the front table did the realization fall upon her, that she too was being honoured for her lifetime of dance.

"Grandmum, your name is written across the stage above beautiful pictures." Mia gasped.

Speechless, Fiona set the brakes on Edith's chair in front of the seat bearing her name on the place card, next to one with hers.

Single red roses tied in elegant satin ribbons lay next to their sterling silver flatware. Scrolled parchment with the evening's program rested on fine white china plates.

One look at the stage changed everything. Massive black and white posters canvassed the wall with one photograph after another of the ballerina and her mentor. Pictures alone, together, with the Royal family, the Queen, and dignitaries from other countries. Opaque glitter lettering in artistic cursive spelled out both of their names for all to see—Dame Edith and Fiona Rose.

"My beloved friend," Edith told Fiona, "I share this night with you."

Fiona collapsed to her knees, her face resting on Edith's plum chiffon gown, a waterfall of tears bursting forth that she could not stop. A weathered hand caressed her trembling head.

"Come, sit beside me and share our cherished memories with your granddaughter."

Mia paused in absolute wonder. She leaned and whispered in Fiona's ear. Stunned to silence, Fiona rose and let Mia seat her, and push her chair in toward the table, then join them herself. Frederick and Tessa were seated across the round table of eight with the director and his associate, beside the Prima ballerina assoluta. The Company's music director led the symphony in the opening instrumental.

So began a magical evening.

Fiona's name was called to come on stage and speak after two hours into the program. An escort came along side of her and led the way up the stairs to center stage where the podium waited as it had for Dame Edith before her.

Fiona adjusted the gooseneck holding the mic, and cleared her throat. "Gracious Company, fellow dancers, and supporters of ballet, my sincere gratitude for this unmerited honour. Truly this acknowledgement solely belongs to my dear mentor and friend, Dame Edith. She spoke with eloquence and benevolence minutes ago. She changed many of our lives with her committed instruction, and guidance through the ranks all the years she gave unselfishly from her heart, body, mind, and soul, to continue to make the Royal Ballet the treasure it is today. And I hope, will be for generations yet to come."

Mia's heart filled as she absorbed her Grandmum's words.

"I stand before you, so undeserving in this capacity." Her voice wavered, her body trembled. She steadied herself and gripped the podium edges for support. Lifting her head, she scanned the room and gazed directly into the faces of the many she knew seated before her.

A hush settled throughout the room as Fiona stood mute.

"I left you with a bitter spirit." Her voice wavered. "Not appreciative for the decades of privilege bestowed upon me by my teachers, directors, choreographers, and the love of one dear woman who saved my life when I fell from the sky." Her arm extended toward Edith.

"Before my injury, many expected me to achieve the position of Prima ballerina assoluta. As did I." Fiona paused. "The true joy does not come in the final accomplishment, but in the journey. And mine was blessed beyond measure both in dance, and in the gift of family. Tonight I am honoured to introduce to you my granddaughter, Mia." Fiona directed the spotlight off herself toward a shy, surprised Mia who rose, and curtsied in perfect form toward the audience.

"How proud I am to tell you Mia loves to dance, and takes ballet lessons in America where she lives with my son and his wife." Fiona paused as if the moment took her breath away.

"In brevity I will close with my deepest expression of gratitude, so long overdue." Fiona struggled to keep her composure, her voice straining, years of suppressed emotions surfacing unguarded. She lifted an arm to the photographs behind her. "This woman will always fondly remember her Royal family, and hopes to encourage others to use their talent, their gifting, to learn the hard work of dance to bring that beauty and grace into the lives of people around the world. Ta, dear ones. And a heart of thankfulness to our patron, Her Majesty the Queen."

The room rose to thunderous applause to bid her farewell. The same gentleman approached to escort Fiona back to her seat.

She stood behind Dame Edith in her wheelchair, Mia at their side, and curtsied.

Back at the cottage, Edith and Fiona chatted after Mia dozed off in her gala frock. Tucking her in bed, Fiona slipped off her ballet flats and slipped a hot water bottle she'd requested upon her feet. She covered her with several heavy, handmade quilts, fluffed her pillow, turned off the light, and closed the door.

"Did you tip the driver? Has he left?" Fiona asked.

"Yes. We were most generous in gratuity."

Earl Gray steeped in a pot on the table between the two women.

"Tonight, dear Fiona, you once again soared through the air." Edith commented with obvious pride.

"Those words, my admission, should have happened decades ago."

"They were quite timely tonight." Edith stated, and drew her blanket up over her flannel jimjams and shabby fleece-lined slippers. "Some people never free themselves as you did."

"Many came up to me afterward to express their own sense of gratitude despite losses due to injury or falling down in the ranks too." Fiona relaxed in her thermals and slip-on booties. She clasped the toasty wool blanket she cozied up in, and pulled it snug to her neck. "And this is perfect tonight for our last evening in the Cotswolds, before Mia flies back to the States."

"She reminds me of you, the same spark of determination illuminates in her eyes, in her drive and endurance. She will excel at what she puts her mind to." Edith raised her feet to rest on the table. "Time to elevate after sitting for most of the day in the limousine and at the gala."

"You were so kind to have them include me. I know this event was meant for you alone." Fiona drew a pillow to her chest and leaned her chin into the soft feathery stuffed fabric.

"Once I told the company you had returned, and offered my suggestion, they immediately acted to create a duel celebration." Edith reassured her. "You never grasped how dearly you are considered and remembered. Think of your friend Frederick. He is a lifelong devotee."

"He and Tessa are the only true friends I've made since I came home." Fiona declared. "And you, you have always been my kindred spirit. The faithful one when I myself strayed."

"I saw several of your Londoners there, in the back. What they must have paid to acquire those tickets at the last minute to get a table added. The event has been sold out for months."

"Money talks." Fiona frowned, her pale brow wrinkled in furrowed rows that smoothed out with her next sentence. "I saw Edward with that young ballerina Lydia beside him. His latest acquisition. He can talk and buy his way into anything, anywhere."

"He did greet you then?"

"Oh, my, yes. How pompous. He appeared when I was with the company directors for publicity photos." Fiona's tune changed. "But did you see my Mia shoot with the mobile she'd slipped in and out of her little clutch purse?"

"She could have been issued a correspondence press pass this evening." Edith commented with earnest admiration. "Though she was dignified in her every approach, respectful to ask permission first to take each new photograph."

"She took lovely shots with Frederick and his Tessa, and you and me with her. That is all I care about. And those selfies she is so adept at taking."

"Your Mia is poised in how she carries herself, and in her speech." Edith complimented. "Very articulate for one so young."

"Edith, will you reconsider spending tomorrow evening at the Townsend's villa in London?"

"Tomorrow is for you and your granddaughter to say ta to each other and her new friends too. I had tonight and we have all next morning and afternoon to bid our farewells. You and I shall ask the lovely Townsend couple to the cottage many a time after Mia returns to California." Edith sipped her tea. "We have much to discuss, papers to sign. It is important to me that you carry on my legacy."

"I am honoured to fulfil my commitment." Fiona set her cup on the table.

"I tire easily these days. At my age one must limit their out-of-town excursions with a rest in between no matter how delightful."

"I hope we did not weary you to exhaustion this evening." Fiona patted the toes of Edith's slippers.

"It is a pleasant kind of tiredness." Dame Edith basked in the afterglow of a once in a lifetime presentation. "I will sleep well this night." She rested her head against the chair pillow.

"Mia certainly is slumbering without a care."

"As we should, Fiona dear. Leave our tea to be tended to in the morning. Will you help me to bed now?"

Fiona rose to aid Edith out of the chair, then walked her slow and steady to her room. One arm looped under the wobbly old woman's shoulder for a firm but gentle hold. Then a second time, she prepared a hot water bottle in its cozy cover, then she pulled covers up snug, turned off the light, and closed the door.

Fiona and Mia shared their final dinner together at the charming villa of Fredrick's Grandmum. "Frederick, dinner was better than any restaurant in Londontown." Fiona acclaimed. "Mia and I have so enjoyed this visit. You and Tessa have made us feel at home." She hugged husband, then his wife warmly. "Ta, my friends."

"It's going to be hard for me to leave tomorrow." Mia spoke up. "Ta, for everything."

"You are both welcome anytime. Please do come back to see us young Kensington."

"Maybe my parents will let me come on holiday in the summers from now on." Mia looked hopefully to her grandmum for approval.

"Oh, how lovely that would be." Fiona wholeheartedly agreed.

Tessa and Frederick stood in the bedroom doorway with an extra quilt. "If you need hot water bottles, they're in the bathroom linen cupboard. Should be warm enough temps tonight. Sweet dreams." Tessa kissed Mia on the cheek.

"We'll be in the room across the hall." Frederick added before leading his wife there.

Fiona asked. "You don't mind that we are sharing the guest room?" She and Mia settled on the queen-size bed heaped high with crocheted and patchwork quilts after she'd filled bottles for them.

345

"Our last night slumber party." Mia answered. "We can talk until we fall asleep."

Fiona turned over the bedding and Mia crawled in first after slipping out of her comfy lamb's wool house shoes, the ones Miss Edith got her on their only shopping trip. Fiona left her tatty pair next to Mia's. They cuddled for warmth, sheets and quilts pinched up to their noses, and hot water bottles toasty on their feet.

"This is not like July in California. If the sun is out, it's hot, one hundred degrees." Mia shivered. "It's a trick when you see sunlight, like, 'Ha, ha, fooled you!'"

"You are just getting used to things here." Fiona was heartsick thinking of her departure.

"Not the crazy, drivers on the wrong side of the road!" Mia said. "I will miss calling trucks—lorries, pajamas—jimjams, cell phones—mobiles, naps—kips, and referring to 'the continent'. I love the way people talk on this side of the pond."

"You probably understand your Gramps better now."

"I think I do, though I already knew not to call him anything but Cornish." Mia giggled.

"I'll miss you more than I can say." Fiona whispered.

Mia hesitated. "You aren't moving back to live with us again, are you?" She turned from her back to be face-to-face, hands still holding onto the covers for warmth.

"No. I'll be helping Edith with some things for a while."

"I never saw you cook and clean like this at Mom and Dad's, the way you do in Miss Edith's cottage." Mia stated rather factually. "She needs someone to rally round her."

"She gets tuckered out. I earn my keep doing the wash, scrubbing, cooking, and I bake too." Fiona fluffed her fingers through the short layered hair she was still getting used to.

"I don't mean to be disrespectful, but the folks back home would be way surprised." Mia thought better of what she'd said. "In a good way."

"Oh, don't worry. I know I behaved badly. That's not a secret." Fiona turned to face Mia. "Please carry this memory of me in your heart too."

Mia curled under Fiona protective wing. "Grandmum, you know the circus is not the same since you left. We can't put on a performance without you." She buried her head to muffle a weepy burst of tears. "What am I going to do without you?"

"I'm coming for your sister's birth. I promise." Fiona drew Mia to her chest, cleaving close. "I've made some mistakes in the past. This distance will not come between us. We are stronger because of this fortnight together. You keep writing in your journals, share them when you arrive home. And always know I am a mobile call near." She paused. "And keep praying."

"I will pray for you." Mia hugged her. "Gramps does too."

"He does?" Fiona pulled back in surprise. "Someone sure has been. Please be sure to give Ian the books, and my others gifts. And do remember me to him."

"I will. All is packed up in my suitcases. I'll give everyone their presents." She assured her.

"What an adventure we've had." Fiona reflected.

"I just wanted to be with you, but so much more happened." Mia looked up into Fiona's eyes. "And, I love the short hair."

"I guess you can say I've been reborn in more ways than one. The hair is still an adjustment for me."

"It's very California." Mia encouraged. "It will grow on you."

"Are you excited about your sister?"

"Yes! I can't wait to hold her. I asked if we can share my room. Mom and Dad have a bassinette next to their bed, for when they bring her home."

"Your dad sent me the surgery date they got yesterday, so I can get my ticket and be there a few days before she's born."

Mia snuggled. At this moment all was right in her scrap of a world. She closed her eyes dreaming of her family all together again under the big top. Drifting off to sleep, she tried to imagine what a cute baby acrobat her sister would be.

Chapter Forty-Six

Summer passes, and the temperatures cool, though August is by far the hottest month. Being nine months pregnant at the end of a season of one hundred plus degree heat can be unbearable. Relief comes in limited ways; swimming pools, spiked air conditioners, popsicles, and pretty much living in your pregnancy swimsuit with a tank top overlay. Easy to do at home. Venturing out means shorts and that same tank top, flip flops, and frozen bottled waters that thaw in your SUV cup holder, and sweat as much as you do. ~ Elisa's pregnancy lament to Ian's third trimester groupies at her doctor's office.

Delivery

The baby's scheduled August nineteenth Caesarean delivery date was two days away. Elisa carried up front and could barely waddle. Troy had to help her on and off the sofa. Complications so far had been edema, high blood sugar, and blood pressure. Concern for possible placenta previa was under watch. The temperature was in the one hundreds and Elisa was appropriately miserable.

Fiona flew in the previous day and was dealing with jet lag. She took a kip in her old room which had remained as it was before she'd left. She and Ian had gone to Streets the night before for fish and chips while Troy and Elisa packed the bags for her maternity room at the hospital.

"I'll get it." Troy called out when the landline rang. "Hello."

"I've been trying to reach you all day on your cell." Robert Stanton's voice sounded frantic.

"Forgot to charge it this morning. What's up?"

"The police are coming to arrest you. I've done everything I can to stay this off until after the baby's delivery. Blair's lawyer started pushing yesterday because of some possible new evidence."

Troy closed the bedroom door where Elisa lay asleep, and walked downstairs to the empty family room. "Can't anything be done?"

"I am so sorry. Legally no. He has to copy this information to me when he gets it, but the police will act on what they've already received." Robert paused. "You need to tell Elisa."

"How?" mumbled Troy as he disconnected. He dropped the phone, missing the cradle. The room floated around him, swirling and shifting in jagged movements. He gripped the chair cushion under him and kicked the ottoman into the coffee table, then picked up the phone and slammed it in place.

Fiona stood in the hall. "It is bad news isn't it?"

"I'm going to be arrested today for a crime I didn't commit." Bleary-eyed, he stared past his mother to the wall behind her. "My baby girl will be born without me there. Elisa will go through this alone."

Fiona moved slowly to the couch across from him and sat. "I can't believe this is happening." She cleared her raspy throat. "What can I do to help?"

"No one can help." Troy sat stoic. "I have to wake up my wife and tell her." He rose as he spoke and headed upstairs, then turned. "Mum, please take Ian and Mia to the store, to the park, anywhere. I need some time alone with Elisa. Take my keys."

"I'll go out back and get them. We'll pick up groceries for dinner. Mia wanted to go for a drive anyway." She walked over to hug him. "Text me when you're ready for us to come home."

"Thanks." Troy straightened his back. "Thank you for being here to help. Elisa is going to need you more now than ever before." He kissed her cheek and took slow steps to the top landing.

Fiona lingered until she heard the master room door click shut. She uttered a prayer for help and grabbed her purse and Troy's keys before opening the patio slider. Mustering up all she had in her, she called out cheerily. "Three on a mission to market for dinner."

Troy watched Elisa sleep fitfully. She tried to shift her cumbersome body to the right, then to the left, but ended up in the same position where she began. Her breathing seemed labored to him. He sat beside her on the edge of the bed. She did look huge but he'd never tell her. It wasn't a negative kind of big, it was quite beautiful. The baby slept in front, he imagined pretty much curled up in the safety of her womb the same way she curled to accommodate the life within her. He wanted to remember the two of them like this so he took the picture in his mind and stored in in his memory before awakening her.

"Elisa." Troy whispered. "Can we talk for a few minutes?" He stroked her straggly hair.

"How long have I been asleep?" She batted her eyelids open trying to focus in on the blaring light. "I'm still tired." Her head fell back to the pillow.

"It's mid-afternoon. You've been up here for a couple of hours. Lean on me, he gave her a gentle tug forward."

"Impossible task. Baby daughter does not want to wake up either." She grunted in a low moan, then struggled to raise to a sitting position. "It's the swelling. Makes movement laborious." She lifted one leg, with great effort. "I have cankles, enormous, ugly cankles. I want my real ankles back."

Troy said nothing.

"I thought you would make a joke or something." Her eyes searched Troy evasive ones.

"We need to talk."

She'd been waiting for this the closer it came to the day of the baby's birth. It had been quiet for a while on the legal front, blissfully quiet. All they needed was a few more days. "Okay."

"My lawyer called." Troy hedged before continuing. "He believes the police will come to arrest me today because Blair is supposedly handing over new evidence."

"This incriminates you?" Her head shot up.

"It must. So far it has been his word against mine. His claims I altered the books, not him as I stated. Claiming all is in my handwriting. You know the lies."

"I do." She scooted to sit next to him. "Are you sure they'll come for you today?"

"Robert is certain. He called to warn me so I could prepare you."

"We both knew it could come down to this." She blinked at the bright light. "I have dad and your mum here to help. Mia too."

"It should be me."

"I can't stand the thought of you in jail." Her voice cracked. "Will they take you away in handcuffs, in a patrol car?" The walls seemed to compress in on them. She held her breath.

"That's pretty much how they arrest people."

"Will it be better if you and I go to the station and you turn yourself in?"

"I don't know. It may spare Mia and Ian the trauma of witnessing my arrest. My mum can handle it. She took them out on an errand so I can talk with you."

"Fiona is changed, for the better." Elisa blurted without giving thought to what she said. "I'll be okay. No labor this time. In the hospital for a few days with help around the clock. Don't worry." *She didn't know how to comfort him and she dare not tell him the truth—she was scared, more than she'd ever been in her life before. What if something goes wrong?*

"My place is to be with my wife when our daughter is born." Troy punched a pillow. "Blair did this on purpose."

Elisa flinched and instinctively threw her arms over her belly. "Troy, I need you to stay calm. We both know we're in trouble if I'm the stable one in this family."

"Please forgive me." Troy's torso trembled. "I will see you through this as best I can. I promise."

She tried to hold him but the baby was in the way so she lowered her head to his shoulder. "When will your mum return?"

"When I text her to bring them home." Troy turned to reassure her. "Only she knows, Ian and Mia are in the dark about this."

"Okay, that's where we work from for now."

"So you want them at home or out for this next step?"

"Maybe we should hold a family meeting?" She suggested. "Go ahead and text Fiona and I'll shower before they get here."

Troy pressed his lips on hers before she got up. He stood and offered his hands to hold onto. At first she waved him off, but after trying on her own, she accepted his help.

"Thanks, this fat lady needed a lift off." She waggled her waddle to the bathroom doorway. "We will get through this, together." Elisa tried to blow a kiss.

Troy tapped in his mum's number. *Come home. We'll do this together. Will tell them when you get here.* He stopped, then wrote. *Thanks for assistance. I needed you. Love, Troy.*

"Big top meeting for all family members." Troy announced when the traveling troupe arrived home with the dinner groceries. "Everyone in the family room."

Ian and Fiona hauled the bags to the kitchen counter. "We thought beef kabobs might be the ticket for tonight. Simple, healthy, and light enough for Elisa." Fiona put the prepared packages in the meat tray and closed the fridge.

"Is this about the baby?" Mia pressed. "Is she coming early?" Her eagerness was obvious.

"No." Troy caught his breath. "This is about me."

"Oh." Mia sat between her grandparents on the couch. The excitement drained from her voice as she nestled in the snug space available in the middle.

Elisa and the baby joined Troy on the loveseat.

"My lawyer called to warn me what to expect." He inhaled a deep breath, then exhaled a slow, long draft of air. "The police are coming to our home to arrest me sometime today."

Silence buffeted the room.

Ian spoke first. "Be there nothing to be done?" He placed a protective arm around Mia.

"Apparently not." Fiona mumbled.

All eyes fell upon Mia. She scooted off the sofa, went to her father, and sat on his lap. "I know you are innocent, Dad." Her arms enveloped him. She said nothing more.

"I am so sorry you have to go through this." Troy held her, visibly shaken.

"Will I get to go see you, in the jail?" She whimpered.

"I don't know what is ahead. I hope so." His large hand intertwined with hers.

Fiona hung her head and began to cry. Ian reached over to comfort her, but he had no words. The harder he tried, the more nothing came to mind, so he let her lean on his shoulder when she drew near. Without thinking, he stroked her hair, then rested his head on hers. The quiet in the room held all their thoughts and fears captive without protest. The outside world was a distant entity, and for the time being, they encamped, alone.

Elisa rose with great effort, pushing herself against the sofa arm. "Fiona, will you help me prepare dinner? We can eat a little early today."

"Yes. Of course." She brushed a sleeve across her cheeks and stood. "I'll turn on the broiler. You want to toss the salad ingredients?" She asked.

"Sure."

Ian joined them in the kitchen and opened cupboards gathering plates to set the table. The clang of the flatware against the dishes fragmented the room.

The doorbell rang once. Then a second time.

Mia dug her face into Troy's shirt. "No, Daddy, don't answer the door." Tears flowed freely, streaking her flushed cheeks. Mia's face turned to the image of an adult standing at the edge of the slender window in the entryway, and back again.

"Go to your mom now," Troy kissed Mia and looked for Elisa to come for her. Mia clung tighter. He lifted, and carried her into the kitchen. The five of them stood huddled together. The bell rang, a third time.

"Come, Bean." Ian stepped forward for her. "Your Dad has to answer the door."

Troy lowered Mia to the floor, and let go.

Elisa and Fiona moved forward to form a small circle.

Troy left them, grabbed the handle, and flung the door open.

"Marilyn?" Troy gasped, exhaling the breath he didn't realize he was holding. He certainly hadn't expected to see Blair's wife at his doorstep.

"Do you have a few minutes to talk?" She asked.

"I, I don't know if we are supposed to talk." He stepped back.

"Please, may I come in Troy?"

"The police are on their way to arrest me. My lawyer called, and I'm probably telling you more than I should." He stopped himself short of saying more.

"They aren't coming to your home because they already went to mine." Marilyn stated in a reserved tone. "I gave evidence against Blair last night."

"What?" Troy's mouth gaped wide.

"I turned my husband in for embezzling his own company."

Troy froze. *It sounded too good to be true. Could he trust Marilyn? She'd been somewhat absent throughout this entire ordeal. Never on the news with Blair.* "Okay, we'll talk."

Marilyn entered. She caught sight of the rest of the family clustered across the room. "I am so sorry you have gone through so much pain. My sons and I are struggling too."

Elisa came to her side. "Please, Marilyn join us at the table." She waited for Troy.

Fiona suggested she and Ian take Mia to the back patio so they had privacy. Troy nodded.

After the slider door shut. Marilyn shared her story.

"I figured out Blair had been tampering with the figures, but I never imaged to what degree. He didn't need to either. We had plenty of money, we both come from money." She sat shrunken by the big wooden arm chair, navy blue pants and a long sleeve blouse hung loose on her petite frame. Her once stunning features were haggard and pale. "This has just about killed me."

Elisa asked. "How did you find out?"

"I'd hired a detective to follow Blair last year. I was pretty sure he was cheating on me with his secretary Beverly. And he was." She swallowed hard. "It wasn't his first affair."

Troy expressed sympathy. "You don't have to tell us anything you don't want to."

Marilyn said. "I know." A weak smile appeared briefly. "But I figured you already knew. Most of the office knew. At least that is what came out in the police investigation."

"But, what does that have to do with the embezzlement?" Elisa asked.

"Blair has been living a double life for a long time. That costs money. And he started gambling at the local casino with his girlfriend. Basically, he was never home." She spoke almost incoherently. "I got a lawyer to see what my rights were in a divorce."

"Did he know you were planning to leave him?" Troy asked.

"I don't think he cared." Marilyn answered, body slouched to one side. "All that parading our sons on the news—that was the most the boys were with him in ages."

"Can I get you some water, something to drink?" Elisa realized she hadn't offered, and Marilyn swooned like she was about to faint.

"Yes, thank you." She answered. "I think I'm a bit dehydrated."

"Oh, no ice then?"

"No, thank you."

Elisa got a tall glass, and water from the fridge. "Here you go. I'll fill a pitcher for the table. Do you want one too?" She asked Troy.

"Sure, Honey, thanks." He took a glass.

Marilyn drank half the glassful in one long gulp before resuming the conversation. "I noticed Blair hiding these work ledgers at home. If I walked in the room, he'd whisk them from view. But he never put them in the same place twice."

"Is that what you gave the police?" Troy pursued.

"Part of it. He'd hidden one of his laptops. I almost gave up searching, thought he'd stored it at Beverly's. Then Trevor accidentally found it in his room." She scowled. "In the bottomless abyss of the Legos trunk. I can't believe he invaded his children's lives in that way."

"So the police have all this?" Troy asked. He tried not to push, to be patient with Marilyn. She was obviously traumatized. She'd lost a lot of weight, and her hair looked—patchy.

"Yes, and their computer guy broke the passwords. They have everything they need to convict him not only of embezzling, but of plotting to frame you." She broke down. "I'm so sorry, Troy. I almost came to you before this happened, but I wasn't sure then if you knew."

"I think I figured it out about when you did, but I didn't believe he could do this."

"Blair played us all for fools. Even Beverly." Marilyn added. "I think the gambling took over, and he just nosedived." She drained the rest of the water in her glass.

"What did he do with all the money?" Elisa asked.

"The police techie found two hidden bank accounts. They think he was planning to flee the country after Troy caught him off guard by going to the police first."

"Wow." Elisa blurted out.

"I'm going on TV tonight to publically announce the evidence I turned in and your innocence, Troy." Marilyn got weepy. "I needed to ask your forgiveness first, in person. I wish I'd discovered more sooner, or come to you earlier."

"Now makes all the difference. I can be with Elisa for our daughter's birth."

"I hope your family can start to heal as the boys and I are trying to." Marilyn stood. "You should share this news with your parents and Mia. Blair's in jail and he's going to be for a long time." She took Troy's hand. "You have your lives back."

Chapter Forty-Seven

I did not know what to expect from a C-section birth. Mia was a mite six pounds and my labor a mere five hours when she arrived two weeks early. Being checked into the hospital the night before the surgery was not what I wanted. It ended up being what I needed. My water never broke, I went into early labor before the epidural, and Troy was grumpy from sleeping on the extendable chair-bed all night. The next morning I ended up having a nine pound, fifteen ounce screaming baby boy. That's right, no ultrasound is one hundred percent correct. We turned down the amniocentesis test at full term because, in our opinion, it put our child at higher risk. So we are taking home a son that we are in no way prepared for to share a room with his older sister. Did I mention he'll barely fit in the bassinette? ~ Elisa experiencing the wonders of motherhood again at thirty-five.

Bringing Home Baby

Ian sat on his bed with his shoes on the floor in front of him. He'd switched them once already, to the right, then back to the left. It was his favorite and most comfortable pair. Still something was not quite right. He picked up one by the heel, and angled it side to side, examining the inside tongue and fingering each eyelet hole the laces ran through. After closer inspection, he placed the soles on the bottoms of his socks to match up the proper shoe to the correct foot. He just finished tying the strings when Fiona knocked on the door.

"Hurry, they're home." She stood and waited. "Ian!" Fiona rushed in and grabbed him. "No poking around today." They exited together.

"I be going as fast as I can." He tagged along at a clipped pace.

Mia had wheeled the bassinette out to the center of the living room. She stood ready, Nikon in hand set to video when Troy and Elisa brought a squalling bundle of green and yellow receiving blankets through the front door.

"Look at him." Fiona all but melted. "He's the size of a three month old."

"Surprised us all this newborn bruiser." Troy led Elisa to the chair prepared for her.

"Hello, Jory." Mia recorded. "Welcome to the Kensington Big Top." She hit pause. "Wow, he's not little at all."

"He's got Mick's mop of dark hair." Ian laughed. "Me mate would like that."

"Yeah, he does, Dad." Elisa unfolded the blankets so they all could get a better look.

"Jory be Cornish for George. Jor-ee." Ian said it slow and distinctive.

"You named him after your father?" Fiona asked.

"We just decided on his full name this morning. They wanted his birth certificate filled out before we were discharged." Troy answered. "And yes Mum, Jory is for my dad."

"What's the rest of his name?" Mia kept filming.

"Darrow Kensington." Elisa presented the baby for her Dad to hold. "We decided to give him the grandfathers' names.

"How wonderful." Fiona let go an emotional sigh.

Ian took the squirming babe in his arms and sat on the sofa. "You be carrying on me family name. To be remembered after I be gone." He pressed the lad to his chest and whispered something in his ear. Jory calmed down, his limbs no longer stiff and jerking. Ian kept speaking to him in a low soothing tone until the baby lie still, gazing at his face.

"He knows your voice." Elisa took in a deep breath, and let it go. "From our walks."

"Are you doing okay?" Troy asked her.

"Just tired, and sore." She held a protective pillow over her abdomen. "One of the repeat C-section moms told me you can never have enough pillows after the surgery."

Fiona offered. "I can bring you more."

"Thanks, I'm good for now."

Mia zoomed in with the camera and asked her Gramps. "How does it feel to have a grandson?"

"It be a dream come true." He beamed.

"Not-so-little grandson," she got closer, "how does it feel to have a Gramps?"

"He says these be hard fisher shoes to fill, but will try his best." Ian answered for the lad. "Fiona, you want to take next turn?"

"Do you think he will let me?" She was quick to sit beside Ian.

"Is he not the reason you've come back to us?"

"You all are, but this chunk, he's my new number one fella." Fiona lifted the baby from Ian's chest onto hers. "I am so pleased to welcome you home, Jory. And I must say how glad I am that your middle name, is not—Elizabeth. Someday I will tell you why."

"And you, Mia." She asked herself and turned to aim the camera inches away from her face. "How does it feel to get a chubby, bubby brother instead of the sister you thought was coming home from the hospital?" She leaned her head near his for the shot. "I think I am in for the adventure of my life!" She phased out and away.

"He already is changing lives, that's for certain." Elisa commented.

"Oh, I almost forgot. Your friend Maddie dropped off bags of baby clothes she exchanged from your shower. She returned dresses and bonnets. Lots of monkeys, puppies, and Giants baseball prints in there. She said the stores were most accommodating." Fiona cooed at Jory.

"Troy, we should wash a load so he can wear them." Elisa suggested.

"Here, you take your son. I'll go do the laundry." Fiona handed over the baby and went to get the bags. "Would you like to look through the clothes first?" She asked Elisa.

"I would, thank you."

Fiona set the bags next to the chair for her. "Let me know when you're done." She headed to the kitchen. "We feast on beef Wellington and Yorkshire pudding to celebrate tonight. And Victoria sponge cake for dessert."

"Mum, I am impressed." Troy blinked twice.

"You might want to wait until you taste it first. But I gave it a go."

"Grandmum is a good cook. At least Miss Edith and I think so." Mia complimented her before focusing the camera in. "How do you feel to have a grandson?"

Fiona tried to form a sentence but the words eluded her. When she opened her mouth to speak, the back of her throat choked up. "I'm a blubbering old woman." She struggled to gain her speech. "I am blessed." That was all she could manage. "Sorry to be so blustery."

Mia turned off the video. "You are blessed."

"I haven't seen you cry since Dad died." Troy walked over with Jory and hugged her.

"Afraid I'm a bit teary these days." Fiona flustered.

"No need for apologies, Mum. And I have to say your new hairstyle is growing on me. It was an adjustment at first when the cell pictures came through. I don't think I've ever seen you without long hair to pin up in a dancer's bun."

"I like it too." Elisa agreed. "It is softer feathered that way." She changed her position. "Maybe I will take those extra pillows. Sure miss the adjustable hospital bed."

"Is this the pile of clothes to pre-wash?" Fiona asked before taking anything to the laundry room.

"Yes. Everything except the Giants black and orange outfits. They need to go in a separate load." She raised the bags she'd refilled.

"Careful not to lift too much weight." Troy rushed over and grabbed them in mid-air while cradling Jory in the crook of his other arm. "Thanks, Mum." He gave the sacks to Fiona.

"I think it is breastfeeding time." Elisa reached for her son.

"You are the Mom for mealtime." He laid a rooting-about-Jory, on her chest.

"And you are the Dad when it's nappy time." Elisa joked. "That won't be long after he nurses." She quelled the baby's frustrated cries by directing his mouth so he could latch on.

"And that ends the first segment of, *The Day my Baby Brother Joined the Circus*." Mia powered off and asked. "Is there anything I can do to help?"

"Can you hand me that burp cloth and blanket?" Elisa answered.

"Well that was easy enough." Mia placed both on her mom's chair.

"Oh, sweetie, it gets a bit harder tonight."

"What do you mean?"

"He'll wail about every two hours for his food source." Elisa swathed the receiving blanket over Jory's head, and draped the cloth on her shoulder.

"Uh, Mom? Is he slurping?" Mia asked. "He sounds like a piglet." She peered closer to see for herself. "That is him making all that noise."

"He is quite voracious." Elisa laughed. "Oh, my incision. Ouch!" She stuffed a pillow on her lower abdomen and applied light pressure, wincing. "You made the same sounds, Dearie."

"No way." Mia crinkled up her face.

A sudden explosion blasted under the covers.

"What was that?" Mia closed in, curious. "Oh, my word!" She pulled back, hands pressed on her mouth and nose. "There are no words to describe that smell." She cringed.

"That is my call to bum duty." Troy took Jory and hooked the diaper bag.

Ian doubled over in stitches. "You can change the lad in me room, but leave the door open. Air it out good, mate."

"And that my Mia, is what parenthood is all about." Elisa snapped her nursing bra flap closed. "And again in another couple of hours." She sighed.

Mia gasped as terror struck. "Is he going to do that while he's sleeping in my room?"

Chapter Forty-Eight

A peaceful hush settled throughout the house. Beams of light from the sturgeon full moon illuminated the darkness. Elisa drifted to sleep, Jory sheltered snug in the warmth of her arm. Ian wandered from his room to check on them. He sat spellbound. Joanie and their Michael floated in his thoughts, then floated away. A hazy glow shone about Elisa and the baby's face. He wanted to remember this moment forever, take it home to heaven with him. But he be already forgetting again, little things, maybe some big things too, he didn't know for sure. It be a blessing to live to see your children's children. Nothing be said about remembering. Ian took note of Jory's pursed pink lips, his smudge of a nose, the distinctive curl of his ears, and the near lack of an earlobe. He smiled thinking of his mate Mick when the babe's little head tufted in thick black hair, bobbed while dreaming. He be grateful to be a part of this new generation, of hope.

~ The beginning of the end.

Remembering to Remember

Elisa's bed for the night was the living room chair and ottoman. She sat, legs elevated on a mountain of pillows that also buffered her on every side. Her newborn lay swaddled in cotton blankets in an air-conditioned house bearing up under the hot August heat. Troy stretched head to toe on the sofa across from her, zonked out in a deep, exhausted slumber. Big sister Mia hunkered down in the adjacent love seat, legs dangling over the armrest, her pink ballet flats swaying.

Ian wandered down the hall, Fiona's door was shut and the thin line of light underneath had gone black. He continued to pad lightly into the living room. Family members slept on every piece of furniture except the recliner across from Elisa. She stirred when he settled into the wide glove of the leather seat, the coils creaking making more noise than he'd intended.

"Is that you, Dad?" Elisa rubbed weary eyelids.

"Tis me. I be not intending to awaken you, just checking to see you be okay."

"I think Troy and Mia are more tired than I am." She whispered.

"You be up to a chat?" Ian leaned closer.

"Actually, I would love to chat." Elisa shifted the sleeping baby to her shoulder. "Is there something in particular you want to talk about?"

Ian hesitated, tightened his robe belt, and wiggled his knee-hi socks through the open toe of his slippers. "These days me not be sure what sort of man I might wake up each morn. The doc upped my meds dose to help but, we soon be seeing if be able to help."

"Is your memory getting worse?"

"I now be struggling to make sense of some words and other things. The drug be a temporary fix."

"It gave you a second chance." Elisa's voice cracked.

"When I first arrived in America, all me wanted to do was go home to Cornwall, be with me mates. Now—."

"You feel different?"

"Yes. It would break me heart to leave Bean behind, you, the baby, even Fiona."

"And Troy?"

"Of course." Ian did that nervous shuffle with his feet. "I be needing a promise from me, daughter."

"What?" Elisa asked.

"If me be forgetting all again, as before, Ian be not wishing to be a burden here." He hesitated and opened his mouth, then closed it. "Put me in a home." Ian gazed directly in his daughter's eyes.

"Absobloodylutely not! This is your home, with us." Elisa strained to speak low.

"Please, you and Troy be having two to be raising now."

"No Dad, I cannot agree to that. Tell me, would you ever do that to me?"

"What?" Ian's face clouded over.

"If I was the one with Alzheimer's."

"Never." He responded immediately.

"Neither can I." Elisa said. "We will remember for you, the forgotten pieces." She tried to reach over to him but the baby began to fuss. She rocked Jory on her shoulder until he calmed down.

"One day coming Ian be not able to walk, talk, dress or feed by himself." Ian pressed his hands on his chest.

"Dad, I know more hardship is ahead. We'll deal with it when we get there. One day at a time for now." She stroked the baby's back, and downy hair.

"When drugs no longer work?" Ian rung his hands in his lap.

"We will take care of the person."

"What kind of person be that man then?"

"The kind we love." Elisa drew air in deep, and held her breath before letting it go. "We face the unknown together. We make the hard choices as a family."

Ian pursued. "I, I be trusting your word me daughter. Tell me you be honouring these wishes."

Elisa nearly crushed Jory to her heart. "I can't do that. Place you in a home with strangers. No family around you that loves you." She struggled to find words to help him realize this could not possibly be an answer.

"Elisa Jean." Ian wept. "I *would* do this for you. It just be a different kind of a home. You come visit me. Bring Bean, she be reading to me from books she knows me love, and from her journals. Jory be coming with you too. Troy, maybe even Fiona." Ian waited for her to answer. He did not budge. He'd thought this through. He'd done research on Bean's computer. He knew.

Elisa clung to the infant in her arms. After the C-section it physically hurt to cry. This was a deeper pain, watching someone you love disappear. Looking into vacant stares. Caring for an adult who becomes a child again. It was but a matter of time. She knew that. "Yes, Dad. I give you my word." Elisa whimpered. "I promise to honour you. I will always honor you."

"You be setting me free." He rose and kissed her moistened cheek. "Remember me, and me always be this close, as this moment." His head bowed next to hers.

Elisa squeezed his hand and held on before releasing him. Lowering her line of vision as he walked away, she noticed his slippers were on the wrong feet.

Ian caught a glimpse of Fiona near the hall doorway just as she turned to leave. "Wait." He urged. "Come, sit under the moon with me."

"That sounds lovely."

"Will we be troubling you if we go to the back porch?" Ian quietly asked Elisa.

"No." She motioned them on. "I'll be nursing Jory soon."

Ian quietly inched the slider door open for Fiona. She stepped out, her blue satin robe flowed in the ripples of a gentle summer breeze that embraced them. The two sat side-by-side on a wrought iron bench near the edge of his garden. Fiona's bare feet didn't quite touch the ground.

"You asked a hard thing of her."

"This be true." Deep sorrow echoed in Ian's voice. His heart ached to say more while he remembered, but he knew Elisa could not bear the rest. He wished to say many things to Fiona too, things he worried he would forget. His tongue stuck to the roof of his mouth each time he tried to speak. The moon hung above them like an immense guardian orb in the starry dark of night. Wisps of clouds misted in swirls across the vast universe.

"The sky be like a stormy sea this night." Ian told Fiona. "Many times me sailed such an ocean."

"You speak poetically." She searched the canopy mapped overhead for what he saw.

"Ta for the novels you sent me home with Mia." Ian remarked. "The gardening book be me favourite."

"I regret not being your friend before." Fiona blurted out. "I fear I've wasted precious time. Time we cannot get back."

"It never be too late to begin a friendship." Ian perked up only to withdraw, subdued.

"I would like that." Her glassy eyes twinkled at him.

"You would?"

"Yes, very much."

Ian gazed upward and stuck his legs out, heels anchored on the slate rock patio. "You know Ian will be forgetting you."

"Yes, I do." She leaned her head down on his shoulder. "It might be a good thing if you don't remember everything about me." A mischievous smile played on her lips.

"Do you mean your hoity-toity behaviour? Thus far that all be crystal clear." Ian grinned and slipped an arm about Fiona.

Elisa watched Ian and Fiona sit under the stars. Somehow seeing them together mended an ache piercing her heart. Who knew after all the years of battling, they'd end up friends? For today they shared a small victory in the Alzheimer's war. This memory, she tucked away in a safe place.

And he arose, and rebuked the wind,

And said unto the sea, Peace, be still. And the

wind ceased, and there was a great calm.

~ Mark 4:39

Excerpts from the journal of Mia Kensington

A story about my Cornish Gramps and me.

Journal entry: page 1

My Gramps calls me Bean, short for Beanie. I love the sound of his voice when he says my name out loud. Mom wanted him to come to America when I was born, but I think he was afraid to travel across the ocean he sailed at home in Cornwall. What matters is that he is here now. I will always have this time, our time together.

I am learning that there is much I did not know about my Gramps. We share a love of reading, good books, a lot of books. He shares classics with me that take me on adventures in new places. Then we talk about what we like and didn't like in the stories. Gramps has many opinions, I am discovering, so do I.

Journal entry: page 12

Today Gramps repeated something to me three times and I don't think he realized it. I didn't tell him because I thought it would embarrass him. Besides it was a terrific story about when he was a lad thrashing about the Cornish coast with his childhood mates. I learned a new word: thrash.

Journal entry: page 20

I really want a baby sister. Gramps is hoping for a grandson. Mom still seems surprised to be pregnant at thirty-five. Dad is over the moon. Grandmum bought a pink bonnet. Well, someone is going to be happy when the new baby joins the family circus. We need another acrobat.

Journal entry: page 22

On our walk today in the neighborhood Gramps got lost. He was so scared. I knew better than to let him get ahead of me, but Mrs. Crothers grilled me about the lemons disappearing from her tree. She really should have planted it in her back yard. I don't know who is taking all those lemons. I held Gramps hand the entire walk home.

I didn't tell anyone he got lost. I'll just stick closer to him from now on. When we hung up our coats, he took six lemons out of a pocket.

Journal entry: page 29

Why can't my Grandmum and Gramps be nice to each other? They quarrel like little children.

Journal entry: page 36

At first I thought Alzheimer's was someone's name—Al Heimer. I wish it was. It is a disease that makes people forget who they are, and who they love. Today, Gramps called me Elisa for half of the day, then he just started calling me Bean again. I can't figure out what changed, and he didn't know. He saw me crying and asked if he'd done something wrong. I just kept hugging him.

Journal entry: page 41

Gramps had the best day ever! We went back to Fairytale Town. He loves that place. I think it reminds him of home in England. He remembers more now so he misses it. We sat at the round table in King Arthur's court at the castle. Gramps told me all about the Arthurian legends and history of Cornwall. Some parts he acted out, drawing a sword and fighting knights of "questionable character". He knows so much history. He is smart. He is funny. He is silly like me, that's why we get along. I want to remember today for him. When he forgets again, I'll tell him all our stories. And when the baby is born, I'll tell her about the Gramps she'll never know.

Book Club Discussion Questions

This story has complex characters dealing with various personal growth, cultural and economic, and physical issues. Did this resonate with you?

1) Who was your favorite character, and why?

Alzheimer's has no boundaries. It transcends gender, race & nationality.

2) Do you have a family member, friend, or neighbor diagnosed with Alzheimer's?

You travel from America, to England, and back again throughout these pages. During those journeys, Elisa, Ian, Fiona, Mick, and Mia, learn more about themselves and others, and the two countries that connect them to those they love.

3) Do you think these characters would have learned what they do without their experiences in both America and England? What did they discover?

Family is a central theme in The Wrong Ocean. This is not your average family, or is it in today's world?

4) Do you think families in modern times live together by choice, or by necessity? Are multi-blended families' lives enriched by communal living, or compromised?

Integrity and honesty are tested in various ways in different characters lives. Troy's job is on the line either way he goes. Fiona makes wrong decisions, but one in particular affects her entire family.

5) Can you think of other characters and decisions they make that impact another individual, several people, or a community? Can you identify with a character, and/or situation they face that is universal?

Love is the thread binding this family together. Does that thread break and need mending? Does forgiveness seem impossible at a certain point?

6) Sometimes people hurt the ones they love the most. Why?

Prayer is another continuous thread in some of these characters' lives.

7) Who prays, and who does not? Does it make a difference, for the better, or do things get worse? Why keep praying if things get worse?

What surprised you the most at the end of the story, when Ian asked Elisa the hard question? Do you think when the time comes that she will honor her word even though Ian won't know by then? Why?

Acknowledgements

My mother Mary fought a brave sixteen year battle with Alzheimer's. It was a devastating journey for me and my six sisters. Most of all for my sister Shannon who was mom's main caregiver. All Ian's mates, especially Mick, in the village of Cagwith, Cornwall represent my sister Shannon to me. I hope my readers see those around them who live the unselfish, daily life of loving while caring for someone who cannot reciprocate or remember them.

Thank you Amador Fiction Critique Group: Judy Pierce, Debbie Mackey, Becca Fischer, Carrie McAlister, Betty Ruth Weatherby, Carolyn Bakken, Lydia Cameron, Pam S. Dunn, Jess Moore, and Sarah Garner for their tireless reads, in-depth critiques, and commitment to venture across the pond into uncharted waters.

Thank you beta readers Marlene Risse Johnson, and Amber Morgan, my gratitude for your time, comments, wisdom, and encouragement. A big thanks to my amazing editor, Bonnie Miller.

Thank you Mokelumne Hill, and Lake Tahoe workshop writer friends: Antoinette May, Monika Rose, Genevieve Beltran, Sally Henry, Kevin Arnold, June Fern, Linda Field, and the late Sandy Towle and Jennifer Hamilton.

So grateful to the care homes that offer a needed sanctuary and provide for the dignity of those beloved ones we entrust to them when living at home is no longer an option. They help to make the heartbreaking decision to meet the needs required when that devastating time arrives uninvited.

Thank you Ophir (Buddy) Vellenowith, family historian, for booking passage for a fortnight across the pond in telling the family stories of Cornwall; Carol Newell who hails from Cornwall, and not only took time to share her Cornish life, but also taught me how to make pasties. All the people who shared their broken hearts and shattered lives, ravaged by this relentless disease that alters both physically and mentally, the person they once knew.

With a grateful heart I thank the many intercessors including: Ruth N. Keppeler, Karen Snook, Debbie Walker, Cindy Boyd, Marlene Johnson, Vicki Byassee Hurley, Dale Lavely, Glory Potts, and Lydia Cameron who prayed me through one of the hardest writing endeavors of my life. Only by the grace of God did I walk through the firestorm and finish this book unsinged, especially when I was near the end of the novel, and my mother passed away.

Sincere gratitude for the patience, information, and corrections encompassing all my research adventures in Nevada City, Grass Valley, and Sacramento, CA; Streets Pub, downtown Sacramento, CA; Fairytale Town, Funderland, and the Sacramento Zoo, in William Land Park, Sacramento, CA; The Royal Ballet and Opera House, London, England, and to Becky, owner of the Secret Cottage Tours in the Cotswolds, Gloucestershire, England.

In loving memory of my rescue granddogs Jake and Missy, my faithful office assistants who sat at my feet while I wrote this book from beginning to end.

Alzheimer's Association: Home Office: 225 N. Michigan Avenue Floor 17, Chicago, Il 60601. alz.org   24/7 HELPLINE 800-272-3900 Since 1980.

Alzheimer's Society in Cornwall & Isles of Scilly cornwall@alzheimers.org.uk tel 01872277963 Contact position; Dementia Connect Local Services Manager, alzheimers.org.uk

Books with a wide variety of approaches to consider reading to help you through the Alzheimer's journey.

The 36-Hour Day: A Family Guide to Caring for People Who Have Alzheimer Disease and other Dementias (A John Hopkins Press Health Book) by Nancy L. Mace MA and Peter V. Rabins, MPH

Alzheimer's Through the Stages: A Caregiver's Guide by Mary Moller MSW CAS

When Only Love Remains Surviving My Mom's Battle with Early Onset Alzheimer's by Lauren Dykovitz

The End of Alzheimer's Program: The First Protocol to Enhance Cognition and Reverse Decline At Any Age by Dale E. Bredesen, M.D. and David Perlmutter, M.D.

The First Survivors of Alzheimer's: How Patients Recovered Life and Hope in Their Own Words by Dale E. Bredesen, M.D.

Learning to Speak Alzheimer's: A Groundbreaking Approach for Everyone Dealing with the Disease by Joanne Koenig-Coste and Robert N. Butler, M.D.

H.O.P.E. for the Alzheimer's Journey: Help, Organizations, Preparations, & Education for the Road Ahead. Carol B. Amos

Picture Book of Psalms: For Seniors with Dementia by Mighty Oak Publishing

Ice Cream with Grandpa: A Loving Story for Kids About Alzheimer's & Dementia by Laura Smetana and Elizabeth B P de Moraes

The Alzheimer's Disease Caregivers Handbook: What to Remember When They Forget by Dr. Sally Willard Burbank and Sue Pace Bell

The Caregiving Season, Finding Grace to Honor Your Aging Parent by Jane S. Daly

Other books author Kathy Boyd Fellure recommends for your TBR pile:

Sanctuary by Patrick Barrett and Susy Flory ©2021

Your Guide to Not Getting Murdered in a Quaint English Village by Maureen Johnson and Jay Cooper ©2021

Katie in London The Best Tour in Town! By James Mayhew ©2014

The Butterfly and the Violin A Hidden Masterpiece Novel by Kristy Cambron ©2014

Kiyo Sato: From a WWII Japanese Internment Camp to a Life of Service by Connie Goldsmith with Kiyo Sato ©2021

©Farrell Photography

Kathy Boyd Fellure

Kathy Boyd Fellure is author of *On the Water's Edge Tahoe Trilogy*. *The Wrong Ocean* is the first book in her new five novel, *Across the Pond Series*. The second novel *Harper House* releases in 2023. These stories travel between England and America in a mix of contemporary and historical times.

Kathy is also a former host of the TSPN TV Authors, Writers, Books, and Beyond Show. She presents an annual literary read in Jackson, California at Hein & Company Bookstore, upstairs in 221B Baker Street West.

Kathy Boyd Fellure is also the author of a series of four children's illustrated storybooks ~*The Blake Sisters Lake Tahoe Adventures*. Kathy currently lives in the foothill gold country of California with her family and two stand-up comedian rescue dogs.

Learn more at www.kathyboydfellure.com. Write to her at P.O. Box 1209, Ione, CA 95640-9771.

Made in the USA
Middletown, DE
06 July 2022